MOONGATE

A NOVEL

William Proctor

and

David J. Weldon, M.D.,
U.S. Congressman

A JANET THOMA BOOK

THOMAS NELSON PUBLISHERS®
Nashville

A Division of Thomas Nelson, Inc.
www.ThomasNelson.com

Published in Nashville, Tennessee, by Thomas Nelson, Inc.

Scripture quotations are from the REVISED STANDARD VERSION OF THE BIBLE. Copyright © 1946, 1952, 1971, 1973 by the Division of Christian Education of the National Council of the Churches of Christ in the U.S.A. Used by permission.

Library of Congress Cataloging-in-Publication Data

Proctor, William.
    Moongate : a novel / by William Proctor and David J. Weldon.
      p. cm.
    ISBN 0-7852-6685-2
    I. Weldon, David J. II. Title.

PS3566.R63 M66 2002
813'.54—dc21   2001056226

Printed in the United States of America

02 03 04 05 06 PHX 5 4 3 2 1

To Nancy and Pam

1

Professor Carl Rensburg's imagination was soaring. As he sped down the open Taconic State Parkway toward New York City, his mind wasn't on the winding road in front of him. He was mostly oblivious to the waning rays of daylight, which caused the canopy of orange and yellow autumn leaves overhead to glow like an Impressionist's fantasy.

For a person who hated heavy traffic, Rensburg was only vaguely conscious of how he had lucked out on this particular road trip. The highway was unusually deserted and the driving unbelievably easy. But he didn't dwell on his good fortune. Somewhere at the back of his mind, he chalked it up to the fact that he was still many miles from the city, and besides, most people had probably already made it home for dinner.

Anyhow, those were minor distractions. Rensburg found he could really focus on only one thing: the moon. When the trees parted to his left, he could see it clearly in the east, hanging full, large, and low in the early evening sky. He was tempted to fix his gaze on the silvery sphere in an effort to make out with his naked eye the shadows on the left side that marked the *Oceanus Procellarum*—the Ocean of Storms. That was his destination. His longtime dream was about to come true.

Then he caught himself. His inattention had caused the car to edge toward the shoulder of the road. *Focus on the driving! Don't run off the road. Not now. Not with just a month to go before liftoff.*

He had just left his wife and two children at their country home in the Berkshires, in western Massachusetts. Tomorrow he was scheduled to board the jet that would take him directly from New York to Houston. There, under the close eye of experts from NASA, he would conclude his final briefings and training for this all-important mission. Then he would head for the east coast of Florida and the Kennedy Space Center—and the historic blastoff that would most likely change the future of the earth.

The pressure to succeed was enormous. Rensburg shook his head as he recalled the laundry list of crises that had literally forced the world's political leaders to schedule and fund the trillion-dollar moon venture, Energy Project Omega. Regular rolling brownouts and full-fledged blackouts had spread from California to New York and other highly populated sections of the United States, not to mention vast sections of Europe and the Far East. Businesses often didn't know from one week to the next whether they would have enough power to run their operations—and the world's economy had gone into a steady downward spiral.

The desperate search for stopgap measures, such as drilling for oil in the Arctic, had backfired with a couple of disastrous oil spills. Some people suspected eco-terrorist involvement in the catastrophes, but that almost didn't matter. Oil, gas, and coal were on their last legs. The scientific evidence had continued to mount to implicate fossil fuel in global warming and other environmental threats. Fossil fuels were running low anyway, so a more permanent solution was an absolute necessity.

It was equally clear that nuclear fission was not a promising alternative. Fission plants were an ongoing source of controversy, with radioactive waste and the constant danger of core catastrophes, such as the 1986 Chernobyl reactor explosion in the old Soviet Union.

But nuclear *fusion*? That was a completely different matter. The fusion process produced no radioactive waste. Also, putting factories on the moon would quell public concern, real or imagined, about nuclear dangers on earth. The moon seemed the perfect answer—and that was why Carl Rensburg was almost euphoric as he sped down the Taconic.

After the initial financial investment to set up the moon factory, the earth would have access indefinitely to unlimited, clean energy. Dirt-cheap fuel. A revolution in world economic growth. The end of air pollution and any threat of global warming. Rensburg knew he was probably being overly optimistic. But everyone agreed that if he and his team succeeded—if they established viable helium-3 mining operations on the moon and made nuclear fusion a reality—the benefits would be enormous. The transmission of limitless power by laser from the moon would solve the earth's energy needs for the next ten thousand years. He chuckled as he mused to himself, *That should be enough time for a future Carl Rensburg to find the next energy solution!*

Then he shook himself and resolved to stop believing his own press clippings. Sure, he was probably the best nuclear fusion scientist in the United States. Maybe even in the world, though he secretly considered Pushkin in Russia to have a slight edge. But as accomplished and brilliant as he was, Rensburg was fundamentally a humble man. He was awed that for some reason—a coincidence, an unexplainable convergence of the right education, career path, and remarkable timing—he now found himself poised to become more than a footnote in world history. Yet he sensed deeply that his professional expertise and good luck were only part of the story. Something beyond himself had surely orchestrated his life and this swirl of events to bring him to this moment.

The siren and flashing lights in his rearview mirror jerked him abruptly back into the present. It was an unmarked police car. Unsuspecting, Rensburg had actually noticed the vehicle several miles back but had thought nothing of it. Apparently, the unmarked auto had been following him for some time, waiting for the right moment to pounce. Automatically glancing down at the speedometer, the scientist felt his stomach turn over.

Ten miles per hour over the limit. Okay, guilty.

But he figured he should be able to talk himself out of this one. The trooper might even recognize him. After all, his picture had been plastered all over the papers in the last couple of months. Any police officer should be willing to give a break to the scientist who was going to provide the earth with unlimited and inexpensive electric power.

Because the Taconic was such a narrow highway, with tight shoulders and numerous sharp turns, Rensburg expected to have some trouble finding a place to stop. But around the next curve, he saw a side road, where he was able to pull off and park.

He waited patiently as the trooper got out of his car and ambled in his direction. They always took their time. Then he saw the second uniformed officer, who was opening the back door and dragging out a couple of red traffic cones.

Two cops? One in the backseat with traffic cones? Odd. But then I don't know anything about handing out tickets on the Taconic.

"Sir, you were speeding," the first trooper said, leaning his head into Rensburg's open window.

"Sorry, Officer," the scientist replied with his most cordial smile. "But I guess I had my mind on other things. You see—"

"Important to keep your mind on the road," the cop interrupted. "This is a very dangerous stretch of highway. Many accidents. Especially in this kind of light."

"I'm sure, but you see . . ."

Rensburg stopped talking because it was clear that the officer wasn't paying attention. The man had straightened up and was watching his companion place the traffic cones on the edge of the highway. Then he turned back to Rensburg.

"Sir, please turn around and look behind you. See those cones on the road? That's what we often have to do when we stop someone on this highway, to protect you and ourselves."

Rensburg dutifully twisted around and looked toward the other officer. He was about to make some ingratiating remark about how much he appreciated the great effort the police in this state made to do their jobs. But he never got the chance. Just as he craned his neck to the rear, the needle entered his neck, and he immediately lost consciousness.

2

The anger inside Congressman Scott Andrews seemed to be building like an internal volcano as he paced back and forth behind his desk, reading and rereading the headline in the *New York Times:*

WORLD'S LEADING FUSION EXPERT DIES IN AUTO ACCIDENT
Rensburg Was Top Scientist on Moon-Mining Team
Russian Will Take His Place on Energy Project Omega

"How is this possible?" he almost shouted to his chief of staff, Colleen Barker. "How could something like this happen, just when everything was coming together for us? What am I working for if everything's going to fall apart at the last second?"

Colleen, who was nursing her usual morning cup of cheap, strong Pilon Café Espresso, shrugged and brushed several strands of tousled black hair out of her face. She knew he didn't expect answers from her. He just needed to vent.

She watched him closely as he spun around just a few feet from her face and gestured broadly. *Impressive,* she mused. *Electable.*

But the tanned, blond good looks didn't sell her. No, it was the brains and vision. *Wants to change the world, and I'm along for the ride. The House today. Senate tomorrow. And then . . . ?*

She suppressed a smile as it occurred to her that Scott had temporarily forgotten where he was. Apparently, he thought he was addressing the entire House of Representatives, and not just one slightly pudgy, late-thirtyish, extremely bright former reporter—who had single-handedly orchestrated his five House-election victories. She had left the New York newspaper scene to join Scott when she was at a career peak, having just won a Pulitzer while still in her mid-twenties. But she'd never regretted the move for a moment because from the outset, she had become a player in the making of history.

As the new chairman of the House Space Committee, Scott Andrews had used all his influence and negotiating skills to get the moon mission approved. He had managed to put Rensburg in charge of the fusion project, even though there were plenty of objections from the Russians and Chinese. He had even succeeded in getting himself a seat on the moon shuttle as *numero uno*, the man in charge of the entire operation. The whole thing had been an amazing political tour de force, with the Russians marginalized, the Chinese barely on the radar screen, and the Americans poised to oversee the earth's energy needs for the next millennium.

But now Rensburg was gone. Over the side of a cliff on the Taconic. Burned to a crisp in his Volvo.

"How on earth do you go off a cliff on the Taconic Parkway?" he asked again, shaking his head.

"Beautiful drive, but those narrow lanes and turns make me nervous," Colleen said. She had driven the highway often when she was working as a reporter in New York.

"I wouldn't really know," Scott said. "I'm a Florida boy myself."

Growing visibly calmer, he idly fingered some papers on his desk and then focused on one in particular. "Police report says he apparently hadn't been drinking—though it's hard to tell about that when your body has been burned beyond recognition. They think he must have fallen asleep. Complete autopsy's scheduled, but they don't seem to expect anything unusual."

Colleen shook her head. "Still, something's not quite right."

"Oh?" Scott said.

He appeared to be half-listening. He glanced approvingly at the definition of his triceps as he eased his lean, muscular frame into his chair. Colleen watched her boss patiently, and with some amusement.

As one of only six or seven former practicing physicians in Congress, Scott was ready at any time to launch into a lecture on how the weightlessness of space travel could take a toll on bone mass. Colleen had heard him expound on one of his favorite theories so often that she now had it memorized: "The more exercise you do on earth to gain additional skeletal mass, the more protection you'll have when you go into space."

Although Scott was only forty-four and hardly a candidate for osteoporosis,

Colleen had to admit he was probably wise to be careful about that extra ounce of prevention. After all, he was scheduled to spend three months on the moon, which had only one-sixth the gravity of the earth.

But Colleen's main concern at this point wasn't the moon's gravity or Scott's physical fitness. She was still trying to sort through the Rensburg accident and its potential impact on the mission. After all, Scott's political future was intimately linked to the outcome of the energy project. Also, Rensburg was dead. Stone-cold dead. Was Scott himself in any danger?

"Volvos don't just burn up in a crash, do they?" she asked rhetorically. "I thought they were supposed to be the safest cars around. And Rensburg was maybe the most careful, conservative guy I've ever met. I can't imagine he'd begin to doze and then fall asleep on the road. And the timing—the timing's just too odd. He dies the day before he's scheduled to begin his final training for the moon mission. Do you believe that kind of coincidence?"

A slightly strained smile played across Scott's lips. "So what are you trying to say, Colleen? A conspiracy? Maybe murder? Or terrorism? We took care of terrorism years ago, after the World Trade Center attack. Come on! You're not a reporter trying to sell newspaper stories anymore."

"But it does seem a little suspicious, don't you think?"

Scott shook his head, almost a little too vigorously, she thought.

"Who could possibly want to get rid of Rensburg?" he asked. "Sure, we've had our differences with the Chinese. And I know the Russians are just as happy that their top scientist—Pushkin—is now in Rensburg's slot, and they even get an extra team member with Pushkin's assistant—what's his name?— Bolotov? But do those gains really justify knocking off our chief scientist and maybe derailing the entire operation? After all, the helium mining and fusion are for the entire earth. Either we all win, or we all lose."

Colleen watched Scott closely. She prided herself on an ability to pick up subtle signals from his facial expressions and body language, and it was apparent to her now that for all his protests, he was trying to convince himself that there was no problem. She raised her coffee close to her nose, where she could savor the aroma. She preferred to brew the Pilon in her office rather than buy Starbucks at the local shop, as everyone else on the staff did. Maybe it was just superstition, but she felt she always thought more creatively when she held a hot cup of this strong Cuban-American stuff next to her face.

"Well, that's certainly one way to look at it," she finally said. "But maybe the Russians are hiding something. I don't trust them."

"Well, quite honestly, neither do I," Scott replied with a sigh. He turned away and began to shuffle papers.

He's getting tired of this kind of talk, she decided. *The moon trip is all he can manage right now. Obviously he doesn't want to throw an international conspiracy into the mix.*

"The FBI's on the case, and there's no evidence at this point that the Russkies are up to any monkey business," the congressman finally said. A conclusive note had now crept into his voice. "Until we have more to go on, we'll have to chalk this whole thing up to bad luck. Very bad luck."

It was clear to Colleen that the conversation was over, so she got up to leave. But as she closed the door to Andrews's office, she resolved to put out a few feelers among some of her reporter friends and also law-enforcement people she knew in the New York area.

Always been told I have a nose for news, she thought as she took another sip of her coffee. *And this one just doesn't smell quite right. Not right at all.*

3

"Congratulations, Doctor!" Prime Minister Demitry Martov exclaimed as he hurried toward the door to greet the rumpled scientist, who was walking uncertainly into his office.

Martov knew the look. As well as he could remember, Sergey Pushkin had never been in his expansive office before, and the reaction visible on his face was typical of other first-timers. Awe. Deep respect. Even fear. Everyone with political access in Russia knew that he was the real power behind the president. In effect that meant near-absolute power in the society—and a right to expect groveling obedience and homage, even from accomplished scientists like Pushkin.

Legacy from the Communists, he thought. *At least one reason to thank them.*

"Please, have a seat and let me look at you," Martov said in the paternal tone he had cultivated during his five years in power. "Our new international celebrity—and cosmonaut!"

Pushkin, who slowly lowered his thin, angular frame onto the edge of a chair in front of the prime minister, seemed genuinely embarrassed. "I'm hardly a cosmonaut, Prime Minister. And I don't feel like a celebrity. I just want to live up to your expectations. Dr. Rensburg was truly a great man. Hard for anyone to equal."

"Nonsense!" the prime minister objected with a scowl. "Everyone regards you as the better scientist. No one in the world knows as much about nuclear fusion as you. Believe me, I have reliable sources, and they all agree."

"Still, it's an extremely heavy responsibility," Pushkin said, wringing his hands nervously.

The prime minister leaned forward so that his large, square head, set on an equally large and muscular neck, almost seemed in danger of bumping against the scientist's nose.

"You must remember who you are!" he said, an edge of reprimand in his voice. "At this moment, you are the most important scientist in the world. And your importance will grow as your work proceeds. As such, you carry the reputation and future of Mother Russia with you. I have chosen you, Dr. Pushkin, because I believe you are the man for this historic moment. Don't disappoint me!"

Pushkin averted his eyes and shook his head. "No, no, I'll do my duty," he replied. "I'm aware of my skills. We know the fusion technology we've developed works."

"Of course, of course!" Martov said with a broad smile. "That's what I like to hear. Confidence. That's the Pushkin I've come to respect."

Then the prime minister grew serious again. "But of course, you know there's more. The fusion project is just the first step. Your additional experiment may be even more important for us."

"Yes, yes, I'm quite excited about that," Pushkin said, growing more animated as the thought took shape in his mind. "That's really my passion."

"Every Russian should have a passion," Martov murmured approvingly.

"I'm so grateful for this opportunity," Pushkin replied, almost looking as though he might embrace the politician—before he thought better of it. "It's a scientist's dream. But of course, it's speculative. The formulas work perfectly on paper, but we don't know if we can really do it in the laboratory."

"Confidence, Professor!" Martov reminded him sternly. "What works on paper will work in practice—if you remain confident and make it work."

"Yes, Prime Minister," the scientist said quietly, looking down at his hands.

"And remember, this experiment must be kept very secret," he reminded Pushkin. "You'll be working with several handpicked specialists, but only you will understand the full import of what you're attempting. We'll let them all think this is just a sideline, a sop given the Russians to ensure their full participation. Everyone must believe that the fusion project is your sole priority. If they should learn too much about your other experiment prematurely, that could result in unfortunate publicity for us—and perhaps the end of your special research opportunity."

"Yes, yes, of course," the professor replied, looking rather nervous. "But I'm concerned about the Americans. They're not stupid. Won't they insist on knowing the details of our special experiment? And if we refuse to tell them, won't they try to stop us? I'm just one man—and I'm not in charge of the mission. How can I hope to overcome such opposition?"

Martov patted him on the arm with a hamlike hand. "Don't you worry about that, Professor. I've taken care of the Americans already. Anyhow, they know they can't proceed with the fusion energy mission without you. If anybody tries to put pressure on you, just be firm! Remember, I'll be giving you my full support from earth, and I'll be sure you have plenty of help on the moon—good, strong help. We've already provided you with a top assistant, Vladimir Bolotov."

"Still, I'm not entirely clear about the priority you're giving to the secret project," Pushkin said. "The fusion energy mission seems so much more useful for the world's population. If we succeed in the experiment, what use do you plan to make of our discoveries?"

The questions were beginning to irritate Martov. "Don't worry about the specifics, Professor. Just do your work. The practical applications will take care of themselves. Understand?"

"Certainly, Prime Minister," Pushkin replied, bowing slightly. "Please forgive my curiosity. I fear I've overstepped. And I do want you to know how deeply grateful I am to you."

"Well, as the Americans say, you now have a blank check. The best way to thank me is to proceed diligently—and to succeed."

Even as Dr. Sergey Pushkin was nodding his assent, the prime minister hastened to usher him out the door. Martov felt he had made it completely clear what he expected of the scientist, and any further conversation was likely to be counterproductive—or even dangerous. The less Pushkin suspected about possible "uses" of his scientific discoveries, the better it would be for Martov's ultimate plans—and Pushkin's health and well-being.

4

When Sergey Pushkin finally arrived at his modest apartment on the outskirts of Moscow, near the extensive research facility where he spent most of his waking hours, he quickly closed the door behind him and heaved a sigh of relief. These meetings with politicians, especially top-ranking officials like Martov, were quite stressful. Some of his colleagues loved the notoriety and publicity that accompanied great scientific achievement. Pushkin didn't. Not at all.

He lived alone. Though in his late forties, he had never been married, and he liked it that way. Some of his colleagues had wondered, only partly in jest, if he might be a secret Russian Orthodox monk. Others whispered behind his back that he was homosexual. Neither bit of gossip was true, though he had to admit that the monkish idea was attractive. He had risen to a preeminent position among Russian scientists by paring down the trappings of life to their bare essentials and immersing himself in a minimalist environment, with as few distractions as possible.

Solitude is my natural state, he thought.

He collapsed into his favorite padded chair, which he had placed in the precise middle of his living room. Spread around him, all within easy reach, were strategically placed reading lights and several small tables holding a wide variety of a scholar's basic tools. On one surface writing materials lay before him in a neat arrangement; current books he was reading rested next to the pens and paper. Another table held remotes for a huge television screen, VCR, and DVD system that were set up across the room. The latest-model notebook computer lay on a shelf underneath.

The scientist had even placed a miniature refrigerator nearby so that he wouldn't have to miss a beat if he wanted a snack while he was working or watching the TV screen. Especially thirsty this evening, he immediately reached into the refrigerator, pulled out a container of bottled water, and took two or three long quaffs before he settled back into his chair. He had given up drinks containing alcohol and caffeine two years before, mostly as a matter of personal discipline and restraint.

One of the first steps in my current journey, he reflected.

Surveying his surroundings, an incongruous thought entered his mind: *bachelor's pad.* He had first heard those words from one of the few Americans who had visited him here—a Bible scholar, named Michael James, whom he had met in an underground church he had been attending for more than a year.

Pushkin reached across to one of the small tables near him, the one that contained the books he was currently reading. Five volumes were stacked one on top of the other. Typically, he kept several books in play at once, shifting back and forth, depending on his mood on a particular day. He had found that because his interests were so wide-ranging, he couldn't limit himself to only one particular area of science . . . or classic fiction . . . or theology . . . or philosophy—at least not for more than a couple of days at a time. To keep a sharp edge, he had to stimulate his mind from several different directions at once.

The book he selected, which was at the top of the heap, was an obscure, long-out-of-print work in English entitled *Faith for a Lifetime,* by the former Greek Orthodox primate of North and South America, Archbishop Iakovos. Pushkin had been reading it with a couple of purposes in mind.

First, it was written in a popular American style—and he had been working hard on his American English. He was scheduled to fly to Houston, Texas, in only two days, where he would undergo about a month's final training at the NASA astronaut facilities there. As Rensburg's backup, he had already been preparing himself at cosmonaut facilities near his laboratory—just in case.

After he finished with the program at the Johnson Space Center in Houston, he would be ready to blast off to the moon in the company of a team largely controlled by Americans. He looked down at the book in his lap. The better he could understand and communicate with these Americans, the more effective he would be in executing his duties.

But more important, this book and several others in the stack—including a Bible he studied every day—were helping him nurture his renewed faith, the faith to which his American friend, Michael James, had introduced him.

Pushkin had been quite cautious in making this commitment. He knew that religious cultural styles could sometimes be confused with true inner belief, and he wanted to be sure that what was happening inside him was authentic and if possible, permanent.

So he had met with the American scholar several times, here in this very room, in an intense tutorial in the practical implications of the Christian faith. The more he heard and studied, the more convinced he became that he had caught hold of a force that could change his life for good. He felt he was now linked to the true spiritual roots of Christianity, not just stale, dead traditions. But at the same time, he was still wrestling with the best way to merge his new understanding with his deeply ingrained Russian Orthodox heritage.

He stood up, walked over to one of his own wall shelves, and surveyed some of the very same icons, small statues and oil portraits that his parents had passed on to him years before. One representation of Jesus caught his eye, a flat piece of wood that had been painted at least three hundred years earlier. One of his favorites as a child.

Picking it up, he cradled it in both hands and then touched his forehead lightly with the artwork. Almost immediately, he felt tears well up in his eyes and an involuntary prayer escape from his lips.

It's as Archbishop Iakovos said. The power lies not in the image, but in the Power beyond the image. Just as the words of the Bible have no power in isolation, but only as God gives them meaning and transforms them into the Word in my life.

Still holding the small image of Christ, Pushkin returned to his chair, picked up his Bible, and turned to one of his favorite passages in Exodus, the story of the artisan Bezalel who had built the ancient Hebrew tabernacle and the ark of the covenant:

> *I have filled him with the Spirit of God, with ability and intelligence, with knowledge and all craftsmanship, to devise artistic designs, to work in gold, silver, and bronze, in cutting stones for setting, and in carving wood, for work in every craft.*

Suddenly, he felt incompetent to handle the challenges that lay ahead in space. He dreaded the physical danger. He trembled as he contemplated the scientific hurdles, barriers that no human being had yet been able to scale.

Solving the earth's energy needs forever. Then the secret experiment—attempting to create a rip in the fabric of space-time, in God's very handiwork. Who am I even to contemplate such matters?

"Do I really have the capacity to become a modern-day Bezalel?" he wondered aloud. "Will You give me the ability and intelligence I need to work in submolecular space, in the ultimate artistic medium that Bezalel himself couldn't have imagined? Or is this to be just another instance of human hubris, a failed attempt—perhaps with cosmic consequences—to explore realms that men and women were long ago commanded not to enter?"

Exhausted from the inner turmoil, Pushkin closed his eyes and began to doze. But before sleep completely overwhelmed him, a final thought lingered in his fading consciousness, a command of sorts that he remembered vividly until his departure from Russia two days later, a command that promised to sustain him in the weeks beyond:

Fast.

Fast and pray.

Guard your spirit, for that is your only protection, and your only hope for success.

S cott Andrews struggled to maintain his position in the massive water tank at the Johnson Space Center in Houston. The exhausted congressman was now in his fifth hour of submerged labor, yards beneath the surface in NASA's Weightless Environment Training Facility, or WETF. His assignment: seal a hole in a mock spaceship hull, which simulated the outside of the new lunar shuttle, the *Moonshot.*

This specialized spaceship would take him and his crew of international scientists to the moon, where they would set up their nuclear fusion shop at one of the lunar outposts now in operation. Their specific destination—the *Oceanus Procellarum,* or Ocean of Storms—was a huge mare or dark-shaded "sea" on the left side of the face of the moon that was always visible from earth. The scientists would board the *Moonshot* at its usual docking point, the new Deep Space Station (DSS), which served as a companion to the latest International Space Station (ISS). The ISS continued to be the focal point for orbital scientific research, while the DSS was a separate launch platform designed to handle missions to the moon and other parts of the solar system.

Scott's fatigue had erased any traces of good humor or excitement that might have sustained him at first. In fact, he found himself wondering exactly what he was doing here, wearing a cumbersome space suit underwater (in preparation for microgravity), engaged in what looked suspiciously like a make-work project. But then he remembered what he and his fellow scientists had been told at their introductory meeting at the Johnson Space Center.

"It's quite true that you're *not* astronauts—we're well aware of that," noted a senior astronaut-instructor, who had made countless trips into space. "But these moon trips are still risky business. Anything can happen—a puncture by a micrometeoroid, an equipment malfunction—anything. So we have to prepare you as well as we can in the short time available to us."

But the instructor didn't stop there. "Who knows?" he continued. "Your pilot and other trained mission specialists on board could be injured or killed. You might have to do a space walk and make repairs to the hull of the ship— all by yourself. And if you can't do it, you'll die in space."

Okay, okay, that got my attention, Scott conceded grudgingly to himself. *But that doesn't mean I have to like this glorified construction work.*

He turned to his task with renewed vigor—but without warning, he felt a sharp pain stab through his left side. Simultaneously, he was knocked up against the hull. Turning his head in an effort to find the cause of the problem and perhaps defend himself, he saw Vladimir Bolotov, floating only a couple of feet away. The Russian, who had been working nearby with a double-pipelike attachment, was holding one of his hands up in what seemed to be a rather halfhearted "I didn't mean to do it" gesture. As Scott peered into Bolotov's partially obscured face through the transparent visor on his helmet, the Russian appeared to mouth, "*Prahsteetyee!*"

Yeah, sure, Scott thought, drawing on his rudimentary knowledge of Russian. *If that guy ever really meant "Excuse me," I'd die of acute surprise. And was that the trace of a smirk on his face?*

One of the scuba divers assigned to monitor the training exercise had already arrived at Scott's side and was motioning him and Bolotov back to the surface. After the congressman had been pulled out of the water and the bulky tank-space suit had been removed, a medical team began checking him closely for injuries. Scott could tell from his own cursory self-examination that even though a couple of his ribs had been bruised, nothing was broken. But that didn't make him feel any kindlier toward the Russian.

"Exactly what did you think you were doing down there?" Scott asked sharply when Bolotov had removed his helmet. "I heard that the Cold War was over."

"Indeed, I am so sorry," the Russian scientist replied casually, with a decided lack of conviction. "The apparatus I was using slipped."

Without bothering to wait for a response, the Russian, his neck muscles bulging just above the suit, turned away, lowered his close-cropped, white-blond head, and began to remove his tank suit. He seemed the picture of unrepentant nonchalance.

"There can be no such slipping in space," retorted the head NASA instructor, who had rushed over to check Scott's condition. He was glaring at Bolotov, but the Russian ignored him. "Space suits are tough. But a blow with a sharp instrument might puncture the fabric. We've got backup oxygen systems to keep it inflated for thirty minutes, but that's assuming only an eighth-inch hole. If there's a bad rip, you might not get a second chance."

"Hey, you could puncture one of these underwater suits too—and that could mean big trouble!" added the scuba driver, who had been listening closely to the interchange.

Then, apparently annoyed that the Russian didn't seem to be paying attention, the diver stepped over and pulled on Bolotov's sleeve with enough force to shake the Russian off balance. "Hello! Are you still awake? A hole in this suit underwater could drown a guy!"

Bolotov, obviously not happy that he was the target of criticism, jerked his arm away. Scott watched out of the corner of his eye as the Russian quickly finished stripping down to the special, insulated long johns worn by the spaceship crew and passengers. He then stalked wordlessly back toward the locker room.

Bolotov measured six feet, two inches, according to the medical records Scott had seen, but the muscular Russian moved effortlessly for a big man. *Couple of weird scars on his back too. Run-ins with other Americans?*

Only Scott was still watching when the Russian glanced over his shoulder and looked back directly at him. The expression was not exactly friendly or remorseful.

"Did you see him hit me?" Scott asked the instructor.

"No, but I'm sure one of our cameras caught the incident." Then the instructor shook his head. "Chances are, though, you won't be able to tell much from the video disk."

"Too bad," Scott said. "I'd like to nail him red-handed."

"Why? Is there bad blood between you two?"

"He's not a real cuddly guy," Scott replied noncommittally, watching as a medic taped a cushioned pad over his bare ribs. "I have no reason to think he'd attack me on purpose. At the same time, though, I want to be very sure about the people on my team."

The medic now stepped back from his first-aid patchwork, and with the NASA instructor, he surveyed Scott's bare torso critically. "I think you're okay, sir," the medic said. "But one of our physicians will have to give you a more extensive exam. We have to be sure you're completely okay since you've got only ten days until you blast off."

"Yeah," the instructor echoed. "Can't have a half-healthy congressman going to the moon."

"You mean this could knock me off the team?" Scott replied incredulously.

"Any last-minute health problem could do you in," the instructor said. "Virus, sprained ankle, you name it."

"But, but . . . ," Scott spluttered, torn between frustration and growing anger toward Bolotov.

"Don't get upset until we have you checked out," the medic cautioned. "I've seen plenty of bumps and bruises in this final training phase, and they usually don't knock anybody off a mission."

"Bolotov!" Scott muttered to no one in particular.

"Well, the Russian's not exactly a careful worker when he's underwater," the NASA instructor said offhandedly. "This is probably just an accident."

Still, Bolotov will bear watching, Scott reflected glumly as he headed toward the lockers. *Close watching.*

6

The meal on the plate in front of him looked appetizing enough. But Scott was too tired to eat, and that wasn't all. Even with the painkillers, his bruised ribs hurt, making it almost impossible for him to find a comfortable position in his chair.

A preliminary exam by a NASA flight surgeon had tentatively cleared him to continue his training. But the doctor had advised him to go on light duty for a couple of days so that the healing could proceed swiftly and smoothly.

"I think you're going to be okay," the doctor had said. "But that depends on how well you take care of yourself."

That reassurance meant something, but Scott remained preoccupied about his uncertain position with the mission. Even the reasonably good food and comfortable setting at the team's private dining room in the Johnson Space Center couldn't relax him completely or relieve a nagging concern at the back of his mind. With some distaste, Scott eyed Bolotov, who was eating at a nearby table with his Russian colleague, Pushkin.

Friend, these ribs had better heal quickly. If I'm not cleared for this mission, someone will pay.

Scott's two dining companions—Jeffrey Hightower, an Australian nuclear physicist and engineer, and Shiro Hiramatsu, the Japanese laser engineering specialist who was Scott's second in command—seemed unaware of his worries. They were embroiled in an intense discussion about the outlook for mining helium-3 on the moon, which would be a key ingredient in triggering the nuclear fusion process.

Hiramatsu sucked air between his teeth—a sound that Scott knew signaled

the scientist's frustration—and then voiced his anxiety. "Ah, even if we succeed in establishing the fusion plant, many problems remain. Our plan hinges
on generating massive power on the moon and getting it back to earth on a
laser beam. But much is still not known about lasers."

"You're the world's main expert on lasers!" Hightower said in mock surprise. "Are you saying that we're trotting up to the moon, risking our lives in
space, pouring billions into this project—and you don't know if you can jolly
well pull off your end of it?"

"*Hai*, of course I know lasers," Hiramatsu replied quietly, looking down at
his plate. "But much is still experimental. We see it works on paper. But will
it work in fact?"

"Just don't point your lasers at me," Hightower said, ducking his head
down to one side.

"Now *I'm* starting to get nervous," Scott chimed in, glad for an opportunity to take his mind off Bolotov and his own aching rib cage.

"Ah, no, you see, you see . . . ," Hiramatsu began nervously, apparently
sensing he was under some sort of professional attack. "Ah, *tasukete!*"

"What's that?" Scott said.

"I think he said, 'Help!'" Hightower responded.

"Shiro, we're joking," Scott said. "Bad American and outback humor."

The banter had gone a little too far, Scott realized.

"Let me get serious for a moment," Scott said in an effort to make
Hiramatsu more comfortable. "Jeff understands this stuff, but I'm relatively
new to fusion energy, lasers, and the like. So tell me again—in the simplest
possible terms—what you guys will be doing up there on the lunar surface.
The more I hear, the better."

Now the Japanese engineer was on firm ground. He adjusted his large,
black-rimmed spectacles, pursed his ample lips, and reached into his ever-
present briefcase for a sheet of blank paper. Then he began to draw.

"We all know, of course, that the engineers who were sent to the moon last
year have established a well-equipped facility for us on the Ocean of Storms,"
he began. "All the physical material we need to construct a fusion plant and
lasers is already up there. Also, our technicians are even now on a lunar shuttle
heading for the moon. This preparation makes everything so much easier. But
still, we face challenges. Very great challenges."

He stopped talking for a few seconds so that he could put the finishing
touches on his drawing.

"This is crude and simple," Hiramatsu apologized. "But perhaps it will help. You see, it all begins at the moon, where the fusion plant will be built. Our Russian friend"—he pointed toward Pushkin at the nearby table—"will oversee the construction of the plant."

"And remember why we're building it on the moon instead of on the earth," Hightower added. "It's because there's a lot of helium-3 on the moon, which is an essential ingredient in the fusion reaction."

"Yes," Hiramatsu agreed. "There is almost no helium-3 on earth. Our magnetic field makes the molecule unstable. But because of the lack of a magnetic field and atmosphere on the moon, helium-3 has accumulated in significant amounts on the lunar surface. We're already setting up a moon mining operation to extract the helium-3 from the surface for our fusion fuel."

"At what point do you get personally involved in the operation?" Scott asked the Japanese scientist.

"At the beginning," Hiramatsu replied. "Dr. Pushkin needs a powerful laser to heat up the helium plasma to approximately 400 million degrees Celsius."

"Seven hundred and twenty million degrees Fahrenheit," Hightower echoed.

"Pretty hot," Scott said quietly.

"So our laser mate here is the key player in kicking off this operation," Hightower said.

He wrapped a large, freckled arm around Hiramatsu and pulled him so close that the Australian's fine, unruly reddish locks almost mingled with the Japanese engineer's well-combed black hair. Hiramatsu stiffened and tried to lean away.

"Hey, come to think of it, Shiro's also responsible for maybe the most important part of this project—getting the electrical power from the moon to the earth!" the Australian said.

With that, Hiramatsu pried himself loose from Hightower's grip, straightened his blue, short-sleeve shirt, which was the uniform all the team members were wearing at the space center, and turned back to his drawing.

"Now you see I have drawn this laser line from the moon to the earth," Hiramatsu said, looking expectantly at Scott to be sure he was following the explanation. "That laser beam is generated by an extremely powerful x-ray device, which we must create from the fusion power."

"By the way, Scotty m'boy, do you know where we get the word *laser* from?" Hightower interrupted.

"I'm not a complete dunce," the congressman replied. "It's an acronym, standing for, let's see . . . Light Amplification . . ."

"... by Stimulated Emission of Radiation,'" Hightower finished when Scott hesitated. "L-a-s-e-r."

"This will be the most powerful laser that humans have ever created," Hiramatsu continued. "It will consist of a coherent stream of x-rays, which will be directed toward an artificial satellite circling the earth."

"Then the satellite will convert the superpowerful x-ray laser beam into multiple microwave laser beams, which will be transmitted to earth," Hightower interjected.

"And as I understand it, the reason for using the microwave beams is that they'll be safer for people and animals on earth," Scott noted.

"Correct," Hightower said. "No point in cooking old Mum and Dad and the kiddies. The microwave lasers are much weaker than lasers made from shorter, more powerful electromagnetic waves—such as visible light, ultra-violet, or x-rays. So they're less of a threat if anyone gets in the way."

"Still, we plan to be extracautious with these devices," Hiramatsu said. "The microwave laser beams will be redirected to these major power centers on earth—what the public utility people call 'central stations.' And to add to the safety, those central stations will be positioned in clearly posted, unpopulated areas, where it's highly unlikely that people or animals will pass through. At those stations, the microwaves will be converted into electricity through rectifying antennas—or 'rectennas,' as they're called. These contain special photovoltaic cells like those used to convert solar energy."

"And that electricity will supply the earth's energy needs for ten thousand years," Scott finished.

The three men studied the diagram quietly for a few moments.

"Of course, this is all very new technology," Hiramatsu finally said. "But the powerful x-ray laser seems best to cover the vast spans of space. All lasers tend to spread out the farther they are projected. With more powerful lasers, the beams will hold together better over long distances."

"Still, the great power of the x-ray laser does pose some possible problems," Hightower said.

"So you were saying," Scott replied.

"We fully expect we can control it over such vast distances—an average of about 240,000 miles from the moon to the earth," Hightower said quietly. "But if anybody or anything gets in the way, the intruder could get fried. Totally vaporized."

"Like a third rail in space," Scott mused.

"How's that?" Hightower asked.

"A third rail. That's the live rail on New York City subways. You touch it, you die."

"Right," Hightower said. "So there must be strict safety protocols for this moon-to-earth laser."

"*Hai*, very strict," Hiramatsu emphasized. "One major accident early in this project, and we could encounter serious public opposition."

"Believe me, I know," Scott agreed. "I'm already getting resistance from some of my constituents in Florida."

"What's the worry?" Hightower asked.

"Some see military uses for such a laser," the congressman said. "If it's really as dangerous as you say, what happens if the technology gets into the wrong hands? What if a hostile nation or terrorist group turns the beam on one of our military installations or a city?"

"What sort of hostile group?" Hightower said.

Scott rubbed his sore ribs and looked toward the Russians.

"You're not serious, Scotty old man," Hightower said, an incredulous smile playing across his face. "I mean, our Russians are respected scientists."

"Bolotov?" Scott replied. "You think *he's* a respected scientist?"

Hightower shrugged. "So maybe he's KGB."

"FSB," Hiramatsu corrected, referring to the post–Cold War term.

"Whatever," the Australian said. "A spy's a spy. Scotty old man, I think you're still into the Cold War mentality. You've got to shake that."

Then a mischievous gleam came into the Australian's eyes. "But who knows? Maybe you're right! No point in taking any chances. I don't like the idea of watching my back in a moon suit. Let's check 'em out." He stood up abruptly and swaggered toward the Russians' table before Scott could react.

"G'day, cobbers!" the Australian cried, stopping in front of the two scientists and slapping a frowning Bolotov on the shoulder.

"What did he say?" Hiramatsu asked Scott in a low tone.

"I think that's Australian for 'Hello, guys,'" Scott replied, shaking his head.

"Well now, Vlad and Serg," Hightower said, leaning into the Russians' faces with a broad grin and rubbing Bolotov's back with a familiarity that made the Russian visibly tighten up. "I was talking to my mates over there, and they started to get a mite jittery when I told 'em I really love you cobbers. We're all one-worlders, ain't we? All for one and one for all. I told 'em there's no way you boys would be planning to double-deal up there on the moon. After all, we're a team—total trust and all that, right?"

"What do you mean?" Bolotov asked with a growl as he shook Hightower's hand away from his shoulder.

"What is this 'double-deal'?" Pushkin said.

"No offense, mate," Hightower said, plunging forward with hardly a breath. "We're just assuming, as I'm sure you are, that everything up there on the moon will be aboveboard. On the table. In clear sight. We're scientists first, right? So when we work together up there, we'll all share all our findings, eh? Open books, no secrets? And everything we discover is for peaceful purposes. I'm sure we agree on that, right?"

Both Russians stared at the Australian physicist with slightly open mouths.

Finally, Pushkin found some words: "We can make no special agreements. We are Russians. We work for our government, and if our superiors give us special orders, we must follow them. We—"

But Bolotov placed a hand on Pushkin's arm to stop him.

"You are out of line, Dr. Hightower," Bolotov said sharply. "Our government and yours have negotiated the present arrangement. None of us have the authority to change that understanding."

Now it was the Australian's turn to stare with an open mouth. He had clearly been half-joking for the benefit of Scott and Shiro, and had apparently expected the Russians to laugh with him. But their serious, rather hostile response had thrown him off balance.

"You're not helping my confidence," Hightower finally replied.

"Our objective is not to make you confident," Bolotov said gruffly. "Your training was supposed to do that."

At that, the Australian threw up his hands and seemed on the verge of saying or doing something he might regret. But just then, a woman in a wheelchair rolled up to the Russians' table. It was Ruth Goldberg, an Israeli laser expert who had been assigned to the team to assist Shiro Hiramatsu.

"Room for me?" she asked. Then she looked around at the men in some puzzlement when she noticed that something seemed to be wrong. "Of course, I can sit over there with Scott and Shiro . . ."

"No, no, there is plenty of room here," Pushkin replied, in a tone that betrayed some relief. "Please sit here with us."

Hightower took her appearance as his cue to retreat back to the table with

Hiramatsu and Scott. But as he drew closer, Scott could see that all humor had disappeared from his eyes.

"What was that all about?" Scott asked.

"Perhaps you're not so paranoid, Scotty old boy," Hightower replied, obviously seething. "Something's going on here that I don't understand."

"They're obviously not into diplomacy," Scott said, mildly amused at the Australian's discomfort. *At least now, somebody else is seeing a problem with these Russians.* "It's strange. It would have been so easy for them just to say, 'Sure, we'll work together.' Or 'Sure, our goal is peace and great economic benefit to the entire earth.' But they sidestepped your questions."

"And they weren't particularly nice about it," Hightower muttered.

"No, they weren't," Scott said. "But the question is why."

The three men sat silently for a few moments, stealing a glance or two at the other table.

"There are still suspicions about the Russians among many American policy experts," Scott finally said. "The thinking is that President Dalton trusts them too much." Once more, he looked over at Pushkin and Bolotov, who were now huddled in an intense discussion with Ruth Goldberg. "When I stand for re-election to Congress next year, I'll have to respond to some of those concerns. I must admit, I have many unanswered questions myself."

"Um, there have been rumors about the close ties your president has with Russian Prime Minister Martov," Hiramatsu suggested tentatively.

Scott looked at him curiously. "What sort of rumors?" he asked, suspecting that the Japanese scientist might be trying to pump him for information, perhaps on behalf of his own government.

"Rumors about possible economic interests between Americans and Russians, business agreements that may not have been made public as yet," Hiramatsu said, apparently still probing to see if he could learn more.

"I really don't know about any of that," Scott said, then decided it would be best to change the subject. "The main thing I'm worried about is keeping healthy—and staying away from Bolotov."

"Think the bloke whacked you on purpose?" Hightower asked, pointing to Scott's injured ribs.

Scott shrugged. "Hard to say. It sure felt like he meant it. Actually seemed annoyed I was still functioning. Anyway, it wouldn't hurt them to get rid of me. That would certainly make this more of a Russian show."

"They're a strange pair," Hightower said, gesturing toward the Russians. "Look at Bolotov. Those muscles and scars on his arms—"

"And his back," Scott added, remembering the sight of the old, deep wound on the man's bare shoulder as he walked away at the tank. The blond Russian was looking intently at Pushkin with the same hard, cold expression that seemed to mark the usual fault lines of his face.

"Doesn't look like any serious scientist I know," Hightower continued. "What researcher do you know is that fit and skilled at underwater work? And he maxed out on every physical test they gave him here at the center, didn't he?"

"Former cosmonaut," Hiramatsu said. "And wrestler."

The Australian jerked his head toward the Russians again. "And then there's his odd twin, Pushkin," Hightower said. "The anti-Bolotov. Thin, unathletic, almost fragile. I sometimes wonder if he has the strength to make it to the moon and back."

"He's a philosopher," Hiramatsu said to no one in particular. "And he appears to be some sort of spiritual radical. I think perhaps a cult member."

"Oh?" Scott said, startled at the observations of the Japanese laser expert.

"I've talked with him over coffee, and he seemed especially interested in violent groups," the Japanese scientist continued. "Such as the one that placed nerve gas in the Tokyo subway system several decades ago. Back in 1995, I believe. The Aum Shinri Kyo cult."

Scott didn't know what to make of this information, but it was worrisome. As the other two scientists returned to their discussion of complex laser technology, Scott lapsed into silence, immersed in his effort to sort through this new information about the Russians. It was hard enough trying to fathom the role of Bolotov, who was looking more and more like a Russian government plant, maybe even an FSB agent.

But Pushkin was now posing other knotty questions in his own right. Did the Russians know about the man's odd philosophical inclinations? Was he really some kind of religious nut, or was that idea just part of a Russian strategy designed to keep Americans off balance during the moon operation?

Scott's train of thought was shattered as a familiar, disheveled figure burst through the dining room door and headed directly for him. It was his chief of staff, Colleen Barker, and she obviously had something on her mind.

7

I've got to talk to you," Colleen said in an intense whisper that Scott was sure could be heard around the room. "*Now.*"

"Sure, sure," he said, somewhat embarrassed by the intrusion. Colleen knew that the Houston facilities were off limits to everyone except team members—and that included her. But obviously, she had elected to sidestep normal procedures, and he had to assume that something important was on her mind.

After they had quickly exited the dining area, he motioned her into an empty, private room that had been made available for reading and study during the team's training.

"Okay, so what's up?" he asked, pulling up a couple of chairs next to a table.

He knew better than to become annoyed with Colleen because she never violated his privacy unless there was very good reason. Still, he had to fight his impatience as he watched her struggle to peel off her wrinkled, wet trench coat—a summer shower had been drenching the Houston area. Finally, she pulled her wavy, not-quite-combed, damp black hair back from her face and looked him straight in the eye.

"Here's the deal," she began in a whisper. "There's something going on with the Russians, something I don't know a thing about, even with my clearances. I just want to be sure you're on top of it."

Scott was puzzled. Colleen was usually a step ahead of him and rarely seemed to become nervous about anything. Sometimes he wondered if she really cared if disaster struck or the world blew up. Instead of getting flustered in a crisis, she usually reacted like the investigative reporter she had been before joining his staff—more than delighted with the extraordinary, and more than ready to unleash her journalistic skills to solve any problem.

But this was different. He had never seen her in such a state. Her round, full face was wet with perspiration as well as raindrops, and her cheeks were deeply flushed, as though she were just coming off a two-mile run. The problem was, she wasn't a runner.

"What are you talking about?" he asked. "What's with the Russians?"

"It's not just the fusion or the energy issue," she replied. "There's something else. Something bigger. A special experiment of some sort."

"What could be bigger than solving the earth's energy needs for thousands of years?"

"That's just it. I don't know. What they're doing is classified way beyond my personal clearances. Actually seems to be classified black."

Scott knew that "black" meant the information was so secret it wasn't even supposed to exist. Even he didn't know about most black matters.

"If you know and you can't talk about it, just tell me to get lost," Colleen continued. "I'll head out that door without looking back."

Scott shook his head. "I don't have any idea what you're talking about. The fusion and laser projects are all I've heard about. I was just talking with Hiramatsu and Hightower, and neither said a thing about any other Russian experiment."

"What about the Russians? Have they given any indication?"

"I don't talk much with the Russians," Scott replied ruefully. "Bolotov practically disabled me in the training tank earlier today."

Colleen winced as he lifted part of his shirt to show her the bruise and patch on his ribs.

"And apparently Pushkin is dabbling in religious cults," he continued. "I probably should have made more of an effort to get to know him, but both those guys seem to want to keep to themselves."

"Maybe for good reason," Colleen said. "Look at this note a CIA source passed on to me. Seems the Russians have been authorized to carry on an unidentified, highly classified experiment—by our president and the national security adviser."

"Are you kidding me?"

"I wish."

"And when am I, as the moon-team leader and a senior member of the U.S. Congress, supposed to be informed about this top-secret plan?" Scott asked, growing angrier by the second.

"Apparently when your dear friend President Bobby Dalton says the time is right," Colleen said. "Actually, according to this memo, you and the other team members are supposed to learn about this at the end of next week, just before you blast off."

"So we don't have a chance to ask questions or protest."

"Seems that way."

"Well, they'll hear from me well before that," Scott said. "And if I don't get good answers, I may go public."

"That'll rattle some cages," Colleen said, savoring the prospect. "And it won't hurt your election prospects. It will make you look strong and independent."

"Of course, this may be so serious that I won't be able to mention it," he reflected. "That's the problem when the president starts classifying things."

"But at least you now have some leverage to pry more information out of them," she replied.

"Any indication about what the Russians will be investigating?" he asked.

Colleen sighed. "Unfortunately, I don't have anything official. Nothing else from the CIA. But I did come up with this," she said, pulling a sheaf of additional papers from her briefcase.

"I asked some of my contacts to check on Pushkin—his research, interests, and so forth," she continued. "Also, I did a Lexus-Nexus search on him. Seems he's written a number of papers for obscure international scientific journals on wormholes."

"What?"

"Wormholes, as in science fiction, superfast space travel, that sort of thing."

"And?"

"The interesting thing is that one of his main theories is that the way you build one of these wormholes is by using a huge energy source. His preference is nuclear fusion."

"And we'll be setting up a nuclear fusion facility on the moon," Scott said.

"You got it."

Scott fell silent for a few moments. He scoured his memory for scientific articles he might have read about wormholes, which he knew were theoretical rips in the fabric of space-time. As a former practicing physician and biochemical researcher, he had always tried to stay current on the latest scientific developments. Now as chairman of the House Space Committee and an active senior member of the Science Committee, he was *expected* to be on top of things.

But why should Pushkin, Bolotov, and the Russians be interested in such theoretical experiments? And why would an American president be involved—and not want to let Congress know about it?

Possibilities cascaded through his consciousness. *The military? Could Bobby-Boy and the Russians be planning research with a military use? Or do they have some economic benefits in mind?*

The money motive seemed as likely as anything. President Dalton was known for using his office to build his net worth with shady fund-raising schemes. And his links to corporate and entertainment industry moguls, who would be willing to put him on the payroll when he left office, were legendary. *But how in the world—or in space—could you use a wormhole to make money?*

There were too many unanswered questions at this point. But one thing Scott did know was that the president shouldn't be operating behind his back.

"I'm calling Dalton right now," he finally told Colleen. "And I want you next to me to feed me the facts, just in case I forget anything you've said. Okay?"

"You bet, boss," Colleen said, now relishing the excitement.

Scott could see that even though this new wrinkle in the moon project had temporarily stymied his normally intrepid chief of staff, she was now back on track with a vengeance. As a journalist, Colleen had always been ready to cover the most difficult stories and dig as deep as necessary to get the facts. But as the right hand of one of Congress's most influential committee chairmen, she knew she was answerable to a higher authority, and the weight of this civic responsibility sometimes made her quite uncomfortable—even nervous.

"I'm not one who likes to start wars," she had once said to Scott.

But now that her boss was up to speed on the facts and in a position to speak authoritatively on what was shaping up as a major national security issue, Colleen's confidence returned.

"So should we put the call through to Dalton now?" she asked.

"Yes," he said. "There's a secure phone in the next building. Let's go right over."

They made their way to the next building, where Scott dialed the White House. As Scott waited for the president to come to the phone, he glanced at Colleen, who was sitting on the edge of a chair just across the desk from him. She was obviously enjoying the action. *Especially since the ball is now in my hands.*

"Hello, Scott," the smooth southern voice finally said. "From what I hear, you're staying pretty busy there in Texas. Hope those ribs are mending okay."

"Thanks for the concern, Mr. President. You must be getting minute-to-minute updates on me. My unfortunate encounter with Dr. Bolotov happened just a couple of hours ago."

"Oh, I'm keeping close tabs, Scott. What you're doing is probably the most important program in my entire administration. Why, maybe even in American history or world history. We're on the verge of achieving something truly great for mankind—uh, humankind." The president cleared his throat, realizing he had made a minor politically incorrect blunder. "Anyway, you should know I'm completely behind you."

"Yes, then perhaps you could fill me in on something," Scott replied. "I've heard that the Russians are going to be working on some highly classified project up there on the moon. Something I haven't been told about. Anything to those reports?"

"Ah, well, you see, Scott . . ."

Answer: Yes.

"Because I really need to know everything that's going to happen up there, Mr. President," Scott said. "After all, the success of this mission and the safety of the people here are in my hands. I don't think my fellow members of Congress would be too happy to learn that something is going on with the Russians behind our backs."

"Now see here, Scott," the president protested. "I trust you're not implying that *I'm* involved in doing anything behind your back. Not on your life! Not on such an important mission! I know we're in different parties, Scott, and we haven't always seen eye-to-eye. But that doesn't mean we're not both *Americans*, with the interests of our great nation at heart."

Yeah, yeah. I can already hear "The Star-Spangled Banner." Scott rolled his eyes, and Colleen, who was watching him closely, grinned. Even though she couldn't hear what Dalton was saying, she knew the conversation was heating up.

"Of course I know we're *both* patriots," Scott said, not trying to disguise the irony in his voice. "But there's a problem of full disclosure. Disclosure to the elected official who is in charge of this mission—namely, me. I have no limits on my security clearances. Yet it seems I have to find out from nonofficial sources that the Russians are up to something—something like a wormhole?"

Scott, who had saved that zinger for the right moment, smiled slightly as he thought he detected a slight gasp on the other end of the line. The response seemed to confirm Colleen's speculations. Apparently, the mysterious research did have something to do with wormholes—and Dalton was aware of more than he was letting on.

"The Russians have been authorized to conduct some special experiment up there," Dalton finally admitted vaguely. "The exact nature of it must remain classified. But—"

"What do you mean, 'must remain classified'?" Scott replied sharply. "How can you share sensitive matters with the Russians on a mission like this, but not with the senior congressman who's in charge of the entire team? Who's running this thing? Us? Or Pushkin and Bolotov?"

"Now, Scott . . . ," the president said soothingly.

"Don't you patronize me!" Scott shot back. "Exactly what's going on with you and the Russians?"

"I won't have you talk to me like this!" Dalton barked, a self-righteous tone now taking over.

"So maybe you'd rather have the entire U.S. Congress talk to you? Or the American people? I think maybe we need an investigation."

"You're being irresponsible," Dalton said. "If you're not careful, I'll take you off this mission."

"Try it," Scott said, seething. "You take me off this team, and I'll have no choice but to go public. What is the *real* purpose of this project, anyway? A joint military venture with the Russians? Some private deal you're working out that's really a treaty—a deal that should have the Senate's advice and consent? Or is it nothing more exotic than some financial windfall designed to line the pockets of high-ranking American and Russian officials?"

Scott let that sink in for a moment. Then he softened his tone before Dalton could respond. "Look, Mr. President, I don't want to create a crisis here. And I'm well aware that you could pull me off this mission. But I hope you're also aware that I could probably scuttle the whole thing with hearings in Congress. Neither of us wants that. Put yourself in my shoes. You'll see that it's essential for me to know more about what the Russians are up to. After all, I'll be in charge of marshaling our resources up there on the lunar surface. If I can't trust the Russians, how can I allow them free access to our technicians and information sources?"

"Right, right, you're absolutely right, Scott," Dalton replied in a much calmer, more unctuous tone, the one he frequently used when he was trying to cajole members of Congress into supporting one of his controversial, big-spending projects. "Our objectives are basically the same. It's mainly a question of timing. In fact, I actually thought I might give you a call as early as today or tomorrow to fill you in on what I know. But of course, you called me first."

Sure, sure.

"Scott, we're both practical men, both deal-makers," the president said soothingly. "In crass terms, I had to do some down-and-dirty bargaining to keep this thing moving forward. After Rensburg's death, the only fusion game in town was Pushkin. You know that. Then the Russians decided to play hardball. In return for making Pushkin available, they insisted that we allow him to do some secondary experiment with his fusion technology."

"Wormholes," Scott said quietly.

"I did hear something about that," the president conceded.

Bingo!

"But who knows anything about wormholes?" Dalton continued. "What could they possibly be used for? My people think the whole thing is a fantasy. So to pacify the Russians and get them on board with us, I said yes to their little experiment."

"Did you require them to share their results with us?" Scott pressed.

"Well, I'm sure if they find anything important they'll let us know."

"You say you're sure?" Scott asked incredulously. "How can you possibly know? This all seems rather remarkable to me. I mean, in a joint project like this, where we're putting up most of the money, are you saying we have no assurance of participating in the benefits if they discover something?"

"I'm sure there won't be any practical benefits," Dalton said defensively. "This experiment of theirs involves pure research."

"And you also allowed them to pad the Russian presence on this mission with Bolotov—was that part of the deal too?" Scott asked.

"Pushkin had to have his own assistant," the president protested. "That's only fair, isn't it?"

"Except we end up with an extra Russian on the top scientific team," Scott said. "And I'm now the only American, even though we started out with three—Rensburg, his assistant, and me. You know that, don't you?"

"Of course, but I have implicit trust in you, Scott," Dalton said in a transparent attempt at flattery. "You'll oversee our interests quite well."

"*If* I'm on the team when it leaves," Scott replied. Then he remembered with a brief flash of horror that Dalton had the power to keep him off the launch for medical reasons. "Wait a minute. Let me be clear. I *expect* to be on that team when it leaves, and if I should be replaced because of what Bolotov did to me in the tank, I'll be a very unhappy camper. In fact, I think I'd be duty-bound to report my suspicions about the Russians to the House Intelligence Committee. On the other hand, if you could guarantee that I'll be on board that lunar shuttle . . ."

Scott winked at Colleen as he heard the president say, "If you're walking, I'll personally see to it that you'll be on board that shuttle."

"That's somewhat reassuring," Scott replied. "But I have to know one thing. Did you attach any strings at all to this wormhole deal—anything that might work in our favor?"

"Of course, of course," President Dalton replied quickly. "For one thing, they can't use their findings for military purposes. Or any other application that would harm American security, and so on, and so on."

"Any way to enforce those restrictions?" Scott asked curtly. "Any inspection procedures?"

"Sure, sure, we have the right to limited inspections in case anything comes of their experiments."

"And who, may I ask, will be doing the inspections on the moon—or presumably, the ones in Russia, if the technology is transferred there?" Scott asked skeptically. "Have you set up an international watchdog group that has some teeth?"

"Still working that out," Dalton replied, rather uncomfortably, Scott thought. "But don't you worry. We're on top of all that."

"I'll tell you straight, Mr. President, I don't like this," Scott replied. "I don't like it at all. And it looks like I'm playing with a hand that's already been dealt. But remember, I have a responsibility to the American people that goes well beyond my relationship with you. I intend to fulfill that responsibility one way or another."

"Wouldn't have it any other way, Scott," the president replied, a sense of relief coming through in his voice. "You're a patriot, a real American. I know that. Makes me feel safe and secure to know you'll be on board, watching over things."

Sure it does.

"Thank you, Mr. President," Scott replied. "I think this has been a very enlightening and useful conversation."

"Same here."

After her boss had hung up, Colleen beamed at him for a moment. "At least now he knows the score," she finally said.

Scott shook his head. "This is just the beginning. And I don't think we have the foggiest notion where any of this will end up. Dalton knows a lot more than he's saying. I have a strong feeling he and the Russians are collaborating on something. He also understands more about the potential for this classified research than he admits. Certainly more than I do."

"So what's next?" Colleen asked.

Scott sighed. "I want you to play bloodhound and get on the trail of Rensburg's killers."

"Killers?"

"Yes. You know we both suspect foul play. Try to run it down. If you get some answers, that'll tell us a lot more about this moon mission."

"So you think the Russians are involved?"

He smiled. "*You* do, don't you? Did you think I wasn't listening to you in my office a few weeks ago? Your idea about Russian involvement is getting more plausible." He winced as he touched his sore ribs. "I'd even say the Russians are prime suspects—unless you can prove otherwise."

"And you?" she asked.

"I'll just keep moving toward the moon, and maybe do a little snooping of my own—into Russian-made wormholes."

8

The Texas sun was just going down over the seventh tee, which was clearly visible through the bay window of the small house Scott Andrews had rented while he was in training at Houston's Johnson Space Center. As he lay back with his head resting in his wife's lap, looking at the waning orange rays of the sun out of the corner of his eye, the congressman finally felt somewhat at peace.

A rather long, stressful day at the office, he reflected. *Astronaut training was tough enough. But when you add in an underwater attack from a hostile Russian, followed by a heated argument with the president of the United States, well, that is a little excessive for anybody.*

Fortunately, he had found a relatively inexpensive cottage in the Clear Lake area near the JSC facilities, and Sara and the two kids had been able to fly in from Virginia and visit him for a long weekend. She, their son Jacob, and daughter Megan might be able to visit him one more time while he was in Houston. Then he would be off to the Kennedy Space Center on the east coast of Florida for the final countdown and liftoff into orbit.

"Still want to bring the kids down to Florida for the launch, don't you?" he asked. "I'll be there for only a couple of days, but I've arranged to rent a place in Cocoa Beach where we can all stay. You and the kids can hang around for a few days after I leave if you like, so they can check out the Kennedy facility and maybe spend a little time on the beach."

"Sure, that's fine," she said with a sigh.

He could tell from Sara's tone that she didn't want to think about his upcoming trip into space. There was always a risk when you chose to sit atop a group of exploding rocket boosters and soar thousands of miles per hour into orbit. And who could say what risks the moon might hold?

The extra pressure in her fingers told him that Sara was worried. He was on the verge of telling her to ease up a little, but then she returned to her usual gentle massage of his forehead, then his temples, then his forehead again. He could feel the tension in his body fading away.

"Sara, I think you've discovered my stress gene," he said. "You've been keeping this medical breakthrough all to yourself."

"Don't talk," his wife said impatiently. "The more you talk, the more uptight you get. Just keep quiet for once."

"Right, don't talk," he repeated, looking lazily up into his wife's green eyes, which almost seemed to glow against the background of her short, dark hair.

Scott's thinking became more jumbled as his wife's strong but soothing finger pressure lulled him nearer and nearer to a doze. "Yeah," he said groggily. "No moon, no lasers, no fusion . . ."

"What's fusion, Daddy?" The girlish voice from the other side of the room jerked him from his near-slumber and caused him to sit up abruptly.

Scott sighed and beckoned to his eleven-year-old daughter. Soon Megan and ten-year-old Jacob were wedged between their parents on the sofa.

"Let's see, what is fusion?" he repeated, trying to think of an easy way to convey the concept to a couple of inquisitive elementary school children. "Think about it this way. You see my finger?"

He held up his right index finger.

"Yep," Jacob said.

"Okay, now what is my finger made of?"

"Skin," Jacob replied.

"And muscles and blood and bones," Megan added.

"Right, but now go a little deeper," Scott said. "What are the skin and blood and bones made of?"

Megan thought for a moment. "Cells. We just studied that at school."

"Right! But go even deeper. What are the cells made of?"

Megan was temporarily stumped, but Jacob surprised them all: "Atoms."

"Not bad," Scott said. "Not bad at all. Where did you hear about atoms?"

"TV, I think."

"Well, you're quite right," Scott said. "Atoms are on a level we can't see with our eyes—but we can detect them with certain measuring devices. This finger is made of tiny cells, and those cells are made of atoms, and arrangements of atoms called molecules. At the very center of each atom is something called a nucleus—and that nucleus is the key to maybe the greatest source of power in the universe."

He reached over to the table next to the sofa, picked up a loose sheet of paper, and wadded it up into a ball. "So let's say this is a very large, blown-up version of the nucleus of an atom. Now suppose we split this nucleus—cut it right in two." He ripped the ball of paper into two parts. "What happens when we split the atom?"

Jacob shrugged, but Megan said, "Boom!"

Again, Scott was surprised, and he could tell from his wife's expression that she had been caught off guard as well. "I wonder if maybe you two shouldn't be giving this little lecture instead of me. Where'd you learn that?"

"TV," Megan replied. "There was something on the other day about an atomic bomb. So I figured—"

"You figured right," Scott said. "When you split an atom, that involves a process called 'fission,' which releases an awful lot of energy. The atomic bomb you probably saw exploding—maybe with a mushroom cloud?"—Megan nodded—"is an example of what can happen when fission occurs. But there's a big problem with fission."

"What's that?" Megan asked.

"When you smash an atom like this, all sorts of dangerous garbage is left over," Scott explained. "That's called 'radioactive waste' or 'fallout,' and the damage radiation can do to humans and other life on earth is huge. So people have been trying to develop another, cleaner way to make use of atomic energy—and that's where fusion comes in."

Scott took the two balls of paper he had split apart and pushed them together again. "Fusion is the opposition of fission. With fusion, you use tremendous amounts of heat to cram the nuclei of atoms or molecules together, so that they form a heavier molecule. When that happens, tremendous energy is also released, but the waste products are clean. They're not radioactive. They won't hurt us or make us sick."

"So why do you have to go to the moon to do this?" Jacob asked.

Scott, avoiding his wife's accusatory glance, said, "Several reasons. First, there's a lot of stuff necessary for fusion up there on the moon. But we don't have enough of that stuff here on earth."

"Like what?" Megan asked.

This was turning into more of a fusion lecture than he had expected. But

Scott was never one to cut off his children's questioning—especially when science was involved. "Like a form of helium," he replied.

"The stuff you and Mom used to fill those balloons at my birthday party?" Jacob asked.

"Yes, almost," Scott answered. "But this is a special kind of helium, called helium-3. And to cause fusion, we combine helium-3 with another molecule, a form of hydrogen. You know, hydrogen is an important part of the water you drink."

"Hydrogen plus oxygen," Megan said.

"Very good!" Sara said. "School science again?"

"Yep. So you put the special helium into the hydrogen, and you get what?" Megan asked, moving Scott's hands together so that the two wadded paper balls were touching.

"You get some normal helium—just like we used to fill Jacob's balloons," Scott replied. "Real clean stuff. But we also get a huge amount of energy, enough to take care of the lights and heat and other power needs around the earth for thousands of years."

"Wow," Jacob said. Both children sat quietly for a moment.

"So you can see why Daddy has to go on this trip," Scott concluded.

"But what if something happens to you?" Jacob asked. He was obviously not primarily concerned about the energy needs of future generations.

"Nothing's going to happen to me," Scott said, putting his arm around the boy. Glancing at Sara again, he didn't like the troubled expression that had crossed her face. "Think of this as a space adventure in the movies or on TV. That's what it is. And when I come back in about three months, I'll have all sorts of stories to tell."

"About aliens?" Jacob asked expectantly.

"Wouldn't that be something?" Scott exclaimed. "I don't expect to run into any little green men—"

"Or women," Megan interjected.

"Or women," Scott agreed. "But who knows? Anyhow, if I see any aliens, you'll be the first to hear! I'll be able to talk to you a lot over some phones they've set up in space. And we can go back and forth with e-mail all the time. I'll be sure to check my mail several times every day to see if I have any important messages from my favorite people. But now, it's time for bed, okay?"

After the children had settled down for the night in their rooms, Scott tried to lean back again with his head in Sara's lap, but the mood had been broken.

"I wish you weren't going," she said, pushing him back to an upright position.

Sara stood up, walked over to the window, and looked glumly out onto the golf course, which now had become a vague, featureless expanse in the twilight. Scott watched her closely as she hugged herself tightly with her long, well-muscled arms. He knew her body language as well as his own. Her lanky body, now wound up like the tightest spring, practically screamed that she was under unusual tension.

"I know you're against this trip, but that's settled now," Scott said with some weariness. "I can't turn back the clock. We do what we have to do."

"You're going to be in places where anything could happen," she pressed. "A glitch in the lunar shuttle. A stray meteoroid. A fusion explosion." She hesitated, and then said what both of them were thinking: "Or a devious Russian."

"I shouldn't have told you about that," Scott sighed.

"It's kind of hard to hide that bruise and bandage on your side."

"It was probably just an accident," he said, avoiding her eyes.

"I don't think so. Both you and Colleen suspect there may be funny business going on with the Russians, and I think you're right."

"That's all just speculation," he replied, but he immediately realized that he wasn't even convincing himself. "We have to plan for the worst-case scenario. But the worst case almost never happens."

"Sometimes it does," she said.

"I've probably made this into more of a cloak-and-dagger deal than it really is," Scott finally replied, hoping to curb her curiosity. "Colleen and I come up with wild ideas all the time when we're brainstorming in the office. Usually, though, we're completely off track."

Sara sighed, but didn't reply.

Didn't convince her, and doesn't convince me either, Scott concluded, settling back onto the sofa and trying to massage his own temples.

His thoughts drifted to Colleen. Maybe she'd be able to set his mind at ease. *If she finally decides she can trust the Russians, I suppose anybody can—even me.*

9

Colleen Barker slid on her backside the final fifteen feet down the muddy embankment, until a birch tree broke her plunge. She swore under her breath, partly from shock and partly from irritation.

"You okay down there?"

When she looked up, she saw Sam Greeley, the off-duty New York City detective who had agreed to accompany her on this little adventure. He was peering over the edge of the cliff about forty feet above her, with his hands cupped around his mouth to form a makeshift megaphone. She knew he was standing only a few feet off the Taconic Parkway, at the precise location in upstate New York where Professor Carl Rensburg's Volvo had gone off the road and plunged in flames to the culvert below.

Colleen stood slowly, held on to the birch for balance, and tried to brush the biggest clods of dirt off her jeans and the back of her khaki bush jacket. She tested her body here and there. *Still working.*

After resolving for the umpteenth time to get her body in better shape, she looked at the metal detector she was lugging to be sure nothing was broken. The circular base, which housed the metal-sensing mechanism, seemed okay, and the three-foot handle was still intact.

Finally, she called back up: "Yeah, I'm in one piece. More or less. Just a ton of mud. And some minor war wounds."

Ignoring the laughs of her companion, who had paved the way for this outing by calling in his chits with the state troopers, Colleen began to wend her way through the scratchy, leafless brush. Fortunately, though there had been a little rain since the accident, it was still October and the first snow hadn't fallen. Soon she reached a clearing marked by a large depression in the ground that didn't seem quite natural. *The car was there. Now let's see what they missed.*

Slowly, she circled the clearing, searching with her naked eyes for any glint or unusual configuration on the ground or the nearby bushes. She moved leaf piles, felt around rocks, scanning for anything that seemed out of place.

Nothing.

Then she switched on her metal detector and covered the area again, inch by inch and foot by foot. Three or four times she got a hit as the detector began to squeal. But each time, when she brushed the fallen leaves aside, or dug a shallow ditch with a trowel she was carrying, she came up with the usual suspects: a beer can, a piece of wire, a coin.

A coin?

At first, she had ignored it, assuming that the dull, silver object was a quarter. It seemed about the right size. But looking more closely, she decided it was too big for a quarter.

Hard to tell, there's so much dirt on it.

To check further, she dug more of the hard soil off. It was then that she saw the coin was foreign. Pulling out a small flashlight so that she could study her find more closely, she was able to make out some sort of victory wreath on one side. On the other side, there was a strong-looking male figure in a long, military-type coat, holding a large, unsheathed sword. Also, some strange-looking letters emerged.

Cyrillic?

She was no Slavic scholar. But if the letters were Cyrillic, the coin could be Russian. Then she quickly put that idea aside.

You want *this to be Russian. That's your problem! Wait for some evidence. For proof.*

When Colleen scraped off more of the dirt, she made perhaps her most interesting discovery: a hole near the rim, apparently punched to accommodate a chain of some sort.

Colleen immediately placed the coin in one of the empty plastic pouches she was carrying, put the container in a roomy side pocket in her jacket, and set to work again with her detector, scouring the area for a neck or wrist chain. *Has to be narrow enough to fit into that hole. But there must be a chain.*

"What're you doing down there, Colleen?" the detective above her shouted. "You've been down there almost an hour!"

"Take it easy!" she yelled, somewhat annoyed he hadn't volunteered to come down and help her. But she knew that would be asking a lot. Besides, she wasn't so sure she wanted anyone else involved. "Give me a little longer!"

Colleen swept the area with the detector again, but this time she concentrated on semicircles that took her farther and farther from the wreck site.

Bleep!

Another hit. Colleen fell to her knees and brushed away the pine needles and rotting leaves. Although much of the autumn foliage was now on the ground, the trees and branches overhead still blocked out much of the sunlight. So she pulled out her flashlight and carefully directed the beam back and forth over the small area where the metal detector had reacted.

Nothing.

She pulled out the detector again and, still on her knees, moved the circular device slowly over the ground.

Bleep!

Finally, she isolated the exact spot on the ground that was causing the response and began digging carefully with her trowel, sifting the dirt through her fingers and examining every little clod and rock with the flashlight.

Then she saw it. A skinny sliver of a chain, so caked with mud and leaf fragments that it had been camouflaged almost to invisibility. The clasp on the chain was still fastened, but one of the links near the clasp had snapped. Colleen carefully brushed away the largest pieces of debris and then fished into her jacket pocket for the plastic bag containing the coin. Fumbling to open the plastic seal, she finally succeeded and extracted the coin. The chain fit perfectly into the hole.

"Okay, Sam, I'm ready to come up!"

The detective threw the end of a knotted rope down to her, and she proceeded to edge her way, sweating and struggling, up toward the road. Finally, just as she neared the edge of the road, Colleen lunged forward and grabbed the base of a shrub. Fortunately, she was now within reach of Sam. With his pulling and tugging, she crept on her stomach up to the narrow shoulder of the road and collapsed on her back for a few moments, catching her breath and rubbing the cramps out of her arms. Sam watched her silently, an amused smile playing about on his face. As she lay on the ground, she knew the questions would be coming soon, and she would have to make a decision: Should she tell him about her discoveries or keep quiet?

"So, find anything interesting?" Sam asked as they climbed into his car.

He was forcing her hand, but Colleen hesitated, trying to buy some time. "Mostly beer cans and wires," she said, hoping to change the subject.

Finally, Colleen made up her mind. "Sam, look, I did find something down there. Something that might be very important. But frankly, I'm not sure you want to get involved."

"Try me," the detective said with a guarded smile.

"Okay, but can you promise me this will stay between us?" she said, searching his face for a clue as to his thinking. "Nobody else in the NYPD can know about it. This could be a federal matter."

He glanced at her and then looked back over the steering wheel at the highway. "You ought to know by now that you can trust me, Colleen. Besides, this car wreck is outside my jurisdiction."

"I found these," she said, dangling the plastic bags containing the chain and coin in front of his face. Sam squinted at the dirty containers, obviously not quite comprehending what he was seeing.

"A weird foreign coin, maybe Russian, with a hole punched through it," she explained. "Also, a chain that fits into the hole. Could be just a coincidence that they were down there where Rensburg's car landed—"

"But probably not," Sam finished. "Could they have belonged to Rensburg?"

"I'll check that out," Colleen replied. "But I doubt it. He didn't seem the type who would wear a necklace."

"Whatever, but you'll have to nail down the source of the jewelry," Sam said. "Find out the exact identity of the coin and the maker of the necklace."

"Can you help?" Colleen asked, satisfied now that she had been wise to reveal her discovery.

Sam thought for a moment. "There's a Russian coin dealer in Manhattan, in the diamond district. He owes me. I'll give him a call after we get back."

As they rode back to the city, the conversation veered away from the auto accident and the necklace, and toward Andrews's impending moon trip. But Colleen's mind was still on the dirty coin and chain. The plastic pouches, which she had returned to her side jacket pocket, began to weigh very heavily. Even though she was glad she had shared her findings with Sam, a bad feeling was welling up inside her. A feeling with origins in that soggy ravine.

10

Whenever Colleen walked along West Forty-seventh, just off Fifth Avenue in Manhattan—through the heart of the diamond district—she had the feeling she was entering a foreign country. During the day, the street was always crowded and claustrophobic, with pedestrians pressing in on all sides, and cars and trucks honking and double-parked as far as the eye could see.

As Colleen elbowed her way slowly along the sidewalk, she glanced up periodically at the signs posted by various jewel merchants, but then quickly looked back into the flow of traffic. To avoid collisions with fast-moving diamond couriers carrying their omnipresent briefcases, she had to keep a close eye on her immediate surroundings.

In some ways, the scene reminded her of a street bazaar where she had browsed on a recent, official trip with Scott to Jerusalem. The prevailing uniform there, as here, was Hasidic black, with forests of Orthodox beards and bouncing *payas*, the curly sidelocks that framed the ears of many pious young men.

Then she looked up and saw the sign she had been watching for:

JOSSEF'S COIN AND DIAMOND EXCHANGE

When Colleen entered the shop, the scene became strangely quiet, at least in comparison to the hubbub on the sidewalk just outside the front door. In fact, as she looked around, she found she was the lone customer in the place. The only other person in sight was a portly, middle-aged man who appeared to be napping. His head, topped by a black yarmulke, was tilted so far forward that his chin, cushioned by a full, bushy gray beard, seemed to be resting on his chest.

She looked away, but then abruptly turned back when a somewhat annoyed, heavily accented male voice asked: "Yes, yes, wha*tiss* it?"

It was the shopkeeper, who hadn't been sleeping at all. She could see now— as he raised his hands and peered closely up at some sort of jewelry he had been holding—that he was actually hard at work.

"Sam Greeley at the NYPD sent me," Colleen said. "He called earlier this morning. Are you Jossef?"

"That's me," the man replied, continuing to look intently at his work. "I got the message."

"Sam said you might be able to help me with something," Colleen said, feeling as though she were pulling teeth to get the jeweler to talk.

"Maybe, maybe not. We'll see."

"I have a coin I'd like you to look at," she said, becoming a little exasperated. "You handle coins here, don't you?"

"Of course. You read the sign, didn't you? So let me see it."

Colleen handed over the plastic bags containing the coin and the chain she had found upstate. Because she had run them under a faucet several times, the pictures and letters on the silver coin were much clearer, and the tiny links in the slender silver chain, now free of the dirt, glistened under the intense beam of light the merchant had focused on them.

After examining each item for a few moments, Jossef cleared his throat and looked up at Colleen with a squint that was magnified by his thick glasses. "Where did you get these?"

"Why do you ask?" Colleen replied guardedly.

"Let me try again," he said with thinly masked impatience. "Did you acquire these together or separately?"

"Together," she said, unsure where the conversation was going. "I, uh, got them in the same place. Except the chain broke."

"I have eyes," the Orthodox merchant said gruffly with a shake of his head. "If they were sold to you together, then clearly they are part of the same necklace arrangement. Because the chain fits through the hole in the coin."

"I figured that out already," Colleen said, now becoming somewhat impatient. She hadn't made a special trip to Midtown just to hear this guy tell her what she already knew.

"But what you apparently didn't figure out is where they come from," Jossef said with some apparent satisfaction.

"So can you tell me?" Colleen said, aware now that she couldn't push the dealer any faster than he was willing to go.

Jossef took at least a full minute to reexamine both the coin and the chain more closely through an ocular lens. Then he stood up abruptly, and holding the coin and chain in each hand, he began to shuffle with disconcerting speed toward a back door in his shop.

"Wait!" Colleen almost shouted. "Where are you going with my stuff?"

"Relax, relax," Jossef said with a sardonic smile. "If I steal your stuff, Sam will arrest me."

Colleen wasn't completely convinced, but when the dealer reached the back door, he stopped and yelled, "Menachem! Menachem! Come here, please."

Seconds later, a younger bearded man in rumpled black trousers and white shirt appeared in the doorway. After Jossef had shown his colleague the coin and chain and Menachem had examined them closely, the two conversed animatedly in Yiddish for a few moments. Then both men disappeared through the back doorway. Colleen waited uncomfortably as the minutes ticked by.

Finally, Jossef reappeared and returned to his perch behind the counter. He placed the items carefully on the flat surface, exactly halfway between them.

"Okay, here's what you have," Jossef said. "The coin is a nickel-silver World War II commemorative ruble, issued by the Soviets in 1946. The chain was handmade in a shop in Moscow. A very special shop."

"How can you tell?" Colleen asked.

Jossef smiled slyly. "You want my trade secrets?" Then he shrugged. "Okay, you can have this one. Several of the links on the chain are etched with the jeweler's initials. He's a one-of-a-kind craftsman. The hole in the coin was of course punched so that the chain would exactly fit through it."

Jossef stopped and looked directly at her. It seemed clear that he knew more than he was disclosing, but Colleen didn't know the precise questions to ask. She knew she had to probe.

"What sort of person would buy or wear this chain?" she asked.

"Ah, now there is an interesting question," Jossef said. "But if we go down this path, I must have some assurances. I wouldn't say another word to you, but I know you are Sam's friend. I called him just now in the back room, just to be sure you were the one he had sent."

Colleen smiled wryly. "I thought maybe you were doing more than just taking a bagel break with Menachem."

"Menachem did examine the items more closely as I was calling," Jossef replied, apparently not particularly impressed with her attempt at humor. "He confirmed what I already thought. So you now have two expert opinions."

"Fill me in," Colleen pressed. "What's the big deal?"

Jossef now became very serious. "First, you must forget you ever came to this shop or spoke to me. You must forget Jossef and Menachem. Yes?"

"Sure."

"And everything I'm about to tell you—if you're asked, you'll say you got this information from somewhere else. Right?"

"Sure, sure," Colleen replied, now completely mystified.

"Okay," Jossef said. "A limited number of these coins were produced and distributed, and they're hard to find today. Collectors do have them, but they're not so easy to obtain. The chain is very rare. In fact, it's made-to-order in that one Moscow shop. The only customers are members of a particular wing of the *Mafiya*, the Russian Mafia. A very secretive and violent group."

"What's this Mafia bunch called?"

Jossef hesitated, as if wondering if he had already said too much, but then he proceeded: "The people who wear this pendant are said to be part of the large *Dolgopruadnanskaya* organization. Called the *Dolgos* for short. They're based in Sointsevo, a suburb of Moscow. Total membership is in the thousands—I've heard about six thousand soldiers. Many of them traffic in drugs, guns, killing for hire. But there's much more to their business. Foreign corporations must pay up to 20 percent of their profits to the *Mafiya* to operate in Russia. The criminals control much of the economy. And the *Dolgos* are right at the center of it. They're the biggest *Mafiya* organization in all of Russia. They have become stronger in recent years, since the anti-terrorist wars just after the turn of the century. They have filled a vacuum left by the elimination of other terrorist groups. Elite wings of the *Mafiya* are even more technologically advanced and dangerous than the earlier terrorists. That's one of the main reasons I left Russia, and it's much worse since I was there."

"And the necklace?" Colleen asked, pointing toward the coin and chain the dealer was holding.

Jossef looked furtively out the window, as though he expected someone to break in and cut him off. "The coin is said to be worn with the chain only by special operatives of this *Mafiya* group. Dangerous operatives."

"Dangerous?"

"Assassins," Jossef said, now speaking in a near-whisper.

"Do they have a name?"

"The *Pika*," he replied. "Means 'knife' in street Russian. Rumors say their specialty is bringing down major political leaders. Even nations. But the exact identity and work of these people are subject to speculation. Nobody knows how many *Pika* there are. I'm told there are only a handful of people throughout the world who wear this around their necks. But who knows?"

Colleen was skeptical. "Are you sure about this?"

"Am I sure? What am I—a *nar*, a fool?" Jossef responded, clearly annoyed that she was questioning his credibility. "I'm from Russia. I'm in the jewelry and coin business. And listen to this, my inquisitive young friend—I've even been to that shop in Moscow. So don't ask if I'm sure, okay?"

"Fine, fine," Colleen said, raising her hands to mollify the temperamental dealer, though she could hardly mask her excitement at his firsthand knowledge about the necklace shop. "Interesting you've been there. Can you tell me anything about how these Mafia assassins operate?"

"Of course not!" Jossef said. "Nobody knows that. Maybe not even the police—or the KGB or FSB, or whatever they're called now. But something I do know. They wear *this* coin and *this* chain. I've actually seen the jewelry on men that everyone knew were feared members of the *Pika*. Believe me, when you see one of those people, you look the other way. You understand? That's why you must never tell anyone you were here."

"My lips are sealed—"

"I should never have talked with you," Jossef interrupted. "I have a family. I must be *narish*. This was stupid. Even for Sam I shouldn't have done it."

"Look, I promise you don't have to worry," Colleen protested as the agitated dealer began to guide her toward the front door. "I've already forgotten I was here. Okay?"

But Jossef didn't say another word, and before Colleen knew it, she was standing on the street again in front of his shop. The crowds were just as large as they had been before. The mix of pedestrians and drivers seemed about the same. But now, Colleen thought she sensed a new, ominous presence. Someone seemed to be watching and waiting, like a stealthy, mysterious force about to surprise an unsuspecting victim.

11

The nearly clear sky promised a perfect Space Coast evening. A few wispy, reddish-golden clouds hung over the Kennedy Space Center on the east coast of central Florida, the only reminders of the sun that had just disappeared into the west. The air was cool, with just a touch of salt in the light breeze. A nearly full December moon dominated the eastern horizon.

Scott Andrews took one last look up at the fading sunset and walked reluctantly into the Space Center Headquarters building. He had arrived in Florida from Texas only two days before, and he had hoped to spend some time relaxing with his family. As planned, they had rented a townhouse in Cocoa Beach for the event, near the living quarters of some of the Kennedy workers, who also had children.

Scott knew he should be feeling something close to inner peace in such a setting. In central Florida, he was as close to his roots as he could hope to get. It was his home congressional district, and the Kennedy Space Center was only about fifty miles from his house in southern Brevard County. Friends and well-wishers were always just around the corner here and in parts south.

But Scott wasn't by nature a serene man. There was always too much turmoil in his life—and too many disturbing memories. He tried to forget that he was within a few minutes' ride of the site of his old family home, where he had lived as a child before he had lost his mother, father, and sisters in that tragic church fire. He had been only twelve years old at the time, but he still could see the flames and hear the screams as clearly as if it had all happened yesterday.

He had become bored with the preacher's sermon and left the pew reserved for his Sunday school class on the pretext that he had to go to the bathroom. But he walked past the men's room and kept going, right out the back door and onto the church school playground, where two of his friends were waiting for him. They knew they couldn't use this ploy for skipping church too often or they would be found out. They also knew they would be safe as long as they limited their escapes to once a month or so.

One of the boys, a fourteen-year-old named Tom, pulled out some cigarettes and offered one to Scott. At first, he refused, as much out of fear as conviction. But when it became apparent that no adults were lurking in the shadows and the boys could conceal themselves effectively behind a wall at the far side of the playground, he went along.

Scott didn't know how long they had been sitting there at the base of that brick wall—puffing away and laughing at one another's bad jokes—before the noise got their attention. At first, he thought that the time had gotten away from them and that church was out. He figured he was hearing the congregation pouring out into the parking lot. Panicking, he ground his cigarette butt into the dirt and stood up, trying to look as innocent and unassuming as possible.

But when he glanced toward the church, he knew something was wrong. Tragically wrong. Flames and black smoke seemed to be pouring out of every window. He could see people hanging out of the top windows, where the church balcony was located. The only doorway in his line of sight was crammed with clawing people, trying to get through the bottleneck.

It was then that Scott realized the noises he was hearing were shouts and screams for help.

"Move it! Get out of the way!"

"Faster! Please, please, faster!"

"Help me! Oh, dear Lord, please help me!"

"On fire! I'm on fire!"

At first, Scott was frozen to the spot. Then he sprinted toward the building, but two men grabbed him before he could get to the church door.

"No, Scott, no! Stay away from there! Let them get out! You'll just make things worse!"

He had fought with the men but couldn't free himself. The screams grew louder, more chilling. Was that his mother he heard? One of his sisters? Finally, the fire engines had arrived. Police lines arose around the blazing building, which was beginning to collapse in masses of charred, glowing timbers.

Scott paced behind the barricades, trying several times without success to slip past them. Finally, the bystanders got the word they had been dreading. A few members of the congregation had escaped. A few had been rescued by the firefighters. But dozens had perished in the flames. Scott's heart was in his throat as he went back and forth, examining the survivors, asking medics for the names of those rushed to the local hospital. But every time he had asked, he received the same answer: no one knew anything about his parents or sisters. Finally, some official-looking woman came over to him and put her hand on his shoulder. That was when he knew. She didn't have to tell him that they were gone forever. That he no longer had a family. That he was an orphan.

After negotiating his way past several security posts at the space center, Scott opened the door to the empty office he had reserved and was mildly annoyed that Colleen wasn't there waiting for him. He began to pace in front of a window that dominated the headquarters office, trying his best to enjoy a final earth-view of the heavens. But as the minutes ticked by, his mood worsened. Glancing down at his watch, he sensed that this perfect Florida evening before his moon trip was about to go to waste.

Colleen had called this conference with him earlier and had insisted that they meet late in the day, when most of the regular Kennedy Space Center workers and journalists would be gone, and unwanted eyes were less likely to observe them. But she was late. That meant he had a steadily shrinking block of time to spend with his wife and family, and to get his thoughts together for the launch, which was scheduled for the following evening.

Scott stalked over to the office phone, uncertain whether to call his wife to apologize or to get Colleen on the line and chew her out. Finally, just as he moved to pick up the receiver, Colleen burst through the door.

"Sorry I'm late!" his chief of staff said, her arms overflowing with papers that she apparently hadn't been able to cram into her bulging briefcase. "Stuff came in at the last minute. And the security here's tougher than I expected. They kept checking my ID, making calls—"

"I hope this is important," Scott interrupted, trying to stay calm.

But Colleen didn't seem to notice the edge in his voice. She dumped her loose papers on the only table in the room, wiped some perspiration off her forehead with the back of her hand, and collapsed into a chair with her open briefcase in her lap.

"Let me get some of this out so we can go over it in detail," she said.

Scott shook his head silently and looked down at his watch again.

"You're not going to believe some of this," she said as she stacked the papers from her briefcase next to the others she had brought in. "I'm really sorry for hitting you with this at the last minute. I know you're busy and time's running out. But you have to know what I've found before you blast off tomorrow. Your life may depend on it."

Scott's mood changed abruptly. "Tell me you're being dramatic," he said, but he knew Colleen well enough to understand that she didn't make such comments lightly.

"This is no joke," she said. "First off, I told you about the coin and chain I found off the Taconic Parkway."

"Right," Scott said, nodding.

"I checked with some contacts at the CIA, and they said they had heard about this coin-and-chain neckpiece, but they'd never seen one," she continued. "Apparently, my friend Jossef knows more than they do. But they knew a little about the *Pika*. They confirmed that the group has two, maybe three dozen members in the entire world."

"Do you have the coin and chain with you?"

"No, but here are a couple of pictures," Colleen replied, handing him three color photos.

Scott studied the photographs for a few moments. "Not quite a smoking gun."

"But close to it," Colleen said. "Close enough that you'd better be very careful. Believe me, that underwater accident at the Johnson Space Center was no accident."

"I think you're right about that," Scott said, rubbing his lips thoughtfully with an index finger. "Did you mention Bolotov to your CIA friends?"

"I had them check both him and Pushkin," Colleen said. "Both their histories came back clean, but Bolotov has some holes in his résumé. Months here and there can't be accounted for. Also, no family or close friends."

"So his main holiday activity could be assassinating people," Scott said.

"Could be," she replied. "In fact, I'd bet on it. That's why I'd be careful around him. Very careful."

"And Pushkin?" Scott asked.

"Also a loner," she replied. "I'm still checking him out. So far, he seems more an egghead and eccentric than anything else. But he has some unorthodox connections, especially with foreign religious groups. One thing especially concerns me—a link with an American Bible scholar who seems to have a knack for getting involved in violent situations overseas. Because Pushkin is such a prominent scientist, our boys have been keeping close tabs on him for years, but they still don't quite know what to make of him."

Scott contemplated his chief of staff's findings briefly and then shook his head. "I don't get it. What could the Russians be after?"

"Yes, the question of motive—I've been thinking about that," Colleen said. "Seems to me, if the Russians really did kill Rensburg, they may want complete control of the world's energy supply."

"Maybe," Scott said, "but that would be a tough order. After all, this moon venture is an international operation. Even if their scientists are in charge, how does Russia get rid of all the other countries—including the U.S.? Their military's not as strong as ours. They certainly couldn't force us out of the picture."

The two sat silently, contemplating the photos and the pile of documents Colleen had spread on the table. Finally, she spoke: "One of the people at the CIA did say something about a move in Russia to form a *Vorovski Mir*."

"A what? Speak English."

"A 'Thieves' World,'" Colleen said. "It's a kind of supercrime family. All the Russian Mafia groups would combine to form their own nation within a nation. So maybe it's not the official Russian government. Maybe it's the criminal element that wants to take over the world's energy—and these *Pika* assassins are their frontline troops."

Scott smiled. "That might make a great newspaper story, but let's not get ahead of the facts."

"Okay," Colleen said. "So maybe this has nothing to do with fusion power and electric energy. Maybe it goes back to that special, secret experiment—and wormholes."

"I can't see the Russian Mafia getting interested in theoretical physics," Scott said with a sigh. "These thugs are interested in money and power—not quantum mechanics. Where's the money in that? Where's the power?"

Colleen shook her head. "I don't know. But I do know you'd better watch your back."

12

What's wrong?" Sara Andrews asked as her husband walked through the
front door of their rented Cocoa Beach townhouse.

"It's that obvious?" Scott said with a wry smile.

He looked around the quarters and was amazed that in just one day she had
been able to make their temporary shuttle-launch quarters look almost like
home. The secret had been to allow Megan and Jacob to bring whatever they
could pack into a suitcase, and then let them spread the toys, video games, and
other items all over the floor.

Sara and Scott had questioned whether it was a good idea to disrupt the
children's school schedule yet again. But after all, how often was it that kids
got to see their dad take off for the moon?

"It's nothing serious," he finally said. "Just that every time I see Colleen,
some new question about the Russians comes up. And there never seems to be
any good answer. Anyhow, I'm not going to worry about it, and I don't want
you to worry either. Are the kids around?"

Sara looked at Scott quizzically, but he was relieved that she decided not to
press the issue. "They're playing out back," she said. "It's a great Florida night.
Here, I saved you a hamburger. Seasoned with chopped garlic and onions, just
the way you like. You can eat it outside." She handed him a plate and a glass
of iced tea.

Munching on the sandwich, the congressman followed his wife out into the
backyard. Megan and Jacob were chasing a soccer ball in a pickup game with
four other boys and girls. Scott recognized the others as children of permanent

Kennedy Space Center employees, whom they had gotten to know on their family trips to the congressional district.

"So they've found some old friends—even on such short notice," Scott said, suddenly feeling somewhat remorseful that his family had become uprooted as they followed him around for his moon-launch training. "I'm sorry this has turned us into such nomads."

"It's a good education for the kids," Sara said with a shrug, "watching their daddy train for a moon launch."

"True," Scott said, now feeling a little less guilty. "Hey, can I play?" he yelled, heading toward the group of youngsters.

"You're too big," Jacob said, waving him off. "Why don't you just watch?"

"Yeah, you could get hurt," another boy about his son's age agreed. "My dad says he's doing everything he can to keep you from getting hurt."

Scott and Sara looked at each other. "Your dad is with security here at the center, right?" Scott finally asked.

"Yep. He runs it."

"Just one part of it," said an older girl, apparently the boy's sister.

"And he thinks I might get hurt?"

"Well, he heard you got hurt once before, so he's going to protect you this time," the boy replied, who was beginning to lose interest in the conversation as he turned back to the game.

"Interesting," Sara said with a frown as she watched Scott concentrate on his hamburger. "Seems you have a reputation for trouble and accidents. I'm telling you, I don't like this business. What's the latest from Colleen?"

It was the exact question he didn't want to answer. "Oh, nothing much," he said, desperately wanting to change the subject. "She's still looking into the backgrounds of the Russians. But nothing to worry about. Hey, look, isn't that one of the kids' fathers heading over here?"

Out of the corner of his eye, Scott saw that he hadn't succeeded in distracting Sara, who was still staring at him. So to cut off further conversation, he waved at the approaching figure, who turned out to be the security official.

"Hey, how are you?" Scott said. "Some game over here. But they wouldn't let me play. Seems you told them it was important for me not to injure myself."

"Yeah, this is a rough bunch," said the official, who had introduced himself as Mal Rodriguez. "You don't want to play ball with them," he said, gesturing toward the children with a smile.

"So why are you worried about my husband getting hurt?" Sara asked, not smiling at all. "Do you know something we don't know?"

Mal shrugged. "I guess most everybody's heard about Dr. Andrews's injury in the training tank in Houston. Probably an accident, but we like to be sure. I've never trusted those Russians. Anyhow, I'm not one to take chances, especially not on a big mission like this. We've always had tight security around here, but we've cranked it up a notch or two for this mission. After all, if this moon project works out, you folks may be able to cut my utility bills!"

Rodriguez had concluded with a wink, but Sara apparently didn't see any humor. She took the empty plate and glass out of Scott's hands—rather roughly, he thought—and marched back inside.

When she had closed the door, Scott turned to Mal and asked, "Is there anything else? Have you heard anything I should know about?"

The security officer looked somewhat uncomfortable, as though he was being asked to disclose top-secret information. But then he replied, "We've had more than the usual number of tips about possible terrorist threats to the center. But that's to be expected, given the amount of publicity for this mission—and what you folks are trying to accomplish. You'd think everybody in the world would be overjoyed that their energy needs could be resolved for all time. But there are always some nuts out there who want to spoil everything."

"Anything believable?" Scott pressed.

"A couple of tips about terrorist activity seemed worth investigating. The FBI is looking into that—but nothing so far. I wouldn't worry."

Mal looked around to be sure no one could overhear. "One caller said we should watch for an attack from the ocean, the Atlantic side. Terrorist frogmen or something like that. But that doesn't seem likely. Anyhow, we've got the Atlantic covered like a blanket with the Navy Seals.

"But another caller, a female who wouldn't give us her name, worried us more. She warned about a specific employee on the launch site, some guy who was supposed to be angry about missing out on a promotion. The caller said he was planning some act of sabotage to get back at NASA."

"Was there anything to it?"

"Doesn't look like it," Mal replied. "But we're still checking. We just got the call yesterday, and a preliminary investigation cleared the worker completely. Matter of fact, he got a promotion and pay raise about two months ago—so there's no obvious motive! We're pretty sure the woman was a quack, or maybe just had it in for the employee. Might have been a jealous girlfriend. The guy was dating several women."

"So you're still looking into this?" Scott asked.

"Yeah, and just to be completely safe, we're keeping the worker under close surveillance and assigning him duties through which he couldn't possibly compromise the mission," Mal said. "It's not too fair, especially since he seems to be completely innocent, but we don't take chances in a situation like this. Also, our greatest concern does happen to be sabotage by disaffected employees. Like insiders who could unscrew a key component of the orbiter or even plant a small explosive. We're not really worried about an armed attack from the outside. We have the sea and air completely covered."

"So we're still scheduled to lift off at 6:00 P.M.?"

"A couple of minutes after six," Mal replied, and looked at his watch. "It's now T minus twenty-two hours. We have a projected launch window of about five minutes, and the weather looks fine." Then the security man turned and shouted to the soccer players: "Hey, kids, it's time to go now! Dr. Andrews has a big day tomorrow, and he has to get a good night's sleep."

As Scott watched Mal and the children troop away across one of the adjoining yards, his mind wasn't really on them, nor was he fully aware when his own son and daughter passed him and slammed the back door. He still couldn't shake a vague sense of foreboding. Maybe those calls about sabotage really were nonsense. *But still, something's wrong.*

Scott followed his children inside. But he wasn't very good company for Sara that evening, and when the lights were out and everything had grown quiet, he didn't sleep too well.

He would find himself dozing off, but then some variation of the same disturbing dream kept jarring him back to consciousness.

Fire on the lunar shuttle! But a familiar fire—the same fire that had stalked him since he was twelve years old. His mother and father and sisters are still trapped in the blaze, crying to him for help. Somehow he is spacewalking outside the ship, searching futilely for some way to quench the inferno inside. Suddenly, a sharp pain in the side. Turning, he confronts a huge, dark figure holding a knife stained with blood. A faceless man—who for some reason isn't wearing a space suit—seems poised to deliver another blow.

Scott looks down at his punctured space suit and feels ice-cold water pouring in through the hole. Water rising inside the suit, up into his helmet, past his neck and chin. Claustrophobic water.

13

Joe Gilbert loved the northern New Hampshire woods at any time of year—even now, in mid-December. Most people might have chosen an earlier month for a hike, before the autumn leaves had fallen off the trees. Or perhaps a somewhat later date, after the first big snow had fallen and the trails were ripe for cross-country skiing.

But Joe actually liked this in-between season because so few other people tended to take to the hills. He was of two minds about people. On the one hand, he liked to go out drinking into the wee hours with his buddies. He especially liked to pick up unattached women. But there was another side of Joe that was a loner. Every now and then, he preferred stretching his legs and communing with nature by himself, unencumbered by crowds or companions.

Solitude seemed to be in store for him today. The conditions this morning appeared particularly unappealing for the average nature walker or backpacker. The weather was cold, in the twenties, and a steady breeze had brought the windchill factor down below zero. Also, Joe had chosen a little-traveled, difficult trail that he expected few other hikers to know about or attempt. The route took him across expanses of treacherous, loose rocks; up steep slopes; and through sections of thick, low-hanging brush and branches.

So Joe was quite surprised when he topped a particularly challenging ridge and found himself face-to-face with two other trekkers, a man and a woman who had stopped to examine a compass they were using.

"Lost?" Joe asked.

The two, who were obviously startled at his sudden appearance, didn't reply for a moment. Then the woman—a real looker, Joe noticed—said,

"No, no, not lost. We are, uh, practicing—orienteering. That's our sport for the holiday."

"Orienteering," Joe repeated. "What exactly does that involve?"

"Footracing across the wilderness," the woman said impatiently, clearly wanting to end the conversation. But Joe wasn't ready to be put off so easily.

"So you're, like, training for competition, maybe like they race in the Olympics or something?" he pressed.

"No, no, just for amusement," she replied, turning her face away from him and looking back at the compass.

"If you're trying to get to a particular landmark or road, I might be able to help," Joe said. "I hike around these parts a lot."

"*Nyet*, no help," the man said harshly.

For the first time, Joe focused on the man and noticed he was about the same height as the woman, only much stockier. Not a very appealing looking sort either, with that flat face, the mashed, crooked nose, and the pockmarks on his cheeks.

"Say, you're not from around here, are you?" Joe rattled on.

He noticed that the woman seemed annoyed with him for some reason, but he couldn't bring himself to walk away. Maybe it was because she was so attractive, with those dark, oval eyes and olive-tinted skin. She looked kind of Asian, but not quite. Even in her hiking outfit Joe could tell she was in pretty good shape, slim with long legs. And she didn't fit in with her companion at all. Joe had already ascertained they weren't married because the woman had removed her gloves to manipulate the compass and she wasn't wearing a wedding ring. Surely this smash-faced guy couldn't be her boyfriend.

"I could show you some good restaurants in this part of the state," he continued. "Great blueberry pancakes. Full stack. All you can eat. Where you from, by the way? That word you said, *nyet* was it? Sounds Russian. I think I heard somebody say that on a TV program I was watching the other night. You from Russia?"

The woman glanced at her male companion with what Joe took to be a distressed expression, but he didn't think much of it. Probably they were having an argument. *Might be an opening for me*, he decided. Joe fancied himself as something of a "babe magnet." He was half a head taller than the man she was with and certainly a lot better-looking, at least in his opinion. If he could make some time with this woman, that would really be something to tell his buddies about.

"Have you seen any other hikers today?" the woman asked.

"Nope, not a one," Joe said. "Not many other folks up in this neck of the woods this time of the year."

Joe was about to ask the two if they wanted him to join them on the rest of their outing. Maybe act as their guide. And who knows? See if he could get the woman to split with him. But the next thing he saw was a blur of movement, and things began to happen faster than he could take them in.

The good-looking woman had gone into a crouch, like a boxer or one of those karate people, and had shifted quickly to Joe's left. More disturbing, and seemingly out of nowhere, a big, mean-looking knife had appeared in her hand.

Joe fell back a step in surprise, but then felt a sharp pain on the right side of his neck. Starting to lose consciousness, he twisted to his right and noticed, with a kind of detached recognition, that the short man had reached toward him with stiff, outstretched fingers. The guy had apparently blindsided him and jabbed him on the right side of the neck, pushing him into the woman's knife.

The woods were getting very dark, too dark for this time of day. The last thoughts that passed through Joe Gilbert's mind were, *Dirty fighter. This guy's a dirty fighter.* Then a dull pain moved through his neck, and he slipped into unconsciousness.

14

The hapless hiker slumped against the tree trunk, life seeping steadily out of his eyes. Finally, he lay motionless on the ice-encrusted ground. Like some sinister Rorschach test, blood from the gash on his throat produced an irregular, widening stain on the shallow snowdrift where his body had come to rest.

"Bad luck," Klaudia Ming-Petrovich muttered as she lowered her blade and slowly rose from her crouch.

"Worse luck if he had lived to talk about us, Colonel," her companion volunteered in Russian.

"You made a mistake, Valery," Klaudia continued in English, not willing to let her team member off the hook. "A big mistake. In this part of the United States you must always speak English. No Russian. At least until we arrive in New York City and get settled with our people. There, we can fit in like other immigrants who don't speak the language well. But in this New Hampshire place, our accents alone could raise questions. And speaking Russian is strictly forbidden. Understand?"

"I am sorry, Colonel," her stocky colleague replied, his eyes fixed submissively on the ground.

"Why would any American be hiking up here in this wasteland at this time of the year?" Klaudia grumbled half to herself, trying to make some sense out of their misfortune. She cursed under her breath as she carefully wiped her knife clean on some loose leaves.

"At least we made it across the border without being seen," Valery said.

"Yes, but that's no great achievement," Klaudia replied. "American border security up here is a joke. Any fool can walk across from Canada. But now there will be a search for this man. A missing person's report. He must not be discovered. Not with that cut on his throat."

Valery shrugged and pulled a short spade out of his backpack. "So we hide him in the ground?"

"Yes, but we do it very carefully," Klaudia said, looking toward Joe Gilbert's body as though she were evaluating a sack of dirty laundry.

"First, we take his money, if he has any," she ordered, reverting to Russian to be certain that Valery would comprehend every point. "The money will make it look like robbery—just in case his body is ever found. Also, drop nothing. Not like you did before."

Valery's shoulders slumped at this criticism. "I'm not sure where I lost the sacred necklace," he objected weakly.

"That's not the point," she replied. "The point is that you did lose it, and you're very fortunate that the Americans have failed to find it. At least we can hope they haven't found it. You have no margin for further error. I assigned you to this mission because you had a good record for us up to the Rensburg affair. And because you have other skills, which you know we will be needing. But there can be no further missteps. Understood?"

"Yes, Colonel."

"Now, let's bury this carcass and get out of here."

Valery immediately set to work searching for a relatively soft, partially thawed area of ground where he could dig a shallow grave quickly. Klaudia turned back to the body and began to go through Joe Gilbert's pockets. She found his wallet, removed all the paper money—nearly three hundred dollars—and also took off a wristwatch and a set of keys. Then she headed toward the sound of Valery's digging, which turned out to be about fifty yards away in a soggy ravine that was exposed to direct sunlight.

"Good," she said as she saw her companion had made considerable progress in digging a grave.

"Maybe luck is with us after all," Valery said. "I thought all the ground would be hard, but the snow has melted here, and the ground is soft. I should be finished in a few more minutes."

About fifteen minutes later, the two Russians dragged Joe Gilbert's body to the hole that Valery had hollowed out of the ravine.

"I would like for it to be deeper, just to be certain no animal finds him," Klaudia said. "But we have no time. This will have to do."

"We can throw rocks on top, and perhaps some leaves and branches," Valery suggested.

Klaudia answered by tossing him the keys and wallet she had taken from Joe Gilbert. "Put those in your pocket. We'll dispose of them in another part of this forest."

"Yes, Colonel."

"Are you sure you have left nothing behind?" Klaudia asked pointedly. "You've dropped nothing this time?"

"No, Colonel, nothing," the flat-faced Russian said.

"Then let's be on our way," Klaudia said. "Our contact will be waiting for us in a van at the designated highway rest stop. He won't leave, but the longer he waits, the more likely it is that he will arouse suspicion."

"Yes, Colonel," Valery replied. His obsequious attitude was beginning to get on her nerves, but she decided she preferred total obedience at this stage of the operation. The more Valery sensed she was watching and evaluating him, the more careful he was likely to be in executing his duties.

As they silently resumed their southward march, Klaudia Ming-Petrovich turned the recent violence over in her mind. Valery seemed to be slipping. Some people were like that. They operated well on routine missions, but in matters of supreme importance, they folded.

Valery would have to be watched very closely from now on. But Klaudia hoped that such extreme discipline wouldn't be necessary. The *Pika* had relatively few members. There were twenty-seven remaining by her latest count, after the loss of the two operatives in Israel, who had died in the assassination attempt on the prime minister.

Klaudia could see no choice but to rely on Valery through their current mission. After all, he was the *Pika's* top explosives expert. And his loyalty was unquestioned. But after the mission was completed, they would re-evaluate. Yes indeed, as the Americans would say, a thorough job review would be in order.

15

"T MINUS 2:58!"

Not quite three hours before liftoff at the Kennedy Space Center. Now in the last stages of the launch countdown, seven of the eight crew members of the *Challenger II*, the latest generation of shuttlecraft operating in the current year, 2017, walked out of the Operations and Checkout Building and headed toward Launchpad 39A.

The eighth, Ruth Goldberg, the Israeli laser specialist who would be assisting Shiro Hiramatsu, was being pushed in her wheelchair. That was one of the things that had impressed Scott the most about the prospect of working in space. The virtual absence of gravity on the International Space Station and the very low gravity on the moon—only about one-sixth of that on the earth—made it much easier for those with special physical needs to get around. In fact, Dr. Goldberg had proven herself one of the most agile and mobile during three previous missions to the space station.

The late afternoon sun glowed warmly down on them from an almost completely clear sky. Unless there was some mechanical problem, a successful launch now seemed almost certain. Shuttles still lifted off from pads 39A and 39B, as they had for decades from this cradle of near-perfect weather on the east coast of central Florida, the birthplace of American spaceflight. Two new pads had been added recently because of the increased volume of traffic into space.

Still, the atmosphere was a little different this time. Scott, who was walking just behind the shuttle mission commander and the shuttle pilot, could see that security was unusually tight. Armed guards, who were part of an Army Special Forces team, were stationed here and there in full view. From his classified briefings, Scott knew that other fast-response military teams were keeping a close watch on things from hidden vantage points, both on the ground and in the air.

As commander of the six scientist-astronauts who comprised the international energy effort, Scott felt a special responsibility to keep abreast of security measures and threats. Like a mother hen, he glanced over the head of Ruth Goldberg, who was rolling along just behind him. His eyes stopped in turn on each of his other charges—Jeffrey Hightower, Shiro Hiramatsu, Sergey Pushkin, and Vladimir Bolotov. They were the core of the moon mission team. The success of the project would depend on their ability to do their respective jobs and work together. He was gratified to see they were all looking fit and alert, even if a little nervous. Nerves, properly managed, could be an asset. But there were also some personal concerns on Scott's mind this particular day— concerns that went deeper than temporary nervousness about a major pending assignment.

"T MINUS 2:45!"

The countdown reverberating in his headset caused him to look nervously at the waiting shuttle, which lay just ahead. Given his family history of death by disaster, Scott had found it difficult to push to the back of his mind the concerns expressed by Mal Rodriguez, the security officer. He knew he was particularly vulnerable to such fears. It wasn't every day that a person lost his entire family to an arsonist at age twelve. Over the years Scott thought he had done a pretty good job of hiding his chronic anxieties from Sara and Colleen, the two people who knew him best. But he couldn't hide the ghosts of the past from himself.

Even this morning, when he should have been focusing exclusively on the mission before him, he found those old fears penetrating his consciousness. He worried about Sara and the kids. Could they be in any danger from terrorists? Were the phone threats Rodriguez had related last night just hot air— or was there really something to them?

Scott kept playing over and over in his mind a series of now-familiar anxiety tapes about the mission. He ran and reran mental scenarios involving potential enemies on the team, especially the Russians, Pushkin and Bolotov. What were they really up to? Would they try to sabotage the project? Would they try to eliminate him?

The congressman also found himself fighting nagging panic attacks that always seemed to be lurking somewhere in the wings of his mind. The same emotions had plagued him in a less intense manner on his only other trip into space—as a passenger to inspect the first space hotel that had been constructed in earth orbit. The idea behind that project had been to stimulate greater interest in space exploration by enticing tourists to visit the hotel. Scott had strongly endorsed the concept from its inception, and the venture had proven to be wildly successful. But that didn't mean he had to like space travel.

As a result of the hotel's offerings, public enthusiasm for space exploration had intensified beyond expectation. NASA had even managed to get funding for a Mars expedition, which was scheduled to be launched in only about two years, in the year 2020. Also, the new government and investment money that had poured into space had helped make possible the funding for this fusion venture on the moon—which promised to change the earth's economy for all time.

But on his earlier trip into orbit, as now, Scott had found that he had to fight back periodic tidal waves of terror. He worried that the shuttle might explode on the pad or just after liftoff. He wondered what the chances were that the crew compartment might catch fire in flight, either as they moved into earth orbit or even on the trip to the moon. All inside might be trapped and die, just as his parents and sisters had died in that church building decades before.

The details of preparing for the actual launch had been a welcome distraction, an opportunity to get his mind off worst-case scenarios, even if for a few moments at a time. Scott was happy to concentrate on the final briefing before the flight . . . on assembling and donning his flight suit and other equipment . . . on following the movements of the seasoned astronauts who would be getting the team into orbit. The two top officers, a female commander and a male pilot, were both highly qualified astronauts with many space missions behind them. They obviously knew what they were doing and regarded this liftoff as totally routine—even if Scott didn't.

Many of the countdown and launch procedures for a trip into earth orbit were the same as those that had been in place nearly twenty years ago, at the beginning of the twenty-first century. The members of the crew—the commander and pilot, plus the six scientists who were part of the moon team— rode an elevator lift about one hundred feet up the side of the orbiter, the winged, airplanelike craft that would take them into space.

As they entered the crew compartment through a side hatch, they heard the disembodied voice echo again in their earphones: *"T MINUS 2:25!"*

Launch Control Center was reminding them they were fast approaching the moment of truth. Scott was very much aware of the importance of each step they were taking in the prelaunch procedure. If anything went wrong in the sequence, the mission would be aborted, and they would have to postpone liftoff and start all over again at a later date.

But everything seemed to be moving ahead smoothly. In a flurry of activity, technicians helped strap them into their seats, using the two shoulder harnesses and the lap belt provided for each passenger. Every crew member's helmet was adjusted and secured. When the crew and passenger loading was finished, Scott found himself sitting in a tilted position on his back. The commander and pilot were strapped in just in front of him and to his right.

At first, his attention was riveted to the maze of instruments all around him. Then he looked to his left—and saw Sergey Pushkin sitting beside him, next to the bulkhead. The Russian was looking directly at him, silently and without the trace of a smile.

Scott looked away, his anxiety now turning into frustration. *Just what I need. With everything else on my mind, I have to blast off with a Russian in my lap.*

"So, Dr. Andrews, we are about to make history!" an accented voice echoed in his helmet. It was Pushkin.

At first Scott couldn't figure out how the Russian was getting into his head. Then he remembered that some recent advances in shuttle equipment enabled passengers to tune in one or more other crew members for conversation. These individual hookups could be overridden by messages from Mission Control or the commander or pilot. So how many other people was Pushkin pulling in to this little town meeting?

"I'm only on your channel," Pushkin added, as if in answer to Scott's unspoken question.

"T MINUS 1:30!"

The countdown announcement from Launch Control jarred Scott. Hoping to discourage any further conversation with Pushkin, he nodded brusquely in the Russian's direction and then turned away. The congressman knew he was in a state of precarious emotional balance, and he feared that an unpleasant encounter with the Russian might push him over the edge.

There was at least one thing about the Russians that Scott could be thankful for. During this phase of the trip, Bolotov was on the other side of the crew compartment, well out of earshot, sitting next to Shiro Hiramatsu. Pushkin would never have been Scott's first choice as a seatmate, but Scott decided that if forced to choose, he would probably give the fusion scientist the edge over Bolotov.

During the training at Houston, Pushkin had seemed more than willing to pair off with his gruff countryman and eschew most contact with the other team members. So it struck Scott as peculiar that the Russian had now become so talkative. The American wasn't interested in camaraderie as they sat there on their backs, waiting for the rockets to explode beneath them. He resolved to keep quiet, speak only when spoken to, and certainly avoid revealing any more than necessary about himself or his government work.

"You have seemed somewhat preoccupied in the last day or so," Pushkin said.

The guy just won't give up.

"Not your usual, jolly self," the Russian scientist continued.

"I never thought of myself as jolly," Scott finally responded, hoping that a slightly unfriendly tone would turn off Pushkin's incessant chatter.

"Forgive me—*jolly* may be the wrong word," Pushkin replied, obviously not getting the message. "I meant you always seem enthusiastic and positive. My English is not so good. I have been working on it. But of course, I found out at a very late date that I would be with you."

"I know," Scott said, thinking how much he wished Rensburg were sitting next to him rather than this Russian. Where was all the chattiness coming from?

"Have I never told you how sorry I was—how sorry I *am*—about Carl Rensburg's unfortunate death?" Pushkin asked. "He was not just a valued colleague. He was a friend. We spent time together at many international conferences. He and his wife entertained me on several occasions. I miss him."

Scott turned to look Pushkin directly in the eye, and then searched his face, which was clearly visible through the visor opening in his helmet. Didn't seem to be any hidden message. No obvious body language to belie his words.

"Yeah, Carl Rensburg was a fine man," Scott finally said. Then, still looking closely at the Russian, he decided to test him: "What exactly do you know about his death?"

Pushkin seemed startled, even uncomfortable with the question. His eyes darted down, and he wet his lips. Scott was certain that he had just learned something important about Pushkin, something he suspected strongly he wasn't going to like at all. The American continued to stare until the Russian physicist looked up at him with what appeared to be a troubled gaze, through deeply wrinkled brows.

"I know only what I've been told," the Russian finally said. "That he ran off the road, where was it, in New York? A tragic accident. Isn't that correct?"

"Of course," Scott said quickly. "A very tragic accident. But it was so fortunate that you were ready to take his place, wasn't it? We didn't lose a beat in meeting our schedule. Yes, that was quite lucky."

"I never regard the death of a dear friend and colleague as good luck," Pushkin said with such force that Scott automatically leaned away from him. "Dr. Rensburg's death was a great loss. I would have been quite happy to continue with my work right here on earth. Bolotov loves the adventure of space travel. But I'm different. I'm quite content to spend my evenings with my books."

Scott glanced across the crew compartment at the other Russian, who looked as though he was dozing. "Yes, Dr. Bolotov is nothing if not enthusiastic," Scott said, again feeling that twinge in his ribs.

"T MINUS 30 MINUTES!"

The voice from Launch Control Center echoed in his headphones, cutting into their conversation.

"Time flies when you're having fun," Scott muttered as some of those old, deeply embedded anxieties began to wash over him again. He didn't particularly like Pushkin, but talking with the Russian had at least kept his mind off his phobias.

"That's an American idiom?" Pushkin asked. "Time flies—"

"Yeah," Scott said, now resigned to talking until one of them fell asleep. "But I'm being ironic. This isn't exactly fun. Too many things on my mind."

"Such as?" Pushkin asked.

A sharp retort was on the tip of Scott's tongue, but then he remembered he was the head of the scientific team. He had to keep relationships on an even keel. Even with the Russians.

"I don't like this sort of trip," Scott finally admitted, and then wondered why he had opened himself up even this much.

"Why is that?" Pushkin asked.

Scott sighed. "Reminds me of something bad that happened to me, to my family, when I was a kid."

"What happened exactly?" Pushkin asked, pushing the edge of the envelope in this conversation.

"I really don't want to go into it," Scott said abruptly. "It's a personal matter."

Pushkin sat silently for a few moments, and Scott closed his eyes, hoping the discussion was finished.

"T MINUS 14 MINUTES, BOYS AND GIRLS!"

This time the disembodied voice reminding them of the ticking clock was that of a male pilot, not Launch Control. Scott's eyes were wide open now, and he started to perspire heavily. Up to this point, he had been somewhat successful in pushing the countdown to the back of his mind during his conversation with Pushkin. But now the immediacy of their departure hit him like a blow to the chest.

Try as he might, he couldn't get rid of the mental images of fire . . . of an explosion in the crew compartment . . . of violence against his family while he was gone. He hadn't really warned Sara, had he? No, he had wanted to prevent her from worrying unnecessarily. Now he was afraid she would be unprepared if she became the target of terrorists. What if Rensburg's killers came after her and the kids?

Involuntarily, Scott began to toy with his shoulder harnesses. He suddenly felt claustrophobic and extremely hot. Had a fire already broken out behind them?

"Dr. Andrews, are you feeling all right?" an accented voice asked in his earphone.

It was Pushkin again. When he looked toward the Russian, he picked up something in the man's eyes he couldn't read. Did Pushkin sense his weakness?

When Scott failed to answer, the Russian placed a hand on the American's forearm and asked quietly, "May I pray for you? Prayer always helps me in difficult times."

Scott just stared. "Well, I don't really think—"

"Even a short, quiet prayer can be very powerful," Pushkin insisted.

"Look, I'm not—"

"What harm can a prayer do?"

"Okay, okay," Scott said, wanting to end this interchange as quickly as possible. He felt he was being manipulated, but he didn't know how to extricate himself. Out of the corner of his eye, he noticed that Pushkin seemed to be bowing his head, though it was hard to tell when both of them were tilted up on their backs. Then he glanced across at the other passengers, hoping no one was watching this scene.

The congressman didn't believe in prayer. Didn't even think he believed in God. The only God he knew about was the God those parishioners had worshiped in his childhood church, the same God who had allowed the flames to destroy his entire family. What kind of a God would do that? Long ago, he had decided that his safety and that of his present family—Sara, Megan, and Jacob— depended on *him,* not on some imaginary divine protector who had proven Himself incapable of taking care of the crowd of innocents in that little church.

Scott barely heard Pushkin's supplication resonating in his helmet. Most of what the man said was in English, but some of it seemed to be in Russian. Immediately afterward, Scott couldn't recall a word the man had said. But for some reason, he began to calm down. Because of some mind-body dynamic—which Scott convinced himself had nothing to do with Pushkin's God—he began to feel that somehow he could make it through this crisis. Maybe the sense of tranquility inside him had something to do with some of those medical reports he had read, which said prayer could be effective in reducing stress and enhancing health. Whatever the reason, he gradually began to believe he could actually survive liftoff without going wacko and forcing them to take him off the shuttle.

"T MINUS 30 SECONDS!"

The voice of Launch Control in his headphones didn't seem to grate as much this time.

"Looks like we have a go," the mission commander said.

The next thing Scott felt was something akin to an earthquake that shook the entire crew compartment. He knew from the launch briefings that it was now six seconds from liftoff because the three main engines of the space shuttle had just ignited and were voraciously burning up the liquid hydrogen fuel and liquid oxygen oxidizer from the external tank. The tank, which was attached to the orbiter, would be jettisoned into the ocean after they were only a few minutes into the flight.

The steady shaking intensified. The place felt like it was coming apart. That had to be the two solid rocket boosters kicking in, Scott decided. Strange. He wasn't feeling apprehensive at all. This was beginning to seem more like a hands-on classroom experience than a ride on a fire-breathing spaceship. Of course, it helped that Scott had been instructed about what to expect, and fortunately, he could still remember vividly that other time he had blasted into space. Maybe he was getting to be an old hand at the procedures.

"SRB IGNITION—LIFTOFF!"

The voice from the Launch Control Center helped him focus professionally, as a medical scientist with some astronaut training, on what was happening. Almost without thinking, Scott translated the NASA acronym: Solid Rocket Boosters.

Moments later, Scott felt the pressure of gravity pushing against his chest. Within the next sixty seconds, it would increase to three Gs, or three times the force of gravity on earth.

Scott thought of his wife and children, who were watching his ascent into the clear early evening sky. What must this look like to them? He had witnessed this scene many times, both as an interested spectator and as an official observer from the House Space Committee. In his mind's eye, he could see the steady stream of fire from the rockets . . . the dramatic, gold-red trail of exhaust smoke . . . the prominent moon rising against the dark blue sky.

But this time everything was different. He wouldn't be staying behind, watching the shuttle until it disappeared into the high, wispy evening clouds. No, he was *on* it—and in charge of perhaps the most important team of scientists the earth had ever produced.

Two minutes into the flight, the commander announced that the two solid rocket boosters had consumed their propellant and were being jettisoned. Scott knew that the boosters would continue to ascend for a little while. Those on the ground would see them separate and then keep going upward, but at different angles to the orbiter. Soon afterward, parachutes on the boosters would deploy automatically, allowing them to descend safely into the Atlantic about 150 miles from the launch site. There, they would be recovered and reused on a later shuttle flight.

Scott glanced down at his watch. By now, they were reaching an altitude where it would be hard for anyone on the ground to follow them with the naked eye. Those with binoculars—such as the ones he had bought for Megan and Jacob—could follow his trajectory a little longer. But soon, he knew the shuttle would be out of sight.

A few minutes later—about eight minutes into the flight—the commander announced that the external tank had been jettisoned. That huge cylinderlike container would also continue to travel upward for a short while, but then would arc back down, where it would be torn apart by the atmosphere. On this particular flight, the debris from the external tank would fall into a remote part of the Indian Ocean, halfway around the world from the Kennedy Space Center.

Now the shaking had stopped completely, and the ride was smooth and quiet. The transition was remarkable. After the rockets were gone, they soared faster than sound into the empty space above the atmosphere. To Scott, it seemed as though they had just shifted from a bumpy covered wagon to a luxurious Cadillac, cruising along on a seamless superhighway.

As Scott sat quietly, feeling the first effects of weightlessness, a surprising thought came to mind. His fears had totally disappeared. For the first time that day, as the shuttle speed approached the orbital velocity of seventeen thousand miles per hour, he actually felt enthusiastic about the adventure that lay before him. The preliminary briefings had definitely been important in helping him focus his mind on the mission, rather than on his personal worries. Also, just getting started—just blasting off and starting to move ahead with their assignment—had been therapeutic in itself.

And the prayer? He looked over at Pushkin, who was gazing out into the darkening sky through one of the portholes, and then, as the shuttle rotated, at the eastern coast of Asia. The earth was beginning to resemble a giant, man-made map or globe, rather than the third planet from the sun. As the blues, greens, sharp coastlines, and cloud-created white shapes slipped in and out of view, the Russian seemed to have forgotten all about Scott.

Maybe the prayer had helped, and maybe it hadn't, Scott decided. *But I know one thing for sure: the success of this mission is up to me, not some God I don't understand and can't rely on.*

Scott's confidence had returned with a vengeance. He could see his objective clearly. His purpose in life was to provide energy for all the earth. For his children, and his children's children.

Also, as he glanced once more at Pushkin, and then at Bolotov on the other side of the compartment, Scott was sure he still knew where to look for his enemies. The two were obviously up to something, and no amount of praying by Pushkin would convince him otherwise.

16

S huttle launches had become so commonplace that news coverage had become spotty. Usually, interested TV viewers had to listen very closely to cable television anchors and reporters to be sure to catch any tidbits of information that were passed on quickly to the public.

The coverage of the current mission to the moon, however, was different. Because the stakes were so high, the event had triggered more interest than the garden-variety liftoff. As the two immigrants sat in front of their TV set at an apartment in the heart of a Russian-speaking enclave in Brooklyn, the CNN Headline News team devoted almost five minutes to descriptions of the liftoff. At every turn, viewers were reminded that if this mission were successful, the average person's fuel and utility bills would plummet.

"They might even *disappear!*" one reporter exclaimed hopefully, abandoning any pretense of being a disinterested observer.

But the black-haired Russian woman listening to the broadcast wasn't concerned about fuel bills. She wanted only to keep track of the mission's progress. Had the shuttle actually departed? Were all the original crew members on board?

When Klaudia Ming-Petrovich heard Dr. Scott Andrews's name mentioned as one of the mission specialists, she sat back in her chair, an involuntary scowl crossing her face. So the injury hadn't sidelined him. It was obvious that Andrews could not be easily discouraged with a nonlethal physical attack. Yet eventually he had to be neutralized, because he was the only one on the moon team with the resolve or political connections to offer any serious opposition to the clandestine Russian experiment.

So now, it seems, plan number two must go into effect. She knew that even now, Martov was taking steps to reach out into space with his long arms to deal with Andrews — either through Bolotov, or "other means," as he had suggested enigmatically. She hated the thought that her man Bolotov had been unable to resolve the Andrews problem before liftoff. She also was irritated by Martov's suggestion that he might have to use channels outside her control to achieve their goals. But she couldn't allow Bolotov's initial failure to distract her. Other important business remained on her agenda.

Klaudia looked over at Valery, who was barely paying attention to the television set. She shook her head as she watched him search through a New Hampshire newspaper they had bought earlier in the day.

Dunce. He doesn't read English well enough to know what the paper is saying.

"I don't see any pictures of the man, Colonel," he said in Russian. "There seems to be no mention of any missing person. But perhaps you should look."

"I've already checked the paper, Valery," she said patiently in English. "Our friend — Mr. Gilbert, I believe was his name — isn't in there. We'll probably never hear any more about him. Obviously, he wasn't important."

"Still, I'd like to be sure," Valery said, still speaking in Russian. "I'd like to know that my mistake didn't make any difference."

"Mistakes always make a difference," Klaudia replied severely. "And speak *English*, Valery. The more you use it, the better you'll get."

"Yes, Colonel."

It was looking more and more like this was Valery's last major assignment. Maybe his last assignment of any type. It seemed he just couldn't be trusted to follow directions.

At least the amount of damage he could do was limited in this part of Brooklyn, where most people spoke Russian and tended not to pay attention to such a dolt. How had he ever made it into the *Pika*? Then Klaudia remembered Valery's expertise with explosives, a skill he had developed in the *Dolgos's* wars against rival *Mafiya* gangs in Moscow. He had honed his violent talent into a fine art with successful bombings in Israel and stints as an instructor for Islamic radicals. *Hard to replace. Maybe he can continue to be of use to us. But that decision will depend on how well he performs in Florida.*

"You should be concentrating on lining up people to help us in Florida," she said impatiently, absently fingering the coin and chain around her neck. "None of our *Pika* comrades are available to help. But there are other competent Russian *Mafiya* operatives here in Brooklyn looking for work. Have you found reliable drivers and weapons specialists—*Dolgos* people who will do dangerous work for a fee *and* keep their mouths shut?"

"I'm trying, Colonel—"

"Don't *try*, Valery! *Do!* Understand?"

"Yes, Colonel," he replied, hurriedly heading toward the door.

When she was alone, Klaudia went on-line with her PDA—her late-model "personal digital assistant" pocket computer—and placed an encrypted message to Martov. She wouldn't mention anything about the hiker in the woods. But she would attempt to bolster the prime minister's confidence in her and distract his attention from Bolotov's failure to knock Andrews off the mission.

17

Colleen's room in the House office building was so full of papers and files that she had long since given up trying to find open areas to place her feet. Just this evening, she had added a couple of empty containers of take-out Chinese food to the mix of trash and research materials strewn about on the floor.

Having abandoned any hope of being neat or even organized in the usual sense of the word, she just tramped over the materials willy-nilly and filled up her coffee cup at her ever-present Pilon drip coffeemaker. Then she returned the same way, trying not to think about what live or rotting debris she might be stepping on.

Second law of thermodynamics, she muttered to herself.

A few months ago, before Colleen had embarked on her current, self-taught crash course in cutting-edge physics—including nuclear fusion—she wouldn't have had a clue about this particular principle. But now she knew a little something about the revered second law, which said that orderliness in the universe tends to deteriorate steadily into disorder.

"And that applies to me and this office," she said out loud, with more than a little frustration.

Colleen wasn't worried about anyone overhearing her. The other staff members had left hours before, and many were probably already at home getting ready for bed and cuddling with their loved ones. For all she knew, she was the only person in the entire building. It would have been a perfect time to straighten things up, but Colleen was resigned to the fact that she was firmly locked into her mess for the time being. If she tried to organize the clutter now, she might misplace some key piece of paper—and that could actually put Scott Andrews's life in danger. She might not have someone waiting for her at home, but at least she had a worthy boss who relied heavily on her, one to whom she was completely loyal and devoted.

She breathed a sigh of relief as she switched on the TV in her office and watched Scott's shuttle lift off safely into orbit. But she knew that was only the beginning of his dangerous venture. She had to continue with her research to assess the exact nature and magnitude of the threat against him.

Leaning back on her couch, she picked up a classified report she had been reading on Professor Sergey Pushkin. By now, she had read and reread the document several times and had put out some feelers with her intelligence contacts in an effort to get a better handle on the details. But the report—and especially a short transcript of a secretly recorded conversation in Moscow—continued to puzzle her.

Until Pushkin had been picked for this mission, the intelligence on him had been rather sparse and unenthusiastic. But now he was emerging as a somewhat strange and mysterious man. The background searches and analyses were pouring in—and Colleen was becoming increasingly puzzled and disturbed at what she was learning.

The report contained the transcripts of several conversations, which American operatives had picked up by focusing a parabolic microphone through the window of a Moscow coffeehouse. "Nontraditional intellectuals" and "political malcontents" frequented the place regularly, according to the researcher who had produced the document. In one of those discussions, Pushkin had engaged in a puzzling interchange with a noted, if not notorious, American professor, a Wheaton College Bible scholar named Michael James.

In a few lines buried in the footnotes to the report, Colleen had read with some interest that this was the same James who had been connected more than a decade earlier with the scientific investigation of a strange light that had appeared in the eastern sky. Though she had been a lowly suburban reporter on Long Island at the time, Colleen still remembered many of the details, and the footnotes in the report also helped jog her memory further.

James had claimed that the light, which inexplicably could be viewed in the east from anywhere on earth, was somehow supernatural—and might be related to the ancient Star of Bethlehem. In fact, certain events provided fodder in support of James's views, at least in the opinions of religious and spiritual leaders and their followers. According to news reports, dramatic healings and paranormal events had been associated with the light, and some of these sightings had actually been corroborated in secret government documents.

More ominously, apparently in direct response to the appearance of the light, a rash of riots and other forms of social and political unrest had broken out for a time around the world. Predictably, many religious people had become convinced that somehow the light was an apocalyptic sign of the end times and the return of Christ. But then the light had abruptly disappeared, and everything had more or less returned to normal.

References to Michael James—and some Harvard and Amherst professors he had worked with on the study of the light—had quickly faded from the news. Until now, Colleen couldn't remember hearing another word about any of these investigators. But as her eyes raced down the transcript of his conversation in that Russian café with Pushkin, it became apparent that James might once more be at the center of another set of international machinations.

Transcript

Location: Grand Moskva Café, Moscow

Date: January 18, 2016

Participants: Sergey Pushkin, Michael James

[Ellipses indicate where clanking of dishes and background voices have obscured words and phrases of conversation.]

James: . . . Certainly, as we say in America, you are an old hand in the Russian scientific establishment. But you must remember that you're quite new to the movement.

Pushkin: Yes, new. Quite new. Though I have deep family and social connections.

James: . . . connections. Those may or may not be helpful.

Pushkin: So I have discovered. But overall, I have become more—how do you say?—sensitized. More alert to problems and inconsistencies, especially between the movement and my work.

James: Anything you can discuss?

[A pause]

Pushkin: I must be careful. For your sake as well as mine. There is a potential conflict here. I want to know more about this movement and how I can participate. But there are government restrictions.

James: I understand.

Pushkin: I am also worried about how my government will use my work. Especially some of my recent investigations. In some areas, we are probing the very foundations of life and reality. That is the nature of theoretical physics . . .

James: Believe me, I understand. This work involves issues and principles that reach far beyond national boundaries. You and I are not citizens . . . Are we safe here? Can we really talk freely?

Pushkin: . . . but it's better than my rooms, which are probably—how do you say?—bugged up with microphones.

James: What specifically about your work puts you in this internal conflict?

Pushkin: Again, I must be very careful. I do have a responsibility to my government. But there is no one in my circle of colleagues I can talk to about my reservations and doubts. Yet I do sense I can trust you.

James: We've known each other for . . . I believe that. Otherwise we wouldn't be having this discussion.

Pushkin: You ask about my personal conflicts. Let me just say this. If I told you that I'm involved in research that could provide human beings with knowledge that once was thought to be in the domain of God alone, what would be your response?

[A pause]

James: I guess I'd have to know more. It's a little vague.

Pushkin: I can't say much more.

James: It's hard to advise . . .

Pushkin: I can say this—that we may be opening doors that can provide certain nations or international organizations with powers beyond anything humans have imagined before. Nothing less than control of the entire . . .

James: Okay, I'd advise you to determine for certain how your research will be used. Then if you learn the objective is contrary to basic . . . principles, you must take steps to counter the enemy. The enemy must not prevail . . .

Pushkin: At this point, their objectives are not entirely clear.

James: It often takes decades, doesn't it . . . ?

Pushkin: True. But I sense that in this case, the political forces may be far ahead of me in devising practical uses.

James: Again, until I know specifically what you're talking about, my advice may not be very helpful.

Pushkin: . . . more helpful than you realize. I've probably told you more than is wise for either of us. Let me change the subject. Have you seen ancient Russian Orthodox icons?

James: Only in Eastern Orthodox churches.

Pushkin: I have some family pieces that might interest you. And I'd like your views on using them in private devotionals. Would you like to see them? They're in my flat, only a few blocks from here.

James: . . . an honor. Do you have family here?

Pushkin: No . . .

James: Ah, so you live in a bachelor's pad.

Pushkin: I don't understand.

James: [laughs] . . . figure of speech . . .

End of transcript

Colleen let the report flop down into her lap and rested her head against the back of the sofa. The interchange was too general and vague to tell her much about Pushkin's research. She couldn't tell if he was talking about his fusion experiments, which certainly involved groundbreaking work, or about the fuzzier stuff they had picked up about wormholes.

But there were interesting—and rather disturbing—bits and pieces of information she felt she could now glean from the short, fragmented conversation. On her all-purpose PDA, she began to scribble notes to help her organize her thoughts. First, Pushkin was clearly bothered by some sort of political or moral conflict related to what he was doing. Were the Russians using certain scientists to execute some major power play, which would give them a decisive advantage on the international scene?

Second, Pushkin was obviously deeply committed to an unidentified "movement" that he apparently suspected the Russian government wouldn't appreciate. Was this a *Mafiya* connection? Or could this movement be related to the reports American agents had received that he had a connection with some radical religious group? Perhaps he had some formal link to such a group through James. Given the Wheaton professor's background and also the drift of this conversation, that possibility seemed more and more likely.

Third, the two men had referred to some "enemy." Was that Russia? The United States? Or her own boss, the Honorable Scott Andrews?

Finally, Colleen didn't believe for a minute that the two had gone back to Pushkin's apartment to look at family icons. That was too transparent. Had that been a ruse to allow Pushkin to pass on documents to the American in private? Could Michael James be some sort of undercover operative? Maybe for the Russians? Or perhaps even a covert soldier for the *Mafiya*?

Whatever the answers, Colleen decided, Pushkin's presence introduced a volatile, unpredictable factor on the moon team. If he could be linked to Russian organized crime—and if Bolotov was also involved with a *Mafiya* group—that could only spell big trouble for Scott and the others. On the other hand, even if Pushkin was just a religious nut, he might also be part of the violent wing of a bunch of true believers. Muslims, Christians, Jews—in Colleen's view, it didn't matter once the violence started.

As she looked back down at the classified report, another item caught her eye, a footnote in a related report that she had somehow overlooked. It seemed that this Michael James was a former Navy Seal. Not only that, he had been involved in a major-league shoot-out in Israel when he was investigating that strange light in the sky years ago. Also, he currently did undercover work for some sort of clandestine international Christian organization. James's specialties included protecting and even physically extracting foreign missionaries who were in trouble in hostile overseas situations, promoting political action programs, and who knew what else.

Colleen sighed. *Sounds like a fundamentalist Christian version of Islamic jihad. Osama bin Laden revisited.*

What could she tell Scott? The best advice still seemed to be what she had passed on at their meeting the day before he had blasted off into space: *"Watch your back!"*

18

Soon after *Challenger II* moved into earth orbit, the commander announced that the passengers could unbuckle their seat harnesses and do some sight-seeing through the viewing ports, which had been inserted at regular intervals around the shuttle walls, or bulkheads. They would have an hour or so of free time before they reached the earth-orbiting Deep Space Station. At that recently constructed shuttle platform—a companion to the older International Space Station, which was used primarily for research—they would transfer to another spacecraft, the *Moonshot,* which would take them from earth orbit to the moon.

"But be careful as you move about," she cautioned. "For most of you, this is your first real experience with microgravity. You have to get used to floating and drifting rather than walking."

Then the pilot took a route that gave the passengers a close view of the rotating space hotel, the giant, wheel-shaped tourist site that was modeled after Wernher von Braun's "wheel-in-space" space station concept. The slowly spinning structure—which contained living quarters, observation decks, exercise areas, and amusement centers—produced gravity close to that on earth through centrifugal force.

"Think I'll take the family up there when I get back," Hightower said as he and Scott viewed the sight.

"No matter what you may have read, it's still a work in progress," the congressman replied. "After I had been up there for a couple of days, it got a little boring. They hadn't yet built the entertainment sections, like the High-Rollers' Casino."

Hightower chuckled. "I've heard about that. Where they play those outer-space gambling games—three-dimensional roulette, holographic poker . . ."

"Right," Scott said. "You can't escape human nature. It's Las Vegas in orbit. But it's making the entrepreneurs behind it rich. Private investment and tourist money is flowing into space like a raging river. We probably wouldn't be making this trip if the orbital hotel hadn't been built—and if rich travelers weren't willing to put down a small fortune for a short stay in orbit."

"What exactly does it cost to visit the hotel?" Hightower asked. "I heard the prices have come down."

Scott laughed. "The shuttle flight alone is now down to a bargain-basement, round-trip fare of $900,000 per person."

"It still costs that much?" Hightower exclaimed. "That's outrageous!"

"They're expecting the price to go down, though maybe not into our price range," Scott replied. "Still, it's not much money for the very rich. You remember that guy Dennis Tito, who paid the Russians $20 million back in the 1990s for the right to become the first space tourist? He was just the first in a long line of adventurers with deep pockets."

"So for high rollers, paying less than a million may seem like a real bargain," Hightower said, shaking his head.

"I can still remember the congressional hearings on this subject," Scott said. "Of course Tito's name came up. But also our witnesses cataloged what thousands of wealthy tourists had been willing to pay routinely in recent years for exciting vacations. One guy produced a brochure from the Harvard Museum of Natural History—I think it was circulated back in 2001. They were charging almost $37,000 per person back then for a twenty-five-day trip in a private jet to exotic locations around the earth."

"And there were takers, of course."

"Plenty of takers," Scott replied. "But the excitement of those trips pales next to flight into orbit."

Hightower laughed. "The guys in this business must be raking it in. We're in the wrong business."

"They're making plenty of money, but their expenses are high," Scott replied. "With the new technology, they've managed to lower the total cost of one shuttle flight from about $100 million at the turn of the millennium to about $50 million today. That's still a lot of money, but the profits are starting to roll in. They've been successful in filling their quota of about a hundred passengers per flight, which is the maximum capacity on the new class of shuttles they're using. At $900,000 a pop, that means they can gross about $90 million for every round trip."

"So they probably net close to $40 million every time they go up," Hightower mused.

"Yep. And on top of that, the space hotel owners charge plenty for their rooms and gourmet space meals—such as 'Jupiter sundaes,' 'Europa cappuccino,' 'moon muffins,' and 'sun-flare steaks.'"

Hightower smiled wryly. "Not to mention the activities and tours I've heard they offer. The tourists even get to do space walks."

"You bet," Scott replied. "One of the first things they set up was an 'extravehicular activity' station, called the 'Guest EVA Platform.' After providing a little instruction, experienced former astronauts take entire families outside the hotel for a space hike. But there's an additional fee, of course."

"Of course," quipped Hightower. "It's amazing that so many people have the money for this sort of thing."

"Still, it's the wave of the future, and many well-heeled people want to be at the cutting edge," Scott said. "They also see it as a major advantage for their children. After all, for decades people have been willing to pay thousands for SAT preparation for their college-bound kids. Can you imagine what it would look like on a college application for a kid to say she's spent time in earth orbit?"

"I read that the second and third hotels are already in the planning stages," Hightower noted. "Maybe they'll give us poor scientists a special rate." He was obviously still intrigued by the idea of a family vacation three hundred miles above the earth's surface.

"I understand they're planning minicourses in astronomy and space science for both kids and adults," Scott said. "I must admit, that would be a fantastic experience. Beats anything I can imagine for you and your family in Sydney."

Before Hightower could reply, the *Challenger II* commander directed them to return to their seats and buckle up. They were now beginning their approach to the Deep Space Station, which had been quite successful in relieving the burdens on the revamped International Space Station. The Deep Space Station, which specialized in servicing lunar shuttles, would also be the site where the first manned Mars spaceship would be assembled and launched.

If the passengers had been hoping for a tour of the Deep Space Station, they were disappointed. Their earth shuttle, the *Challenger II*, docked smoothly on one side of the Earth Arrival Platform, which was rigged to receive shuttles from earth. Then they were hustled through hatches into a passenger-waiting-room compartment, and they immediately exited through other hatches that led into the lunar shuttle, the *Moonshot*.

Scott was beginning to get somewhat used to the weightlessness, in part because he had experienced the phenomenon on his previous trip. Also, he had learned a great deal on the astronaut training flights in transport planes, which had gone into a controlled dive to simulate a lack of gravity.

"It's like riding a bicycle," one seasoned astronaut had told him. "Once you learn to maneuver in microgravity, you don't forget."

Scott had also learned to refer to this condition as "microgravity" rather than "zero gravity" because even in earth orbit, where you tended to float about, there was a tiny bit of pull on your body from the earth. Some scientists he had consulted actually argued that zero gravity was impossible throughout the universe. They said that even though in some places the force of gravity might be only one-millionth as strong as gravity on earth, some slight gravitational pull was exerted by any object with mass, including planets, moons, and even spaceships. But as a practical matter, even in low earth orbit, Scott didn't sense any gravitational pull. He felt weightless, pure and simple, and it had taken some getting used to.

As soon as the crew had entered the lunar shuttle, another commander and pilot joined them. This time, the genders of the officers were reversed. The commander was male and the pilot, female. Immediately after they were strapped into their seats, the Deep Space Station crew detached the *Moonshot* from its moorings, and the lunar shuttle began to accelerate to an earth-escape velocity of almost 25,000 mph. They had finally embarked on their long-awaited trip to the moon—a journey that Scott hoped would prove to be less eventful and threatening than his other experiences as a neophyte astronaut.

19

Scott, who had anchored his drifting body in front of the porthole on *Moonshot*, one of the two lunar shuttles in regular use, quietly contemplated the receding earth. Suddenly it dawned on him that they were now more than halfway to their destination, the Ocean of Storms, the vast plain on the lower left side of the moon.

During the hours since they had left earth orbit, Scott had become intimately familiar with the three main chambers of the lunar craft. At the back of the shuttle was the "bedroom," with separate sleeping compartments and a quiet space for work, but he had seen little of that area. There had been far too much to observe and discuss.

Scott and most of the others were now floating around in the larger middle chamber, which had been designed both as a dining area and a common room to promote social interaction and space observation. As the shuttle streaked toward the moon, the pilot tilted the craft so that the portholes in the middle chambers provided spectacular views of both the moon and the earth.

An earth-moon television hookup in the common room enabled passengers to engage in press conferences at designated times and also to carry on semiprivate conversations with family members or colleagues back on earth. Scott had already participated in one international press conference about the mission, and then had talked for about ten minutes face-to-face over a video monitor with Sara and the children.

Speaking from a special private communications room at the Launch Control Center at the Kennedy Space Center, Sara had tried to put on a good face. But Scott could tell she was still worried about him. The kids, on the other hand, were enthralled at the idea that they were actually talking to Dad in outer space as he was speeding away from them at many times the speed of sound.

Scott smiled as he remembered Jacob's mantra, repeated over and over from Florida during their conversation: "I can't believe this. I really can't believe we're doing this."

The third main chamber of the lunar shuttle, the flight deck, was located at the front of the craft. There, the commander, the pilot, and a scientific officer/navigator carried out all the flight functions. A spot on the flight deck had also been set aside for science-team members to engage in private telecommunications and encrypted e-mail links.

As Scott looked up toward the passageway leading to the flight deck, he saw Ruth Goldberg squirt gracefully through as she came into the common room. It was amazing, watching her move effortlessly about in the weightless environment. Having lost the use of her legs as a child as a result of a fall during a rock-climbing holiday, Ruth had been forced to rely exclusively on her arms and back to move about and do most chores on earth. As a result, her upper body was far stronger and more agile than that of most men. *Hard to believe she's confined to a wheelchair on earth. Space may be her natural milieu.*

When Goldberg's legs disappeared through the passageway leading to the sleeping chamber, Scott turned back for one last look out of his porthole, which provided a spectacular view of the expanse of space they had been traversing for the previous few hours. The blue, green, and white globe that was earth dominated space from its perch in the heavens 120,000 miles away. He began to understand the attempts by Armstrong, Aldrin, Irwin, and other earlier moon travelers to wax poetic as they groped for the right words to describe the overwhelming vistas of space.

Now more accustomed to the weightlessness, Scott gave the bulkhead near him a light, confident push and began to drift slowly toward the opposite side of the middle chamber, where Jeff Hightower and Shiro Hiramatsu were contemplating the moon. The earth's satellite was glowing with increasing brightness against the black backdrop of the airless heavens, and the craters and ripples on the surface had become much more visible to the naked eye.

But Scott was too tired to savor the scene further. Usually the Australian could get a laugh out of him, but suddenly he felt dead tired. In seeming response to his thoughts, the voice of the *Moonshot* commander came over the speaker system in the crew compartment: "Commander to crew. Commander to crew. We have a good fifteen hours to go before we enter lunar orbit. I'd suggest you get some sleep. We like to have alert passengers during a moon landing."

Scott and the others had been awake since they had left earth orbit—in fact, since the liftoff from the Kennedy Space Center—and fatigue was now catching up with most of the mission scientists. Everything had been moving so quickly, and no one had wanted to miss a moment of the adventure. But now, Scott was having trouble thinking clearly; he knew he needed some shut-eye.

The congressman pushed himself through the short passageway leading to the rear chamber, where the sleeping compartments were located. Each compartment, which had reminded Scott of bright blue coffins the first time he had seen them, could be closed off to keep the sounds and movements in the vicinity from disturbing the sleeper. Space stations and lunar shuttles could become noisy places, as drifting tools, clipboards, and utensils banged regularly against the bulkheads. When trips to the moon became a regular event, complaints from sleep-deprived astronauts had quickly led to innovations like the mostly soundproof sleeping compartments. The tiny spaces had been designed so that the only clearly audible outside noise would be a sharp "wake-up" rap directly on the compartment door.

Scott opened the sleeping compartment that had been assigned to him and pulled himself into his narrow berth, which was just large enough to accommodate a high-tech sleeping bag. When he had first seen one of these sleeping slots, he thought he was looking at some sort of enclosed tanning bed. He was old enough to remember these "skin-cancer machines," as many dermatologists had called them, before they were largely eliminated as health hazards about a decade before. Scott slipped feetfirst into the bag, which was attached to the side of the bulkhead in the compartment, and then closed the cover behind him. He noticed immediately that most of the stray noises in the shuttle had been shut out.

Looking up at some controls that had been built into the compartment, Scott made sure that the vents that piped fresh air into his area were working properly. He had been warned that when you're sleeping in space, the air may become motionless because there's no gravity or natural breeze to move it around. As a result, carbon dioxide can accumulate in different pockets of a compartment, including those around a passenger's head. With excess CO_2, Scott knew it was impossible to breathe properly. In fact, if a passenger steadily exhaled carbon dioxide and somehow failed to "push it away" from his nose and mouth, he could become unconscious and suffocate.

"Fortunately, you have a built-in alarm system in your mind and body," a NASA instructor had told them. "If there's too much CO_2 and not enough oxygen, you'll automatically wake up."

Still, Scott wasn't interested in taking chances with his oxygen supply. He checked the vent carefully to be sure it was open. Then he shut off his light and found himself in total darkness.

At first, a mild feeling of claustrophobia gripped him, but soon the weight-lessness provided a feeling of spaciousness. Sleep was slow in coming, however. The main problem was that as Scott floated within the sleeping bag, he was disconcerted by the lack of pressure on his back. He had been warned that in some people, even seasoned astronauts, the absence of a sense of physical heaviness at bedtime could prevent the onset of sound sleep. He also knew that many astronauts had to rely on sleeping pills to get their rest.

But other concerns were also keeping Scott awake. As he drifted inside his compartment, the events of the past few hours swirled about in his mind, vivid sights and sounds, and sharp memories that almost made him feel he was reliving the liftoff and ascent into earth orbit. Gradually, almost imperceptibly, his muscles relaxed in the microgravity, and his thoughts became more fragmented and disorganized.

———————

Scott wasn't sure exactly when he fell asleep. But he was acutely aware of the point when he woke up, because he couldn't breathe. Gasping for a breath that wouldn't come, he jackknifed his body inside his sleeping bag and immediately bumped his head hard against one of the walls of his cramped compartment.

The first rational thought that came to mind was the carbon-dioxide problem. But if that was the difficulty, he couldn't figure out why waking up hadn't resolved it. He had believed those NASA instructors. When the inner alarm bells aroused you, a shift in positions was supposed to expose you again to good, oxygen-filled air. But that wasn't happening to him. Even though he was awake, he was still gasping for air.

To make matters worse, he was tangled up in his sleeping bag, with arms and legs caught inside as though he were in some kind of straitjacket. Some sort of cloth or covering seemed to be wrapped firmly around his head. As Scott's panic intensified, every survival instinct in his being took over.

In a desperate act of shoulder strength, he widened the bag opening near his neck just enough to be able to force one arm outside. Then he swept his free hand back and forth against the sides of the compartment in an effort to find the air vent. Finally, he thought he had located it—but it wouldn't turn.

That's impossible! If that's the air vent, it has to turn!

By now, Scott had become completely disoriented in the dark. He had no idea where to find the light switch. Then he thought he had identified the compartment door, but he couldn't open it. Was he pushing against the bulkhead instead?

He was breathing in short, ineffective bursts, and his mind was becoming fuzzy. Very, very fuzzy. Though he could feel consciousness slipping away, panic kept him awake and somewhat focused. He sensed that the only chance he had was to try to kick out the compartment hatch, and he knew he had a limited amount of strength left. Then it would all be over.

He rotated his body around sideways in the compartment, braced his back against what he thought—and hoped—was the bulkhead, and began to bang away with his feet against the other side of the sleeping container. But the hatch held firm.

Then Scott relaxed. The panic faded. Feeling unusually sleepy, he thought how nice it would feel not to have to fight and bang against this impossible little prison. Perhaps he should stop and rest for a moment, only a moment, no longer. Just as he closed his eyes, a blast of air woke him up. The compartment door flew open, and arms reached in to pull him roughly into the main crew area.

Gulping in the fresh oxygen, Scott floundered for a few moments in the arms of his rescuer. When he looked up, he saw the blurry faces of two concerned-looking women. He was sure the one on his right was Sara—until he blinked and saw that Colonel Anne-Marie Coquillat, the lunar shuttle pilot, was holding him firmly by his right arm.

Then he looked down and noticed that Ruth Goldberg had an iron grip on his left leg and arm.

"Are you all right, Dr. Andrews?" the pilot asked in her distinctive French accent. She proceeded to free him from the sleeping bag, which was still impeding his movement.

"I think so. What happened in there?"

"That remains to be seen," the pilot replied. "I happened to be conducting a routine check of the craft, and Dr. Goldberg called me over to your compartment. She'd heard banging noises inside and decided something was wrong."

"I didn't want to violate your privacy," Goldberg said. "But something didn't sound right."

"Frankly, Dr. Goldberg was the one who saved you," the pilot said. "When we decided to break the compartment open, I wasn't strong enough to do it. Somehow, she braced herself against the bulkhead and pried it open all by herself."

"If you hadn't opened the cover, I'd be dead," Scott said, looking at the Israeli scientist, whose physical limitations on earth had apparently become a major advantage in microgravity. "I would have suffocated."

Goldberg nodded self-consciously and pulled the still-dazed congressman to one side as the French pilot turned her attention toward Scott's compartment. Colonel Coquillat carefully inspected Scott's sleeping area, looking closely at the air vent and the latches on the compartment cover.

"See anything?" Scott asked, now feeling more like himself. He drifted to the pilot's side as she examined his sleeping bag and the instrument controls in the compartment.

"Your air vent is definitely stuck," she replied with a frown. "Broken, it seems. It's twisted so tightly that the screw is off its threads. And Dr. Goldberg actually had to break the latch on the compartment cover to get you out. That seems to have been jammed as well."

"But the door to this thing was working fine when I opened it and got inside," Scott said. "So was the air vent. I checked just before I went to sleep. The air was flowing nicely."

"The vent is broken now, see?" She indicated the vent control.

"Also, I think you were too tightly laced in your bag," she continued. "This head flap, which is available for extra warmth if you need it, had apparently become wrapped around your face. So with the vent broken and your head covered up, the carbon dioxide accumulated rapidly around your nose and mouth."

"How could that happen?" Scott asked. "I wasn't laced up very tight when I went to sleep. And I don't remember putting the flap over my head at all."

Colonel Coquillat, who was anchoring herself in front of him by holding on to a handle on the bulkhead, just shrugged. "It's impossible to re-create now exactly what happened. But I'll have to file a detailed report so we can study this and prevent it from happening again."

By now, Hightower and Hiramatsu had joined the group.

"Did either of you notice anything unusual around Dr. Andrews's sleeping compartment?" the pilot asked the Australian and Japanese scientists.

Both shook their heads in the negative. "Scott was the first into the sack," Hightower said.

"Then I followed soon after," Hiramatsu added.

"I watched the moon a little longer," Hightower said. "Then I decided to retire myself." Suddenly, he raised his hand. "Hold on! When I got into the sleeping area, something struck me. Both Pushkin and Bolotov were talking next to Scott's berth. At first I thought they might have found another viewing area for the moon or earth. But there was no porthole on that side of the shuttle. Nothing really, but Scott's little drawer."

Scott looked around the crew area. "Where are the Russians?" he asked, feeling a wave of anger well up inside.

The pilot immediately pushed off in the direction of their sleeping compartments, which were built into the opposite bulkhead, and knocked on the covers. Bolotov emerged immediately, but it took several more knocks before Pushkin responded.

"What is it?" Bolotov asked gruffly.

"We've had an accident," the pilot said.

By now, Pushkin had moved out to join the others and was drifting near Bolotov's elbow. Both seemed to notice Scott on the other side of the sleeping chamber at the same time, and both looked startled.

Scott pushed off from his bulkhead and shot right up into Bolotov's face, only a few inches from his nose. "So, you guys seem surprised to see me. Why would that be?"

Bolotov scowled and backed off slightly, but Pushkin maneuvered himself closer to Scott. "What do you mean? What's happened?"

"Maybe you should tell me," Scott said. "Why were you hanging around my sleeping compartment after I went to sleep?"

"We weren't interested in you," Bolotov said with a smirk. "No matter what you may think, you're not the focus of our lives. We were discussing the fusion issue."

"But why in my sleeping area? Why right next to my compartment?" Scott pressed.

"Because that's just where we wanted to talk," Bolotov said defiantly.

"I didn't really think about where we were, Dr. Andrews," Pushkin said. "In this weightless environment, we drift about. I often end up in a place far from where I originally planned to be."

The pilot nodded, evidently satisfied with this explanation for the time being. But she asked. "Did you see anyone open Dr. Andrews's compartment cover?"

"No, no one," Bolotov said, looking away from the others. The discussion appeared to be boring him.

"I didn't see anyone either," Pushkin echoed.

"So nobody knows anything," Scott said sarcastically. "Well, one thing *I* know is that I almost suffocated. Somebody broke my air vent and jammed the cover to my compartment."

"So what are you saying, Dr. Andrews?" Bolotov said, looking back at him with a sardonic smile. "Are you saying one of us is to blame? I think you are— how do you say in English?—paranoid. Yes, paranoid."

Scott felt anger boiling up inside him. He tried to reach for the Russian, but the female pilot and Ruth Goldberg, both of whom were more skilled at maneuvering about in microgravity than Scott, easily diverted him to one side.

"*Remettrez-vous!*" the pilot warned. "Easy, easy. It's an unfortunate incident, but there's no evidence of foul play."

"What do you mean, 'no evidence'?" Scott spat out, but then caught himself. He remembered he was still the leader of the scientific team, and he had to exercise some self-control. "Okay, okay, we'll let this pass. But I want a full report entered on this incident, understand?" he said to the pilot.

"Of course," she replied. "We always make out full reports on such matters."

Scott, still seething, turned away before he said anything he would regret and floated back toward his sleeping compartment. The Russians, Ruth Goldberg, and Hiramatsu climbed back into their compartments for another hour or so of rest, and the pilot propelled herself toward the passageway that led to the common room and then back to the flight deck.

Hightower, who had followed Scott, said with a chuckle, "I don't imagine you plan on any more sleep just now."

"You imagine right," Scott said, not returning the humor. "Look at this."

He pointed to the control for the air vent, which resembled the vent controls used on most passenger airplanes. "There seems to be a mark, a cut on this thing, as though someone used a tool, maybe a pair of pliers, to twist it.

The thing is completely stuck. Can't move it at all with my bare hand."

"Are you sure you adjusted it before you went to sleep?" Hightower asked.

"Definitely," the congressman said. "It turned easily. I adjusted it so that a steady stream of air was coming out."

Hightower placed a finger under the outlet. "Now there's nothing. It's closed up tight."

"I'm telling you, I didn't wrap that sleeping-bag flap around my head. And when I fell asleep, I was only loosely strapped at the neck into my sleeping bag."

"You're sure?"

"Absolutely," Scott replied.

Hightower contemplated the vent and the sleeping bag silently for a few moments, and then he shook his head. "But why? Why would anyone want to harm you?"

"*Kill* me," Scott corrected. "If the pilot and Goldberg hadn't happened by, I'd have been a goner. All the sleeping compartments are soundproof. Nobody could hear me—and I was on the verge of losing consciousness. The more I breathed, the more carbon dioxide I inhaled. There was almost no oxygen inside there."

"I still don't see a motive," the Australian scientist protested.

"I don't really understand either," Scott said quietly. "All I can think of is that I'm the only American, and I'm in charge. So if I'm out of the way, leadership of this mission—and maybe control of the entire energy program—could go by default to the Russians."

"But Shiro would take your place, not a Russian," Hightower said.

"Look, no matter what that pilot says, I'm convinced somebody tried to kill me," Scott replied. "Somebody damaged that air vent and twisted me up in my sleeping bag. And as far as I'm concerned, Bolotov is the prime suspect. After all, he was responsible for my injury in the Houston water tank. But I'm not ready to rule anybody out, not even Shiro. The more I think about it, the Japanese may have as much to gain as the Russians by reducing American influence."

Hightower shook his head and turned toward his sleeping compartment. "Your suspicions are running wild, mate," he said.

Scott decided not to pursue the issue because he knew the Australian might be right—maybe he was becoming paranoid. Also, as the leader, he didn't want to poison the team atmosphere. But he had a strong sense that he was encountering too many threats for them to be mere coincidence.

With Hightower now tucked away in his compartment, the congressman found himself drifting alone in the weightlessness of the sleeping chamber. Yet he didn't feel like getting back into an extra sleeping drawer that had been made available for him. Instead, he sensed an urgent need to contact Colleen and get her feedback. Fortunately, with the sophisticated communications system available to him on the shuttle, he would be able to transmit the latest news and then receive an immediate reply, assuming that she was in a convenient place to respond.

As Scott made his way toward the passageway that led out of the sleeping chamber and into the common room, he remained deep in thought. So it was understandable that he failed to notice the pair of eyes watching him closely through an open crack in the door to one of the passenger sleeping compartments.

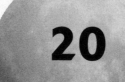

20

When Colleen first drove onto the peaceful, green Wheaton College campus, just south of Chicago, she thought she had entered a kind of time warp. The place reminded her of what she had read and heard about America in the 1950s. There were open, grassy areas, crisscrossed by country-like roads with little traffic, and conservatively dressed students. None of the cacophonous, blaring music or weird outfits and body jewelry she was used to seeing at most universities in cities on the eastern seaboard. Then she did a double take. One group of young people was planting small white crosses in an open section of lawn on one of the green commons.

"What's that all about?" Colleen asked a young man who was watching the activity.

"The crosses are for babies killed by abortion," the student replied.

Feeling even more out of place, the chief of staff decided not to follow up on that one. She quickly asked directions and hurried on her way, past the Billy Graham Library and toward the building the young man had pointed out. Soon, she was knocking on an office door with the nameplate she was looking for: Michael James, Professor of Biblical Studies.

"Come in!" a firm male voice commanded from behind the closed door.

When she opened the door, she saw there was only one occupant in the small, single room—a medium-sized, wiry man wearing prominent spectacles and a somewhat goofy grin. She knew from her research that he was in his early fifties, but he looked younger, with a relatively unlined face and a full head of wavy, steel-gray hair. He had already left his neat, nearly clean desk and was walking vigorously toward her with outstretched hand.

"Ms. Barker, I presume!" he said, with rather too much enthusiasm and friendliness, Colleen thought. "I'm Michael James. Please sit down."

"Thanks for seeing me, Professor James," she began. "You know something about why I'm here."

"Only what you said—that you have some concerns about Professor Sergey Pushkin. I'm not sure I can really be of help, but please go ahead."

"I have some information about a conversation you had with Pushkin a year ago, in the Grand Moskva Café in Moscow," she began carefully.

"And where might you have obtained that information?" James asked, now growing serious and locking his eyes on hers, to the point that she began to feel slightly uncomfortable.

"Can't say," Colleen said. "It's classified."

Then, even though she didn't possess any particular authority over him, she decided to try some intimidation. "And I'll have to ask you to keep our conversation to yourself. It could be important to national security."

"Afraid I can't promise a thing," James said pleasantly but unequivocally. "At least not unless you can present me with some sort of formal order from a government agency. Let's face it, Ms. Barker, I don't know you from Adam— or Eve."

"Look," Colleen said, realizing she had to take a different tack. "If necessary, I can get all the authority I need. Because there are indications that you may be working against the best interests of your country."

Colleen hesitated, hoping to provoke a reaction—perhaps a nervous swallow or a shift in the seat. Nothing. James just sat there silently, staring directly into her eyes.

So she continued: "I haven't passed on my suspicions about you to anyone else. Not yet, anyway. Because I think in the long run it might be best for both of us to keep this thing as informal as possible. So here's the deal. Pushkin said something to you in Moscow that suggested the two of you were working together on something. What was it?"

James shrugged. "I'm not free to discuss my conversations with a person I'm, um, counseling. Priest-penitent privilege, you know."

"You're an ordained minister?" Colleen asked, unable to conceal her surprise. She had missed that item in her research.

"Yes, among other things."

"Such as a Navy Seal," she said.

Score! This time, James looked a little startled. "My, you have been looking into my background, haven't you, Ms. Barker?" he finally said with a wry smile.

"I try to do my homework," she said pointedly. "Okay, so maybe you can't disclose what a sinner says to you in confession. But I don't for a minute think you were hearing Pushkin's confession in that conversation. You were pumping him for information about his work. And the interchange indicates you two might have been conspiring about something—with those references to some sort of 'movement,' and an unidentified 'enemy.'"

James frowned. "You have the advantage over me, Ms. Barker, because you obviously are in possession of some sort of detailed, verbatim transcript. I know enough about undercover work to know that you're making use of a recorded conversation. What authority did you have to record my discussion with Pushkin—if, in fact, I had such a discussion?"

"I didn't record anything," Colleen blurted, and then wished she had kept her mouth shut. She was under no obligation to give this man any information at all.

"So who did the recording?" James pressed.

"Let's just say we're in the area of serious, classified intelligence—matters that I can't discuss freely, and you shouldn't be involved in at all," Colleen said heatedly. "You shouldn't be collaborating on foreign soil with an enemy of the United States."

"Who says Pushkin is our enemy?" James asked, a slight smile crossing his face again. "I thought he and his Russian colleagues were working with us to solve the energy needs of the world. At least that's what the newspapers are saying. Are they wrong?"

Colleen could see that regardless of this man's real agenda, he was too experienced to disclose anything to her by accident. Then she remembered that her main objective was not to spar verbally with James, but to do all in her power to assure Scott's safety. If his recent e-mail disclosing the new attempt on his life was any indication, the danger to him was escalating. Because she was coming to the end of her options, she decided to take a chance.

"Look," she said, "I'm mainly worried about my boss. And believe me, Professor James, if I decide you pose any danger at all to him, I'll bring the wrath of the U.S. Congress down on your head. You'll be tied up testifying at hearings from now till the next millennium. On the other hand, if you think there's any way you can help me, I'll listen."

"I'm certainly willing to help Dr. Scott Andrews or anyone else, so long as I don't have to violate confidences," James said mildly.

"Not the most promising answer, but I guess I have to take what I can get," Colleen replied, and then decided to try to throw him off balance. "From all I've learned, your methods and background are unorthodox, to say the least. What with international political incidents, killings, and bombings in that Star of Bethlehem business in Israel a few years back."

"Perhaps my reputation outstrips reality," James said. "My real mission in life may disappoint or even bore you, Ms. Barker. I just want to help people in need and perhaps introduce a few to Jesus Christ."

"Yeah, yeah, I know," Colleen said, dismissing this answer as most likely part of a cover story. "Anyhow, please contact me immediately if you hear anything about Scott. It could be a matter of life or death."

As she stood to her feet and picked up her briefcase, she couldn't resist a parting shot. Pointing her finger directly at James's chest, she said, "Just remember this. I've alerted my federal law enforcement contacts about our little talk here today, and I'll report to them again when I return to Washington. If you know something about Pushkin and the Russians that you're not telling me, that could be bad for your career."

Michael James smiled amiably and shook his head. "Ms. Barker, please, not so dramatic. I won't tell you more about my relationship with Sergey Pushkin, no matter how much pressure you apply. But I will say this. I have no designs on the life or well-being of Dr. Scott Andrews. And I would be stunned if Professor Pushkin wants to harm Andrews either. I don't believe he's that kind of man."

"And Dr. Vladimir Bolotov?" Colleen asked, trying one last test.

"Professor Pushkin's colleague—the one with cosmonaut training who was included in the team at the last moment?"

So you have been following the news stories.

"Yes."

"I don't know him personally," James said noncommittally. "But be assured of this: if I determine that Scott Andrews is in any sort of danger from any source, and I feel I can be of assistance, you'll be the first to know."

She nodded grimly, and he smiled. "You're quite an enigma, Ms. Barker. I can't decide if you're trying to woo me as an ally or you want to put me behind bars."

"The answer to that depends on whose side you're on in this business," she replied.

"There may be more than one side," he said.

She almost asked him what he meant, but then she decided he was likely to get too philosophical. Colleen had already determined that the only way she would get anything more out of the man was through a congressional subpoena, and she wasn't ready to take that step. At least not yet.

In the end, as she walked away from his office, Colleen concluded that Michael James was unreadable. Either he was telling the truth and really was willing to help her, or he was a superb liar. She simply couldn't decide, but she also couldn't take a chance because her boss remained in danger. Until this crafty Wheaton Bible professor could convince her otherwise, she had to assume that she couldn't count on him for any help—and it would probably be wise not to trust him with any more information.

21

As the *Moonshot* passengers crowded around every available porthole, the gray-white, pocked, and rippled surface of the moon passed slowly before them, filling their viewing windows with a parade of empty valleys, silent mountains, and dusty, dry seas. For a moment, Scott almost thought he was watching a panoramic science-fiction movie unfolding in front of his eyes. But then it registered on him that he was witnessing the real thing—and seeing sights that he had only dreamed about since he was a child.

The lunar shuttle was just starting its journey around the far side of the moon, the surface that only space travelers could see since most of one side of the cratered satellite was always turned toward the earth. As the spacecraft slid through the vacuum—and the setting earth gradually sank and then dropped out of sight behind the moon's horizon—Scott noticed a decided difference in topography. The surface of the far side was whiter and smoother than the near side because, scientists surmised, the thicker crust of the far side had been able to absorb and disguise the constant asteroid and meteoroid bombardment more effectively than the thinner-crusted near side.

In the early days of space exploration, this first phase of establishing a moon orbit had always been disconcerting, if not frightening. As the astronauts passed behind the moon, they lost contact with earth for the first time in their long flight. The moon itself got directly in the way of radio and television signals and made communication with the home planet impossible. As a result, there was suddenly a disturbing new sense of being all alone in the infinite wasteland of space.

In the last decade, all of that had changed. Now, transmission signals could be bounced off one or more of the artificial satellites that were circling the moon, and then redirected back and forth to earth. Voices and pictures from the earth were constantly available.

From earlier briefings, Scott knew that the procedure for landing on the moon was also somewhat different from that employed by Armstrong, Aldrin, and the early astronauts. Like the old Apollo class of spaceships, *Moonshot* first went into a high, elliptical orbit, and then established a lower, stable orbit. But unlike the earlier craft, *Moonshot* didn't carry a lunar lander. Instead, the new lunar shuttle headed toward the permanent lunar space station, an orbiting platform similar to the Deep Space Station that now circled the earth.

The moon station, which had been constructed about five years before, functioned as a service platform for the lunar shuttle and also housed the new Falcon class of lunar landers, one of which would take the scientific team to the surface. The name for the landers had been chosen to continue the bird-of-prey motif, which had begun with *Eagle*, the first lunar lander that had been carried by *Apollo 11*.

"Passengers, prepare to disembark!"

The voice of the *Moonshot* commander brought Scott back to the present. The members of the scientific team, who had already donned their pressure suits and helmets and had packed their personal gear, moved to the rear hatch of the shuttle. Scott expected the docking procedure and transfer to the lunar space station to take some time. But immediately after he felt a slight bump and heard a muffled *clang!* in the direction of the hatch, the hatch door swung open and a man wearing a red-and-white pressure suit hurtled through from the station airlock.

"Welcome to moon orbit, ladies and gentlemen!" he said, introducing himself as "Jack, your moon-lander guide."

He pointed at the hatch through which he had appeared. "Our other guide, Heather, will meet you on the other side. You'll be taking the *Falcon I* lander on this trip. I'll take care of your gear."

Ruth Goldberg was the first through the hatch, and Scott was the last to enter the lunar space station's holding area. Under Heather's guidance, they were now floating in two lines, holding on to one another to stabilize their positions in the microgravity environment.

There was hardly time to think about what was happening, as Heather slipped quickly through the second airlock and into the lunar lander and Ruth Goldberg and the others began to follow. When Scott finally entered the

Falcon I, he saw that the craft was almost circular, with large viewing windows on every curved bulkhead.

As soon as they were all strapped in, Scott felt a slight jarring and a pull of acceleration as the *Falcon I* disengaged from the moon station and headed toward the surface of the moon. A few minutes into the flight, the *Falcon I* pilot, Captain Hardisty, began to speak through the passengers' headphones.

"If you'll look out the left windows, you can see your destination, the Ocean of Storms," he said as he began to tip the lander in that direction. "It's that big, dark area down there. Soon you'll be able to make out the structures that will be your home for the next three months. We call it Energy City."

From the briefing pictures he had seen, Scott knew the outpost was designed in a rather odd shape, like a huge barbell, with octagon-shaped structures on each end and a long passageway linking them. One of the octagonal modules was the living area, where they would sleep, eat, exercise, and socialize; the other was the factory and work area, where they would build the fusion energy mechanism.

"Does look cold down there," Hightower observed.

"Let me give you today's weather report—which will be the same every day you're here," the pilot said and chuckled, as though reading Hightower's mind. "We know that the temperature can go from about 140 degrees Celsius in sunlight—well above the boiling point—down to minus 170 degrees Celsius in the shade, or during the lunar night. It gets even colder around the polar ice caps. In Fahrenheit, that's a swing of roughly 280 degrees boiling hot, to 275 degrees or more below zero."

Then the pilot cleared his throat for effect: "Just be sure you don't accidentally step outside."

Scott could hear a murmur of slightly nervous laughter from the team members through his headphones, but he wasn't inclined to join the fun. Just hearing the word *accident* made him think of his own mishaps at the Johnson Space Center and on *Moonshot*. Accidents on this mission could be serious, even fatal.

He looked over at Pushkin and Bolotov, whose faces were visible through their open visors. They weren't laughing either—and Scott didn't take that as a reassuring sign.

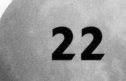

22

The name *Energy City* quickly stuck with the members of the scientific team, and they began to use the term freely as the *Falcon I* descended nearer and nearer to the Ocean of Storms. From a distance the place did indeed look something like a huge, cream-colored barbell. But as they drew closer, Scott could see that the living quarters and work area were much more complex than such a simple description might suggest.

At the ends of the long passageway, each of the octagonal structures was punctuated with a series of glassy plates, which Scott knew from his readings were specially designed, thick, synthetic windows. The walls of the multi-storied living quarters, as well as those of the work area at the other end of the passageway, were constructed out of many layers of plastic, synthetic foam, aluminum alloys, and even a specially designed textile fabric. Scott had learned from his preparatory courses on the mission that the idea behind the design for the "skin" of Energy City was to do everything humanly possible to protect the inhabitants and workers from possible impact of micrometeoroids. These tiny meteors and other space debris, traveling at many times the speed of a bullet, could puncture deadly holes in ordinary spaceships or space suits.

Many of the current energy needs of Energy City were being met by solar power. Scott immediately recognized the large metallic solar receptors that covered much of the open surface of the outpost. Unencumbered by the clouds that made the sun's energy an uncertain proposition on earth, these plates collected solar radiation, and internal photovoltaic cells converted the radiation into electricity.

Falcon I was now going into a landing mode, so the pilot was no longer able to tip the lander for easy sightseeing. Suddenly Scott's view out the windows was obscured by what he thought was a dust storm—but there wasn't supposed to be any wind on the moon! Then he realized that they were only a few yards above the moon's surface, and the exhaust from the lander rockets was kicking up the fine dust from the regolith, or uppermost layer of the surface. The pilot had maneuvered the lander to a spot within a few yards of the middle of the long passageway, or "the bar of the barbell," as the *Falcon I* pilot had put it.

As *Falcon I* settled to a stop, Scott could see through a window in the passageway that a landing crew was working hard to maneuver a short, tube-like device out in their direction. Jack and Heather were already out of their seats, walking toward a hatch just behind the flight deck. Bouncing or hopping slowly might have been a better description of their movement. The moon's gravity had already kicked in—only one-sixth of that on earth, but already things were looking and feeling more normal. Scott couldn't wait to get out of his safety belt and shoulder harness and try his own moon legs.

Scott was grateful that Heather and Jack were available to help them disembark, because it did take each of them a little while to get used to the low gravity. The locomotion technique was closer to that on earth than in microgravity, but it was still easy to lose your balance if you bounded or moved too quickly. Scott brushed his head on the top of the exit tube as he walk-jumped out of the doorway of the lander—and he might have taken a spill if Heather hadn't steadied him.

"You'll get the hang of it soon enough," she said. "Just take it slow at first."

Scott also noticed that the others were weaving about in front of him, some sailing too high off the ground, others lurching sideways instead of moving straight ahead. The only person who seemed in complete control of herself was Ruth Goldberg, who was doing as well in the moon's low gravity as she had in the microgravity of space. She had packed a specially designed, motorized, low-gravity wheelchair, which featured oversized, inflatable wheels that gripped the ground effectively, and special straps that enabled her to propel and maneuver the device as though it were a natural extension of her body. Watching her practice on the full gravity of earth, Jeff Hightower had quickly dubbed the gadget Ruth's "moonchair"—and the name had stuck.

The contraption also came with arm extensions, which she could attach to her hands and forearms like prosthetic limbs. These long, plastic appendages enabled her to push herself about when the wheelchair motor was off, and also to regain her balance if she began to tip too far in one direction or another.

A wider, platformlike surface on the end of each "arm" provided Ruth with the extra benefit of space crutches, which she could employ when she moved on her own, away from the wheelchair. Scott made a mental correction: he decided *crutches* wasn't quite the right word for the arm extensions. Low-level stilts might be a better description. In some respects, as far as Scott could tell, Ruth's powerful arms actually made locomotion on the moon easier for her than it was for the rest of the team, who were forced to use their legs to get about.

The passageway in which the six scientists now found themselves was equipped with moving sidewalks on each side, much like the people conveyors in many airports on earth. A major difference was that the moving "moonwalks," as residents of Energy City called them, were equipped with overhead hand railings, as well as handholds on each side. The architects had obviously made every effort to help earthlings compensate for the challenges of low moon gravity.

Ruth Goldberg, needing no help to board the conveyor, quickly vaulted onto the walkway and pulled her moonchair in behind her. The two Russians, Pushkin and Bolotov, guided by two young technicians who had met the lander, hurried to catch up with her. Before long, the three were huddled in conversation. Hightower and Hiramatsu followed them, and Scott brought up the rear.

As the moonwalk moved steadily toward the lunar hotel that would be their short-term home, Scott looked back pensively in the direction of the gate, which led to the lunar lander. Heather, Jack, and Captain Hardisty had already disappeared back into the *Falcon I*, and presumably they would be heading directly back into orbit.

Suddenly, Scott became acutely aware that a few moments ago a new era had begun for him. An era that somehow he sensed would change his life forever—but in ways that he suspected the brilliant planners of the moon mission had never anticipated.

23

Within a few minutes, the scientists arrived at the end of the moonwalk conveyer belt. As they stepped off into the lobby of the Energy City living area, a blast of party horns, cheers, and slightly discordant but highly festive music stopped them in their tracks.

"Surprise party on the moon," Scott murmured, shaking his head.

Scott counted several dozen people, all dressed in some variation of the blue-and-white uniform that was the design motif for new residents of the colony. In a nod to nationalism, flags representing the countries of the scientists had been planted at the center of the reception area.

A small, ragtag musical combo—featuring a guitar and a couple of electronic keyboards—was playing "When the Saints Go Marching In." A female technician, whom Scott recognized as an acclaimed MIT electrical engineering grad, had draped a "Woman on the Moon" sign across her shoulders and was making a valiant, off-key effort to put words to the music.

Must make a note: Put real musicians on the next spaceflight.

Finally, the six members of the scientific team followed the guides who had been assigned to get them settled in their living quarters. When Scott's turn arrived, he boarded a lift with his aide, a Chinese national named Gao Jhong, and rose steadily to the "penthouse" level, which housed the VIP suites on the fourth and highest floor of the living module.

As Scott stepped off the lift, he looked down the light, sky-blue passageway that linked all their rooms and noticed that Shiro Hiramatsu and Jeffrey Hightower were in the process of entering their quarters. He assumed that Ruth Goldberg and the Russians were already settled.

When Scott entered his quarters, he stopped to stare in awe at the sight before him. Gao Jhong had opened the panel that usually covered the large bay window on one wall of his apartment to reveal a sweeping view of the night sky, with the full, blue-white earth hanging in the center of the vista.

"It almost looks like a painting," Scott said.

"I've been on the moon for almost a month now, and I'm still not used to the spectacular beauty," Jhong remarked.

Scott looked down at the surface of the moon below him and saw several vehicles at rest. Two looked like rectangular trucks, with a cab in front and six wheels spaced at regular intervals, three on each side. A large, open hauling bin in the back of each was half-filled with moon dirt. Another machine, which lay in a broad, shallow ditch that obviously had been created by excavation work, was attached to a series of lines, pulleys, and shovel-like appendages, which reminded him of the backhoes used for construction on earth.

"Moon Mack trucks and a regolither?" Scott asked.

"Correct," Jhong said. "All were produced in China," she added proudly. "The regolither digs out the regolith surface dirt, which goes down about fifteen meters. That's rich in all kinds of minerals and trapped gases—including the helium-3 isotope you'll be needing for your fusion work. Then the Moon Macks carry the dirt over to that processing factory." She pointed to a dark, rectangular structure in the distance.

"And the factory over there separates out the helium-3 and other materials," Scott mused.

"Yes," Jhong replied authoritatively. "The factory has been placed far away so that if there's any sort of accident, the workers won't damage or destroy the main buildings over here."

"Does Energy City have a mayor, in case I have any complaints?" Scott asked.

Jhong's sober reply put him on notice that the international workforce at the outpost had a long way to go before it developed a common, interplanetary sense of humor. "As you know, the supreme authority is Secretary Martin," she said seriously, referring to Archibald Martin, the British diplomat who had become the main administrator for the outpost.

Martin headed the five-person directorate that oversaw the entire operation, including security matters. But since there were only 162 people living in Energy City—including the six team members who had just arrived—and since each worker averaged at least ten hours a day at work, Scott didn't expect that Martin had too many disciplinary problems.

After the young woman had left through the panel door that opened into the hallway, Scott immediately stripped off his pressure suit and floated down onto the bed that dominated one side of the room. Unexpectedly, he bounced just after he hit the surface and almost tumbled off the other side. The only thing that saved him was a set of raised railings on the side of the bed. He had been wondering what those were for—and now he knew.

Scott lay still for a few minutes, enjoying the dramatic view of the earth through his open window. Then he began to feel guilty about resting at all. He had work to do. He bounced up, this time more carefully, and easily hoisted his bags—which had been quite heavy and cumbersome on earth—onto a flat table. *One-sixth G has its advantages.*

After transferring his clothing and other effects to drawers and a closet on one side of the room, he faced the fact that he hadn't communicated with Colleen for almost twelve hours. He was tired and needed sleep, especially since the team was scheduled to meet for breakfast about six hours from now. But Scott knew he couldn't postpone the exchange.

Wearily, he walked-bounced over to the office space, which he saw had been designed so that he could work either sitting down or standing up. *Another advantage of low gravity.* This time, he decided to sit.

Before he left earth, Scott had arranged with Colleen that they would conduct their most sensitive conferences through regular e-mail, or through an encrypted, real-time, instant message system. In both cases, they spoke directly into the computer microphone and watched as their words appeared in typed form on the screen, just as they would show up on the recipient's computer screen. As an option, if they were in situations where their voices might be overheard, they could type messages directly into a computer using a standard keyboard.

He glanced at his watch, which was set both to Washington, D.C., time and to the arbitrary "lunar time" used by everyone on the moon outpost. He and Colleen had established five possible instant message windows during the course of any day, when they could communicate directly with each other. But they were now precisely between two of those windows—so it was highly unlikely she would be waiting on the other end to chat with him. As a result, he knew he would have to rely on regular e-mail.

As Scott began to apply the codes that were necessary to access his e-mail messages, he smiled when he saw a tiny box down in the right-hand corner of his screen, which read *65.6.* That indicated the newly instituted concept of "lunar time"—lunar year sixty-five, lunar month six.

Early in the process of moon settlement, scientists working for weeks or months on the satellite had decided that for convenience, they needed a common time reference. But no one could agree on which earth time zone should prevail. The Russians wanted the Moscow zone; the Chinese insisted on Beijing; the Americans thought that because they had taken the lead in space exploration, Washington, D.C., time should be the chosen time.

Finally, to keep the international peace—and also to make a statement about the special status of moon settlement and exploration—an international committee resolved that they would establish a calendar and time system that would be unique to the moon. When space exploration reached beyond the moon, an interplanetary star-time system would go into effect.

To honor the moon's peculiarities, and at the same time keep the integrity of the metric system, they had settled upon a ten-month moon calendar. One month was based on the time it took for the moon to make one orbit of the earth: twenty-seven earth days, seven hours, and forty-three minutes. As it happened, this was the length of a lunar day, or the time required for the moon to revolve once on its axis. Each month was numbered, but not named, again to avoid controversy. There had been unanimous agreement that Moon Year 1 would begin on July 20, 1969, the year that the first earthlings, the Americans Armstrong and Aldrin, had set foot on the lunar surface.

Obviously, a ten-month year was a much shorter year than a solar year on earth, but moon workers had easily fallen into the habit of keeping two sets of time measurements. Scott looked at his watch again. The digital reading showed that the earth year was 2017, and he also noted the time in Washington, D.C., where most of his earth life was centered. Another digital window on his watch showed, as did his computer screen, that the moon year and month were 65.6. He noted that it was past time to check his e-mail messages and then get a few hours of shut-eye before the first day's work began.

Having now moved past the series of encrypted barriers that gave him complete privacy in his communications, Scott scrolled through two dozen e-mail messages until he came to three messages from Colleen. The first described her meeting with Professor Michael James, an odd, secretive evangelical operative who would bear watching. His connections with Pushkin were particularly disturbing. Scott decided that he would have to decide carefully about how to use this information when dealing with Pushkin—or for that matter, whether to use it at all.

The second message brought him up-to-date on his chief of staff's investigation of the possible connections between President Bob Dalton and the Russians. As good as she was, Colleen was having trouble nailing anything down. She said she felt it was becoming clearer that something "smelly is afoot," to use her unique metaphor, because Dalton was in regular touch with Russian Prime Minister Demitry Martov. The American president had scheduled an unusual number of "summit" trips to Moscow in the past year, and Martov had taken the unprecedented step of visiting the U.S. on three separate occasions in the same period. In each case he had arranged to spend considerable time with Dalton. What was so important that the two couldn't let their staff members help conduct negotiations? And why wasn't the head of state, President Boris Loukachik, a participant in the meetings?

This friendship struck Scott as ominous, and he wished he could find out more about it. But he knew that Colleen and her American undercover contacts could be expected to do only so much.

When Scott brought up Colleen's third e-mail message on his computer, he stopped dead in his tracks. There were only a few short sentences. But the capitals and punctuation marks his chief always used to highlight important names and phrases made his blood run cold:

Solid info says that RUTH GOLDBERG is really TATIANA TIMOSHENKO—RUSSIAN IMMIGRANT TO ISRAEL!! Went through several name changes before moving to Tel Aviv. One report says she knew VLADIMIR BOLOTOV in Russia??!! Still working on this—but BE CAREFUL!

24

The patch of woods at Camp David was overcast and dreary, and a light afternoon drizzle had begun to fall. But President Bob Dalton impatiently waved off a Secret Service agent who approached with an umbrella.

All members of the American and Russian security details had been ordered to keep at least twenty yards from the president and Prime Minister Demitry Martov as they ambled along the dirt path—and a little rain was no reason to make an exception. By mutual prior agreement, this discussion was for their ears only. No hidden Oval Office cameras or microphones. No opportunity for parabolic mikes to record the interchange.

"Demitry, I'm becoming concerned about this special experiment you're planning on the moon," the president said in a hushed voice. "There's no reason for me to be concerned, is there? You told me that Pushkin's secret project would have only economic possibilities, not military. That's right, isn't it?"

"Of course, of course, my friend," the Russian prime minister said, slapping Dalton amiably on the back and causing the American president to miss a step. "We both know that focusing on the military is a bad strategy for both America and Russia—and also for Demitry and Bobby!"

Bob Dalton was well above six feet tall and was several inches taller and much more slender than his squat counterpart, but the muscular Russian would have been the favorite in a street fight. With his long, perfectly appointed white mane of hair, President Dalton was the picture of southern dignity. But he seemed older than his fifty-five years—perhaps the result of years of hard living as he had taken advantage of his political leverage to drink deeply of the world's pleasures. Martov was well aware that the American was more interested in private partying and dallying with available females than he was in solid physical fitness.

But an even more important weakness from Martov's point of view was Dalton's love of money. Although the southerner had succeeded admirably as a politician, he had never accumulated any wealth. In fact, he had incurred so much debt in high living over the years that his net worth now added up to a negative. So, early on, it had become apparent that the best way to keep the American president on the hook was to hold out the promise of personal riches.

"Never forget—we Russians are capitalists now, just like you!" Martov emphasized, slapping Dalton again, this time watching with some pleasure as the president staggered under the blow. "And that means Swiss and offshore bank accounts for both you and me."

"But why can't you tell me more about this?" Dalton said under his breath. He shifted slightly away from the Russian, apparently to avoid another friendly backslap—but not so far that he was unable to continue talking in a near-whisper. "How exactly are you going to make money out of Pushkin's work?"

"How are *we* going to make money?" Martov corrected. "Remember, we are partners. America and Russia will benefit, but so will Dalton and Martov. We will both be out of office at some point. Why should we be just ex-politicians? Why not the two richest men in the world?"

Dalton looked around nervously, apparently afraid that Martov's voice might be carrying. "Not so loud—the trees could have ears," he cautioned, glancing at a Secret Service agent who had moved dangerously close to the twenty-yard limit he had established.

The prime minister laughed, and then spoke more quietly. "Even if we are overheard, who would have any idea what we're discussing? We left all our political aides back at the house. The people around here are merely guards."

"Even so, it's best to be cautious," Dalton said, shaking his head so vigorously that a few strands of his coif fell out of place. "Somehow the word got out about your wormholes. I had a big argument with Scott Andrews just before he blasted off, and he let me know he'd heard something about Pushkin's work. Even mentioned wormholes."

"How could he know that?" Martov demanded. "No one in your government is supposed to know about that except you alone."

"It didn't come from me, that's for sure," Dalton replied defensively. "But let's face it. Plenty of your people know about it. Maybe Pushkin or his assistant said something to another scientist. And Andrews has a snoopy chief of staff. A former newspaper reporter. She may have learned something."

Andrews, Martov fumed. *Why is it always Andrews?*

"Also, let's be frank, Demitry," Dalton continued. "You know our American intelligence network has contacts in Russia. Maybe one of our CIA people picked up something about the experiment from one of your people."

Martov grimaced but tried hard to mask his annoyance at the news that Pushkin's secret work was becoming less and less secret. Now he had to engage in damage control. Dalton was bound to know more than he had revealed so far, and it was inevitable that as the American spies continued their work, the U.S. president's store of information would increase. So Martov had to try to put him at ease.

"I'm no scientist, so I really can't tell you a great deal, my friend," Martov began, forcing himself to smile. "But Pushkin believes there is a chance he can use the fusion technology to open a rift, a sort of hole, in the fabric of space-time—whatever that may mean. Some theoretical physicists call it a 'wormhole.' Personally, I can't imagine such a hole in space. Still, if Pushkin can achieve his purpose, there could be money in it for us—for you and me, I mean. The economic impact could go far beyond our attempt to resolve the earth's energy problems. One possibility is that we could create entirely new elements and molecules. The old dream of the alchemists about turning lead into gold could become a reality."

"Still sounds like science fiction to me," Dalton grumbled. "I'll be dead and buried before you turn this thing into a cash cow."

Greed, Martov thought, smiling to himself. *How do Americans put such people into their highest office? Any Russian knows that wealth is useful only when it leads to power.*

"It may not be fiction, my friend," the Russian said. "But now, let me tell you something new. Something I don't think we discussed before because I didn't know about it."

Dalton leaned so far into his face that Martov knew he had the American's full attention.

"There is a possibility that if Pushkin succeeds, we will be able to develop special molecular technology that could make us rich," the prime minister said quietly, speaking in such a confidential tone that Dalton had to lean even farther in his direction to hear. "This 'nanotechnology,' as it's called, will enable us to create entirely new materials of such strength and versatility that they will revolutionize human industry."

Martov paused and searched Dalton's face. "Our first project—which is already in the planning stages—will involve the development of extremely cheap, diamondlike materials," Martov continued. "These 'diamonoid' substances are many times stronger than any metal. I'm told that a diamond is sixty-nine times as strong as an equivalent amount of titanium. This means that we could build trucks, automobiles, airplanes, and spacecraft that would be much lighter and virtually indestructible for a fraction of what they cost today. Can you imagine the profit potential for those who control such manufacturing techniques? And that's just the beginning, my friend."

Dalton walked in silence as they approached the presidential compound at Camp David. He was obviously pondering Martov's argument. The Russian watched him closely out of the corner of his eye, hoping that the diamonoid picture he had painted would pacify the American for the time being. He had to ensure that Dalton and the Americans would continue to support the moon experiment because the Russians would never be able to underwrite such a venture on their own.

Despite what he was telling the American president, Martov was clear about his *real* expectations for Pushkin's experiment. Working with a handful of political allies, including military experts who understood the full potential of Pushkin's work, Martov had begun to lay plans more than two years before for "Project Moongate." If successful, Moongate could begin a period of world domination that would make the dreams of Hitler or the Caesars seem schoolboy fantasies.

Specifically, if Sergey Pushkin perfected the technology to produce a stable rip in space-time, Russia—or more accurately, Martov's elite international cadre led by Russians—would immediately have access to an absolutely superior weapon that would render any opponent defenseless. Using wormholes created in areas on earth or in space under their control, they would be able to move nuclear devices or troops *instantaneously* from Russian installations to any other part of the planet. There would be no possibility of advance warning. Also, those who controlled the wormholes would control a vast transportation system that would almost certainly lead to economic control of the earth.

Martov was convinced that the nation-state was fast disappearing. International connections had grown so much stronger in recent years, with business cartels and highly organized, sprawling "extralegal" organizations like the Russian *Mafiya* leading the way. Pushkin's wormhole project could cement Martov's position as a genuine interplanetary ruler.

Early on, the Russian had made a strategic decision to mention the wormhole experiment to Dalton, but without going into any details about Project Moongate. Martov knew there was some danger that word about the experiment might leak beyond the president, even to the press. But he had gambled that the president, who was smart but no visionary, would either keep his mouth shut to protect his own financial interests, or would immediately discount the whole idea as too theoretical and implausible to worry about.

In fact, one of Martov's moles in the White House had reported that soon after Dalton had learned about the wormhole experiment, the president had referred generally to the Russian prime minister as "a nice guy with his head in the clouds." Apparently, as Martov had anticipated, Dalton had said nothing about the experiment itself.

Being discounted as an impractical dreamer was fine with Martov because he didn't want Dalton to take Pushkin's work too seriously. On the other hand, if the experiment worked—and if Dalton believed he stood to make a fortune from it as Martov's partner—the American's greed would almost certainly cause him to defend the Russians and downplay any potential danger to the United States. It was a win-win scenario for Martov because of what he perceived as the fatal, venal weakness in Dalton's character. It was sad, but you couldn't seem to find a real statesman anywhere these days!

Although President Dalton seemed to be under control, thoughts of Scott Andrews continued to nag at Martov. The congressman was savvy about international machinations, and chronically suspicious of Russian motives. *What does he really know?*

Then the prime minister relaxed. Most likely, it really didn't matter what Andrews or this annoying former reporter on his staff knew about Pushkin's work, or even about the real Russian objectives. Everything was going according to plan, and carefully orchestrated events were fast converging to create a critical mass. It would take a miracle now for anyone to prevent the expected denouement, which would change the course of world history in ways the Americans could never anticipate.

25

It wasn't exactly the way she had planned to spend the Christmas holidays. The cramped, stuffy FBI surveillance van where Colleen was sitting caused her to fidget so much at one point that one of the two agents who were monitoring the eavesdropping equipment had to tell her to sit still.

"Every time you move around like that, you rock the vehicle," the man had muttered. "Might as well tell everybody on the street we're inside here looking for Russians."

The two men were singularly uncommunicative—even unfriendly. For one thing, the van was built for only two observers, and she was the third who made it a crowd. Also, they had made it clear that they didn't put political operatives on the same high level as real law-enforcement professionals.

Perhaps most frustrating of all for the agents was that their expectations had soared when they had been told they would have to spend some time in Cocoa Beach, Florida. The weather was still warm, both men were avid surfers, and Cocoa Beach was known as the "small-wave capital of the world." But instead of doing undercover work on the beach in their swim trunks, they were stuck in an uncomfortable threesome in a tiny van built for two.

Sighing, Colleen looked down at her loose, short-sleeve shirt and black slacks. She supposed that if she had dressed like a beach babe, they might have been more understanding. But she never felt she came off too well in shorts or swimsuits.

Anyhow, by pulling some serious strings with the House leadership, she had arranged for the FBI to set up this assignment as a matter of utmost importance to national security. Furthermore, Colleen had gained full access to the operation. When a superior put an agent on such a case, he paid close attention because his career in the FBI might depend on his performance. So any dissatisfaction the two men felt toward Colleen was limited to the occasional frustrated sigh or offhanded remark.

"Nothing," said one of the agents, who was fiddling with his earphones and glumly twirling dials on an audio receiver, which linked them to bugging devices in a nearby apartment.

Colleen had finally figured out his first name was Ralph, and she had no interest in knowing any more.

"Absolutely nothing," he repeated. "It's quiet as a tomb up there."

"How long have we been here?" the other agent asked no one in particular. "Three, four hours? Happy holidays."

"You don't have any idea what these guys look like?" Ralph asked Colleen for what she was certain was the fourth or fifth time.

She was so absorbed in studying the view through one of the one-way surveillance windows that she didn't respond immediately. The sunny side street on which they were parked—which was one of the arteries that fed into route A1A on the barrier island—provided an intriguing vantage point.

One location of particular interest to Colleen was a café and sandwich shop on the corner of A1A, which she had been told was used occasionally by Russian agents. The shop seemed an ideal place for spies to merge into pedestrian traffic. The place did such brisk business with such a varied clientele that it was hard to keep track of the customers who were running in and out. The possibility of twenty-four-hour shopping at the world-famous, art-deco Ron Jon's Surf Shop just up the street made the place even more attractive for hungry tourists.

But the most important reason they were parked here was that this was as close as they could get to the suspected Russian safe house—which was no longer so safe, since the FBI had seeded it with a truckload of eavesdropping equipment.

"Nobody has ID'd them," she finally answered, suspecting that it was all the agents could do to hold back the comment they didn't dare articulate: *So what are you doing here in our van if you can't give us any help?*

"Now what's the deal again?" asked the other agent, whose name was Larry. "Some Russians are down here on some special assignment that you can't tell us about . . ."

"And there's an outside chance that I may pick up something you miss because I've been working on this case for a while," Colleen finished, her patience now reaching its limit. "'Course, I may not be able to help at all. Then again, I may recognize one of the people from one of the hundreds of mug shots I've seen. Or I may hear something on the tapes you're making that could help us crack the case."

"Even though we don't know what the case is all about," Larry said sarcastically.

"That's right," she shot back. "So you'll have to put up with me a little while longer. But don't feel left out. There's a lot I don't know either."

What she did know, but couldn't tell her companions, was that top-secret intelligence reports had revealed that foreign agents—possibly renegade Russians or other terrorists—might be planning violence against members of the moon science team when they returned to Florida. When this information had reached her the day before, Colleen's blood had run cold. Maybe it was nothing but a rumor, but she couldn't take any chances. First, she had shot off an e-mail to Scott to inform him about developments and tell him to be on his guard. Then she decided she had to be on-site, in the middle of the action—and that meant sitting in this claustrophobic, hurriedly mobilized van, cozying up to these two rumpled characters.

"I'm getting hungry," Ralph said, and then he looked over at Colleen. "Why don't you get us something to eat?"

"Why me?" she asked sharply.

"Don't get defensive," Ralph said, scratching his stomach. "We know you're the queen bee here. It's just that Larry and I know the equipment, and one of us will have to go up to check the apartment in case our Russian friends show up. So it's best that we don't take any chance of being seen on the street before that."

"Fine, give me your lunch orders," Colleen said with a resigned sigh. "And tell me when it's all clear."

Larry scanned the street carefully through the one-way viewers that lined the walls of the van. "When there's nobody on this side of the street, I'll tell you to take off. After you get the food, don't come back the same way. Walk around the block, and then come at the van from behind. The door will be open, so don't knock. Just get in fast. Got it?"

"Got it," she replied, mimicking his officious tone so well that he gave her a disconcerted glance.

Then he turned back to his surveillance, hesitated another moment or two, and finally commanded, "Okay, go!"

Colleen opened the back door of the van only wide enough to squeeze her body through. Then she quickly dashed across the street, as though she were a jaywalker who had stepped off the sidewalk next to the van. After reaching the opposite sidewalk, she walked down to the corner to the sandwich shop.

Ralph and Larry had told her to keep her eyes open and watch for any out-of-place detail that might suggest something was amiss. She suspected they were probably putting her on, but why take any chances? Trying not to be obvious, she looked over the customers, just to be sure there was nothing suspicious about them. *This whole thing is making me paranoid. I want to get back into politics!*

A half dozen patrons were drinking and eating at tables on the sidewalk. A young man and woman were holding hands, deep in their own intimate conversation. An older pair was sitting quietly, surveying the scene on A1A.

Two other people were lounging at separate tables by themselves. One, a woman with short blond hair and wraparound dark glasses, was deep into some potboiler-thriller. A broad-brimmed beach hat shielded her from the sun's rays, and well-tanned arms and legs, mostly concealed by a loose-fitting beige beach cover-up, suggested she had been enjoying the good weather for a week or more. The other sidewalk customer, a dark-complexioned, heavyset man whose face was almost covered by the brim of a Dodgers baseball cap, seemed to be playing lizard-on-a-rock in the sun, as he dozed between sips of his soft drink.

Four or five other customers were waiting in line for take-out orders, and Colleen took a place behind them. The line moved quickly. Within a few minutes, Colleen had three sandwiches and three cold drinks in a bag under her arm and was soon on her way out onto the street. She looked over again at the people who were relaxing at the sidewalk tables and satisfied herself that no one seemed at all interested in her or in the van, which was in plain sight. Then she walked away from the van and headed down route A1A. She planned to walk around the block, reenter the side street from the other end, and approach the FBI vehicle from the rear.

As the pale, slightly rumpled brunette walked out of the Cocoa Beach sandwich shop with her purchases, the blonde potboiler fan kept her eyes riveted on her book. She was seated close to the street corner with her back to route A1A, so that she could face down the side street, which ran toward the beach. She was almost certain of the woman's identity, but she needed a more careful look.

After the female customer passed behind her, the blonde cut her eyes toward a decorative reflective panel on a handbag lying next to her drink. Using this device as a rearview mirror, she followed the progress of the brunette, who was now walking down A1A.

Still, she couldn't be absolutely sure that the picture she had seen in the file was the same person. When the brunette was out of sight, the blonde's eyes returned carefully to the side street that ran in front of the café. Using a tiny telescopic lens attached to the upper rim of her sunglasses, she studied every detail in her improved range of vision.

A parked van had become her main focus of interest. Then she saw what she had been looking for—a brief flicker of movement through the back window of the van's front cab. A head had flashed into view and immediately disappeared. A few seconds later, the patience of the watchful blonde paid off again—and she got the confirmation she had been hoping for. She sighted the dark slacks and nondescript blouse of the brunette, who was heading back up the side street from the far corner.

Clearly, this woman was out of place. She was walking far too purposefully for any tourist. Also, she had circled the block—by no means normal activity for a resident or even a tourist. No, the blonde concluded, the pale-skinned woman clearly didn't fit into the Florida beach culture. She seemed to be dressed more for an American city or a big-city suburb than for this resort.

The blonde turned the page of her novel but at the same time continued to stare through her dark glasses at the brunette. The picture she had seen fit the face and body on the street before her. The woman had to be Colleen Barker, the chief of staff of Congressman Scott Andrews. Sure enough, the brunette disappeared into the back of the van.

It was now clear to the blonde what she had to do next.

26

When Colleen slipped behind the van and pulled open the back door just wide enough to squeeze inside, she heard that some sort of argument was in progress.

"Will you get down?" Ralph hissed to Larry.

From what Colleen could deduce, Larry had just moved from one side of the van to the other, and in the process he had briefly exposed himself to view through a half-open panel that separated the cab from the listening-post section in the back of the vehicle.

"Relax, man," Larry grumbled. "Nobody's watching us, and even if they are, they didn't see me for that half second."

"Still, you never know, and we've got to keep some discipline," Ralph said.

"See anything?" Larry asked Colleen as he took a sandwich and drink from her.

"Just normal-looking customers and pedestrians," she replied. "The people in line were in and out—nothing suspicious at all. The couples sitting at the tables had eyes only for each other. The woman sitting over there never took her eyes off her book. And the guy taking his siesta near her never moved, at least as far as I could tell. I think I even heard him snoring."

"Wait, they're talking!" said Larry, who was still intently watching the scene outside the café through one of the hidden viewing portals.

"What's that?" Ralph responded, moving to watch through another peephole.

"They're talking—the man and woman outside the shop," Larry said.

The three observers in the van watched quietly as the man, who had been sleeping under his Dodgers cap, leaned over to say something to the blonde.

"Let me see if I can get a mike on them," Ralph said.

He hurriedly adjusted some instruments to redirect a small, state-of-the-art parabolic microphone, which was mounted unobtrusively in the midst of decorative metal and chrome on the top of the van.

"I noticed you like those . . . thrillers," the man was saying. "Me too. Say, you want to . . ."

Noise from the traffic, combined with the man's lowered tones, obscured the rest of his sentence.

"Seems to be making a pass at her," Colleen said with a smirk.

"Shh," Larry responded, holding up his hand for quiet.

The woman, who had apparently said nothing, stood up, patted the back of her short, sandy locks, adjusted her beach cover-up—a loose blouse and matching three-quarter-length pants—and proceeded to gather up her book and handbag, apparently with the intention of leaving.

"Say something, sweetie, anything at all," Ralph coaxed.

As if in response to the FBI agent's request, the blonde's voice come across on the tape recorder's speaker: "Thank you, but no. Good day."

With that, she turned and left. The three watched her walk briskly down A1A until they lost sight of her behind a building. They saw the man shrug, look around self-consciously, and then stand up to leave. He headed down A1A as well, but at a slower pace than the woman.

"The Dodgers strike out," Ralph said.

"Yeah, the guy needs better pickup lines," Larry agreed.

"That was a little odd," Colleen said, still looking in the direction where the two had disappeared.

"What's that?" Larry asked.

"I mean the way she talked," Colleen mused. "Can you play her words again?"

"Sure," Larry sighed. "Here you go."

"Thank you, but no. Good day."

"Sounds funny to me, the way she phrased that," Colleen said. "Kind of stiff. Formal. Who do you know who talks like that?"

"Plenty of women who want to get rid of a pest," Ralph laughed. "When they're not interested, they try to sound cold. Standoffish."

"I don't know," Colleen persisted. "There was something about her tone."

"How many girls you tried to pick up lately, Colleen?" Larry gibed. "You're an expert, right?"

"Nah, Colleen's just got a bad case of spy fever," Ralph said.

"What exactly do you mean by that?" Colleen retorted, feeling defensive and letting her irritation get the best of her.

"It happens to most people when they first go undercover or do surveillance," Ralph explained amiably. "You can't believe it's as boring as it is, so you start to see or hear things that aren't really there. Relax, Colleen! Take our word for it! That was nothing but a put-down to get rid of a pickup artist."

She lapsed into silence. What they said made sense, but she still didn't feel quite right. Granted, the woman had said almost nothing, and none of them had picked up anything beforehand that was suspicious about her. Colleen herself had walked right past the blonde twice and observed her from just a few yards away for the better part of several minutes. There was absolutely nothing about her to make you look twice—unless you were a man who happened to like good-looking blondes in beach outfits.

"You're probably right—most likely it's nothing," Colleen finally said. "But to be safe, let's mark where her voice is on the audiodisk. I may want a voiceprint at some point, just in case we need to make a comparison."

"Fine, fine," Larry said, rolling his eyes to make it clear that he felt Colleen was going overboard again.

But he knew he had to comply with her wishes. She was the one who worked for the prominent congressman. After marking the spot on the disk, he turned back to the dials that linked them to the equipment in the bugged apartment. Again, there was nothing but silence.

Probably should have followed her, Colleen thought as the FBI agents became absorbed again in their surveillance chores. But then she realized that a wild-goose chase could cause her to miss the real dangers that might be facing Scott. On the other hand, how was she supposed to tell what was important and what wasn't?

Colleen settled back uncomfortably on the small stool that had been provided for her. It had been hard to keep her full attention on this surveillance gig, which she suspected wouldn't turn up anything worthwhile anyhow. Her mind was still on an anonymous call she had received early that morning from a man who had been acting as her informant for more than a week now. Another anonymous informant—probably related to one of her CIA contacts—had put her in touch with this new guy, who appeared to be well connected in the White House. That morning, the informant had quickly passed on the gist of a conversation that, if true, could only have come from someone on or close to the president's Secret Service detail.

"President Dalton met with Prime Minister Martov at Camp David yesterday," the muffled voice had said. The sounds of traffic in the background suggested that the man was speaking from a public telephone, which would make him immune to a trace.

"Go on," she had urged, knowing that these conversations tended to be very short, but also very important.

"The meeting was about some business deal the two have cooked up," the man continued. He seemed to be trying to mimic a foreign accent, but the attempt wasn't working. "Martov said the deal was going to make a lot of money for both the United States and Russia—and also make Martov and Dalton 'the richest men in the world.'"

"He actually said that?" Colleen asked.

"Exact words."

"What's the deal? How are they going to get rich?"

"Unknown. Have to go."

After hearing the click of the phone on the other end, Colleen had sat frozen in silence for several long moments on the edge of her motel bed. This *was* news. But what was going on? She immediately sent an encrypted e-mail message to Scott. Maybe he would have a better idea about what all this meant.

Reflecting on this disturbing conversation as she sat there in the surveillance van, Colleen began to fight the old worries. Increasingly, she was sensing that the entire burden for her boss's safety, and perhaps for an array of incredibly far-reaching international political issues, was entirely on her shoulders. Yet she had no idea where this cloak-and-dagger roller coaster was taking her.

27

The blonde in the beach hat continued walking down A1A for several blocks and then turned down a side street that led toward the Atlantic Ocean. Before reaching the beach area, she slowed slightly as she approached a sign for an undistinguished motel, the Surfer Dude.

She stopped casually to look in a shop window, then glanced back down the street to be sure she hadn't been followed. Confident that she was unobserved, she resumed walking for a few steps and swung abruptly into the motel.

As stray rays of sun played across her face, her bare forearms, and lower legs—the only parts of her body not protected by her beach cover-up—she frowned. Not at all a sun worshiper, she regarded the prospect of a deeper tan in her naturally tawny skin as highly undesirable.

Finally, she reached the door to her room and paused to look out over the Atlantic, which she could see clearly between a couple of intervening buildings. *At least there are a few minor fringe benefits.* Then she entered the room, tossed her handbag, paperback novel, and beach hat on the bed, and flung open the door that led into the adjoining room.

He was stretched out on the bed in his swim trunks, dozing before a television set that was blaring in front of him.

Just like the dolt at the sandwich shop, she thought. *They could be brothers.*

She ripped off the blond wig and savored the coolness as her long, black hair tumbled down onto her shoulders. At the same time, she removed her dark glasses and noticed that the rather short, thickset man on the bed was stirring.

"Colonel!" he exclaimed, sitting up abruptly. "How, uh . . . Did you learn anything?"

His English was still halting, though he was getting better. But she knew it would be best for him to spend as much time by himself as possible, so people wouldn't ask questions about his accent.

"Yes, Valery," Klaudia Ming-Petrovich replied, turning back into her own room. "I have learned a great deal. Certainly enough to keep us both out of the hands of the American authorities. And enough to place us in a much stronger position to fulfill our mission when the time for action arrives."

28

As Scott emerged from the small shower and bathroom that had been provided with his room, he was feeling upbeat. They had been on the moon nearly a month, and work on all components of the fusion plant was well ahead of schedule.

Pushkin and Bolotov had finished assembling and testing the nuclear fusion plant. Hiramatsu and Goldberg had set up the lasers, which would be used to generate the high level of heat necessary to trigger the fusion reaction. And Hightower had completed work on the small nuclear fission plant, which would power the lasers. Today Scott would conduct the final official inspection of the first phase of the construction, and they would test the entire system to see how it performed.

With the work on Energy Project Omega in such great shape—and no further threats to his life—Scott actually decided he might be capable of enjoying lunar life. Then he turned to his computer. The latest e-mail messages from earth, which stared back at Scott Andrews on his computer screen, were enough to destroy any good mood. He read them a third time just to be sure he hadn't missed anything.

First, there was the official report from the board of inquiry, which had investigated the incident that had almost resulted in Scott's death on the earth-moon shuttle. The final lines in the report said it all:

Finding:
The incident that occurred 12/20/17 on board the international lunar shuttle *Moonshot* resulted from circumstances beyond human control and is therefore adjudged an accident.

In the text of their report, the board members admitted that it was still unclear exactly what had happened aboard *Moonshot*. But the investigation into the matter had turned up no evidence of foul play. The prevailing theory was that Scott had probably twisted the air vent too tightly in the wrong direction when he had retired for some sleep. Then, when he couldn't open the vent, he had panicked and jammed the door to his sleeping compartment. It was clear from the text that the investigators wanted no cloud hanging over the members of the scientific team and their work.

The report irritated Scott, but there seemed to be nothing he could do about it. He regarded the investigation as a whitewash, probably influenced by friends of the U.S. president who were in no mood to delay Energy Project Omega. *Of course, it's my neck, not theirs.*

With some lingering annoyance, he turned to his second e-mail, which was from Colleen. She detailed rumors that violence might be planned against members of the moon science team when they returned in a couple of months. But there was still no hard evidence.

The possibility of violence upon their return was certainly a concern to Scott. But things seemed to have settled down. Although the Russians continued to keep to themselves, they were cordial enough when Scott approached them, and on occasion, Bolotov seemed almost friendly. Still, Scott resolved he would not let his guard down while he was on the moon, and he wanted security on earth to be tightened further. He might even have to advise Sara and the kids to stay away from Cape Canaveral and the Kennedy Space Center, especially when the time approached for the moon team's reentry.

The third message, also from Colleen, was short and unsatisfying. His chief of staff had run into a "solid brick wall," as she put it, in her attempts to nail down the exact identity of Dr. Ruth Goldberg. The fourth and final e-mail— in which Colleen related a report from an anonymous Secret Service source in the White House—was the most disturbing of all. As Scott read, he became so angry that he picked up a pen on his desk and threw it with blinding speed in the low moon gravity against the door panel to his room.

Multiple questions swirled in Scott's mind. Exactly how extensive were Dalton's under-the-table dealings in trying to feather his own nest before he left office? Could the president's schemes compromise the moon scientists' effort to provide cheap energy for everyone on earth? Most important of all, how far would Dalton be willing to go in sacrificing the safety of the moon team—and of Scott himself—in return for a payoff from the Russians?

Scott felt completely unprotected. If there was ever a classic case study in being out on a limb, he was it. He hadn't experienced such isolation and vulnerability since the church fire. At least at that time there had been relatives who were willing to take him in.

The anger that had welled up inside Scott when he first read the news about Dalton's double-dealing now began to nudge him toward depression. If you couldn't trust your own president, could you trust anybody? Yes, he could rely on his family and a few committed colleagues. But 240,000 miles of space separated him from Sara, Colleen, and everyone else who cared about him.

Hightower and Hiramatsu seemed friendly enough, but Scott expected that when the chips were down, they would give a priority to their own careers and governments. No, he was alone, and the sooner he recognized that fact, the more quickly he would be able to come up with an effective defense strategy.

The usual inner resources that could bolster his moods in bad times weren't working this morning. Maybe it was the incredible sense of isolation that one could feel with an extended stay in space. He looked out of the window at the black, starless sky. It was now daytime on the moon, with the sun overwhelming the lights of the stars and casting an eerie bright glow on the dust, craters, and mountains, which he could contemplate at a distance. With no atmosphere, the far horizon seemed closer than it really was, and also appeared almost unreal, something like a backdrop on a movie set.

The sense of unreality made him feel unusually small, insignificant, even powerless. Without his usual earthly professional moorings and personal relationships, Scott found himself casting about for some other source of strength and support, an energy or force that could lift him out of his current gloom. Only moments before, he had felt optimistic. But after reading the messages from earth, his good mood had turned bad. Wasn't there any way to protect himself from such emotional swings?

Scott thought of Pushkin and the soothing prayer the man had uttered for him just before the shuttle launch. He was still wary, even cynical, about the Russian's motives. But still, the idea that some power, some superior, intelligent being, might exist beyond or above human capacities kept intruding on his thoughts. In his present state of mind, the idea was seductive.

Was it possible that Pushkin had tapped into a spiritual reality that Scott should explore himself? Could he really communicate with a power beyond himself—with God? Something was going on with the scientist that Scott wanted to know more about.

Also, Scott's regular exposure over the past few months to the strange concepts of theoretical physics that first Rensburg, and now Pushkin and the others had been discussing, was forcing him to think outside his normal, four-dimensional channels. What did it mean to say that there was some sort of unpredictable quantum foam that lay beneath ordinary atoms and molecules—a realm of reality that didn't obey the normal rules of chemistry and physics? Did that imply that what he had always regarded as real—what he could see, taste, and touch—was only a small part of reality? Was it possible that there might be extra dimensions beyond space and time, and if so, was there any way to interact with that reality?

Scott made a decision. Looking over his shoulder to be sure no one else was in the room—though he immediately knew the gesture was meaningless because his door panel was locked—he spoke aloud and forcefully: "If You're there, please reveal Yourself!"

He waited a few seconds. He closed his eyes and listened. Nothing. Then he smiled, embarrassed at his show of weakness.

Scott leaned back in his chair, which in the moon's low gravity felt very light against his back, and forced himself to focus on the here and now, the concrete present. He glanced at the moon-time window on his watch. The others would be trickling into the dining room about now for breakfast, and then all would head out toward the work area at the other end of the long Energy City passageway. If his interim inspection proceeded as expected, the way would be paved for the first formal test of the fusion plant.

Before he departed, Scott tapped off replies to Colleen's messages. He gave her the usual compliments on her good work, and reminded her—though he knew it was unnecessary—to be sure to notify him immediately as other developments emerged.

He also asked Colleen to contact Sara and tell her to take extra precautions for herself and the kids. Officials at the FBI had offered to provide discreet bodyguards and round-the-clock surveillance for his family. Sara had objected earlier because she had felt that the law-enforcement presence would be oppressive.

When the final e-mail had been transmitted, Scott took a deep breath and paused for a moment, staring at his computer screen, which had gone into the "sleep" mode. He didn't want any more surprises right now. No word about other disturbing, unexpected developments on earth. No further coincidences or accidents, which would add unnecessary complications to his already complicated life.

But is there really any such thing as an accident? Or a coincidence? Has my life somehow been plugged into a preprogrammed stream of events over which I have little or no control?

To break the disturbing thought stream, Scott stood up abruptly from his computer, grabbed the light blue jacket that he sometimes needed when the Energy City air-conditioning became a little chilly, and headed out his front door and into the hallway—where he ran head-on into Sergey Pushkin.

"Ah, Dr. Andrews, I'm so happy we meet," the Russian said.

29

Scott was not particularly happy about the encounter. His nagging distrust of Pushkin caused him to look the Russian directly in the eye and frown. He wondered just how deeply the man might be involved with the forces that seemed to be putting him, and perhaps his family, in danger. Also, he questioned the extent to which Pushkin might be in on a sub-rosa deal with President Dalton.

Yet Scott knew that his association with the fusion expert remained profoundly paradoxical. Even as he remained suspicious, he was fascinated by the man. Scott also realized that he had to maintain a reasonably cordial and productive working relationship with the Russian. So he decided on the spot to swallow his natural inclination to be hostile, at least for the time being.

"Call me Scott, Sergey," the congressman said, even though the words stuck in his throat. "After all, we're colleagues. So what's on your mind?"

"Our work has proceeded smoothly, no?" the Russian asked.

"I'd say things are going quite well," Scott replied as the two men walk-floated along the hallway of their Energy City penthouse to the lift that would take them down to the dining area. "We're well ahead of schedule, and I'm expecting my inspection today to be just a formality. Then we'll flip the switch and see how this thing works."

Pushkin frowned. As Scott had learned from observing the Russian, that was a sure sign of bad news. "Okay, what's wrong?" Scott finally asked.

"I'm concerned about our next step."

"Why is that?" Scott asked. "Have you run into a problem?"

"Not with the basic operation of the fusion plant," the Russian replied, causing Scott to heave a silent sigh of relief. "Dr. Hiramatsu's ultraviolet lasers should be more than adequate to generate the heat we need for the fusion reactions. Then the next step in the *energy* project will be for Hiramatsu and Goldberg to use the nuclear power to produce the powerful x-ray laser—which will, in turn, carry great stores of energy back to earth."

"Yes, and I understand that the orbiting earth satellite that will receive the x-ray laser is virtually complete," Scott added. "They're just waiting for word from us that it's time to activate their equipment. But what's bothering you?"

Scott had noticed the Russian's emphasis on the word *energy*. He was fairly sure he knew what was coming next—a Russian insistence that they be allowed to take time off to work on their secret experiment.

"I know there is dissatisfaction on the team, even suspicion, about our other project," he said, confirming Scott's suspicions.

Scott nodded as the lift they were on descended slowly to the main floor and lobby of the living area. He decided to run up a trial balloon.

"You mean the wormhole project," Scott said, looking intently at Pushkin to see if he would react.

Sure enough, the Russian's head jerked sharply, causing the American to work hard to suppress a smile.

"I'm not at liberty to go into details, but you seem to be aware of more than I realized," Pushkin replied.

This time it was Scott's turn to be surprised. He had never expected that the closemouthed Russian would be so quick to confirm, even indirectly, the wormhole objective.

"You've never seemed concerned before about anyone's opinions or suspicions about your work," Scott said, stopping short of the eating area so that they could finish their conversation in private. "Why now?"

"Dr. Bolotov and I will have to begin on our special experiment before Energy Project Omega is finished," Pushkin said. "In fact, we must start on it as soon as we finish the first phase of the nuclear-fusion construction. That means the other scientists may question whether we are putting Russian interests before the energy needs of all the earth."

"Well, *are* you planning to put your project first?" Scott asked.

He was deeply concerned about this detour the Russians were about to take, but for some reason he didn't feel angry toward Pushkin. Something about the man seemed genuine and even compassionate. It had become increasingly apparent that his aloofness was as much from shyness, and perhaps the restrictive orders he was under from Moscow, as from any hostility. More and more, Scott found himself willing to give the fusion scientist the benefit of the doubt—despite his general suspicion of Russian motives.

"Please believe me, Energy Project Omega is indeed my top professional priority," Pushkin replied earnestly. "But my situation is complicated. I understand quite well that solving the earth's electricity and fuel needs is of supreme importance—at least in the short term. But our other project—"

"The wormholes," Scott interjected, looking for additional confirmation. Pushkin wouldn't deny that was his goal, but he wouldn't say yes either. He just kept talking, as though Scott had said nothing.

"Our other project is primarily theoretical and experimental at this point," the Russian continued. "But if we succeed, the results could provide even greater benefits for the earth's population in the long term than the energy project. I wanted you to know that, even though I can't be any more specific. If it were my choice, I would bring you and the others into our confidence immediately. But our instructions from our government prohibit that. Also, we have been ordered to begin on our special project immediately."

"In other words, we twiddle our thumbs while you and Bolotov work on your wormhole," Scott muttered.

"Pardon me?" Pushkin said, a quizzical expression crossing his face. "I don't quite understand . . ."

Scott waved him off. "Forget it. It's an American crack. Just tell me—when can we start beaming power back to earth?"

"Oh, I expect no delay with that," Pushkin said. "I anticipate no 'twiddling,' as you call it. Again, for me the energy effort is top priority."

"How about Bolotov's top priority?" Scott asked, but he received no answer.

Out of the corner of his eye, Scott saw Bolotov bounding slowly in their direction from the dining hall. This had been his best opportunity yet to find out more about the Russians' intentions, but the party was almost over.

"What about Ruth Goldberg?" Scott asked hurriedly. "She's working closely with you, isn't she?"

"Yes," Pushkin replied, a puzzled look on his face. "She appears to know a great deal about the fusion process. Really, more than I expected. But of course she is primarily a laser person."

Scott saw he had time for only one more question before Bolotov arrived, so he decided to take a chance. "She knew Bolotov in Russia, didn't she?"

Pushkin looked genuinely startled. "What do you mean?"

The reaction spoke volumes to Scott about Pushkin's lack of involvement in Bolotov's schemes.

"Perhaps we should keep this between the two of us, at least until we can discuss it further," Scott said under his breath.

Just then, Bolotov joined them. "Hello, Dr. Andrews. May I be of assistance to you?" the younger Russian said, with what seemed to Scott an air of forced cordiality. "My colleague, Dr. Pushkin, is so busy. Perhaps it would be best for me to be your liaison."

"I appreciate the offer, and I do look forward to getting to know you better," Scott said with a wide smile, which he hoped masked his real feelings. "I'm mainly interested in ensuring that all our projects finish on time. That's my role—a facilitator. So I'll check in with you regularly just to see if there's anything you need—material, extra staff, whatever—to expedite matters."

"That's reassuring," Bolotov said noncommittally.

"And I know you two gentlemen have some special project you'll be working on," Scott said. "If you need help, please contact me."

"You're indeed kind, Dr. Andrews," Bolotov said. Then he hesitated before adding: "I don't expect we'll need your help, but I trust that our previous, uh, misunderstanding is behind us."

"Why thank you, Dr.—may I call you Vladimir?" Scott said. "Please call me Scott."

"Certainly . . . Scott."

The Russians moved toward a table where Ruth Goldberg was sitting, and Scott headed for the food service line. Despite the outward amenities, Scott wasn't harboring any warm, fuzzy feelings toward Bolotov—and he expected that the younger Russian felt the same way.

As Scott picked up his breakfast at the cafeterialike dispensing station and began to walk-jog in slow motion toward a table occupied by Hiramatsu and Hightower, he was preoccupied with the connection between the two Russians and Goldberg. If Pushkin's reaction in their conversation had been any indication, he apparently didn't have any notion about Goldberg's uncertain identity. But what about Bolotov?

30

Standing on a platform in the huge factory module, Scott surveyed the scores of blue-clad scientists and technicians standing in front him. As far as he could tell, the entire Energy City population of 162 people had turned out for the event, and well they might. After all, this could be a major milestone that would change world history forever.

The "mayor" of the lunar outpost, Secretary Archibald Martin, was praising the remarkable progress that had been made. Soon, it would be Scott's turn. He would shower the team with compliments and toss in a few memorable quotes from Einstein, Bohr, and Heisenberg. Then, he would throw the switch to ignite the trial fusion reaction. But the residents of the moon colony would be the only witnesses to the live event. A strategic decision had been made to record the proceedings rather than run a live telecast back to earth—just in case something went wrong.

"No need to disappoint or worry the folks back home," Secretary Martin had said in conveying to Scott the consensus of the political leaders back on earth. "We're ahead of schedule as it is. If anything goes wrong, we'll just fix it, try again, and no one will get upset."

Or be any the wiser, Scott thought. Fortunately for Secretary Martin and the politicians, a strategic decision had also been made not to send any journalists to the moon for this initial phase of the operation. The excuse had been that there was only room for scientists and technicians, and even though some grumbling had resulted, the press had no choice but to comply. The absence of snoopy reporters made it much easier to control the flow of information out of Energy City, an arrangement that seemed to make Secretary Martin particularly happy.

After the cheering from the short speeches had died down, Scott called the secretary up to take a position beside him. Together, they placed their hands on a large, gold lever-switch that had been rigged up on a table in front of them. "Now, if you'll look up at the screen over our heads, you'll see the best light show of your lives!" Scott exclaimed.

Moon-cams had been placed at strategic locations throughout the laser and fusion operation and then connected to large overhead monitors.

"Let there be light!" Scott cried.

When he and Secretary Martin pressed down on the gold lever, sweeping shots of moving machinery, flashes of light, and streaking laser beams filled the monitors.

Jeffrey Hightower had supervised the construction of a small nuclear fission plant, which was visible not only at different times on the monitor, but also through the bay windows in the distance on the lunar surface. This plant would provide power for the lasers that would generate the fusion reaction.

The team had decided to locate the fission plant in a special shed several hundred yards from the main factory module, both because there was a limited amount of room in the main module and because nuclear fission produced radioactive waste. Most experts felt that it would be easier to dispose of the waste safely if the plant itself was located at some distance from the main work and living modules.

Some environmental groups had objected at the prospect of putting a "dirty" nuclear plant on the moon at all. But a power source was necessary to produce the lasers that would be used to trigger the huge "clean" fusion reaction, and a small nuclear fission mechanism seemed the best answer. The choice was to use nuclear fission or try some other, more cumbersome fossil fuel source, which would also be unfriendly to the environment. So the few environmentalists opposed to fission were quickly overruled.

As the Energy City audience watched, the enhanced moon-cam images focused on events at Hightower's small nuclear fission facility, which provided power to generate the ultraviolet lasers. The nuclear energy, acting on argon and fluorine, provided the power necessary to produce parallel, evenly spaced, equal-size wavelengths of visible blue light—which the audience could see on the screen. These potent beams streaked down a dozen tubes containing crystal rods. Each tube, which was about a meter in diameter, ran from the nuclear fission plant to the main factory module.

When the blue laser beams reached the factory, they entered a series of amplifiers that increased the intensity of the light beyond the visible band of the electromagnetic spectrum into the ultraviolet. A moon-cam focused inside one of those amplifiers recorded fireworks of light as the beams bounced back and forth on mirrors inside the mechanism.

The ultraviolet lasers that emerged from the amplifiers were divided into a hundred separate ultraviolet beams, which were directed toward a well-insulated fusion target chamber. Inside the chamber was one small, hollow sphere, only about an inch in diameter. A tiny moon-cam, positioned to view inside the chamber through a tiny porthole, zoomed in on the sphere. The sphere contained helium-3, which had been mined from the regolith on the moon's surface, and "heavy hydrogen," also known as deuterium.

The instant the multiple ultraviolet laser beams hit the sphere, it disappeared. The lasers had heated the sphere to about 400 million degrees Celsius, or 720 million degrees Fahrenheit—the level at which nuclear fusion could occur.

The deuterium and helium-3 had been transformed into a plasma, or a kind of quantum soup, where the innards of atoms—the neutrons, electrons, and protons—break down and combine in different configurations. In this case, atoms of heavy hydrogen, or deuterium, and the helium-3 fused to form ordinary helium, or helium-4. At the same time, as the atoms fused, stray protons and incredible amounts of energy were released.

The audience watched in awe as the evidence of this energy unfolded before them. Pushkin and Bolotov, with Ruth Goldberg's help, had rigged up a temporary x-ray laser tube to capture the nuclear fusion power and direct it out onto the moon's surface. There, part of the powerful x-ray was converted to hundreds of visible-light lasers. Large batteries and photovoltaic cells on the moon's surface captured another part of the x-ray energy. These provided both a light display and the power source to illuminate that part of the moon's surface with spotlights for the rest of the lunar night.

At first, the audience was struck silent by the dramatic display of power. Then a sustained, deafening cheer began to well up. It was evident that this party wouldn't end anytime soon. But Scott wanted to make one final point before things got completely out of hand.

Holding up a message that had just been flashed to him on his PDA, or personal digital assistant, which combined communications links and other computing functions, he asked for quiet.

"I've just received this notification from our number crunchers," he announced, unable to suppress a growing grin. "The amount of power generated by the nuclear fusion reaction we've just witnessed has exceeded the combined input power of the nuclear fission plant and the lasers by"—he hesitated a moment to build the suspense—"by a factor of more than ten thousand—so we're in business *big-time!*"

This time, the cheering was even louder than before. Everyone understood that the most important objective of the project had been achieved. They had shown that they could generate far more power *in* the fusion reaction than had been required to *produce* the reaction. It was almost as though by striking a single match, they had generated enough energy to light an entire city. In the past, the main hurdle facing nuclear scientists was that triggering the fusion reaction had required as much energy as the final energy output. Now, they had demonstrated dramatically that this obstacle was a relic of the past.

"I hope your people got all this on videodisk," Scott said with a smile to Secretary Martin. "I'd hate to have to do it all over again."

"You can be sure it's all been recorded in living color," the secretary replied. "But remember: when the earth folks see it, the pressure on us will be overwhelming. The first question you'll get will probably be, 'When can we stop paying fuel bills and suffering blackouts?'"

Scott didn't answer. Instead, he looked over at the Russians, who were in a far better position than he was to respond to such questions. They were celebrating like everyone else. But they also periodically glanced over their shoulders and pointed toward a passageway leading to a laboratory that had been constructed for them off the main work module.

It was a strange research facility for a supposedly open scientific community. The closed panel that opened into the laboratory had a warning posted in the seven main languages spoken in Energy City—English, Russian, Chinese, Japanese, French, German, and Spanish. But to get the message, most of the multilingual members of the outpost had to read no further than the English translation, which stated:

DO NOT ENTER—RUSSIAN TERRITORY
VIOLATORS WILL BE SUBJECT TO FULL PROSECUTION
UNDER INTERNATIONAL LAW

31

Scott had called a general meeting of scientists and technicians in the main factory module the next day because he was well aware of the rumors that were flying around about the secret Russian experiment. But the barrage of objections stunned him.

"What exactly *is* this experiment? Why can't you tell us more?"

"Why should California suffer more blackouts just because some Russians want to play scientist?"

"Level with us: Is this really a *military* project they're working on?"

"You mean we have to put the earth's environment on hold while these guys try to prove some physics theory?"

"What about the poor people of the earth—those in the Third and Fourth World countries who lack the basics of modern technology? Why should their needs be sacrificed so some scientists on the moon can play with theories?"

Scott knew he lacked good answers to the questions. In fact, he agreed with most of the objections. He also saw that he now had political and morale problems on his hands because he had seriously misjudged how outspoken the opposition might be to any delay for Energy Project Omega.

As the arguments intensified, Scott, trying to be as diplomatic as possible, explained, "Our Russian colleagues are pursuing some special research approved by the sponsoring governments." He didn't mention the fact that only the United States and Russia had approved this detour, and that the other national leaders had been arm-twisted into acquiescing.

Scott's effort to calm the group seemed only to aggravate the uproar. Soon Pushkin and Bolotov, who had felt compelled to attend because the meeting was really about them, slipped to the rear of the crowd and finally left the area. At first, Scott had to fight an impulse to beat a retreat himself, but gradually he began to see the resistance as an opportunity. He had gone along reluctantly with the Russian experiment only because as a loyal American, he had felt he had no choice but to back his own government. But now, he began to think that the strong opposition from so many of the scientists might provide just the excuse he needed to limit or even eliminate the Russian venture.

He closed the meeting with a series of promises: "Believe me, your objections will definitely be taken into consideration. Energy Project Omega will in no way suffer from the Russian experiment. You'll all be notified when we expect work to resume on the energy project—and that will happen soon!"

These assurances helped Scott extricate himself from the meeting, even though the grumbling continued to echo in his ears as he departed. Later that afternoon, as he was working off the stress of the day with Shiro Hiramatsu in the Energy City exercise room—located on the main floor of the Energy City living module—he could contain his frustration no longer.

"Don't these people know I'm on their side?" he asked rhetorically. "I don't like what the Russians are doing any more than anybody else, but we just have to be patient until they're finished with their nonsense."

He looked over at Hiramatsu as the two of them prepared to engage in their daily weight-bearing exercise routine. Scott was never quite sure where Hiramatsu stood on any given international issue, so he was eager to test the waters to see the Japanese scientist's latest position.

"The Russians are not so good at what you call 'public relations,'" Hiramatsu observed after a brief silence.

Scott stopped adjusting his exercise equipment and stared at the Japanese scientist. "The Russians have kept pretty quiet about their operation up to this point, but I've picked up a few things. I assume you have too. I really need to know, Shiro—what exactly have you learned?"

Hiramatsu drew in a deep breath and frowned. "I know that they definitely want to create a passageway in the fabric of space-time—a wormhole. Pushkin felt he had to reveal at least that part of their plan to those of us in the laser group because they need our help. After all, Dr. Goldberg is working directly with them."

"Did you ever consider refusing to collaborate with them?" Scott asked.

"Briefly," Hiramatsu said. "But my government worries that if we don't help the Russians, they may not cooperate fully with us. Who wants to jeopardize the entire Energy Project Omega just because of a silly disagreement?"

As he spoke, the Japanese laser expert began to exercise on a lift that simulated stair climbing in earthlike gravity. The contraption raised Hiramatsu steadily upward about thirty feet. As it accelerated, it pushed his body downward at a pressure of about one G—much as a rapidly rising elevator might do. As Hiramatsu went up in the artificial air, he simultaneously climbed a short set of stairs attached to the lift. The upward movement, plus the pressure that climbing placed on his thigh muscles, provided him with approximately the same resistance he would have experienced in climbing stairs on earth. Years of research had established that this kind of weight-bearing workout was essential to counter the loss of bone mass in low gravity.

"I realize that the Russians have boxed us in on this experiment of theirs," Scott said, as he watched the Japanese laser expert move up and down on the "lunar escalator," which was the name they used to describe the device. "But given the reaction at that meeting, I'm afraid we may have a rebellion on our hands if we don't take countermeasures. Any suggestions?"

As Scott talked, he himself was going through a series of movements using a resistance machine that several seasoned users had taken to calling the "super moon gym." By fitting strategically placed straps on his hands, upper arms, shoulders, waist, legs, and feet—and then adjusting weight-resistance levels with a computer—he was able to obtain a rigorous weight-bearing workout for every major muscle group.

"Hard question," Hiramatsu said, breathing hard as he went through his thirtieth set of lunar-escalator repetitions.

At that moment, Jeff Hightower poked his head into the entrance to the exercise room. "You blokes are going to kill yourselves before we finish this project if you're not careful. You work too hard!"

"From what I've seen, you work out harder than we do!" Scott said. "If I didn't know better, I'd say you're trying to keep us so weak that you'll be the only one walking when we set foot on earth again."

"Got to preserve the outback image," the Australian replied. "Say, I couldn't help but overhear what you were talking about. What's your real view of what those Russians are up to in their hidden little laboratory?"

Smiling wryly, Scott said, "I can't believe you're totally behind the curve."

"Of course I know about the wormhole rumor," Hightower said. "That's the official line the Russians have leaked out. But do you believe them?"

"Give me a minute," Scott said as he unhooked himself from the moon gym and then moved over to close the door panel to the exercise room.

As they stood in a close huddle, Scott leaned toward Hightower and asked in a soft voice, "You think they're putting us on? They're not really planning to try to construct a wormhole?"

The Australian shrugged. "All I know is, I can't see how you can take some airy-fairy, theoretical physics concept like a wormhole and turn it into anything practical. If you ask me, it ain't worth worrying about. Might as well let them go ahead with it."

Scott frowned. "Maybe you're right. But if we're not careful, they could take too long and get the energy project off track. Frankly, I'd like to pressure them into dropping the whole thing, at least for now."

"I don't think they'll go along with that, mate," Hightower said, shaking his head. "This experiment seems too important to them. They might even pull out of the energy deal—and where would we be then?"

"We at least need a tough deadline," Scott said.

Hightower nodded. "Might work—that is, if you make the deadline reasonable."

"Two weeks is all I can give them right now. Frankly, if it were up to me, I'd can their entire project. Maybe I will appeal to the U.S. Congress to cut off funding. The Russians may have Pushkin, but they also need American money to proceed."

The shocked looks on the faces of his two companions made Scott realize that he was going too far with his threats, so he decided to soften his argument: "Let's face it, the Russians are behaving irresponsibly, aren't they? Remember, we have people back on earth waiting for us to generate cheap power. We can't force them to go through blackouts just because the Russians want to play with theoretical research up here on the moon."

As both men continued to frown at his words, Scott realized he would never get them to agree to block the Russian experiment. Also, he could see he would have to do a better job of selling his viewpoint.

"Okay, look, if they need more time for their little sideline, maybe they can come back to it later," Scott said, shifting his ground once again. "After we have the energy program up and running."

Hightower shook his head. "That's a little better, but the Russians still may not go along with this. You have to be ready for them to object."

"If we stick together, they really won't have a choice," Scott argued.

Both nodded, but Scott could see hesitation in their expressions. Though relieved that they were at least willing to go along with the short deadline, Scott wasn't encouraged by their lukewarm response.

Then Scott remembered Ruth Goldberg—or Tatiana Timoshenko, as the case might be. "What about Ruth? Where does she stand in all this? She seems pretty tight with the Russians, especially Bolotov."

"More with Pushkin," Hightower said with a knowing look.

"Okay, fill me in," Scott said with a sigh.

"Well, you see, mate, it's like this," Hightower said, putting an arm around Scott. "You know about the birds and the bees, and the 'roos and the koalas. I think something's going on between little Miss Ruth and the Russian nuke-man."

"What do you mean?" Scott asked, holding his breath. "An affair?"

"They spend a lot of time together in the off-hours," the Australian said. "She's the only outsider they allow in the special Russian lab. Many times, it's just old Pushki and Ruthie in there all alone."

"Isn't that normal?" Scott asked. "She's their main laser person, isn't she? Didn't you assign her to work with them, Shiro?"

"Ah, initially, yes, on request from the Russians," Hiramatsu said, looking at the floor, clearly uncomfortable with the direction of the conversation. "But my control is limited. After all, she is Israeli, not Japanese."

"You really think she's sweet on Pushkin?" Scott asked, turning back to the Australian. "I can't believe that."

"Look beyond your nose, mate," Hightower said. "In fact, when I left the work area about a half hour ago, our lovebirds seemed to be alone in the Russki lab. Why don't you trot down there before dinnertime and check it out?"

Scott looked at his watch and saw that he had some time. So he bounded over to the shower compartment to clean up and change clothes. Then he headed across the living-module lobby toward the long passageway and moonwalk, which led to the large work and factory module.

32

The work area was deserted. Apparently the crews had already taken their break for dinner, though Scott knew that many would be drifting back to their work in an hour or so.

As he surveyed the scene, Scott could see much had transpired in the few hours that had passed since his tumultuous meeting with the Energy City scientists and technicians. The Russians had been especially busy, as evidenced by the considerable work they had done reconfiguring the fusion machinery just outside the entrance to their laboratory.

At least these guys aren't wasting any time, Scott mused.

They had already added several refinements to the x-ray laser generator that had been attached to the fusion target chamber. Also, they had disconnected the single laser tube that ran out onto the moon's surface and had been used for the light display. In its place, Pushkin and Bolotov, with Ruth Goldberg's help, had set up a series of six new laser tubes and amplifiers, which ran through the side of the work module into the laboratory.

The burst of power from the fusion reaction would be directed onto selenium wires, which had been chosen as the main medium to produce the x-ray photons necessary for the laser. The nuclear reaction caused the selenium to emit stripped-down or ionized atoms, along with x-ray photons. Then a series of special reflectors caused the x-rays to bounce back and forth, increase in strength, and finally result in a highly focused x-ray laser beam.

Both Hiramatsu and Pushkin had been essential to the development of this mechanism. Pushkin had contributed the basic theory and applied technology that had been lacking to produce a controlled fusion ignition. Now that Carl

Rensburg was dead, he was the only scientist in the world who knew how to design the spherical deuterium–helium-3 pellet so that ignition—and a fusion reaction—would occur when ultraviolet lasers hit the pellet in the target chamber.

Hiramatsu had provided the guiding hand in developing both the ultraviolet lasers necessary to achieve fusion, and also the complex x-ray device. Among other things, he had achieved a long-sought research breakthrough by inventing amplifying x-ray mirrors, which were used to increase the power of the x-ray laser to maximum levels.

As Scott walked slowly around the revamped laser generator, examining every detail in sight, he recognized the special configuration and markings on the new devices. From what he had learned in preliminary briefings by the laser specialists, the enlarged housing contained the latest electromagnetic pulse oscillators, which would produce the extremely powerful x-ray laser beams. These beams would not only be used in the wormhole experiment, but would also carry energy across space back to earth. Clearly, the Russians believed that the best way to produce a wormhole was to employ almost the same technology that they would use later in Energy Project Omega.

Scott was still worried about potential postponements in the energy project. But Shiro Hiramatsu had assured him that the Russians' wormhole setup would require only minor adjustments to redirect the x-ray laser into the moon-to-earth energy transmission machinery.

Still, Scott knew there was a need to push for that two-week deadline. Otherwise, the Russians might go on with their experiment indefinitely, to the detriment of the masses of people waiting for adequate fuel and power back on earth.

So, firming up his resolve, Scott walked toward the closed entrance panel that led into the Russian laboratory. He knew he might not receive a welcome reception, especially if Bolotov happened to be on the scene. But he also knew that it was essential to establish—without delay—a time frame so that the Russians would know exactly how long they had for their experiment.

If they get upset, so be it! After all, he was the head honcho in this operation.

At that moment, Scott heard a noise behind him. He whirled and saw to his horror that one of the laser tubes used to trigger the fusion process had been activated. But something was different. Now, the end of the tube was no longer pointed toward the fusion chamber. Instead, the tube had been rotated, and he found himself gazing directly into the open mouth of the laser.

For a split second, he was rooted to the spot. Then, realizing he had to move, he dived to his left, felt a tug and then a quick warm surge across his back, and rolled twice before coming to rest faceup on the floor.

For a moment, Scott had trouble figuring out what had happened. Now, everything in the factory was quiet. The noise, whatever it had been, had disappeared. Had he just imagined that there was a problem? Was he getting as paranoid as Colleen?

He stood slowly and moved carefully over to the laser tube, which was well out of reach, fully twelve feet off the floor. Then Scott remembered that he was on the one-sixth-G moon, not on the one-G earth. That meant he could jump up and check the laser. Looking at the framework around the tube, he noticed that there were a couple of bars near the structure that he might hold on to. So he jumped, grabbed one, and then suspending himself, he reached over and felt the out-of-place tube.

Warm. Not hot, but warm.

To compare, he shifted his position so that he could feel the casing of a nearby tube.

Cold.

Scott released his hold on the bar and drifted slowly back to the floor. It was clear that the laser aimed in his direction had been used recently, even if for an extremely short burst. He checked himself but couldn't detect any injuries, other than a few sore spots from rolling around on the ground. Also, he could find no evidence on the ground of a laser blast.

Great. Another attack. But still no hard evidence.

Scott felt certain that a laser burst of some sort had been directed toward him. Anger welled up deep inside. In Scott's mind, there was only one explanation for this latest attempt on his life—and he was absolutely convinced that there had been such an attempt. *Bolotov. Pushkin.* He turned and lunged toward the closed panel leading into the Russian lab.

33

Though he was furious, Scott hesitated for a moment in front of the sign on the closed door-panel to the laboratory: "Do Not Enter—Russian Territory." Then his emotions took over and he banged on the door. No answer. He banged again, this time even louder. Still no answer.

He tried the door, fully expecting it to be locked, but the panel slid back easily at his touch.

"Hello! Anybody home?" he called into the short passageway that led into the laboratory. Another door panel at the end of the passageway hadn't even been pulled shut.

As he entered the large workroom, the place seemed unusually quiet. He remembered that Hightower had said Pushkin and Goldberg were still working there, but maybe the Australian had been wrong. Maybe they had left.

If so, why was the door unlocked? He distinctly remembered Bolotov and Pushkin leaning over to lock the entrance panel every time he saw them depart from the lab. Then he had a disturbing thought: What if Bolotov were lurking somewhere nearby?

Feeling that he was treading on forbidden ground—but equally determined to settle with the Russians once and for all—Scott stepped slowly through the passageway until he was just inside the laboratory.

"Hey! Anybody here?" he called out again, but still there was no response.

As he glanced around this inner sanctum, he saw that the Russians had been even busier than their impressive work outside, near the fusion reactor, might suggest. Although he had recognized much of the technology on the other side of the door, he now felt lost, as though he had entered an alien world, with technology totally foreign to his experience.

A large silver metal sphere, with a diameter of about ten feet, had been set up in the middle of the room. The six large laser tubes, which were each about a yard in diameter and were attached to the fusion reactor outside in the main work module, ran directly toward the sphere—but they stopped before touching it. Instead, a multitude of smaller tubes, more than Scott could count, connected the six large tubes to every visible surface of the sphere. The setup reminded him of six giant squid that had snaked their way through holes in the wall and fixed their tentacles on one huge, spherical clam.

Almost without realizing what he was doing, he walked slowly toward the strange machine and began to circle it—but then soft voices stopped him short. He took two more steps and was greeted by an unexpected sight. Sergey Pushkin was bending over at the waist and seemed to be talking to someone.

" . . . love for you. The greatest care and love. Can you believe that?"

"I'm not sure. It's confusing, strange to me . . ."

"It's simply a matter of accepting the love that is offered . . ."

Scott couldn't avoid an audible gasp. Pushkin was leaning over Ruth Goldberg, who was seated in her moonchair. The two seemed to be clinging together, with hands on each other's shoulders in an apparent embrace.

Both scientists heard Scott's reaction at the same moment, and Pushkin immediately stood up and looked in the American's direction. Ruth Goldberg looked down, her face turning a deep crimson. She was apparently embarrassed at having been caught during an intimate moment.

Pushkin cleared his throat and said, "Well, Dr. Andrews, you surprised us."

"Yeah, so I see," Scott replied uncomfortably, his anger still simmering. "Guess I should have yelled or rattled something, but I did call out. Maybe I wasn't loud enough. But I *am* wondering what you two are up to."

Pushkin's laugh startled Scott. "We're really up to nothing, but it's best that you don't say anything about this. Not for the reasons you might think, however," he said, looking at Ruth. "You see, I was praying for healing for Ruth."

"What?" Scott said, now completely confused.

"I felt moved to pray that she would be able to walk again," he said. "But it would be awkward if anyone else knew of this just yet. For the past few days, I've been offering prayers over her."

Scott looked at Ruth again. She was still looking down at her hands, seemingly as uncomfortable as he was. If either of them was involved in his mishap outside the lab, they were certainly doing a good job of concealing it.

"Of course I'll keep this confidential," Scott finally said, though he wasn't convinced by Pushkin's explanation. "But I have a question for you two. I just had a close call with a laser outside your door. You wouldn't know anything about that, would you?"

Both stared at him in such obvious surprise that he immediately eliminated them as suspects. "What do you mean, 'a close call'?" Pushkin asked.

"I mean I found myself staring right into one of those lasers, and I almost got hit by a burst from it," he replied.

"But that's impossible!" Ruth said. "The lasers are positioned to hit the deuterium–helium-3 pellet in the fusion chamber. They couldn't possibly strike anyone in the factory."

"Yeah, well, they almost hit me," Scott muttered. "One of them has been readjusted to point directly at your door."

"Please, show me," Pushkin said, pointing toward the passageway into the factory area.

As Scott turned to lead the way out of the lab, Pushkin stopped him. "What's this?" the Russian exclaimed, putting his hand on the back of Scott's jacket, which was hanging loose because he had elected not to zip it up.

"How did you get that?" Ruth asked in wonder.

"What are you talking about?" Scott asked. "I can't see my back!"

"There's a rip," Pushkin said, examining the jacket more closely, and then helping Scott remove the garment.

As Scott held the jacket in his hand, a cold film of perspiration covered his forehead. "That's not just a rip," he said, pointing to a dark streak next to the tear. "It's a burn."

"A laser burn," Ruth echoed quietly. "The beam must have missed your skin by a centimeter. You're lucky. Very lucky."

When the three of them reached the laser tube outside, Ruth immediately said, "That's wrong. This tube's been tampered with. It's pointing in the wrong direction."

"Maybe someone or something bumped it," Pushkin ventured. "Accidentally, I mean."

"Yes, that's certainly possible," she agreed.

"No way!" Scott retorted. "I've had entirely too many accidents on this trip.

Potentially deadly accidents, with the business on the lunar shuttle and now this. The coincidence explanation goes only so far."

Pushkin shook his head. "It's possible that you're right. But who would try to hurt you? And why would they hurt you?"

"Also, it would be hard to make a case that this was intentional," Ruth said, examining the laser tube more closely. "We'll have to start an investigation. But unless there are fingerprints or some other evidence I don't see around here, I'd have trouble concluding automatically that somebody did this on purpose. Those tubes are on swivels that can be moved around. This one could easily have changed position when some other piece of machinery accidentally bumped it."

Scott was becoming extremely irritated at the attempt to explain away the dangers he was encountering. "You still haven't responded to the real issue," he said heatedly. "Fine—you can argue that the change in position of the laser was an accident. But what about the fact that the beam went on just as I reached the door? It's obvious that somebody's gunning for me!"

The other two contemplated the situation silently for a moment. Then Ruth said, "We have been testing each of the lasers with short bursts, just to be sure they work properly as we reconfigure the mechanisms in preparation for the special experiment."

"Did you turn the thing on tonight?" Scott asked.

"Yes, we did," Pushkin said. "But the timing wasn't right. It's true that we tested each of the lasers just before we became deeply engaged in our . . . um . . . other conversation. Still, I'm sure they weren't turned on when you reached the outside door."

"Is there any place, other than here in the lab, where you can turn them on?" Scott asked.

"No, not that I—" Pushkin started to reply, but he was interrupted by Goldberg.

"Wait, there's another control panel out in the factory," Ruth said. "And it's within sight of the door to this lab."

When they checked the alternative controls, they noticed nothing suspicious in the area. But Scott was struck by their proximity to the Russian lab door, and the fact that they would have been mostly hidden from his view.

"I heard something from this direction," he said.

"Unfortunately, we'll probably never know for sure," Goldberg said in a dismissive tone that suggested she wanted to finish this conversation quickly.

Scott shook his head. "Strange. With these little accidents I'm having, there always seems to be a perfectly logical explanation—an ironclad excuse that somehow frees everybody from responsibility or blame."

He watched Goldberg and Pushkin, searching their faces for any telltale hint of culpability. But he picked up nothing. He decided to shift his ground to the main issue that had brought him to the lab in the first place.

"Okay, let's forget it—for now," Scott said. "Let me explain why I came to your lab—why I'm invading your 'Russian territory.'"

The fusion scientist laughed. "As far as I'm concerned, you could have visited any time," he said. "The sign was Bolotov's idea. He worries more about foreign intruders than I do. But what's on your mind?"

"We need to set a deadline for your experiment," Scott replied. "As I'm sure you know, there's bad feeling about your work."

Pushkin nodded solemnly. "The rather hostile response of our fellow moon citizens earlier today, after the celebration that opened the fusion plant, disturbed me. I don't deny that."

"To keep public frustration and hostility to a minimum, I'd suggest you take two more weeks, beginning today, to work on your project," Scott said, looking hard at Pushkin to see if there was any resistance in his face.

He couldn't detect any response, so he continued: "Looks to me like you've already made considerable headway. So if you'll agree to keep at it for only another two weeks, I think I can hold off the opposition for that long. Then, we'll all turn back to the work on the energy laser. When that's finished, you can return to your work here and keep at it for as long as you like. How does that plan sound?"

Pushkin frowned. *Uh-oh, here it comes,* Scott thought, certain that the Russian would dig in his heels. Scott began to search his mind for a reasonable fallback position. He was hardly prepared for the actual response.

"The deadline is fine," the Russian said quickly. "In fact, if you want to make it shorter, say ten days, that would be quite all right. We've all anticipated something like this, even Bolotov. And you're right, we have made good progress setting up our physical plant. It's practically finished."

Scott was so surprised that he was temporarily speechless, and hardly prepared for what came next.

Pushkin sighed. "But regardless of any time table, we have a problem."

"Oh, what's that?" Scott asked.

"The problem is that we need your help with our experiment."

34

What did you say?" Scott asked, not believing his ears.

"We need your help," Pushkin repeated. "Ruth's laser expertise goes only so far. Dr. Hiramatsu must get involved if this is going to work."

"And if it's going to be safe," Ruth added.

"Safe?" Scott replied, a tinge of worry now replacing his satisfaction. "What's not safe?"

"It's easier to understand the challenge if you look at the apparatus," Pushkin said, moving toward the large metal sphere. "You see, the six main x-ray laser beams, which originate near the fusion ignition chamber in the work area outside, terminate a few meters short of the sphere. These six lasers are extremely powerful, near the gamma-ray end of the electromagnetic spectrum."

"Hold on, hold on," Scott said, waving his hands. "I'm just a simple country doctor."

He noticed that Pushkin looked puzzled at the *Star Trek* allusion.

"What I mean is, the last physics I studied was in college, and I don't remember much of that," Scott explained. "Anyhow, what's the deal with gamma rays?"

"I can make it simple," Ruth said.

As she led him over to a computer screen, Scott marveled at her facility with American colloquialisms almost as much as her physical agility. As hard as he tried, he could detect no accent. And she was supposed to be an Israeli, originally from Russia? Where did the English come from? And just how enthusiastic was she about bringing him and the others in on this deal?

As Ruth tapped on the computer keyboard and maneuvered a cursor back and forth on the screen, Scott—with Pushkin observing over his shoulder—watched a simple diagram of the electromagnetic spectrum unfold.

"Okay, let me start with the absolute basics," she began. "As you know, lasers consist of very strong beams of light that usually have the same wavelength. The wavelengths are parallel to one another, and they move along at evenly spaced intervals. There are also other characteristic features of a laser, such as the fact that the beams don't spread out as much over distance as ordinary light beams. Got that?"

"I'm with you," Scott replied.

"Another basic thing is that the invisible electromagnetic waves, such as radio and microwaves, or ultraviolet and x-rays, are part of the same physical phenomenon as visible light," she said. "It's just that they consist of different wavelengths than visible light."

"I'm still with you," Scott said.

"Now, when you look at the chart, you'll immediately see that the waves on the left side of the spectrum are weaker and longer than those on the right side of the spectrum."

"Yes—seems that some of the weakest radio waves may be incredibly long," Scott said, looking at the wavelength numbers at the bottom of the left side of the chart.

"Would you believe they range from about a foot to more than 1,800 miles in length?" Ruth asked.

"Just one radio wave?" Scott replied incredulously.

"Exactly," Ruth said. "But when you move rightward, into the microwave range and beyond, the wavelengths go below one centimeter, and keep getting smaller."

"And as the wavelengths become smaller, the more powerful they become," Scott said, thinking out loud.

"Now consider this," Ruth continued. "In the demonstration this afternoon, the amplifiers intensified the power of the visible blue lasers into the invisible ultraviolet range. When that happened, the wavelengths decreased to incredibly tiny levels—less than ten-to-the-minus-five centimeters. Writing that out in decimal form, you'd have .00001 centimeters."

"You're a physician—so you know how damaging this powerful ultraviolet radiation can be to living tissue," Pushkin noted.

Scott nodded. "Skin cancers. I've seen my share of those from patients exposed to the Florida sun."

"But when that ultraviolet radiation is harnessed as a series of laser beams, parallel wavelengths all focused on one target . . ." Pushkin's voice trailed off.

"Enough to sear the toughest metals—or trigger that incredible nuclear reaction we just witnessed," Scott finished the thought. "Or to cut a human body like mine in two," he added, looking ruefully at his burned jacket.

"And enough to produce these six x-ray laser beams, with wavelengths much shorter and more powerful than those that make up the ultraviolet laser," Pushkin said, pointing to the giant tubes above their heads. "Imagine the power up there."

The Russian paused and silently shook his head. "Again, you're a physician, so you know why I'm so deeply concerned about all this. At this termination point"—he pointed to the end of the big laser tubes—"the six main beams are divided into 360 smaller x-ray lasers, which pass through these smaller tubes into the sphere." He swept his hands in the direction of the multiple smaller tubes, which Scott had likened in his mind to tentacles emanating from six giant squid.

"If we lose control of this process, and an accident occurs, we could be facing serious human tissue damage—at the very least," Scott said quietly. "Nuclear reactions release x-rays and gamma rays, which can produce devastating radiation injuries. And you said that these x-ray lasers will be operating at close to the gamma-ray range?"

He stepped back involuntarily from the nearest tube, as though that might give him some protection. Memories flashed through his mind of pictures of Hiroshima and Nagasaki—from the totally incinerated bodies of those closest to the blasts, to the radiation sickness of those farther away, which led to vomiting, cancers, and agonizing death.

Ruth's next words didn't improve his comfort index: "The radiation from these x-ray lasers will be more powerful than some gamma rays. Look at the electromagnetic spectrum chart again. You can see that x-ray and gamma-ray radiation overlaps in some instances."

"How does Bolotov feel about the dangers?" Scott asked.

Pushkin shrugged. "He's less concerned than I am. But then again, he's more, shall we say, 'political.'"

"KGB—or should I say FSB?" Scott ventured. "Is he a spy?"

Pushkin gave him a hard look. "I can't discuss that. I can speak only for myself. And I might add that we'll face similar risks of radiation or explosion when we finally set up the moon-earth energy transmission system. That project will employ the same fusion and x-ray technology."

"You should tell him the rest," Goldberg said. "I mean, that the immediate human danger is only part of the problem."

"What?" Scott asked, feeling a tingle in the pit of his stomach.

At first, Pushkin seemed reluctant to respond, but then he gestured toward the many smaller tubes that extended from the six main x-ray lasers to the sphere. "Let me explain this way. The theory is that all 360 of the smaller x-ray laser beams must converge at precisely the same point inside the sphere. If any of the beams are even slightly off the mark, we could lose control of the reaction. That would mean failure—or perhaps something worse."

"Like what?" Scott asked. Now he was really getting worried.

Pushkin shrugged. "We really don't know."

"Could there be a chain reaction?" Scott asked, his alarm growing. Suddenly, he had visions of the moon itself splitting in two or bursting into countless fragments.

"We think a chain reaction is highly unlikely," Ruth replied.

"Really not a concern," Pushkin agreed. "But there is always the chance of some sort of major accident. We nuclear scientists face that possibility often, even as we test our theories in the laboratory. But we're willing to take risks because of the potential benefits of the research."

"I'm not sure I want this entire outpost to be exposed to an experiment that may jeopardize lives," Scott said. Then, as nonchalantly as he could, he asked, "Is the safety of the moon a concern? I mean, we don't want to blow up the earth's only natural satellite."

"Oh, no!" Pushkin said quickly. "I really see no problem after we finally tune up . . . uh . . ."

"Fine-tune, I think you mean," Ruth said.

"Yes, fine-tune our system," Pushkin said. "I certainly want to be sure we minimize the risks. And we do feel quite comfortable about our ability to control the fusion reaction. You've already seen how well it worked earlier today. But of course, this reaction, this target in here, involves a greater magnitude of energy."

"By the way, what exactly *is* the target?" Scott asked. "What will these 360 x-ray beams of yours be aiming at?"

"Nothing," Pushkin replied.

"Nothing?" Scott asked, not quite believing his ears.

"That's right," Ruth confirmed. "Nothing. And that's one reason why this experiment is so different—and unpredictable."

Now she seems almost to be trying to talk me out of allowing the experiment. Is she cagey, or just very honest?

"Let me explain," Pushkin said, smiling at Scott's puzzled expression. "Our premise is that by applying this huge amount of energy from the x-ray lasers to one small spot in empty space, we will be able to breach the submolecular levels of that space and disturb the quantum foam in the area."

"Wait, wait!" Scott said. "Slow down. Let me see if I've got this right. You're trying to use this contraption to dig down into the tiniest, most fundamental level of energy and matter—the core of the stuff of the universe, way below molecules, atoms, even electrons and protons. Is that right?"

"Yes," Pushkin said.

"But how can you do that in empty space?" Scott asked.

"Remember, no space is really empty," Pushkin reminded him. "Hundreds of subatomic particles dart about in the atmosphere all around us—even in the so-called vacuum of space. Strange things called 'quarks,' 'bosons,' 'muons.' Also, we're sure that there are even smaller phenomena, which some call 'cosmic strings.' To make matters even more mysterious, theoretical physicists and astronomers have estimated that more than 90 percent of space is filled with what's called 'dark matter' and 'dark energy,' which we can't see. What's more, much of that dark matter and energy is composed of forces that oppose normal gravity."

"Antigravity," Ruth said.

"So suppose you manage to work your way down to this subatomic level," Scott asked. "Then what?"

"By focusing the great energy from these x-ray lasers on a single point of space, we expect to cause some of the subatomic particles to *expand*," Pushkin explained. "And if we're very fortunate, we'll also find a way to mold and shape at least one of them into a wormhole."

"Perhaps a passageway from our position here on the moon, to some other point in the universe," Ruth added. "We could create a tunnel in space-time that might allow travel in an instant to a distant star."

Scott shook his head. "Really sounds like science fiction to me. But if you think you can do this in a couple of weeks—and do it safely—be my guest."

Pushkin looked at him intently. "Scott, I still don't think you fully comprehend what I'm saying—and requesting."

The use of his first name got the American's attention. Pushkin was usually so formal that he wouldn't use first names, even when he had been given permission.

"We really do need *help* to finish this experiment properly," Pushkin emphasized again. "It's absolutely essential that the laser system be adjusted and monitored by the best minds and skills available." He looked at Ruth with an apologetic smile. "With due deference to my colleague here, we *must* have Dr. Hiramatsu's assistance. We are venturing into the unknown, and we must take any measures we can to avoid mistakes."

Scott was disconcerted. His first objective had been to get rid of the Russian experiment entirely. Then he had sought to stymie them with a difficult deadline. He would never have imagined that they would invite him to cooperate in their secret work, but he had no time to chew over his doubts. Pushkin wanted an answer—and Scott saw only one option.

"Okay, I'll agree to having Hiramatsu help you with the lasers," Scott said. "But I also want Hightower on hand to watch over the nuclear reactions. He's not a fusion expert, but he's maybe the best nuclear engineer on earth. Just in case there's any chance of a mistake or an explosion, I want him on hand to head it off. And I think I should be here as well, just to keep an eye on things—and to act as your facilitator if you need extra materials, technicians, or whatever."

"That will mean that the entire team of top scientists will be involved," Goldberg said, sitting back down on her moonchair. "Is that really wise, Sergey?"

Pushkin sighed. "I must conclude that this is the only way. Bolotov will object, of course. And if my government leaders were closer than 240,000 miles from here, my answer might be different. But I don't see that we have a choice. Either we proceed this way, or we take an unnecessary chance that the experiment will fail or end in disaster."

"Should I talk to Vladimir?" Ruth asked Pushkin.

Scott looked at her sharply. He had wondered about the many conversations he had observed between Goldberg and Bolotov. It seemed that she and the younger Russian had become close in the past few weeks—too close to give Scott a feeling of comfort. It was as hard as ever for him to understand how a couple of Russians could take an Israeli—who would normally be an archenemy—into their confidence so completely. Unless she was more Russian than Israeli.

Then stray pieces of the puzzle seemed to fall into place. *Yes! What better cover for a Russian agent than to pass her off as an Israeli?*

"No, Bolotov is my job," Pushkin replied. "But I want to start this collaboration with the other scientists immediately, before anyone has an opportunity to object."

Scott looked at the Russian closely, wondering if he was witnessing the beginning of a break between Pushkin and his political handlers. The only people who seemed capable of erecting a roadblock to this plan were the Russian governmental leaders, and perhaps Bolotov. A quick order from the Kremlin—probably from Prime Minister Martov, who seemed most involved with this venture—could stop the new, international direction of the experiment cold. But if they could distract Bolotov, even for a short period of time, it might become impossible for the Russians back on earth to regain exclusive control over the experiment.

Pushkin put his hand on Ruth's shoulder. "When I talk to Bolotov, it would be helpful if you would be present. He'll need to be convinced, and you can explain to him the difficulties and dangers with the lasers. Besides, I believe he likes and maybe even trusts you."

"Vladimir trusts no one," Goldberg said so forcefully that Scott did a double take.

Now that they seemed to be embarking on some kind of endgame, Scott decided that this would be as good a time as any to probe her allegiances and her identity: "But you and Bolotov seem to get along so well. You're originally from Russia, aren't you?" Scott asked.

Pushkin jumped at the question, but Ruth showed no reaction.

"Originally," she answered cryptically, and then changed the subject. "Anyhow, Bolotov will be difficult. I predict he'll never go along with including the rest of you in the experiment. I'll do my best to pacify him, though I'm not optimistic."

"Then it's settled," Scott said, deciding this was not the best time to pursue the subject of who Ruth really was. "I'll tell the others that we're all now working against a two-week deadline, and I'll notify them to report to you immediately to make plans for a joint venture."

"Let's waste no time," Pushkin said, nervously tapping a pen against one of his palms. "We should contact them right now, and see if they can meet Ruth and me here tonight."

"And Bolotov?" Scott asked, watching Ruth out of the corner of his eye.

"Not Bolotov," Pushkin said, still tapping his palm. "Not tonight. Tonight, we must put our plan in order. The more Dr. Hiramatsu and Dr. Hightower know, the less reason there will be to exclude them from the experiment. Of course, my superiors will criticize me for a failure of judgment."

"You're expecting serious opposition?" Scott asked.

"Very serious. And Bolotov will be quite unhappy because he's very suspicious of non-Russians. So we must make as much progress as we can before we inform him about the change in plans."

To Scott, this was sounding like the strangest and most unexpected of conspiracies—with Pushkin at the center of the plot. Although there was no time to try to tie all the threads together, Scott suspected that the accelerating speed of events might work to his advantage. So he made a quick decision.

"Let's contact Hiramatsu and Hightower right now through the intercom to their rooms," he proposed. "I think they both decided to rest before dinner. Maybe we can get them over here for a meeting tonight."

"And Bolotov?" Ruth asked.

"From what Sergey says, I think we should leave him out of the loop at this point," Scott replied. "Are you expecting him back tonight?"

"No, he said he was tired and wanted to get to bed early," Pushkin said. "He plans on getting an early start tomorrow."

"But sometimes he changes his mind," Ruth said. "What if he shows up unexpectedly when the others are here?"

Scott pondered the issue for a few seconds. He still didn't trust Ruth and knew he had to find a way to prevent her from contacting Bolotov tonight. So he volunteered his services.

"I'm the most expendable to miss the meeting tonight," Scott said. "But you people are essential. So you stay right here, and I'll notify the others about the meeting. Then I'll camp out with some reading material in the lobby of the living module, where I can see anyone who is heading for the passageway leading to the work area. If Bolotov appears, I'll signal you on my pocket computer—and I'll also do what I can to delay him. That should give Hiramatsu and Hightower plenty of time to beat a retreat out of the lab here."

"That will be very helpful," Ruth said. "But of course, Bolotov will find out very soon what's going on."

"More precisely, he should find out no earlier than tomorrow morning, when we all barge into your forbidden 'Russian territory' here," Scott said pointedly, looking her straight in the eye. "After all, the only people who could tell him would be one of us."

Scott decided that this might be a good test for Goldberg's loyalty. He could ensure that no one contacted Bolotov until the all-important first meeting was over that evening. The only chance to tell the younger Russian about the new plan would be during the few hours when all the participants had returned to their private quarters for sleep. So if Bolotov showed that he had learned about the plan the next morning, it would be fairly clear that Ruth, *née* Tatiana, was the one who had disclosed the secret.

Bidding the two of them a quick good-bye, Scott beat a hasty retreat through the short passageway that led from the Russian lab to the main Energy City work module. Bolotov was at the top of his immediate priority list. But still, he couldn't get the strange network of these Russian relationships out of his mind.

35

"H alt! You will proceed no farther!"

With Shiro Hiramatsu, Jeffrey Hightower, and several technicians hovering behind him, Scott stopped abruptly, just outside the Russian laboratory. He found himself staring directly into the eyes of an extremely angry Vladimir Bolotov. Sergey Pushkin and Ruth Goldberg, who were at work in another part of the lab about thirty meters away, looked up wide-eyed at Bolotov's outburst.

The meeting the previous night involving Pushkin, Goldberg, Hiramatsu, and Hightower had apparently gone well, at least according to the report Scott had received. While the others were having their discussion in the laboratory, he had spent a boring four hours in the spacious lobby of the living module, on the lookout for Bolotov. But the younger Russian scientist, who had apparently been desperately in need of sleep, had not appeared during Scott's vigil.

This morning, however, Bolotov had obviously recovered all his energies with a vengeance—and was as aggressive and hostile as Scott had ever seen him. From the man's initial reaction, however, it was unclear if he had prior knowledge of the new plan.

"Now, Vladimir, we have an understanding—" Scott began, but Bolotov interrupted.

"No understanding! There can be no understanding! You have no right to enter our space. This is Russian territory."

"Seems to be a disagreement about that, mate," Hightower piped up.

Surveying the scene over Scott's shoulder, the Australian was already edging his way into the lab. Scott figured that because Hightower's philosophy

166

must be that possession is nine-tenths of the law, he was intent on moving in physically to stake a claim on some part of the Russian lab.

"Seems that you and Professor Pushkin have a different point of view," Hightower said, continuing to slide, step-by-step, into one side of the Russian work space.

Bolotov looked over his shoulder and scowled in the direction of Pushkin. Apparently Pushkin hadn't yet informed his associate of the new arrangement.

"Look, Vladimir, I think we have the same goals in mind," Scott said, trying to be as diplomatic as possible. "Nobody intends to encroach on your space or your project. This is a Russian experiment. Nobody disputes that. We're just responding to a call for help."

"I never made any such call," Bolotov said gruffly, taking a threatening step toward Scott and simultaneously watching Hightower's movements out of the corner of his eye.

"But Pushkin and Goldberg did ask for help," Hightower said. "You seem to be outvoted."

"Votes are not counted in this situation," Bolotov spat back.

At the same time, he placed his hand on a long, heavy riveting tool that lay on a work surface next to where he was standing. Russian technicians had been using the device, which resembled a light assault rifle, to set up the laser casings. Becoming alarmed at the movement, Scott could only think of how a similar tool in the same Russian's hand had almost put him out of commission in the underwater tank in Houston.

"Vladimir, we want to handle this issue peacefully," Scott said, deciding that he had to ratchet up his response. "But you should know that Secretary Martin and his security force are aware of our entry here. They are prepared to respond—though I've assured them that this certainly won't be necessary."

Scott then pulled out his PDA, switched on the video screen, and turned it toward Bolotov so that the Russian scientist could see the image. The screen showed Archibald Martin sitting at his desk, with two armed security guards clearly visible in the background.

"Is everything all right, Dr. Andrews?" Martin asked over the computer speaker, which Scott had tuned to a high volume.

"I think everything is fine, Mr. Secretary," Scott replied. "But we may want you to participate in this discussion, so please stand by."

Scott then held the computer and screen to one side but still clearly in view, so that there would be no question in Bolotov's mind that the secretary was aware of everything that was happening. He was about to try to offer some solution that would allow Bolotov to save some face, but Hightower, who was now several yards inside the laboratory, interrupted again.

"Give it up, mate!" he said to the Russian, who had removed his hand from the riveter but still seemed unwilling to back down. "You've lost this round! Now let's get on with business."

The Australian's remarks caused Bolotov to become even more agitated, and his hand edged back toward the tool. Scott found himself giving thanks that the man wasn't carrying a real pistol. The time had obviously arrived for Scott to take a firmer hand—and to get the pugnacious Australian out of the picture.

"Let me handle this, Jeff," he said curtly. "Look, Vladimir, we already know about your experiment—trying to create a wormhole and all that. And we all agree that you Russians have a proprietary right to what you discover. But as team leader, I must insist that every possible measure be taken to ensure the safety of this venture. We can't have this experiment jeopardize the life or health of everyone else at this outpost."

"There is no danger," Bolotov shot back.

"You know that's untrue, Vladimir," Pushkin interrupted. Moving at a slow moon-lope, the senior Russian scientist was on his way to the scene of the argument. "Both Dr. Goldberg and I recognize a *significant* danger—and I think we are in a better position to evaluate that than you are."

This was the first time Scott had heard Bolotov's scientific credentials called into question. Now there was no question that he was primarily, if not exclusively, a political operative.

"You cannot proceed with this," Bolotov spluttered. "I will report this. Prime Minister Martov will not allow it."

Apply a little pressure, and it's no telling what will spurt out, Scott reflected. This was the first confirmation that the Russian prime minister was directly involved with this project. He resolved to e-mail Colleen as soon as this current matter was settled.

"The politicians are on earth, and we are up here," Pushkin replied sternly. Looking Bolotov directly in the eye, he added: "If you feel you must file a report, go ahead. But I believe our primary mission is to succeed with this project. If we fail—or worse, destroy ourselves and our research—that would be worse than seeking some help. And if we should fail but survive, I don't think you would like to be the one who bears sole responsibility for the failure. Am I right about that?"

Bolotov dropped his eyes. For the first time in the encounter, he appeared stymied. Scott had been certain that the man would immediately notify Moscow about the change of plans and the involvement of foreign scientists in the Russian experiment. But now he wasn't so sure. Pushkin had apparently picked just the right tone and strategy to deliver his warning. For the first time in Scott's experience, the younger Russian seemed intimidated.

At heart, Bolotov, whatever else he might be, was a field operative who had been trained to follow orders. Now he was obviously in a quandary, trying to decide if he should follow Pushkin, or dig in his heels and insist on rigid adherence to his original instructions. Scott suspected that the junior Russian knew that deviating from an original plan—and showing a little imagination— might be rewarded handsomely, but only if that deviation led to success.

Scott suppressed a smile as he speculated on the inner turmoil suggested by the silence and darting eyes of his muscular, blond adversary. Bolotov's bulging trapezius muscles, which ran from the base of his neck across his broad shoulders, flexed and relaxed as the tension inside the man seemed to build.

For once, Bolotov was on the defensive. Most important of all, the younger Russian's uncertainty might buy them a little time, a short delay from interference by the Russian higher-ups on earth. A day or two might be all they needed. From what the American congressman could tell, it shouldn't take any longer than that for the team to determine if Pushkin's wormhole concept was merely a figment of his imagination—or a truly viable enterprise.

36

"A re we alone?" the prime minister asked, his image flickering on the videophone.

Klaudia Ming-Petrovich's first reaction was that this was a strange question to ask a professional undercover operative, whose stock-in-trade was secrecy. But then she remembered that Martov wasn't used to the new communications technology, which enabled them to engage in a secure conversation spanning continents, from Cocoa Beach, Florida, to Moscow. Also, she realized that he probably wanted to be certain that Valery wasn't in the room with her—though that would have been a major lapse in discipline on her part.

"Of course, my love," she replied. "As you know, we have moved into an apartment here in Cocoa Beach—a much more secure location than the temporary motel quarters. Now we don't have to worry about maids or the motel management intruding on our privacy. So you can be confident that my words are for your ears only. And yours, my prime minister, are just for me."

"Please, not so familiar, even if this message is encrypted!" he reprimanded. "And don't use titles. Are you sure no one can overhear us? There's no way any of their FBI surveillance people can eavesdrop? Displaying our pictures seems highly risky."

She shrugged and smiled slightly, hoping the full impact of her dark eyes and shiny, flowing black hair would come across on the picture he was receiving. Klaudia always felt that if she could be seen, she automatically had a huge advantage in any conversation with a man.

"The FBI is incompetent," she replied. "I've already identified several of their agents here in Florida and have had no trouble at all avoiding them. As for the technology, there are multiple safeguards in place to alert us and immediately shut off this link if any eavesdroppers, viruses, or other electronic intruders try to enter."

She paused and smiled again. "Electronics aside, I find that seeing your face is more reassuring than threatening. When I watch your expressions along with the familiar tones of your voice, I know I'm talking to you and not someone who just sounds like you. So don't worry. At least for the foreseeable future, this satellite channel is completely secure. We know the Americans can't listen to us."

Klaudia made it a point to shake her head and sweep her long hair back over her shoulders. She was well aware that Martov liked that, and she felt certain that his view of her during this videophone conversation would enable her to magnify the impact of her message.

"The Americans may be well ahead of us in a number of scientific and engineering areas," she continued. "But they think the era of big-power international intelligence operations is essentially over. So as you know, my . . . my colleague, they have neglected their surveillance technology. As a result, we have kept our communications systems well in advance of theirs."

She shifted her position and stood up slightly so that Martov could get a fuller view of the flattering silk bodysuit she had chosen to wear for this conversation. "We simply understand covert international operations better than they do," she replied in a soothing, confident tone. "I become increasingly convinced of our superiority every time I'm in the field."

"Still, we must be cautious," he said irritably.

He obviously didn't like to be lectured by a subordinate—even if that subordinate was the beautiful Klaudia Ming-Petrovich. But she could tell by the change in his tone that the image she was projecting over thousands of miles via satellite was having the desired effect.

"This must be an important call," she said.

"For your ears alone," he emphasized, involuntarily looking over her shoulder, apparently in an effort to be certain that there really was no one else in the room with her. "No notes. And there will be no e-mail follow-up. I still have trouble believing that this videophone is the most secure way to transmit a message, but I must rely on the assurances of our communications engineers."

"Only a personal meeting is better, and there are dangers even with that," she replied, remembering a couple of occasions when conversations of her associates had been picked up by parabolic microphones or bugs placed in rooms.

"Then here is my concern," Martov said. "I have just received a strange message from our special friend."

Klaudia immediately became dead serious. The designation *special friend* was the one thing in the moon operation that had remained beyond her security clearance. Because she had chosen Bolotov and had organized all forays onto American soil, she was somewhat annoyed that Martov had withheld the identity of this individual from her. But she could understand his reasoning. Power depended on knowledge and information, and the individual who possessed the most information would be most likely to retain that power to the end of the game.

Though she had wheedled and cajoled in their times alone together, trying to pry the identity of this other operative out of Martov, he had remained unmoved. He was a master at moving his operatives around like chess pieces on the most complex, multidimensional, international chessboard.

Klaudia also knew quite well that Martov insisted on some degree of deniability when an operation veered into criminal activity. He didn't want to know the names or circumstances of those who had to be killed, such as the hiker Klaudia and Valery had neutralized in northern New Hampshire. But when it came to knowing and being in a position to manipulate the essential people and actions that were necessary to control the entire operation, he exerted full authority and control. So it was understandable that he had chosen not to disclose even to her the name of the "special friend" working in the background on the moon project, alongside Pushkin and Bolotov.

Klaudia had a few good ideas about who this person might be. After all, there were only six main participants on the team. The backgrounds of Andrews, Pushkin, and Bolotov were clear. That left only Hiramatsu, Hightower, and Goldberg as leading candidates to be the secret Russian operative. Of course, the agent could also be one of the lower-level technicians or scientists. But Klaudia tended to discount this possibility since those people didn't have full access to the special Russian experiment.

As for the main scientists, the extensive background checks Klaudia had conducted had left her without a clear answer. She had learned that Shiro Hiramatsu was a confirmed Japanese nationalist, who seemed to have no inclination to give Russia any advantage. If a connection with Russia would benefit Japan, that was fine. Otherwise, he could not be expected to help Moscow with anything. But that was Hiramatsu's surface identity—the information that had been easily accessible to her investigators. What facts about his background might they have missed?

Jeffrey Hightower, though Australian by nationality, had been established as a solid American ally. Furthermore, reports from Bolotov and other Russian operatives on the moon had pegged him as a staunch friend and supporter of Scott Andrews. Deep background research before the launch from earth had revealed that in some respects, Hightower seemed even more American in his allegiances than the Americans. But that didn't necessarily settle the matter. Sometimes, being the most ardent public supporter could provide a convenient cover story for what lay beneath.

That left Ruth Goldberg as a potential candidate for the Russians' "special friend" on this mission. Granted, she was an Israeli national. But Klaudia knew through Bolotov that she had been born in Russia, and he had known her at the university in Moscow. It seemed possible that she might be a Russian mole, cleverly planted as a double agent on Israeli soil. After all, who would ever suspect a handicapped Israeli of helping the Russians?

But regardless of who the special agent was, what had this person communicated that was worrying Martov so much?

As if in answer to her unspoken question, Martov said, "Our special friend has disclosed that over Bolotov's strenuous objections, Andrews, Hiramatsu, and the other top scientists will intervene in our experiment."

"How can they do that?" she asked, stunned at the news. "They can't operate without Pushkin!"

"Pushkin has agreed to go along with them," he replied, obviously doing his best to control his anger.

"The traitor!" she cried. "What does Bolotov say?"

"That's another worry," he said. "Bolotov hasn't reported to us about this. Have you heard from him?"

"Not a word!" she cried, now forgetting about being coy or seductive with her superior. "That's a direct violation of my orders!"

"So it would seem—a serious breach of discipline," Martov replied darkly. "He'll have to answer for this. But still, the report from our special friend indicates that Bolotov was adamantly opposed to this collaboration. At one point, he seemed willing to resort to violence, but Andrews arranged for a security backup by Secretary Martin. So perhaps Bolotov really had no choice but to back down."

"Andrews! Always Andrews!" Klaudia snarled through lips that had suddenly switched from soft petals to hard edges framing the slit of her mouth.

"We need a new strategy," Martov said. "I considered suspending the experiment entirely, but then we would lose an opportunity that we may never have again."

Klaudia thought for a moment. "I agree. The obvious solution is for us to wait and see if the experiment produces anything worthwhile. If it does, then I would propose a quick, decisive measure. Our main objective should be to secure the research—by force if necessary. As for the scientists and technicians on the project, only those who are unquestionably loyal to us should be allowed to live. All others should be terminated."

Now it was Martov's turn to pause. "Drastic," he replied after a few moments. "But logical. All right, consider your assignment revised. If our secret experiment succeeds, you will acquire the research and . . . take the other necessary steps. That is, ah, reduce the size of the scientific team."

"And who should be in the final, smaller group?" she asked. "Obviously, Pushkin and Bolotov remain. Obviously, Andrews goes. But the others . . ."

Klaudia waited expectantly for the answer because she knew that she might be on the verge of learning for certain who the secret Russian operative on the team was. But all she elicited from Martov was a smile.

"You think I'm so stupid?" he asked. "You think you're the only wily one? I'll tell you that when the time is right. In the meantime, prepare for all contingencies."

"Yes, my"—she almost said "master of the universe" but caught herself— "my esteemed colleague," she finished.

Unexpectedly, Martov smiled, and unless she was mistaken, he touched his ample lips with his fingertips. *A kiss?* Klaudia could never be sure about the man, but the gesture seemed a good sign, an effort at least at affection. She knew their relationship was 90 percent professional. If she failed as a field agent, she would almost certainly be on her own, out from under his protective umbrella. No matter how much he cared for her personally, he was unlikely to risk himself to try to rescue her.

What about that other 10 percent? Was there any amount of love or personal loyalty there? She would probably never be sure. But she suspected that the tenuous emotional connection between them might someday be her insurance policy. The fact that he cared for her as much as he could care for any woman—and that wasn't much—might just save her life at some point. Certainly, Martov was cold and calculating—but was he as cold as she was? She was betting that he might provide a safety net for her at some point—even though she knew quite well that she would never provide one for him.

When the connection had been severed and the room had grown quiet again, the only sound Klaudia Ming-Petrovich could hear was the pounding of the distant Atlantic surf. Some might have used the moment to relax, to allow the tensions of an encounter with one of the most powerful men on earth to subside somewhat.

Instead, the Russian agent began to think and plan. Calling up the extensive personnel files in her computer documents, she found the folder labeled *Moon Team* and then scrolled through the pictures, biographies, and intelligence reports for the members of the expedition. As she read, she contemplated the best venues and methods to take out each top scientist—even the Russians. *You can never tell, even with those who you may feel are your allies.*

A beep signaled an incoming e-mail message, so Klaudia pulled up her mailbox screen. It was a heavily encrypted communication from the moon. *Bolotov. About time.*

After snaking through the encryption sequence to unlock the message, she finally had Bolotov's words before her:

A difficulty has arisen. The other scientists, led by Andrews, have forced their way into our special project. I resisted to the point of threatening violence, but Andrews was supported by Secretary Martin's security force. Also, Pushkin joined with Andrews, so that I was alone in opposing the intrusion. Pushkin claimed that the experiment was too complex for us to handle alone. He said he fears not only failure, but also serious safety problems. But I suspect there may be more to his decision than meets the eye. Instructions?

Klaudia contemplated the message. Bolotov had included the main facts as she had learned them via Martov from their other moon operative, but he had sat on the information for almost twenty-four hours. Why? Fear? Inefficiency? Knowing he had to be warned without delay, she shot off an immediate answer:

You are late. I learned these same facts well before receiving your message. Why did you delay? Provide a full explanation. Although this is a serious breach of your responsibilities, your past record of service has caused me to overlook your lapse, but there must be no further insubordination. I require no action by you at this time, but I do expect *regular* reports as matters proceed. I do not expect to hear secondhand from my superiors. I trust this is clear.

Her anger at Bolotov still smoldering, Klaudia clicked the *send* button and watched the graphics on her screen, indicating that the e-mail had been successfully transmitted. Then, feeling a little calmer, she returned to her files on the moon team.

One by one, she began to construct scenarios that she believed would be most likely to pull each of the scientists into her web. The main objective: to understand the precise circumstances that would make them vulnerable to the cleanest and most effective assassination attempts. Finally, she amused herself with a relatively easy, even recreational task: formulating additional strategies for playing her own successful game of cat and mouse with the FBI agents and Colleen Barker.

From her own personal reconnaissance, Klaudia knew Barker and at least two FBI agents were still in the area. Wearing modest, unmemorable disguises—certainly not her blond wig—she had observed the FBI men on the beach as they ogled women who were walking the shoreline. As for Barker, Klaudia had actually brushed shoulders with her in a local supermarket. When Andrews's chief of staff had obviously run into difficulty trying to find a store item, the Russian had almost intervened and pointed Barker toward the shelf with the nonfat yogurt products. *So predictable, these slightly overweight American women. Always on a diet.* But seeing no reason to tempt fate too far, Klaudia had deferred to another customer who was eager to help.

She had also managed to keep her rather limited colleague, Valery, safely out of the way. She had assigned him the regular task of using their extensive computer resources several hours a day to research the floor plans and personnel rosters at NASA. Also, he was required to spend an hour or so every afternoon in a local gym to keep in shape.

On a few occasions, Klaudia had ordered him to watch the FBI contingent from a distance. On paper, Valery was supposed to be highly trained in tailing enemy operatives. In practice, she didn't completely trust his techniques. This Florida situation posed unusual challenges, and they couldn't afford to make any mistakes. So the first few times, she had secretly watched him as he was observing the movements of Colleen and her FBI associates.

Having satisfied herself that he could do an adequate job, Klaudia had decided to allow him to operate occasionally on his own. That's what he was doing right now—watching and surreptitiously photographing the FBI people, who had entered their temporary headquarters four blocks from the beach, and less than a mile from where she sat.

When Valery was unoccupied, Klaudia had told him he could entertain himself at an out-of-the-way video-game arcade, visit a couple of bars, or sunbathe on an obscure stretch of beach. Klaudia's preliminary reconnoitering of these locations had given her confidence that they were secure havens where her rather uncreative associate could enjoy his leisure hours without being detected.

With her anger toward Bolotov now under control, Klaudia pulled up the pictures and files she had assembled on Colleen Barker and the two FBI agents, Ralph Jefferson and Lawrence Murphy. If these people were actually looking for her and Valery, they were doing a miserable job of it.

The more she thought about her present assignment, the more amused Klaudia became that she and Martov could communicate face-to-face at their leisure, while she sat completely undetected near one of the most sensitive technological centers in the entire United States—the Kennedy Space Center. Incredibly, the country had become complacent again, despite the devastating terrorist attacks at the beginning of the century. How, she wondered, could a nation that was supposed to be the most powerful and astute in human history, possibly place its political and military security in the hands of blockheads who were obviously incapable of discovering her identity or whereabouts? Even more important, how could such incompetent Americans hope to keep up when Russians were quickly shifting the field of action beyond the earth to the farthest reaches of the universe?

37

The fuzzy, distorted video patterns that played across the screen in front of them were maddening. Given the power and direction of the signal, they knew they were dealing with something well beyond ordinary communications technology. In fact, well beyond anything so far encountered in the most advanced government or commercial research-and-development laboratories.

Now operating out of a temporary command center in an unassuming Cocoa Beach office building, the FBI agents had first picked up the readings on their own listening equipment. That's why, at Colleen's urging, they had decided to report the phenomenon to scientists in Washington.

"It's almost like this comes from aliens," observed Sheila, the FBI tech specialist from Washington whose fingers were moving quickly across the keyboard. "Like something the SETI researchers would love to find."

"What's that?" Colleen asked, hoping not to appear too dumb.

Her expertise was in politics and investigative journalism—not electronics or surveillance technology. But she had learned long ago that even if she looked stupid, it was important to ask the questions and get the information. She was confident that in the end, her analytical skills would overshadow any silly mistakes she might make in gathering the facts.

"Search for Extra-Terrestrial Intelligence," Ralph answered, rather seriously for him, Colleen conceded. At least his initial reaction to her ignorance hadn't been the usual rolling of his eyes. "There are some astronomers who monitor radio signals from space in the hope of finding alien civilizations out there. Wouldn't that be something—if we had caught us an alien?"

He, Larry, and Colleen were standing behind Sheila, who was too absorbed in her work to do more than share an occasional thought out loud. Finally, she sighed and stood up. "I really don't have the foggiest what that was all about," she said. "I recorded the whole thing, and we'll analyze it back in the lab. Maybe we can adjust the frequencies and come up with something."

"Any guesses?" Colleen asked.

"If my life depended on it, I'd guess we're dealing with some sort of very strong video signal," she replied. "It seems to be traveling up into space, probably to a satellite, but I can't break it down into a picture, or even a recognizable audio transmission."

"Could it be an encrypted message?" Larry asked.

"Could be," Sheila said. "But not like any I've run into before. There are certain clear signatures you run into if you're dealing with known encrypted communications technology. But this has none of them. That's why I wonder if it's really a communication at all."

"What else could it be?" Colleen asked.

"Oh, maybe stray signals coming off some powerful electronic equipment in the area. After all, we are in the heart of NASA country. They're constantly in touch with every sort of orbiting space technology you can imagine. Maybe we're just seeing a leakage or feedback from one of those systems."

Colleen looked at her closely. "But you don't really believe that."

Sheila smiled. "You read me too well. No, I'm not satisfied with that explanation. This is a little too weird to dispose of that way. Seems to appear at irregular times and has a focus or direction that makes me think it's not just an accident. That's the way a communications signal would look. But, of course, you have to take my biases into account. I'm always suspicious, always looking for spies and counterspies. After all, I work for the FBI."

"So you'll take it back to your lab . . ."

"And waste my time and that of other colleagues and agencies—probably including NASA—trying to figure the thing out," Sheila finished.

Colleen nodded and began to gather her materials for the short hike back to her Cocoa Beach motel. Another tantalizing dead end. The east-central Florida barrier island seemed to be the stage for that result far too often.

But despite the frustrations she had experienced with the FBI in the last few weeks, Colleen had to admit that this wasn't such a bad place to be on assignment. The early spring sun was pleasantly warm, and the weather had been gorgeous. Hardly a cloud in the sky. In fact, she was thinking about spending an hour on the beach today before dinner—but then she turned around and saw him leaning against the doorway.

"How'd you get in here?" Ralph growled, moving quickly toward the wiry, bespectacled man who was surveying the scene with some amusement. "This building is off-limits to civilians. Who let you in?"

"I let myself in," the stranger answered with a sardonic smile. "If you need a security clearance to enter, you really should have somebody downstairs to stop people like me. The FBI seems to be slipping."

His identification of them as FBI agents seemed to take them by surprise. Colleen could understand why. There were no signs on the doors or downstairs. Nothing in the phone book. How could the man have known?

"You'll have to leave—*now!*" Larry finally said, moving to the right side of Ralph.

They were obviously assuming some sort of tactical configuration with an eye to putting the man out of commission quickly if he failed to obey them.

"Very interesting equipment you have there," the man commented, ignoring their orders and moving a step into the room. He didn't seem at all intimidated by the warnings of the agents.

Ralph drew his pistol and held it in a safe position, with the muzzle pointed toward the ceiling. But with his free left hand, he motioned vigorously to the man to move back. By this time, Larry had moved several paces to Ralph's right and was holding his own weapon in a similar position. Sheila had pulled out a handgun and had taken a station on the left side of the other two.

"One more step, and we'll have to shoot," Ralph said, lowering his pistol toward the man's legs. "You're trespassing in an area protected by national security. I want you to raise your hands above your head—*now!* And very, very slowly get down on your knees!"

"Is that what they're teaching the FBI now?" the stranger replied, raising his hands but not sinking to his knees. Still smiling, he seemed unperturbed by the pistols that were pointing in his direction. "Do they say you should first use deadly force against a peaceable, unarmed man, who wanders into an unmarked room where you happen to be chatting about a mysterious video— which, by the way, may be an encrypted message between renegade Russians? And then maybe you finally get around to asking who this unarmed man is, after he's bleeding at your feet on the floor?"

The muzzle of Ralph's weapon sagged toward the floor, away from the man's body. "Okay, who are you?" Ralph barked. "I want some answers!"

"His name is Michael James," Colleen sighed. "Put your six-shooters away, cowboys."

The emotional intensity had finally subsided to the point where she felt that she could say something without upsetting the delicate balance that gripped the room—and perhaps causing one of the FBI agents to lose control and resort to violence. Colleen was relieved to see that when she spoke, they all turned their heads abruptly in her direction. She decided that must mean that the tension had been broken enough to keep James's head from being blown off—at least for the time being.

"He's a college Bible teacher," she continued, shaking her head with some disgust. "And a former Seal. And a major player in the investigation of that unexplained light in the sky several years ago—the one that he said was the Star of Bethlehem come back to haunt us. Unfortunately, he's not quite in sync with the Prince of Peace. Wherever he goes, mayhem seems to follow. That star thing resulted in several killings in Israel and probably the riots that occurred soon afterward in other parts of the world. And by the way, Professor James, I don't for a minute think you just wandered in here by accident."

"You're right, of course," James answered, lowering his hands as the agents lowered their weapons—though they still didn't holster them. "And it's always nice to run into you, Colleen. By the way, FBI Director Saunders told me where you were. His street directions were quite good, but he wouldn't give me your phone number. Otherwise, I would have called."

The three agents surrounding James immediately holstered their weapons and fell back a step or two.

"You're trying to tell us that the director himself told you how to find us?" Ralph asked incredulously.

"Yes, as a matter of fact," James said. "But don't worry about that. Mum's the word on this little tiff. I completely understand your nervousness. I certainly apologize for not giving you a ring to let you know I was on my way."

Larry was already on the phone, checking with the director's secretary in Washington, D.C. After listening for a few seconds, with no response other than an occasional "Yes, sir!" he held the phone out to Michael James.

"Director Saunders wants to talk to you," he said, a chastened expression fixed on his face.

"Hi, Arnie," James began. Then after a brief pause, he said, "Yes, an extremely efficient group you have working here. I'm impressed. They wouldn't give me the time of day until they were pretty sure I was on the level. And to be absolutely certain about me, they had to get the green light from you. Yes, I'm quite impressed. Fine, Arnie, I'll drop in next time I'm in the area. Best to Martha."

Colleen shook her head in wonder as she watched the fallout around the room from this minidrama. Ralph was still standing near the door, with his mouth half-open. Larry was leaning against the far wall, watching the Wheaton professor as though he were some sort of alien. Sheila, a newcomer to this peculiar little surveillance family, had retreated to the seat next to her computer screen and was contemplating Michael James with a fixed, perplexed frown.

James was indeed a cool customer, and remarkably unpredictable, Colleen concluded. Where did these political connections of his come from? He actually knew the FBI director and his wife on a first-name basis? Not even Scott Andrews was that intimate with the man.

From her research she had assumed that James was just a kook who had almost started World War III—or the Apocalypse, if you believed some of the interpretations the tabloids had put on the Star of Bethlehem incident. But clearly, she had been wrong. This was a man to take seriously. Maybe even a man who could be helpful.

"So are you in the mood for a cup of coffee, Ms. Barker?" James asked her unexpectedly.

When she recovered, Colleen replied, "Sure, why not? Let's celebrate your survival. Not everybody mixes it up with these guys and lives to fight another day."

Out of the corner of her eye, she saw him smile, a wry expression that revealed a few teeth as one corner of his mouth rose slightly higher than the other. *Not a bad-looking guy for a fifty year old. But also not a guy you automatically want to trust with all your family secrets.*

As they walked out the office door and toward the stairs that led down to the first floor and the street, he asked, "Did you arrive through the front door?"

"Sure," she said, not certain where he was going with this line of questioning.

"Then this time, we go out the back way," he said firmly.

At first, she didn't question him but just followed obediently through a rear door, which led into a small parking lot for the building. Finally, she couldn't contain herself. "Okay, what's this all about?"

"Follow me and I'll show you," he replied, motioning to her as a squad leader might signal one of his troops.

Silently and quickly, they walked around the block until they approached a street corner one block up from the FBI headquarters. Just before they reached the intersection, James darted into a beachwear shop and pulled Colleen in behind him.

"What are you doing?" she whispered.

"Let's check out the sarongs," he said, walking over to the women's section near one of the windows. "Yes, I think one of those would look smashing on you," he said, pointing to one of the garments.

"I don't wear sarongs," she said crisply. "But that's not why we're here."

"You're right," he replied in a low voice. "As you're contemplating the sarongs, look out the window to that surf shop on the other side of the street. See that short, stocky man with the high yellow socks and narrow-brimmed, straw hat?"

Colleen scanned the storefront and immediately noticed the man James was referring to. He was lolling around just inside the front door, now glancing at one of the surfboards, now looking out onto the street.

"Yep," she replied.

"Does he seem to belong in a surf shop?"

"Now that you mention it—"

"Of course he doesn't!" James said, answering his own question. "I've never seen a surfer who looked anything like that—and I've seen quite a few in my day, though you might not guess it."

"Southern California. Seal training. Surfer country."

"I wish you'd forget that Seal business."

"Not part of your self-image anymore? The killer-assassin-warrior doesn't quite fit into the Bible-teacher mode?"

"That's part of it," he said wearily. "But it might not be healthy for you or me if the wrong people overheard you. It's best that we just come across as a couple of tourists."

Now Colleen became serious. For the first time, she sensed the man was on her side—and the side of her boss. And she had known from their initial meeting that he could help her if only he were willing.

"Okay, if I had to guess, I'd say that maybe he has a son who surfs, and he's looking over the equipment for a gift," she said.

"If I had watched him only for the few seconds we've been in here, I might agree," James replied. "But I observed the man for nearly a half hour before I ran into that FBI army down the street. For the entire time, he did exactly what you see him doing now. Looking at the same couple of surfboards, and then looking down the street—in the direction of the FBI office."

"So you think he's part of some sort of stakeout?" she asked, looking at the man more closely.

"I think he doesn't belong in that surf shop," James said. "He's no shopper. And that outfit he's wearing wouldn't be right for any beach resort. Also, he doesn't have the right kind of tan. You can tell that he's been spending time in the sun, but he has more of a burn than a tan. I doubt he ever takes his shirt off. See the white skin peeking out from his upper arms, just below the edge of his short sleeves? And watch him move. A little awkward, not your conventional sportsman. But very strong. You can see that in the neck and forearms and the way he holds his back."

Now Colleen was looking at James, not the man in the surf shop. The ice water in his veins had impressed her when those pistols were trained on him a little earlier. But at first, she had wondered if he was a little dumb, provoking armed FBI agents that way. Now, she could see that she wasn't dealing with a foolhardy nincompoop. The more Michael James spoke, the more confident she became that the guy had field-operative intelligence skills that surpassed those of the government agents she had encountered so far.

"So who is he?" Colleen asked.

"That, I don't know," he said. "But it's clear that he's watching movement in and out of that makeshift FBI office. Any other business of note in the building?"

"Not really. It's a regular small-office building. I've seen a couple of real-estate agents. And a college application consulting firm. But why would anyone watch a parade of real-estate clients and students trying to get into a good school?"

"That's my question," James replied. "He has to be watching the FBI."

"That's why you wanted to leave by the back door," she said.

Immediately, she felt like kicking herself for making such an obvious observation, but then she caught herself. *Why do I need to impress this guy?* Anyhow, he ignored her comment. His attention was focused exclusively on the short fireplug of a customer—or noncustomer—in the surf shop.

"It would be interesting to follow him," James finally remarked. "He might lead us to bigger game."

"I don't mind hanging around," she said.

"No, chances are he's seen you. Matter of fact, if he's really on a stakeout, and he's part of a professional operation, he probably knows all about you. I'm an unknown entity. I saw him before he saw me. So I'll make him my little project and see where that takes us."

"You've changed," Colleen said, watching his face closely.

"How's that?"

"When I first met you in your office, you put me off. You didn't want to talk about Pushkin at all."

"Still don't," James said, fingering the price tags on a rack of wraparound skirts.

"Yet you're willing to work with us," she pressed. "Something turned you around."

"Yes," he admitted in a near-whisper, looking around to be sure there was no chance they would be overheard. "Something did. Things are happening on the moon that have led me to offer my services."

"You mean you went directly to the FBI director?" she asked.

"He's only one among many who are becoming involved in this thing," James replied evasively. "Look at yourself. What's the chief of staff of a leading U.S. congressman doing here, working on a surveillance operation in Florida with the FBI? My interests are much broader than one man, or one agency. Broader even than one country."

She looked at him curiously. "I think I know better than to ask, but are you directly in touch with Pushkin?"

"Right the first time," he replied. "It's better not to ask. Our quarry is on the move. I'll be in touch."

Before she could protest, James was out the door, moving unobtrusively like any other tourist about a half block behind the short, stocky man who was now walking purposefully away from the surf shop.

Colleen observed the two men until they were both out of sight, and then she turned to leave as well. Michael James was certainly full of surprises. And she knew from her own professional background as a former investigative reporter that she should be suspicious of every move he made. But somehow, he made her feel comfortable and confident. She sensed that she was no longer the last line of defense in protecting the interests of her boss.

38

The bright lights in the Russian laboratory caused the casings surrounding the 360 spidery x-ray laser tubes to flash and flicker, as though parallel electromagnetic beams were already coursing in tandem through them. Although Scott had surveyed the scene in the lab many times by now, he continued to be fascinated by the way the laser tubes snaked out and grasped the large silver sphere. It almost seemed they were about to devour it.

All the sphere's interior air had been sucked out, so that now, there was no artificial atmosphere inside at all. Nothing but a vacuum, similar to what existed on the moon's surface, just outside the laboratory walls.

Like the laser tubes, the sphere seemed almost alive under the lights, which had been positioned to help observers pick up any changes in the physical appearance of the area with the naked eye. In addition to the visible lighting, technicians had scattered spectroscopes and radiation detectors about the large room to monitor any changes that might occur in the room's levels of electromagnetic radiation. The spectroscopes could detect most parts of the spectrum, from the weaker microwaves through the infrared range, and into ultraviolet wavelengths.

At the last minute, Pushkin had even set up equipment that could detect gamma rays and cosmic rays, "though this will be primarily for historical purposes, for the record," he had noted. "If radiation that strong gets loose in here, none of us will live to tell about it."

Sobering, Scott thought, *but nobody ever said making history is easy.* He continued to be amazed at how easily Pushkin had acquiesced to Scott's demand that he orchestrate this experiment to meet a quick deadline. The American had been certain that the Russians would refuse or at least protest, but Pushkin had done neither.

Then Scott looked at his watch and sighed. Despite the incredible progress the team had made setting up the Russian experiment, he was beginning to wonder if they would ever get started, much less change history. So far, nothing had happened—for one reason only: Sergey Pushkin, the only person with the authority to start things rolling, was still puttering around the equipment, making last checks and adjustments to this dial or that setting.

The Russian scientist had talked more in the last fifteen minutes than Scott could recall in the short time he had known the man. It almost seemed that Pushkin wanted to put off the ultimate moment of truth, arguably the most significant juncture in his entire life. Perhaps he just wanted to savor it as long as possible. Or maybe he was so fearful of the outcome—of potential danger, ignominious failure, or some unforeseen complications—that he couldn't bring himself to take the final step.

Whatever the reason for his hesitation, all the others knew that the final call was up to Pushkin. He was the only one who could determine that all systems were "go." He was the only person in the room who could issue that momentous, almost laughably civilized order that the scientists on this project had come to expect from him: "Ready! Proceed!"

Shiro Hiramatsu, wearing heavily tinted protective glasses like everyone else in the area, sat patiently at an expansive console a few meters from the large silver sphere. In this position, he constantly scanned a laser-monitoring panel, including a screen linked to a small moon-cam that gave him a view of the inside of the sphere.

Perhaps the most important responsibility had fallen to Hiramatsu. He had to calibrate an intricate set of reflectors at the center of the sphere, which would amplify the power of the x-ray lasers far into the gamma-ray range. When the hundreds of these "hyped-up" laser beams hit a single, predetermined point in the vacuum, the fireworks would begin. The prospects were staggering. Subatomic structures, which no human had ever witnessed, even with the most sophisticated instruments, might emerge from the mysterious quantum foam.

"What does a cosmic string really look like?" Pushkin had asked at dinner the night before. "How about a muon or boson particle? Will we be able to pull dark matter or dark energy up to our level of reality? Will it be visible? Perhaps we'll have the answers to some of these questions tomorrow."

Now, tomorrow had arrived. The multiple x-ray lasers that Hiramatsu was checking were within minutes, even seconds, of being fired up. His perfectionism gave Scott some comfort because each beam had to land simultaneously at countless finely calibrated points on the array of small x-ray reflectors in the center of the sphere's vacuum. There was only one correct symmetrical geometric configuration, one perfectly orchestrated set of pathways for the lasers to follow. Variation by a fraction of a centimeter in any single beam would almost certainly doom the experiment to failure—and might trigger a quantum catastrophe.

As he waited for Pushkin's signal, which would launch the main event, Scott reflected how unthinkable it was that the Russians had almost proceeded without Hiramatsu. Somehow, they had assumed they could build this device on their own, using the Japanese scientist's research findings and Ruth Goldberg's practical expertise. But in fact, no living scientist other than Hiramatsu could have put this part of the experiment together.

"We will be releasing a level of energy that the world has hardly dreamed of," Hiramatsu had confided somberly to Scott the night before.

Fortunately, Pushkin had recognized that Hiramatsu's expertise was essential. Even so, it had been obvious to Scott that Hiramatsu was worried they might be transgressing frontiers of science that humans were not quite ready to harness. But like the other researchers, who were all at the top of their scientific games, the Japanese was willing to take the risk. An unspoken reason had to be that he was uncertain he would ever be given a second chance, given the monumental cost of the project. Pushkin's voice brought the American congressman back to the present.

"Remember," the Russian was saying for what Scott was sure must be the twentieth time, "empty space is not empty! So don't become complacent. Don't assume that we are directing all this energy at nothing. The tiny point where the lasers will converge contains untapped energy estimated to equal that of millions upon millions of our suns. Countless particles and strange forms of matter dart in and out of that space every moment. It's some of those quantum fluctuations and tiny specks that we intend to capture and expand through the vast heat released in the laser blast."

Ruth Goldberg, who periodically had to wipe traces of condensed fog off her protective glasses, was perched on an elevated chair near Hiramatsu. A thin veil of perspiration covered her face, and the steam from the evaporation process seemed to be the source of her fog problems. Scott wondered why she was the only one who seemed to be sweating so profusely. *Things on her mind other than this experiment?*

Actually, all the participants seemed on edge in one way or another: Goldberg with her drippy forehead . . . Pushkin with his talkativeness . . . Hightower with yawns and bored looks that were beyond the pale, even for his carefully cultivated, laid-back outback persona.

All were aware that they were about to move into entirely new and potentially dangerous scientific territory. To one degree or another, they also realized that they might be part of a dramatic new scientific breakthrough, perhaps on the order of those made by Newton and Einstein. It would take them into a dimension of achievement well beyond the Nobel. On the other hand, in venturing into this uncharted and energy-charged region, they might trigger a reaction that would blow humankind out of this end of the galaxy.

Maybe that was the main thing that was worrying Ruth Goldberg. Her specific assignment was to watch the action in the sphere closely on her monitor. If an encouraging shape seemed to be emerging from the quantum foam, she was supposed to help "catch" it by using a separate set of lasers to create a positively charged electromagnetic field inside the sphere. This field would operate as a kind of invisible outer envelope to contain the shapes and charges that popped into view.

But what if her effort to establish the electromagnetic field failed? For example, what if the field she generated wasn't strong enough, and the quantum fluctuations broke through? No one had any idea of the magnitude of energy that could be released by this experiment. What might happen to the people in this room? Would they be blown out into space? For that matter, what about the integrity of the moon itself?

No one knew the answers to any of these questions. Yet this phase of the operation was entirely in the hands of one Israeli scientist. Scott shook his head. He tried to imagine his own emotional state if he happened to be wrestling with the scientific responsibilities now on Goldberg's plate.

I might be suffering from a serious case of flop sweat myself, he thought, remembering the slang term used by actors to describe their debilitating nervousness before the footlights went on and the curtain went up.

As Goldberg was sweating out her impending role, Hightower, as the resident nuclear engineer, sat poised to work with Pushkin and Bolotov on the delicate task of trying to pull subatomic structures up into the visible arena. It was obvious that Hightower was becoming increasingly impatient. His nervous yawns were occurring more frequently, and the wearied looks were becoming more exaggerated. He reminded Scott of a superbly trained athlete waiting in a locker room, just moments before being summoned to sprint out onto the playing field to vie for a championship. Studied outward composure, but inner turmoil that could erupt without notice at any moment.

Bolotov's expression, in contrast, was completely impassive. The anger that had almost exploded into violence less than two weeks before was not in evidence. Now, he appeared to have a much better understanding of his role. Had Moscow issued new orders?

Unable to answer his own question, Scott turned to look at the console where Pushkin, Bolotov, and Hightower would be working. They faced perhaps the most formidable task. As parts of the quantum foam expanded, they would confront multiple, split-second decisions that had to be made correctly, or crucial opportunities would be lost—and the entire experiment would probably fail.

First, when a shape or form appeared, they had to avoid confusing it with an expanded piece of dust or an extraneous molecule. The process of identification by itself presented a huge challenge—because no one had ever studied a quantum structure before. Only a few hundred subatomic particles had even been detected, and there were multiple theories about what each might look like under extreme magnification. Unfortunately, the most powerful electron or atomic microscopes were unable to provide a picture of the subatomic realm. Also, although huge particle accelerators had been useful in previous experiments on earth, no scientist had access to the incredibly high levels of energy needed to explore this realm in depth. But now, with the fusion power and lasers at their disposal, the moon scientists were about to change all that.

The scientists had already agreed that if they determined that something had actually emerged from the quantum level, they wouldn't worry about trying to make a precise identification on the spot. No point in getting sidetracked, with speculation about whether they were looking at a muon . . . or quark . . . or boson . . . or kaon . . . or fermion . . . or gluon . . . or whatever.

The first order of business would be to stabilize the particle. So long as the material could be kept in view, it might be possible to work with it—to shape and redesign it, and perhaps transform the substance into the long-sought wormhole passageway to another part of space.

According to theoretical mathematics and physics, wormholes would have a tendency to collapse immediately after they appeared. The tension from gravitational forces inside the wormhole was so great that ordinary matter or energy could never keep it open.

But scientists believed the "door" to the space-time passageway *could* be kept open if its walls were lined with what physicists called "exotic" material—antigravity particles or energy that repelled ordinary gravitational pull. In effect, this exotic stuff would have a "negative average energy density" when measured by a special beam of light. Another way of thinking about this exotic material would be that if it could be weighed on a specially calibrated scale, it would have a negative weight—say, minus-one-hundred or minus-one-thousand pounds.

The best candidate for exotic matter seemed to be the smallest, most basic subatomic particle anyone had imagined—the cosmic string. If Pushkin, Bolotov, or Hightower, in working the controls of his subatomic console, decided that such a negative-energy, "exotic" phenomenon had popped into view, they would take immediate steps to spin it with a laser and "paste" it to the inside of the walls of a potential wormhole. At the same time, the positive electromagnetic envelope that Ruth Goldberg was creating with her laser would suspend the entire structure in the center of the sphere.

Or so the theory went. Of course, no one knew for certain whether these ideas would really be proven in practice. Some scientists back on earth believed that research in this area hadn't proceeded far enough to warrant such a far-reaching experiment. But in his briefings with the moon team over the past two weeks, Pushkin had made it clear, he was convinced that sufficient evidence for the theories was visible in tests with particle accelerators and other technology. These findings, he believed, warranted a sweeping conclusion that exotic material existed in abundance somewhere down there in the mysterious ocean of "dark energy," which was thought to fill much of the quantum level. Now, working with Hiramatsu's laser technology, Pushkin seemed on the cusp of proving or disproving much of the mystery and speculation that had surrounded the theory.

Apart from a few technicians, Scott was acutely aware that he was the only American on the scene. Furthermore, he was a physician-turned-congressman—not a physicist, laser specialist, or nuclear engineer. From a purely scientific viewpoint, he barely knew what was going on in the fusion and laser arenas. It was even worse with the wormhole business. Discussion of "subatomic structures," "quantum foam," and "exotic material" often left him scratching his head.

Clearly, the Russians were still far ahead of everyone else in this particular area of research—even ahead of the United States, which was supposed to be the most scientifically advanced nation on earth. With Carl Rensburg gone, American fusion leadership and know-how had slipped significantly. As for laser technology, no nation could match Japan.

In a desperate attempt to calm his growing anxieties and order his thoughts, Scott began to focus on Jeff Hightower, who was tipping back precariously in his chair and at the same time watching Pushkin roam up and down in the laboratory. Hightower seemed a good barometer to monitor the pressure that was building to get this wormhole experiment under way. When Hightower's patience reached its limit and he began to question the delay, Pushkin would have to act.

The Australian was now leaning so far back in his chair that he seemed in serious danger of tipping completely over. An involuntary smile relieved Scott's mounting tension. Though a little embarrassing, a fall wouldn't hurt Hightower much in the minimal moon gravity—and it would certainly get Pushkin's attention. Maybe the Australian was actually *planning* to fall over. But it didn't come to that.

"Let's move it, Sergey old boy!" Hightower called out, his voice slicing through the tension in the room. "It's time to give it a go!"

Various other researchers and technicians had now assumed their assigned posts and finished the final checks on their own computers and other equipment. To Scott, the scene that he was watching from his seat, on a raised platform about twenty feet from the center of the traffic, reminded him of a huge operating room, with nurses and technicians poised to place scalpels and syringes into the hands of the master surgeons and anesthesiologists.

Finally, the Australian's prodding had the desired effect. Pushkin raised his hand and began to move toward a seat between Hightower and Bolotov. "Attention! Attention!" he cried.

With hand still raised, he took his seat and looked around at the scientific team for the last time. "May God save us all!" he said and lowered his hand toward the sphere.

"Ready! Proceed!"

39

At Pushkin's signal, Hiramatsu switched on the lasers—but as long seconds dragged by, nothing happened.

Following the guidelines that had been laid down during the planning stage, the scientists and supporting technicians maintained utter silence. Both Pushkin and Hiramatsu had foreseen possible disruptions if cheers, shouts, or even chattering broke out during a crucial phase of the operation. So they had insisted on a strict discipline of noiselessness, with only Pushkin and Hiramatsu having the authority to speak. The only exception allowed was if someone else needed to signal the onset of a true emergency. Consequently, only the Russian and Japanese experts had unlimited access to a public address system in the laboratory. Anyone else who felt the need to make a general announcement had to press an icon on an instrument panel to communicate.

The silence was nerve-racking. Scott almost wished they had decided to play background music, or at least allow low whispering to break the tension. Now Ruth Goldberg was not the only one suffering from flop sweat; a thin film of perspiration had also covered his forehead and was beginning to run in rivulets down his protective glasses.

Finally, the action erupted.

Streams of bright, white light began to shoot through transparent apertures that had been built into the sides of the sphere. Recent advances in molecular engineering had provided scientists with the tools to fashion windows from altered diamond molecules. They were stronger than the strongest metallic alloy, much less ordinary reinforced glass or plastic. Yet it was possible to see through these quasi-diamond windows with the naked eye, even though the images were somewhat fuzzy. Computer programs attached to the photographic equipment could produce video or still pictures that were far superior to those transmitted by the unaided human eye, and fairly close to the actual shapes and colors of the objects inside.

Using this new technology, the scientists had set up cameras just outside each aperture, as well as an array of minicams inside the sphere. This way, they could be assured of recording at least the first part of the experiment with the on-the-scene internal cameras. If the internal energy in the sphere shattered the inside cameras, they could then shift to the outside cameras for the remainder of the filming.

"A real fireworks display," Scott said to no one in particular, and then caught himself. *Discipline of silence.* But he knew he was not alone in his lapse. Murmurs were breaking out all over the lab.

"Quiet, please!" Pushkin barked.

As if on cue, his command was followed by more intense flashes of light, from blue to red to violet. But probably that was just electromagnetic leakage in the visible spectrum from the potent x-ray laser beams that now were coursing through the sphere. Scott knew that he couldn't see the most powerful electromagnetic waves—the x-rays, and perhaps even gamma rays—that were now bouncing around in the small reflector array that Hiramatsu had set up in the center of the sphere vacuum. The array, with its multiple, opaque-gray panels arranged in a small, spherical configuration inside the large sphere, was clearly visible through both the inside and outside camera transmissions. Scott carefully monitored the action on two separate screens before him. But other than the flashes of visible light, the picture of the true electromagnetic events inside the vacuum remained invisible to the human eye.

Then, as every eye was riveted on the reflector array, it disappeared. At first, Scott thought his TV monitors weren't working. He even tapped one to see if he could get it back on-line.

But then Scott heard Hiramatsu cry out: "It's gone! Where did it go?"

"Dust," Pushkin said. "See the streams of tiny particles circling about inside? They weren't there before. It exploded. There's also something else . . . Dr. Goldberg, please get ready, but only on my command," he added, an urgent tone now in his voice.

Suddenly, one of Scott's two TV screens went blank. The sound of a huge intake of air swept across the room—an involuntary gasp from the twenty or so scientists and technicians in the room. The minicams inside the sphere had apparently gone the way of the x-ray reflector array. What would be next? The sphere itself? *And then us?*

Disconnected, highly disturbing thoughts flooded Scott's mind, thoughts about the realm of reality they were now probing. He remembered some of Pushkin's worries, which he had always assumed were primarily philosophical. Now, he wasn't so sure.

With the inside cameras out of commission, the other cameras, which were set up at various stations outside the sphere, continued to record the events adequately. But the pictures were somewhat distorted because the shots were being filtered through the transparent diamond alloy.

Unfortunately for those scientists and technicians expecting a fireworks display, there was little to see at first. Then, near the center of the sphere, a roiling, undulating, liquidlike mass began to emerge. First it was the size of a marble. Then a golf ball. Then a baseball.

"What is it?" Hiramatsu asked, his voice reverberating over the public address speakers.

"Maybe plasma," Pushkin replied.

From the physics texts he was now constantly studying, Scott remembered that plasma was often referred to by scientists as the fourth state of matter—different from solid, gas, or liquid. In plasma, electrons and photons become unstable, and molecules began to break down. In the midst of this atomic soup, electrons, protons, and neutrons might recombine to form new atoms and molecules.

"The heat in there now is massive," Pushkin said, sweeping the image with a pointer.

"Millions of suns," Hiramatsu murmured.

Pushkin again pointed to the target area for the lasers with his pointer. "All 360 lasers converge in precisely the same spot. The sustained electromagnetic intensity is reaching historic dimensions."

"Yes," Hiramatsu said. "The lasers are still operating in the high x-ray range. That's equivalent to the low gamma-ray level—a new achievement for human science."

"Don't want to stick your hand in there, mate," Hightower cracked. "Wouldn't be in one piece when you pulled it back out. Fried on the barbie."

Pushkin frowned at the unauthorized comment, but said nothing. He was too intent on events inside the sphere to allow himself to become distracted by the Australian's attempts at humor.

Another communal gasp erupted in the room, followed by a ripple of low exclamations and excited murmurs. The ball of plasma was now throwing off a striking display of particles and flashing colors. Then, the colors began to subside, and rough, grainy features began to appear.

"Dr. Goldberg, it's time!" Pushkin ordered. "Engage your lasers!"

Ruth immediately pressed icons on her console to activate another set of lasers, which would create a positive magnetic field envelope for any emerging subatomic structures. At first, the multiple x-ray beams that were now crisscrossing the sphere were invisible to the naked eye. But with the adjustments Pushkin was making to the TV monitor's computer program, the configuration of the electromagnetic shield soon became apparent. To Scott, the field seemed to resemble a moving, mostly transparent cloud that billowed and surged around the small but growing plasma ball. Increasingly, the ball displayed a rough, undigested mixture of solid materials and strange shapes.

"What are we seeing?" Hiramatsu asked.

"Unsure," Pushkin replied tersely. "Could still just be plasma. Could be the beginning of foam."

Scott's gaze was now riveted on the plasma ball. If Pushkin was correct, and quantum foam was really emerging, they might be about to witness the main event.

Then he wondered if he had blinked. The ball had doubled in size without his seeing how it happened.

"Shiro, that branch on the right," Pushkin cried. "Looks like a pair of stubby prongs. Like a cooking utensil. See?" He pointed with his cursor. "Cut it out. I'll get that cylinder on the other side." This time, he indicated a skinny, cylindrical structure on the opposite side of the steaming ball.

The two men worked in almost total silence for what seemed like minutes, but what Scott knew was a period of about eight seconds. He had decided to time some of the events as they occurred.

"Bolotov!" Pushkin said, his voice becoming more strident and excited. "The strings, the webwork emerging on top! See it, like a thin spiderweb? Pull it out in one piece. No shredding. Those may be the strings. The cosmic strings. Goldberg, pay close attention to your outer envelope! If you're not careful, the strings may tear it apart."

Scott was glad now that he had listened closely to Pushkin's explanations and had read as much as he had in the dry, boring physics books the Russian had recommended. Now, the readings he had done didn't seem boring at all.

He immediately understood that the "prongs" and the "cylinder" might be subatomic structures that could be transformed into wormholes. In fact, they might *already* be tiny wormholes that were now expanding under the laser heat to human scale. The "spiderwebs" that Bolotov was manipulating so carefully could be the negative-energy cosmic strings—the exotic matter that was required to stabilize the wormholes and keep them open for human use.

But, of course, nobody's sure about any of this, Scott pondered, shaking his head. For all any of them knew, this experiment was a complete exercise in futility. Then he looked at the boiling, bubbling mass in the sphere, which now almost filled his monitor—and out of nowhere, a disturbing thought struck him.

Are human beings supposed to enter this unmapped region? Are we trying to gain access to forbidden territory, where only tragedy can await trespassers?

He quickly shook the notion off. That line of thinking was completely unscientific. You couldn't put limits on scientific inquiry. At least he'd always been taught that, and nothing had occurred so far in his life to give him any reason to change his opinion. Education was potentially the salvation of humankind, wasn't it? It was human know-how and power that had put them up here on the moon and moved them to the edge of solving energy problems for centuries to come. What else in the universe could compare with the human mind and creativity?

"Spin it, Bolotov! Spin it!"

Pushkin's cries jarred him back into the present. The skinny cylinder and double-ended prongs had quadrupled in size under the laser heat, so that now, they were each about a meter in length, with their endings as wide as dinner plates. The cylinder had broken almost entirely free from the quantum ball, but an end of the prongs was still firmly embedded in the stuff.

Bolotov was struggling to catch up with the process. He had slowly teased a large clump of spidery strings out of the pulsating quantum ball and was now moving them outward, toward the positive magnetic envelope that Goldberg was still holding in place less than a meter away.

"I think it's a little too early," the younger Russian said, never taking his eyes off the strings.

"We can't wait!" Pushkin cried again. "The ends of the structures are beginning to collapse. If this is exotic matter, we must use it *now*. Otherwise, we lose everything. Use your lasers! Spin it—*now!*"

Scott could hear a low moan coming from Bolotov's direction, but he knew the man would comply with orders. Sure enough, as Scott watched his monitor, the webwork of strings began to move. Slowly at first, then faster and faster, until they began to swirl around and around the boiling ball and the two enlarged atomic structures like a miniature Ferris wheel moving at Mach speed.

"Hightower, there are more strings emerging from the foam!" Pushkin said, placing his pointer at a spot toward the bottom of the foam ball. "Capture them! Move them out toward Bolotov's wheel!"

The Australian, not in the least bored now, immediately used the lasers at his disposal to pull and cut the other set of subatomic spiderwebs off the shimmering ball. Then he pushed them up toward the spinning strings controlled by the younger Russian.

"Now spread them out!" Pushkin ordered. "Spread the strings out so that they surround and cover the two objects!"

Gradually, Bolotov and Hightower, with Pushkin's close direction, created a thinner coating out of the spinning strings, which enabled them to construct a kind of tubelike roof around the cylinder and prongs.

An uneasy but expectant silence settled on the room again, as Pushkin made other adjustments in the various lasers. Finally, his shoulders seemed to relax, and Scott was almost certain he saw a glint of satisfaction in the man's eyes, even though the men were about twenty feet apart.

"We've done it," the Russian finally said. "I think we've actually done it."

He raised no objections, no demands for silence, when a deafening cheer filled the laboratory. Then he raised his hand.

"But let's be cautious," he said. "Let's be certain. Hiramatsu, can you measure the energy density of the strings?"

The Japanese scientist nodded and switched on a special laser-related measuring device, a controllable, finely calibrated beam of light that he had invented specifically for this purpose. Because the forms and structures inside the sphere seemed to have stabilized, Pushkin was obviously convinced that the strings Bolotov and Hightower had spun around the quantum ball and its subatomic structures were negative-density exotic matter. But the only way to tell for sure was to measure the material at the speed of light.

In moments, Hiramatsu turned to Pushkin. "It has negative density. They must really be cosmic strings. And they must be exotic."

Another cheer broke out, but this time, Pushkin signaled for silence. "Good, but we mustn't waste time. We have no idea how long the exotic material will hold up. And if it collapses, we lose those two objects."

He turned to Ruth Goldberg. "Now, we must open a hole in your magnetic envelope so that we can probe the ends of those two objects. But make your incision away from the exotic material, at one end of the tube Bolotov and Hightower have created. And move slowly."

He paused and rubbed the back of his neck. "I expect the exotic material to keep the structures stable as you work, but we don't know. And above all, we must not interfere with the exotic field itself. Understand?"

"Yes," Goldberg said, tension lacing her voice.

She immediately began to rotate the computer image on the screen so that everyone was now looking down one mouth of the tube created by the spinning exotic material. Then, to "cut" a hole, she began to disengage the lasers on the tube-mouth side of the structure. One by one, she took them off-line. Finally, the computer-enhanced imagery displayed her handiwork as a cloudy magnetic-field envelope with a clear opening that led directly to the first enlarged atomic structure, the thin cylinder.

"Good! Excellent!" Pushkin exclaimed. "And now, to the heart of the operation."

With Hiramatsu's assistance, Pushkin began to probe inside Goldberg's magnetic envelope with another set of laser tools. Hiramatsu and his scientists had fashioned these so that there was actually an end to the lasers, reminiscent of the imaginary light-saber weapons used by the Jedi knights in the old *Star Wars* movies. In other words, the laser beams didn't extend indefinitely in one direction but were fitted with modulators that gave them a specific length-range. With this technology, Pushkin could limit the extent to which he probed into the strange space. An ordinary laser beam could have penetrated deeply into the structures and might have destabilized or destroyed them.

Moving closer and closer to the end of the cylinder—which had now drifted entirely out of the quantum foam so that the entire object was visible—Pushkin tested the surrounding area extensively with his laser probes. Then, he said, "Ten degrees' rotation to the right."

A computer specialist rotated the mouth of the exotic tube in the required direction so that the end of the cylinder was facing almost directly toward the monitor viewers.

Then, "Three degrees to the right."

Again, another slight shift.

Then, "One to the left. Perfect!"

Everyone watched expectantly as Pushkin moved his laser probes in micromillimeter steps toward the end of the subatomic cylinder.

"Contact!" he said, indicating that he had actually touched the structure with his probe. "Seems solid. Hard."

He tried several other locations on the end of the cylinder with similar results.

He took a deep breath and in a strained voice said, "All right, we'll excavate."

With the laser now spinning something like a drill, Pushkin pushed the end of the electromagnetic instrument against the face of the cylinder. When he withdrew, a slight hole was clearly visible.

"Seems to be solid," Hightower volunteered. "I'm not sure I'd go any deeper. Might crack the thing."

"Also, it seems unlikely that this would be a wormhole," Hiramatsu volunteered. "By theory, they are supposed to be open, correct?"

"By theory, yes," Pushkin replied. "But we are beyond theory here." The Russian hesitated and then nodded. "Still, I agree. That's enough for this object. Let's try the other one."

The computer technicians rotated the screen image so that the observers in the laboratory were now looking down the end of one of the two prongs. The base of this structure was still firmly fixed somewhere inside the quantum ball, the surface of which continued to roil and billow, like an unsettled sea.

"Wonder where it ends?" Scott asked a Canadian scientist who had moved next to him and was viewing the action on the American's monitor. "The prong-thing, I mean."

"No telling," his companion replied. "But since it hasn't moved for a while, I'd say it has roots in there. Maybe very deep roots."

"Quiet, please!" Pushkin ordered, glancing with an annoyed expression in Scott's direction. "This is the crucial moment! Concentration and focus are essential!"

Though stung, Scott knew the Russian was right. They could afford no distractions at this point. So he settled into a chastened silence and watched closely as the Russian began to move his laser probe toward the end of the pronglike structure.

Once again, nothing happened as he swept the area around the structure with his instrument. Then he made contact with the gray-blue, opaque end of the object, which seemed more or less circular in shape, at least when the computer image was viewed with the unaided eye.

"Nothing registers," Hiramatsu said. "Are you sure you're in contact?"

"We are, according to all our calibrations," Pushkin replied. "Right, Goldberg?"

"That's correct," she replied, tension gripping her voice. "You should be touching it now."

"Then let's go deeper," Pushkin said.

Scott could see no change from the computer monitor, but Goldberg announced, "You're past the face of the structure. You're inside."

"Any responses from any of the instruments?" Pushkin called out. A chorus of voices answered in the negative.

"Then we go even deeper," he said.

Now, Scott could tell that the laser probe was growing shorter and shorter. Obviously, Pushkin was moving farther and farther into the face of the prong.

"Any resistance at all?" Hiramatsu asked.

"None whatsoever," Pushkin replied, excitement now permeating his words. "It's like empty space. Let's withdraw and see if there's been any effect on the probe."

He pulled the laser tool out, but a thorough examination revealed no damage. In fact, no change in the instrument at all.

Pushkin took another deep breath. "I think this may be it," he said quietly. "I think this may be a bridge. An Einstein-Rosen bridge."

"A wormhole!" Hightower exclaimed, using the more popular term. "It's really a wormhole?"

"Perhaps it is," Pushkin replied tentatively.

The cheers and applause were more muted this time as the enormity of the event sank in. If this was really their long-sought wormhole, where did they go from here?

"But we'll have to do further tests," Pushkin cautioned, causing the enthusiasm to decrease further. "And we'll have to do them now. Again, we have no idea how long we can maintain stability. This will be a long day."

Scott looked at his watch. They had been at this experiment for nearly five hours, and signs of fatigue were starting to show in many of the scientists and technicians. He knew that the emotional tension had taken at least as great a toll as the actual work.

Although he wasn't participating directly in the technical part of the work, he was acutely aware of his position as administrative leader of the top moon scientists. So he had arranged to have food and refreshments brought in on a few moments' notice—and this seemed the opportune time.

"Professor Pushkin, it's time to feed the hungry hordes," he called out.

Pushkin waved him off at first, but then Scott walked over and pressed his point in a low voice. "Look, Sergey, if these people don't have something to eat and drink, they're going to start hallucinating. You're going to lose them mentally. I know what I'm talking about. Not everybody can run on fumes like you do."

Reluctantly, Pushkin agreed, and Scott quickly notified the food services team—an action that triggered a discreet thumbs-up acclamation from most of the scientists and technicians.

"But it will be a working lunch," Pushkin announced sternly. "We can't take time off to eat. This moment may come and go quickly. Remember Esau."

Scott and the scientist standing next to him looked at each other in puzzlement. Then an extraneous memory from one of Scott's old Sunday school lessons on the book of Genesis clicked into his consciousness, and he nodded.

"What does he mean?" the scientist whispered.

"Esau sold his birthright to Jacob for a bowl of soup," Scott said with a wry smile. "Obviously, our Russian professor doesn't want us to lose this wormhole the same way."

All eyes had now returned to the monitors, as Pushkin began to probe even more deeply into the end of the prong structure with his laser. He had recalibrated the length of the beam so that it was now three times as long as the original. Slowly, he inserted the electromagnetic ray into the mouth, but even when the opening had swallowed almost the entire length of the beam, there was still no resistance.

"Nothing," Hiramatsu said, looking at the instruments. "It's as though we're moving through nothing. Lasers don't behave that way when they're cutting through something."

"Shall we lengthen the laser probe again?" Goldberg asked.

"No need, I think," Pushkin said. "But I would like to try several different electromagnetic intensities."

With Hiramatsu overseeing the operation this time, they inserted the laser probe and proceeded to move it through several wavelength ranges of the spectrum—from the weaker infrared wave, to the visible, the ultraviolet, and finally the x-ray range. Still, there was no measurable response on any instruments.

"Can we take it safely above the x-ray level?" Pushkin asked Hiramatsu.

The Japanese scientist shrugged. "The probe has been tested for gamma rays, but not cosmic rays. The cosmic range may be too powerful. We could lose the probe itself, and I can't say what an exploding laser probe would do to the inside of that structure."

Pushkin nodded. "Let's try the gamma-ray range, just short of what you've tested in designing the probe. Then, we'll move on to the next phase."

Once again, even as the instruments showed that the laser had reached the gamma-ray range, the highest of any working laser technology in history, nothing happened. No recorded measurements. No response at all.

"That could be extremely important information for the future," Hightower commented. "If we ever have to employ technology that powerful, we'll at least know this particular structure can handle it."

Pushkin stood up abruptly, and at first, Scott thought the man was finally taking a stretch. But he quickly realized he should have known better.

"The disk, Bolotov," he said to his colleague. "It's time to try the disk."

What are they up to? Scott thought, alarm bells now going off in his head.

He watched as the younger Russian reached under his console, pulled out a dull metal container about three inches in diameter, and removed an unusual-looking disk, which he handed to Pushkin. Scott immediately recognized the disk as the latest example of nanotechnology. Just one of these new disks was supposed to have the capacity to store every piece of human knowledge several times over. Scott had seen only a few of these in highly classified settings at the Pentagon, but they were hard to forget because of their flashy gold color and their relatively small size when compared with regular computer disks.

Scott cleared his throat and took a step toward the main control consoles where the top scientists were working. "Just a second. What are you going to do?"

"It's none of your affair!" Bolotov said, moving to intercept Scott.

"It *is* my affair if issues of safety are involved," Scott shot back.

Pushkin stood and waved both of them back. "There is no danger, Scott," he said in a calm, friendly tone. "This disk just represents the next step in our experiment. We now know that this enlarged subatomic structure has an opening. It seems to be a passageway, and we have no idea where it leads. So we plan to use this disk to probe still deeper, farther than any laser can go. And the disk will contain a message."

"A message?" Scott asked, a bewildered expression on his face. "What kind of message?"

"A message like the *Voyager* probe you Americans sent into deep space decades ago. Information about our culture. Music. Samples of the world's languages. Even a copy of the human genome."

"You're expecting some alien civilization to pick this up?" Scott asked.

Pushkin smiled. "It's—how do you say?—a big long shot. After all, there has been no response to your *Voyager*. But who knows? Perhaps this time, things will be different. And we'll never know, will we, unless we try?"

Unable to articulate a reasonable objection, Scott finally muttered his assent and returned to his seat to watch the procedure. He had a vague feeling of unease about this, and he preferred to go more slowly. But he could offer no compelling scientific reason for them not to transmit the message.

Of course, as a nonphysicist, he could follow only the broad outlines of what was going on. The orders that Pushkin was issuing to Goldberg and Hiramatsu for the complex procedure were so technical Scott soon became lost in the scientific jargon. But at least he could see clearly the results of what the scientists were doing.

As he watched, Bolotov inserted the disk into a gray metallic case, which had apparently been designed to protect it from the radiation inside the sphere. Then, the Russian placed the metallic case, with disk inside, into an entry slot built into the side of the sphere. The slot resembled a floppy disk drive in an ordinary computer.

With the disk firmly in place in the outside slot, Goldberg, using what might best be described as laser pincers, opened a small door inside the sphere and removed the case containing the disk. Then she transported the package slowly toward the mouth of the pronglike structure that Pushkin had been testing.

"Very careful, very slow," Pushkin directed. "Don't get the disk near the exotic matter at the edges of the envelope. Even with the protective container, that would destroy it. Move it directly toward the mouth of the prongs."

Finally, the disk case, which seemed literally to be floating in space under the power of the laser pincers, reached the edge of the prong mouth. Goldberg stopped the movement of the laser and waited.

"All right, now move it slowly into the opening," Pushkin said tensely.

Goldberg edged the disk into the aperture until it disappeared from sight, seemingly swallowed by the foggy, immaterial quintessence that guarded the opening. Still holding on to the closed laser-pincers, Goldberg moved her laser instrument to a depth of about a half-meter into the hole, and looked at Pushkin again for instructions.

"All right, give the disk a push and release it," he commanded.

She manipulated some icons on her console, and then withdrew the laser pincer back into view of the monitor. The disk and its container were gone.

"Now what?" Hightower asked after a brief silence.

"Now, we wait," Pushkin replied, sitting down and picking up a sandwich that had been placed on the table next to him. "We wait. And perhaps we pray."

They didn't have to wait long.

Scott managed to get only one mouthful of his sandwich into his mouth before the inside of the sphere exploded before their eyes. In one flash, all the strange structures, including the prong that everyone had thought was a wormhole, disappeared. All that remained was the clean, uncluttered inside of the empty sphere.

40

Nearly twenty-four hours after the disaster in the Russian lab, the six top members of the science team sat glumly around a large table in the main, ground-floor conference room in Energy City's living module. Meals that had been brought in to them by the food services section lay half-eaten in front of them.

"So it seems there's nothing we can do," Hiramatsu said, summing up the hours of discussion that had gone before.

"Apparently not," Pushkin said, shaking his head slowly.

It had been obvious at the beginning of this meeting that the unexplained collapse and disappearance of the phenomenon in the sphere had profoundly shaken the Russian physicist. All had agreed that the two-pronged structure had almost certainly contained a wormhole, or something very much like it.

To come so close to success, yet be unable to grasp it, must have been devastating for Pushkin, Scott mused. But as disappointed as the Russian had been at first, he had become visibly calmer as the new day's conversation had progressed. Now, Scott thought, Pushkin was responding almost philosophically to the failure. For someone who had so much at stake, the relatively quick emotional recovery was remarkable.

"There seem to have been no mistakes in our execution," Hiramatsu noted.

"No mistakes at all," Scott confirmed. "I've already interviewed everyone who was present. And each of you has questioned all the scientists and technicians under your supervision. So some people have been examined two, even three times. It's been a short but very thorough investigation. More certainly needs to be done. But at this point, there's absolutely no indication of human fault or error."

"What about the smell?" Hightower asked.

Everyone knew that he was referring to a strange, cloying aroma, a mixture of heavy sweetness and singed metal, which had wafted out into the lab when the sphere had been opened after the failed experiment.

"Was the atmosphere inside the sphere analyzed?" the Australian pressed.

"We brought some technicians in, but they couldn't find anything unusual in the air," Scott said. "They speculated that the intense heat inside the sphere may have melted some of the protective metal lining and caused the metallic aroma. Of course, the smell was gone by the time they arrived. No explanation for the sweetness, though."

"Quantum flowers," Hiramatsu said, and for the first time that morning, everyone chuckled. Because the Japanese laser engineer rarely joked, every attempt he made at humor somehow seemed funnier than it actually was.

"Still, we have no leads at all as to the cause of the accident?" Hightower asked. He seemed to be the only one who hadn't laughed.

"None," Scott said. He was puzzled that Hightower couldn't seem to get it into his head that the experiment had failed.

"It's just fate," Hiramatsu said. "Karma."

"Perhaps something deeper," Pushkin said cryptically.

"You're sure there's no possibility of reviving this thing?" Hightower pressed earnestly, no trace of the Aussie banter in his tone. "Any way to put the pieces back together? I think we should do anything we can—"

"Yes," Bolotov interrupted, "maybe there *is* something we can do. Some way to use the equipment to try once more."

"We lack the resources," Pushkin replied, a note of resignation in his voice. "Some of the x-ray laser mechanisms were burned out. Dr. Hiramatsu's x-ray reflectors disintegrated. They would have to be rebuilt, at great cost and effort."

"And remember the time factor," Scott reminded them. "We agreed on a deadline to begin our energy production. Many of the same facilities we used for this experiment now have to be employed with the moon-to-earth laser. The needs of the folks back home are now our priority."

"I disagree!" Bolotov insisted. "Our success with the experiment demands that we try again! We could eliminate some steps this time. Use less laser power . . ."

"Vlad may have a point," Goldberg said. "Maybe we could cut some corners and have another go at it."

"We really have no choice but to return to the energy project," Scott said quietly but firmly.

"Circumstances have changed with our success," Bolotov insisted.

Scott was mildly amused that Bolotov kept referring to the disaster in the Russian lab as a success. He imagined that he could detect the voice of Prime Minister Martov in the background, giving the younger Russian his cues.

"Now, Vladimir," Scott said, almost slipping into an ironic use of Goldberg's "Vlad" but thinking better of it. "I wouldn't really call what happened in the lab an unqualified success. Maybe we learned something, but we certainly didn't achieve what we hoped to. And we all agreed to clear ground rules before we got involved with this wormhole business. You don't change an agreement just because you feel like it—"

A rumbling and shaking of the structure beneath them cut off his response. Cups, plastic plates, and uneaten food bounced onto the floor of the conference room. Scott started to stand but lost his balance and almost fell.

"Moonquake!" Hightower cried.

"Impossible!" Pushkin said. "The moon's geology is inactive."

"Asteroid?" Goldberg asked.

"Possible," Bolotov replied, striding unsteadily over to the only window in the room and scanning the lunar surface.

"Or an explosion," Scott said. "What other work's going on around here now? Any nuclear testing?"

"Nothing's scheduled," Hightower said, picking up an intercom to check the condition of his fission facility, which lay some distance away from the main Energy City modules. After a few seconds' conversation on the phone, he turned back to the group. "My people say they felt only a slight tremor, and they're not that far away. Seems we're near the epicenter."

Ruth Goldberg bounded slowly over to the door that led into the living module's lobby and pulled it open. "It's the same smell!" she cried, falling back a step into the room.

"What's that?" Scott replied.

"Hot metal and rotting roses," she said, using terms she had used in one of their earlier discussions to describe the aroma that had filled the lab when the sphere was opened just after the failed experiment.

"Wormhole perfume," Hightower said, a smile now back on his face. "Maybe we're not finished with science fiction after all, Scotty my boy."

41

Though the lapsed time was less than ten minutes, it seemed to take hours for the six team members to rush out of the conference room, board the moonwalk conveyor to the factory module, and reach the entrance to the Russian laboratory. Bolotov was on the verge of sliding the door open, but Scott Andrews put his hand on the panel.

"Wait!" he cautioned. "We don't have any idea what's happened in there. There may not even be any atmosphere."

He had already checked with Secretary Archibald Martin, but the Energy City administrator was as uncertain as they were about the source of the disturbance. Scott pulled out his pocket digital assistant and began talking face-to-face with Martin once again. "Archie, can you pull up a picture of the inside of the Russian lab on our monitors?"

Martin spoke to an assistant sitting next to him, and almost immediately, Scott was looking at a small picture of the inside of the lab on a split screen on his own portable monitor.

"Are you getting the picture?" Martin asked.

"Yes, yes," Scott replied. "Scan the area for me."

He watched the picture as the camera inside the lab swept slowly over the area. By this time, all the other team members had also pulled out their communicators and were watching the surveillance themselves.

"How's the atmosphere in there?" Scott asked.

"Everything seems normal, except that we are picking up some extra carbon in the air," Martin replied. "And the balance of oxygen and carbon dioxide is a little off. But it's breathable."

"Something burning," Hightower said.

"Yes," Martin said. "And we're getting similar readings on the ground floors throughout the outpost, though not as strong."

"We smelled it," Goldberg said.

"No! No!" Pushkin shouted so loudly that everyone was frozen to the spot. "Go back!"

"What's wrong?" Scott asked.

"It's changed!" the Russian scientist cried, looking wide-eyed into his monitor. "The sphere! It's not the same!"

By now, the cameras inside the lab had moved past the site where the sphere had been situated. Even though Scott had only glanced at the spot, he had to admit that something hadn't looked quite right.

"Archie, go back! Give us a picture of the center of the lab, where that sphere is located!" Scott ordered.

Sure enough, when the cameras retraced their path, they confirmed Pushkin's observation—and more. In fact, the huge metallic globe hadn't changed. It had completely disappeared. Now, another spherical object was in its place.

"Zoom in!" Scott said. "As close as you can get, Arch."

Scott had now adjusted his monitor image so that the pictures of the strange new object filled the screen. He also fiddled with his controls to produce as clear a picture as possible.

"It almost looks like a large, cleaned-up version of that subatomic structure you created yesterday," Scott said.

"Yes, very interesting," Pushkin replied, his mind obviously consumed by the video picture he was viewing. "Can we get an even closer look, Mr. Secretary?"

"Afraid not," Archibald Martin replied. "That's the maximum for our cameras."

"Appears to be the same, prong-shaped structure, and a similar quantum foam ball," Hiramatsu observed. "But when you compare the scale with nearby structures, I would estimate this is about ten times as large. The ends of the structures, through which we inserted the disk, are wide enough for a man to walk through, standing up."

"Something on the floor," Scott said.

"Looks like dust," Hightower replied, squinting into his own monitor. "White dust."

"Remains of the sphere?" Scott asked.

"Perhaps," Pushkin said. "But we can learn that only through an on-site examination."

"Mr. Secretary, any reason you can see why we shouldn't go in there?" Scott asked Martin.

"No," Martin replied. "I'd just suggest caution. Our instruments may not be picking up everything. For example, we have a limited ability to gauge radiation levels. You people were ranging up into the gamma-ray levels with your equipment. Who knows—you may even have cosmic waves in there now. Our technology isn't advanced enough to do adequate measurements at those levels."

"Good advice," Scott said. "Sergey, any thoughts?"

Pushkin pondered a moment, looking down at the door panel in front of them. Scott imagined that he could almost see the man's mind working.

Finally, the Russian said, "It is likely that this is the same subatomic structure, possibly a wormhole. If so, that means exotic matter is stabilizing the entire object. Any contact with that negative-energy-density material would be fatal, perhaps for all of us at this facility. But because we lack the proper instruments, we cannot know for certain. As a result, I believe that one of us should enter first, just to be certain that all is safe inside."

A warning bell went off somewhere in Scott's head. The mental alarm became almost deafening when Bolotov volunteered: "I shall be the one."

"Wait, I think two of us would be better," Scott said, rather weakly.

"No point in two!" Bolotov replied brusquely. "Why risk two when one is sufficient? It's logical for me to do it. I know the experiment, yet I'm expendable."

"He's right," Pushkin agreed. "If there's a problem, he'll pick it up as fast as anyone."

Then he put a hand on his countryman's shoulder. "I would never sacrifice another in place of myself. But I agree that we cannot afford to lose any of the other scientists on the team. They will all play irreplaceable roles with Energy Project Omega."

Scott almost responded that he was as expendable as Bolotov. But he knew what the immediate—and unanswerable—objection from the others would be. Namely, that he had no background in physics and wouldn't be nearly as equipped to pick up potential dangers as the junior Russian scientist. So reluctantly, Scott assented to the arrangement, with the understanding that as soon as Bolotov determined that the air was truly breathable and radiation levels were safe, the others would enter without delay.

Within a few minutes, Bolotov had been fitted with a radiation suit and instruments that could provide an adequate evaluation of radiation levels. Then the others stood back as he prepared to open the outer panel to the short passageway that led to the lab door.

"Good luck, Vlad old mate," Hightower said, slapping the Russian on the shoulder.

Scott thought he detected some sort of smile through the visor on Bolotov's protective helmet. Then the Russian slid open the outer panel and closed it behind him. Scott heard a clear click, and again a warning signal sounded in his mind. He glided over to the door and tried it. It was locked.

"What's he doing?" Scott cried, rattling the door in frustration.

The others gathered around him, puzzlement and consternation evident on their faces.

"What's going on here, Pushkin?" Scott demanded, looking over his shoulder at the senior Russian. "What are you two up to?"

"I don't know," the elder Russian replied, a frown wrinkling his brow. "Perhaps . . . I don't know . . . but perhaps Dr. Bolotov worries that we might enter before he determines all is safe."

"In your dreams!" Scott spat out. He immediately adjusted his computer communicator so that the Energy City mayor was in view again. "Archie, do you have a speaker that Bolotov can hear inside the lab?"

"I think so," Martin replied, and after a few seconds, they all heard the secretary's voice reverberating over their own monitors: "Attention, Dr. Bolotov! Attention, Dr. Bolotov!"

On their split screens, they could see Bolotov moving slowly through the lab, directly toward the strange new structure that had appeared in place of the sphere. But he gave no indication that he heard Martin speaking to him.

"He's ignoring us!" Scott said, anger now welling up inside. "Archie, can you patch me in on the PA system?"

"Yes, I believe so . . ."

Within seconds, Scott was talking directly to the Russian: "Listen, Bolotov, this is an order! You stay away from that thing and come back here and open the door for us! Do you understand?"

No response. Bolotov continued to move slowly toward the enlarged prongs without so much as glancing back toward one of the cameras.

"You—" Scott couldn't use the language he wanted to because he knew that if he appeared to have lost control, he might also lose all claim to authority and leadership on the team. So he took a deep breath and tried to come across as angry but firm.

"Listen to me, Dr. Bolotov! Unless you return immediately, you will be removed from this team. Under my authority as the leader of this project, I'll send you back to earth. Do you understand me?"

The Russian stopped his forward movement, but he didn't turn around or acknowledge anything that was being said to him. He was now standing about ten meters from the object. Scott could see his helmet swivel to the right and then the left.

"Perhaps he can't hear you," Pushkin said. "His earphones may not be working."

"Dr. Bolotov, I mean what I said," Scott repeated, ignoring Pushkin's attempt at an excuse. "I want you to turn around and come back here."

Simultaneously, the congressman motioned to two of several technicians who had drifted near the door. He shut off his microphone and ordered the technician: "Break open that panel! Fast!"

As the man and woman worked on the door, Scott switched his microphone back on. Bolotov was now standing like a statue in front of the structure. "Dr. Bolotov, you could be endangering everyone in this facility. Unless you return immediately, you will be placed in confinement and shipped back to earth."

Scott looked around and saw five of Secretary Martin's security guards heading toward him. "The security guards have arrived, Bolotov. I mean what I said. If you—"

"The radiation levels are acceptable, at least at this distance," Bolotov interrupted in a detached tone, as though he had heard nothing Scott had said. He held up a portable radiation detector to make his point.

Then he removed his protective helmet and placed it under his arm. His short, white-blond hair and thick, muscular neck were clearly visible over the monitor. "Air is fine, too, though the smell is still here."

He looked around and then faced directly toward the strange object. "It should be safe for me to proceed farther," he said, and took a tentative half step closer to the subatomic structure.

"Stop, Bolotov!" Scott shouted.

"Yes, Vladimir, you must go no closer!" Pushkin said.

At Pushkin's command, Bolotov stopped.

So he can hear us. No excuses now. Scott also thought it peculiar that Pushkin had failed to take his side up to this point. Maybe he had wanted to gather as much intelligence as possible for the motherland, but now he realized that things could begin to get dicey. No telling what might happen if Bolotov got too close or made contact with that weird object.

At that moment, the technicians broke the lock and pulled the panel back. Scott moved in front of them and took a few steps down the passage until he reached the door that led directly into the lab. Locked again.

"Okay, same thing here," Scott said, gesturing at the two technicians. "Break it."

Within seconds, the final door lock had been disengaged.

"Now you get back, and get the security force up here," Scott said to the technicians.

He stood back until the five security guards had crowded into the passageway with him, their weapons at the ready. They were armed with stun guns that could quickly knock a perpetrator unconscious.

"I want you to spread out next to me when we go in there, and you act only on my command, got that?" he barked to the small squad. "I hope I can talk him out of there, but we have to be prepared for the worst.

"This guy's tough and athletic. Probably better trained in hand-to-hand than any of you, and I have every reason to think he knows how to kill. So it'll probably take several of you to bring him down. I hope it doesn't come to that, but you have to be ready for anything."

"Anything else we should know if we have to take him out, Dr. Andrews?" the squad leader asked.

"The main mission is for at least two of you to get between him and that object that's throbbing in the middle of the floor—the thing he's looking at," Scott said. "That thing is very dangerous. Under no circumstances are you to let him get any nearer to it. And you're not to get any closer than necessary yourselves, and certainly do *not* touch it. Is that perfectly clear?"

Tense nods all around assured Scott that the time had arrived to move. He pushed back the inner door and burst into the Russian lab, with the five security guards on his heels. The squad members moved quickly and smoothly in the low gravity, their weapons held at the ready. Obviously, they had been well trained for just such an emergency as this. Scott had some trouble keeping up with them, but soon, they were all within ten feet of Bolotov, who was still facing the structure, almost as though he had heard nothing of the commotion behind him.

"Vladimir!" Scott called out in a firm, but what he hoped was a friendly, tone. At the same time, he motioned to the squad members to begin to circle the Russian. "Vladimir, you have to come back with us now. If you'll just back up slowly, and join the other scientists, we'll forget this happened, okay? Now just back up . . ."

Vladimir Bolotov still didn't turn or speak. Annoyed, Scott was on the verge of ratcheting up his intensity and issuing a direct threat when he looked down at the floor in front of the Russian and muffled a gasp. Less than two feet from Bolotov's right foot was a small object, which looked exactly like the disk case that Pushkin had inserted into the wormhole that had collapsed on them.

Scott looked back up at Bolotov, who was apparently unaware of the container. Instead, the Russian seemed so mesmerized by the new structure before him that he was uninterested in anything else. He nodded his head in the direction of the open end of the now greatly enlarged prong. Scott followed the line of Bolotov's gaze and saw that the irregular circular opening at the end of the prong was larger and more striking than they had thought when viewing it outside the lab, over their monitors. The thing was at least ten feet in diameter. The face of the opening, reminiscent of the smooth waters of some fuzzy, blue-gray pool, seemed to shimmer as he watched it.

"Vladimir," Scott said with as much gentleness as he could muster, "it's time to leave the room. Now just come on over and—"

"I understand," Bolotov said.

"Good," Scott replied, assuming that the Russian was finally recovering his senses. "Now let's—"

"I understand perfectly," Bolotov said again, in such a detached tone that an odd thought crossed Scott's mind, a notion that the man wasn't answering him at all, but rather was responding to someone or something else.

Suddenly, Bolotov dropped his protective headgear on the floor, threw his portable radiation detector to one side, and sprinted directly toward the object.

"No!" Scott yelled.

The security team was immobilized, too stunned to take a step or lift an arm.

Scott took two quick steps toward the shimmering mouth and screamed, "No, Bolotov! No!"

The public address system began to crackle, as Secretary Martin's shout also echoed through the room:

"Stop! Dr. Bolotov—"

But they were too late. All that any of the onlookers could do was watch helplessly as the younger Russian reached the lip of the foggy, blue-gray window, leaped into the air, and plunged headfirst through the yawning mouth. For a fraction of a second, his body seemed suspended in midair, and then he appeared to shrink in size. In an instant, he became a faraway pinprick and vanished from sight. Simultaneously, a blinding flash and a sound like the roar of a tornado knocked Scott and the guards onto their backs.

Rubbing his eyes to clear his vision, Scott struggled back to his feet, but he was unprepared for the sight that greeted him. Everything—Bolotov, the quantum ball, and its strange, pronglike wormhole with its mysterious mouth—had disappeared without a trace. Only the small disk container remained, resting lonely and unimposing at the same spot on the floor.

42

Sergey Pushkin sat in a despondent heap on the floor of his room. Neither the periodic knocks on the door, nor the buzzing of his intercom—which had subsided and finally ceased—had roused him. At first, the hunger pangs from a short-term, self-enforced fast had provided a distraction. But now the waves of anguish and guilt had flooded back in.

Occasionally, he lifted his head to gaze through his window at the full earth, which nestled majestically in the dark night sky. But mostly, he sat cross-legged, with head bowed and eyes closed. A handful of times when he had opened his eyes, he had contemplated his Bible, which was open to Psalm 91 on the floor in front of him. Disconnected verses struck his eye:

> *. . . who abides in the shadow of the Almighty . . . My refuge and my fortress . . . You will not fear the terror of the night . . . nor the destruction that wastes at noonday . . .*

"Forgive me!" the Russian cried aloud. "Please forgive me."

Images of Bolotov flashed in and out of his mind. It had been more than half a moon day since the tragedy occurred. But the mental picture of the lone blond man, first standing completely still, and then diving and being swallowed by the aperture, haunted him.

Pushkin was well aware that Scott Andrews and the Americans had viewed Bolotov with great suspicion, if not fear. But the older Russian had seen his younger colleague in a somewhat different light.

Sure, he knew Bolotov's assigned role on this trip had been to serve as a political watchdog for Pushkin himself, and probably as some kind of independent operative on behalf of Demitry Martov. But the fusion scientist had also begun to get to know the younger scientist as a lonely, isolated man-boy, who was having increasing problems functioning in the moon environment.

"I had something to offer him," Pushkin muttered, now staring up at the earth and the black sky beyond it. "But I failed. My work took precedence. And now he's gone. An opportunity has been lost forever. Forgive me."

Slowly, feeling resistance from the stiffness in his back and legs, he rolled over to an all-fours kneeling position and then struggled to his feet. Even in the one-sixth gravity of the moon, it had been an effort for him. Now that he was standing, he glided over to his desk and opened his computer.

"*Koinonia*," he muttered. "I must have *koinonia*."

Three years before, he wouldn't have known that the word meant "community" or "fellowship," much less that he somehow needed it. He tapped in a code, spoke a greeting into the computer mike, and breathed a sigh of thanks that a real-time answer came back on the screen.

Greetings to you as well.

"Trouble, disaster up here," Pushkin said, knowing that his encrypted words were now appearing on the other's computer screen.

What's wrong?

"This is for your ears and eyes only," Pushkin said. "Don't rely on ordinary deletion after we finish. Use the annihilation program to get rid of all traces of this message."

I always do.

"The wormhole reappeared by itself, much larger than our creation," Pushkin explained, speaking rapidly, his voice quavering so much that he feared the computer might fail to transpose his voice correctly into type. "Ten times as large as the original. I agreed that Bolotov should be the one to investigate it in the lab, but he locked himself in the room. Something happened in there that I don't understand. He became drawn to the wormhole opening, almost intoxicated. He wouldn't respond to any of our warnings or orders. I thought he was just behaving as a good Russian political officer, gathering intelligence before anyone else. But then he went berserk. He ran toward the wormhole and jumped through the opening. That's the last we saw of him— or of the wormhole. The entire structure has disappeared."

There was a pause on the other end. Then the answer began to appear on the screen in front of him:

Strange. So what is your personal response to all this? How do you feel?

"Terrible remorse," Pushkin replied, stifling a sob. He had no idea how that would be transcribed on the receiver's screen. "I think I might have prevented this. I was too consumed with the experiment. I should have been more cautious. And I should certainly have spent more time with Bolotov."

You're just one man. We all fall short. It's more difficult when somehow our decisions or actions are linked to the loss of life. I know that all too well. But death is inevitable for all of us—if indeed Bolotov is really dead.

Now it was Pushkin's turn to pause. "How could he not be dead?"

You can answer that question better than I. You're the theoretical physicist. But I thought wormholes were supposed to be passages to another part of this universe, or perhaps even to another universe entirely. Clearly, Bolotov has taken a trip. It's just that we don't know his destination.

"That's all pure hypothesis!" Pushkin objected. "All speculation! Most likely, if he did travel to another location, he ended up in the vacuum of space, or on a world or star hostile to our form of life. Bolotov is gone forever."

Maybe, maybe not. But regardless of what happened to your colleague, his fate is the result of events that were largely out of your control.

"That thought doesn't wipe away the remorse," Pushkin said. Michael James replied:

Thoughts never wipe away remorse. Only God can do that. By the way, is there anything you haven't told me about the new wormhole?

Pushkin realized that he had been so wrapped up in his feelings of guilt that he had forgotten the case with the computer disk.

"They found an object that we inserted in the original wormhole," he said. "On the floor of the laboratory. It was a metal case containing a disk with information about humanity. I decided to send it out as a message of sorts."

He shook his head, realizing that his own emotions had prevented him from seeing the possible enormity of this event. "Either the new wormhole simply regurgitated it, or something or someone has decided to reply to us."

Then I think if I were you, I'd check that disk. You may learn more about what's happened to your friend Bolotov.

After terminating the communications link with Michael James, Pushkin felt better. James had provided him with some perspective—and some hope. He splashed water on his face, shaved, sponged off, and put on some fresh clothes. But he was hardly aware of what he was doing. All he could think about was the disk.

Was there a simple explanation for the reappearance of the disk? Had the container just gone to a shallow depth and been spit back up by the strange opening? If so, they probably weren't dealing with a genuine tunnel through space-time. Instead, it was likely that they had encountered some kind of sub-atomic pit with an unreceptive bottom that just bounced foreign objects back, addressee unknown.

But what if the opening really had been the mouth of a wormhole? In that case, it was possible that the disk had actually traveled from this part of the universe to some distant location. If that was the case, why had it come back? And why did the wormholes always disappear when something or someone was placed in them? Was there something that caused space-time to behave this way—something that Einstein and those who had gone before had over-looked? Or had someone or something *returned* the container?

Pushkin zipped up his jacket, picked up his pocket-size personal digital assistant, and headed toward the conference room, where he hoped to find some answers—or at least find someone who would help him solve the mystery of the wandering data disk.

43

The end of one of Ruth Goldberg's aluminum-alloy moon crutches shook threateningly in Scott Andrews's face, to the point that he had to lean back in his chair to avoid being hit.

"Are you trying to brand me with that thing?" he asked, half in jest, but also half-annoyed.

"Of course not," she said, withdrawing the formidable instrument, but still leaning aggressively over the table in Scott's direction. "But you're overstepping your authority! You have no right to meddle with that disk unless Professor Pushkin approves."

The four remaining members of the moon team, who were sitting, standing, or leaning around the conference table in the living module lobby, glanced at the center of the large table, where the small metal container lay.

"He's disappeared!" Scott protested in exasperation.

"He's in his room," Ruth said.

"Maybe, maybe not," Scott replied. "He doesn't answer knocks, intercom calls. For all we know, he could be hiding out in the factory, or out taking a stroll on one of those craters." He pointed through a window toward the stark lunar surface outside.

"Don't be ridiculous!" Ruth argued. "You know he's in his room. I'm sure he's coming to grips with Vladimir's tragedy."

"Weird thing," Hightower said, shaking his head. "I still can't figure that one out. Lost his marbles, that one."

"It's a personal tragedy," Ruth reprimanded. "And it's up to us to give Dr. Pushkin a little time to recover."

"But how much time?" Shiro Hiramatsu asked. "Events have been moving very quickly. What if it's important for us to know more about this container, and to act on that knowledge—quickly?"

"This is Russian property," Ruth said defiantly. "We can't touch it unless Dr. Pushkin gives us permission."

Scott looked at her curiously. Now seemed a good time to press her a little.

"Ruth, is it possible you've lost your objectivity because of a conflict of interest?" he asked.

Watching her expression closely, he was sure he picked up a start in her eyes and perhaps an involuntary intake of breath.

"What are you getting at?" she asked, looking at him suspiciously.

"Your real name is Tatiana Timoshenko, isn't it?" he asked, still studying her face. "And you're Russian, not Israeli, right?"

She froze, a gesture with her free arm becoming fixed in midair. Then her arm relaxed, but her eyes darted to one side. Up to this point, her eyes had stayed locked on his, but now she had obviously become somewhat flustered.

Finally, she shrugged. "A little knowledge is a dangerous thing, Dr. Andrews."

"But that's correct, isn't it? I mean about your nationality and name."

"You already knew about my Russian background, and my name is none of your business," she said, a note of anger rising in her voice.

"But it *is* my business," he said calmly but firmly, not giving her an inch. "I'm in charge of this team, and I have to know the people I'm dealing with. I've been operating on the assumption that you were Ruth Goldberg, an Israeli laser specialist, but apparently you're not. So if you're not Ruth, who are you?"

Hiramatsu, who had clearly been stunned by the revelation, finally found his voice. "It's obvious, Ruth, um, whatever the name, that you are a competent laser specialist. But we are dealing with sensitive matters here. Dangerous issues that can quickly destabilize anyone, as we saw with Bolotov. There must be a level of trust. We are all scientists, and I assumed that we were developing open relationships with one another. So I think we have a right to answers to some of these questions."

She sighed and sat down. "All right, my real name is Tatiana Timoshenko," she confessed. "And I was born in Russia. But that's nothing. Many Israelis were originally from other countries, including Russia. I took the name Ruth Goldberg when I immigrated. Now, I am an Israeli citizen."

"And a friend of the late Vladimir Bolotov," Scott said, trying to pry more information out of her. "Are you really Israeli?"

She looked at him sharply. "I won't be interrogated, Dr. Andrews."

She glared at Scott, this time not willing to back down. Her eyes stayed riveted on his. The tension was abruptly broken when the door to the room slid open and Sergey Pushkin walked into the room. Everyone fell silent and watched the Russian as he glided quietly to an empty chair at the table.

"I apologize for my absence," he said after taking a seat. His eyes remained focused on some point on the table just in front of him. "I was greatly troubled by the incident, the loss of Bolotov. I feel responsible. I should have seen this coming. I should have helped the man, embraced him more. I think he needed a friend, but I failed."

"It was nobody's fault," Scott said. "Bolotov was out of control. Now we have to move on." He nodded toward the container that was still resting at the center of the conference table. "We have to understand what that's all about."

"That was the main reason I decided to join you," Pushkin said. "Have the radiation levels of the container been checked?"

"Yes," Hightower answered. "It's completely safe, at least on the outside. Very low levels."

"Has anyone tried to open it?" the Russian asked, still not taking his eyes off the object.

"No," Goldberg said. "We were waiting for you."

"I think we should open it, but after taking precautions," Pushkin announced. "There may be radiation—or something else—on the inside."

"So what do you suggest?" Scott said. "Radiation suits?"

Pushkin thought for a moment. Then he replied, "We should open it in the lab area, which is a reasonable distance from this living module. All workers in the factory module should be evacuated back to this location. That should give us a margin of safety. Then one of us scientists and two technicians, both volunteers—one a nuclear specialist, and one a computer expert—should open it."

"I'd like to be the scientist," Goldberg said.

Scott looked at her suspiciously. He didn't feel he had enough against her to toss her off the team, but he wasn't about to trust her with his life.

Suddenly, he remembered the incident on the *Moonshot*, when he had almost died from suffocation. Goldberg had been the first to help him—or was that just a cover? Had she been nearby because she was the one who had jammed his air vent and sleeping compartment door? He looked at her broad shoulders. She had certainly shown she had the strength to make that attempt on his life.

He was glad when Pushkin saved him from objecting to her request for the disk assignment. "No, I must be the one, both because of the risk, and also because I have the most knowledge about the experiment," Pushkin replied.

"I can accept that, but with a couple of conditions," Scott said quickly, with considerable relief. "This time, the doors to the lab must remain open. Also, I'll be just outside in the factory area with a security detail, just in case there are any problems."

Pushkin contemplated the American for a moment and then nodded. "I understand your concerns. Those seem reasonable ground rules. So I agree."

"Hold on, now," Hightower said, raising his hand. "I think everybody in this group should be allowed to join you, Scott. Volunteer thing, of course. But we don't know what kind of science may be required when the thing is popped open. Better safe than sorry."

"Sounds fine to me," Scott said, relieved that he didn't have to rely exclusively on another Russian. "If it blows up, I guess we all go at once."

"Or join Bolotov, wherever he may be," Goldberg said.

"So who's on board?" Scott asked.

Everyone raised a hand.

"Then that's settled," the congressman said. "Now let's get moving. The faster we resolve this thing, the faster we'll be able to return to the business of providing energy for the earth. I've been getting some inquiries from the highest levels about our progress, and I'm tired of doing a dance to keep the politicians happy."

"What do the authorities on earth know?" Goldberg asked.

"Secretary Martin is required to report any serious accidents or dangerous events up here immediately after they happen," Scott said. "But he has some discretion, especially if the circumstances still aren't clear and an investigation is under way. So I asked him to wait until we got our act together, but I think he's reached his limit," Scott added, glancing down at his watch. "It's been about twelve hours since Bolotov disappeared, and he hasn't returned. So we've got to start putting out reports. I'm assuming that no one else has notified any earth authority." He looked around at the faces surrounding him again. "We've all been together since the disaster, either in the lab or here in the conference room. Except for Dr. Pushkin, of course."

Pushkin abruptly looked down at his computer screen, as though he didn't want to respond. The move seemed suspicious to Scott, and he almost asked the Russian directly if he had made any outside contacts since the Bolotov incident. But for the sake of maintaining a workable relationship, he thought better of it.

"I'll ask Secretary Martin to report only the bare outlines of the lab events to the key political leaders of the nations of those sitting at this table," Scott said. "He'll also advise them that because the investigation is continuing, it would be best for them not to publicize the recent occurrences on the moon until we have more information. At the same time that the secretary is sending this message, we'll proceed with our plan to open the disk container. Agreed?"

Everyone murmured assent.

Scott stood and pushed back his chair. "Then let's do it!"

44

B ut Bolotov was your choice!" Prime Minister Martov shouted over the video screen.

Even with the slightly distorted colors on the monitor, Klaudia could tell he was red-faced. She also knew that reason, not flattery, was the best way to handle this crisis.

"Sir," she replied—deciding to show special deference but knowing he didn't want any reference to his office over the airwaves—"I'm convinced that something happened up there that we haven't been told. Perhaps Bolotov was drugged. Or there may have been some side effects with this experiment that affected his mind, his emotions. We know so little. Too little to make a judgment at this point."

"What was his psychological profile?" Martov asked, still angry but becoming more rational, to Klaudia's great relief. "Was there anything in his file that could predict this?"

"Nothing," she replied. "I've been over it several times since you alerted me to his disappearance. He was stable and committed to our cause. What he did was completely out of character. If he had a fault, it was to follow orders to the letter and not adjust to changing circumstances."

As Martov sat back in his chair and rubbed his chin, Klaudia relaxed, knowing that for the time being, she was off the hot seat.

"You remain certain that this connection is completely secure?" he asked. "I've done my own checking, and the communications people seem to agree with you that it's safe. But this technology still makes me nervous. I'm relying on your assurances."

"It's absolutely secure," she declared. "Our experts have no doubt."

"All right," he replied, "then let me say this: there is still much we don't know. I have a brief report from Secretary Archibald Martin, the United Nations bureaucrat who is the administrator of the moon settlement. He says that Bolotov somehow collided with some structure that had been created during our experiment, and then he vanished. They're still investigating exactly what happened to him—but they don't affirm that he's dead."

"What about Pushkin?" she asked. "What does he say?"

"I can't reach him," Martov replied, throwing up his hands in frustration. "I sensed the man was unreliable, too much the pure, airheaded scientist, and also too religious. Not truly loyal to us. But I had no choice. I had to send him. He was the only qualified expert who could handle the energy mechanism and also the . . . special experiment. Bolotov was supposed to be my eyes and ears—and Pushkin's watchdog."

He hesitated. "Fortunately, as I told you before, I have provided for another backup agent, one who is still operating in deep cover. But there's a limit to what we can expect from that direction. The more aggressive this person becomes, the more likely it is that the identity will be revealed."

Klaudia noticed that Martov was being extremely careful not to reveal a thing about this other operative, not even the person's gender. "Perhaps we just need to be patient," she said, and immediately realized she had made a mistake.

"Patient?" he shouted. "How can you talk about patience at a time like this? Time is at a premium! For all we know, as we chatter down here, all our secrets are being delivered to the Americans!"

"What can I do to help?" she asked solicitously. "I'll do anything you suggest."

That seemed to soften him somewhat. "There's nothing you can do right now. Just stay alert and be ready to act if need be. The way the situation is developing, it seems increasingly likely that your services will be needed. And as I have promised, you will have additional help, even though Bolotov is now gone."

"Yes, my"—she almost said "prime minister" but caught herself—"esteemed colleague."

"Do you have any fear that your presence has been detected?" he asked.

"None at all," she said with a controlled smile. "Valery and I continue to watch the other side, but we have been extremely careful not to let them know we're about."

"Good," Martov said somberly. "Keep it that way."

When the prime minister had signed off, Klaudia Ming-Petrovich picked up a shoe and hurled it at her bed. She would have screamed and broken the nearest piece of furniture with the calloused edge of her hand if she hadn't been afraid that neighbors would hear the racket through the paper-thin walls and call the building management or even the police.

It was stressful and frustrating, always having to tiptoe around, trying to keep Martov happy. She knew it was in her long-term best interests to keep her relationship with the prime minister on an even keel. But that didn't make the effort any easier. Klaudia had been in hiding for more than a month now in Cocoa Beach. The tension of having to stay in a cramped apartment—or on the few occasions when she was out, to have to look constantly over her shoulder, not to mention supervise Valery—was beginning to wear on her.

Klaudia had elected to spend most of her time inside the apartment, with only occasional, once-a-week forays out onto the public streets. She knew that when the time arrived for the truly important action, it would be up to her to take the lead. So at this stage of their operation, it seemed best to expose Valery more than herself to the risk of discovery.

As a result, Valery had performed all the surveillance on the FBI headquarters, and he did all the errands, such as shopping for food. Klaudia felt uncomfortable about giving the man so much responsibility because she knew he was more likely than she to make mistakes. But given the circumstances, she had concluded she had no choice.

On the few occasions when Klaudia left the cheap apartment complex, she exited by one of the back or side doors. By careful design, she and Valery were never together in public. They had even registered under separate names in different apartments, though a common inside door linked their quarters.

Their effects were always packed, so that either operative could gather all the clothing, computers, and other belongings in seconds and take the materials directly out of the building. As another backup, Klaudia, using one of her disguises, had leased a third room on the ground floor of the complex. If necessary, they could shift their personal effects temporarily to that location. Then a separate Russian cleanup team stationed in the area would sweep in and take the property to a safe house. Klaudia had even gone to the extreme of insisting that both she and Valery wear light gloves or wrap pieces of tape around their fingertips while they were in their apartments so that they could avoid leaving fingerprints.

After the tense discussion with Martov, Klaudia felt she had to get some release from all these constraints. She needed to get out of the apartment immediately, or she feared she would go over the edge—and commit a fatal mistake. So she grabbed one of her wigs—the blonde one was the first that came into her hand—and adjusted it quickly over her naturally black hair. Then she slapped on a beach hat, put on a pair of sunglasses, and strode through the door into the hallway.

After reaching the lobby, she glanced at the back entrance, which she usually used, and decided to break her rule and use the front door instead. There were plenty of people out there on the front sidewalk. The sun was shining more brightly. An ice-cream vendor was hawking his wares. Her mouth began to water. Swiss chocolate was one of her few weaknesses. *Anything to ease the tension.*

Just as she passed through the revolving front door, she came face-to-face with Valery, who was returning from one of his surveillance missions. There was a moment of hesitation on his part. A look of recognition crossed his face. He raised a hand slightly, as if to wave or speak. Then he remembered and looked quickly away from her and hurried into the apartment.

Fuming, she walked directly to the ice-cream stand and ordered the chocolate cone. Then she stood to one side, licked it carefully, and allowed her eyes to dart back and forth, in and out of the stores and doorways that punctuated the buildings across the street.

Nothing of interest. Continuing to savor the cone, she walked slowly down the street in the direction of the beach.

I should do this more often. She even mused that perhaps it was possible to become too cautious, especially if you didn't allow your nerves time to settle down.

Then she realized her mistake. The flash of a woman's face through a store window across the street was all too familiar. Klaudia Ming-Petrovich cursed under her breath. But careful not to signal her awareness, she continued to lick the ice cream and walk at the same pace, focusing on the street directly in front of her—a street that she knew she would never be able to use again.

45

I know her!" Colleen exclaimed under her breath as the blonde woman in the sun hat sauntered away from them on the opposite side of the street.

"Who?" Michael James asked.

Then he saw that she was leaning too close to the window and pulled her back into the shadows of the store. He could only hope that she had escaped observation.

James had been concentrating on the lobby of the apartment to see if he could catch a final glimpse of the short, chunky man he had been shadowing for three days. He had lost the man the first two days because of the fellow's adept movements through the Cocoa Beach streets after he left his station outside the FBI headquarters. He would hurry through shops and motels, in and out of back and side doors. It quickly became clear to James that this individual had been trained well in surveillance techniques, and especially in shaking a "tail" who might be trying to follow him.

Finally, today James had figured out the man's tricks and had managed to stick with him until he entered a coffee shop next to this apartment complex. Figuring that now might be the time to bring Colleen in on his discoveries, he called her on his cell phone. Fortunately, she was nearby and able to join him in about ten minutes, before the stocky man with the inappropriate, knee-length shorts and dark socks had left the restaurant. As a result, they had both witnessed the man's entry into the apartment building—and his strange encounter with the blonde in the beach hat.

"What do you mean, you know her?" James asked as Colleen continued to observe the blonde.

"I think one of us should follow her," she replied without answering him directly. "She may have known the guy you were following."

"I would say it's likely," James said. "He almost seemed to wave to her."

"We can't be sure," Colleen said, still distracted by the blonde, who continued to walk away from them. "But it's too much of a coincidence that she was sitting at a café near the van where I was first doing surveillance with Ralph and Larry. Now she turns up again. Are you going to keep on her, or should I?"

"I'll do it," he said, moving toward the shop door. "She might recognize you, but she won't know me. Meantime, you might check on our would-be surfer dude. See if you can get his name or the woman's from the apartment manager. Use the ID the FBI gave you, and tell the building manager to keep his mouth shut about your inquiry."

James headed quickly after the blonde woman, who was almost a block away now. He wanted to keep her close but not too close. And he had to be alert. If she was working with the man, he would have his work cut out to keep up with her.

She turned into a chic restaurant at the end of the block, and he hurried up to the door in an effort to keep her in sight. Looking through the pane, he could see her walking toward the back of the establishment. He immediately assumed that she was about to pull one of the man's tricks by heading out the back door. So he rushed around the building, located a back exit, and waited for her to emerge.

Seconds ticked by, but no blonde. Realizing that he had made a mistake, James walked back to the front of the restaurant, found the hostess, and asked about the woman.

"She asked for the ladies' room," the hostess said. "I haven't seen her since."

Without comment, James walked quickly to the back of the restaurant, found the restrooms—and saw another back exit, which led into an arcade that connected to another street. Obviously, his quarry had done a thorough job of planning ways to shake a shadow.

Not the first time I've lost a target, he thought. He remembered a failed covert operation near Moscow, just before he had decided to leave the military for a higher, though still largely clandestine, calling—social-service work, as well as rescue operations to extricate trapped missionaries in closed, totalitarian societies. The new work fit in well with his duties as a Wheaton College Bible professor—and his curious background as a covert operative.

When Michael James reached the apartment complex again, Colleen was just walking out onto the street.

"Lose her?" she asked.

"She lost me," he said. "I think she knew I was behind her."

"Probably saw me through the window," Colleen said, chagrin in her voice.

"Maybe, but don't worry about it. What did you learn about the apartment?"

"Near as I can tell, the man and woman are registered separately," she reported.

"Figures," Michael said. "They're professionals. What else?"

"His name is listed as Walter Jones. Hers is Samantha Murphy. They live next door to each other."

"Yep," he said, not at all surprised at the information. "Both phonies. And I'll bet my tenure at Wheaton that by the time we get a search warrant, the apartments will be cleaned out, and they'll both be long gone. She's probably already called him."

Dutifully, he placed a call to the FBI team, who were still puzzling over another recent encrypted video transmission that had originated in Cocoa Beach. They immediately got a judge to issue a search warrant, and within an hour, FBI agents were swarming all over the two apartments.

But as James had predicted, the rooms were clean as a whistle. Not a tell-tale piece of trash. Not a telephone calling record to trace—because regular phones had never been installed. Apparently, the two relied exclusively on cell phones. So far, not even a stray fingerprint had turned up, other than those left by a cleaning service that had done the original cleaning on the two sets of rooms. That was really remarkable—and a sign of incredible discipline, James reflected. In desperation, the FBI had dispatched a team of specialists to search for DNA evidence.

"We'll turn up something," Larry promised. "Don't you worry. Everybody makes a mistake. We just have to be patient. Before long, they'll slip up."

But Michael James wasn't so sure.

46

I t's safe!" Pushkin announced, and the four other team members immediately entered the Russian lab.

All gathered around the container, which had been tested for radiation and then opened by Pushkin and two technicians. But they were not prepared for what they saw. Instead of one small disk, there were six.

"What does this mean?" Scott asked.

Pushkin shrugged and frowned. "Something is going on here that none of us expected. Yet it gives me hope for the fate of Bolotov. You see, either we have created some kind of magical portal, which multiplies things that you insert, or we have received a message."

"Who could have sent it?" Hightower asked.

Again, Pushkin shrugged. "Who knows?" he said. "Perhaps it's from the other side of the universe. Or maybe even from some other dimension. To find out, we must learn what is on these disks."

"But these are *yours*, not ours, Dr. Pushkin!" Goldberg protested. "These are Russia's. You are the only one who has a right to these."

Scott scowled, wishing he had acted on his first impulse in the conference room and thrown Goldberg off the team. She seemed intent on creating problems—usually in Russia's favor. He was strongly considering calling her "Tatiana" from now on.

"Look, this has become a team effort," Scott replied. "An international venture. It's taken expertise from many different countries to reach this point. We should proceed together."

He looked over his shoulder at the security team that was still lurking just outside the lab door, where he had told them to wait. He had resolved that if need be, he would use force to keep access to this information in the open.

"I agree," Pushkin replied. "It's best that we continue to work together. In many advisers there is success, someone has said. And who knows which set of skills will be needed as we move forward?"

Hightower cleared his throat. "Good of you, mate. But just be aware that we know you're the alpha kangaroo here. This is your party, and we're along for the ride."

Scott looked at the Australian curiously. What was he trying to do? Change Pushkin's mind? But after bracing for another argument, Scott was relieved to see that Pushkin was prepared to proceed as he had suggested.

"We'll do it together," Pushkin said resolutely. "But where should we work? The wormhole seems to prefer our lab for its unannounced appearances. I don't believe I'd like to be working too near the spot where it might reappear. Perhaps we should vacate the space for now, just in case."

Scott looked warily at the empty space where the large, pronglike structure with the yawning, blue-gray mouth had been only hours before. "I agree. This place makes me nervous too. Almost seems like some kind of magic circle, where time and space are out of whack."

All fell silent and contemplated the floor area in question. Scott wondered what Bolotov might be doing right now—on the other side the wormhole. That is, if there *was* some "other side." Was he still alive? If so, was he in touch with other intelligent life? Could they expect him to return? If so, would he be the same person, or would he be different?

The thought disconcerted Scott. *Six* computer disks had come back instead of one. He wasn't sure he could deal with six Bolotovs. He shook off the idea and quickly proposed that the best place to work would probably be at a computer center outside the lab, in the main factory module.

Everyone agreed, and within an hour, they were all hovering around a console in the computer center. To be sure they handled the disks properly, they had enlisted the help of the leading lunar computer expert, Robert Wang, an American with the top-secret clearance necessary for this kind of assignment. Multiple monitors, keyboards, and control panels surrounded them, and the door to the area had been locked to prevent curious eyes from intruding.

Pushkin carefully opened the disk container and handed it to Wang.

"The six objects in there appear to be versions of the very latest nanodisks," Pushkin said. "Are you familiar with the technology?"

"It's the newest thing," Wang replied. "They're called nanodisks because they operate on such a small scale. Name comes from the word *nanometer*, which is a unit of measurement one-billionth of a meter long. That's the scale used to measure molecules. I worked with disks like these in Washington just before I came up here. Cost a fortune. The information on them is stored at the molecular or atomic level. You could get every human book and article on half of one of these disks." He looked at them again with a puzzled expression. "Wonder why there are six?"

"That's one thing we want to find out," Scott replied, who was becoming increasingly impatient to solve the mystery. "You're pretty sure these are like the disks you worked with?"

"They seem the same," Wang replied. "But the only way to find out is to boot them up."

"Get to it," Scott directed.

Everyone watched silently as Wang carefully removed each disk from the container, checked for special markings, and then picked one up and held it in front of Scott. "There are no numbers. But they seem to be distinguished by dots. One has one dot, another has two, and so on, up to six. I think we should assume that the single dot indicates disk number one."

"Fine," Scott replied, looking at Pushkin to be sure he agreed. "Insert it."

Wang slipped the disk in a special disk drive that had been fitted to handle the new nanodisks, and clicked the command to bring the first one on line. Immediately, all the screens lit up with complex sequences of letters, diagrams, and pictures.

Again, total silence descended in the alcove as the team studied the screen. "I'm not sure I recognize this," Hiramatsu said.

"I do," Scott said with a slight smile, knowing that he was finally on familiar ground. "This was my home turf when I was a medical researcher and physician before I entered Congress. My friends, we're looking at a diagram of the human genome—the same diagram on the original disk Dr. Pushkin sent through the first wormhole."

"What does it mean?" Hightower asked.

Scott was so absorbed scrolling through the first few pages of the disk that he didn't answer immediately. Then he leaned back and looked at the others. "If this means what I think it does, these six little disks may provide humanity with something a lot more important than unlimited energy."

47

As Scott led the team members farther into the first disk, they encountered an extensive summary and table of contents for all the information and disks that followed. The text was written in the seven main languages spoken on the moon outpost—English, Russian, French, Japanese, Spanish, German, and Chinese.

After examining the material more closely, they discovered, much to their amazement, that they were looking at thousands, or more likely, millions, of pages containing medical terminology and apparent instructions for treatment of diseases. For the first time since Energy Project Omega had been launched, Dr. Scott Andrews became the leading team expert; as the only physician, he was the only person who could evaluate the material.

As he spot-checked the huge volume of material, Scott—who had spent fifteen years doing research and also practicing medicine in Florida, mostly with elderly patients—could not believe his eyes. The text actually purported to provide cures for all the diseases he had fought for so long: degenerative arthritis, high blood pressure, diverticulitis, and Alzheimer's, just to name a few. There were gigantic chapters dealing with each of these diseases, and also with other maladies that he had rarely or never treated.

Perhaps most amazing of all, the disks included genetic information explaining why some humans suffered from these conditions and others didn't. In addition, there were instructions about how to alter the genetic code so that no one would ever have to suffer from these diseases again.

The basic impact of the information was summed up in an introductory statement near the very beginning of the first disk—a section that the other team members, who lacked Scott's medical background, were still contemplating:

These computer disks contain all the information and practical instructions needed for human beings to eliminate the process of telomere loss, to preserve the action of telomerase, and to eliminate unnecessary apoptosis. Other practical instructions are provided to banish specific diseases or other threats to human health.

"Translate, please, Dr. Andrews," Pushkin said. "Just so that we can be sure that we are all, to use the American cliché, on the same page."

"Sure," Scott replied. "To make it simple, you all know that we have chromosomes that contain our genes, including DNA molecules. Humans have twenty-three pairs of chromosomes, with each pair twisted in what's sometimes called the double helix. Together, our chromosomes make up our genome, or our entire genetic package—which determines whether you're a man or woman, have blue or brown eyes, or whatever."

"And the telomeres," Pushkin said, apparently feeling that Scott was speaking at too basic a level. "Tell us about the telomeres—which seem to be at the heart of this message."

"Yes, certainly," Scott said. "Telomeres are the end sections of each chromosome. During the course of our lives, our chromosomes are copied, oh, several hundred times. The telomeres help ensure accuracy in the copying process. But every time a copy is made, the chromosome strand gets shorter, and a little bit of the telomere tip chips off. Finally, in old age, the telomere disappears completely, and cells begin to die off."

"And *we* age and die off," Hiramatsu said.

"Basically, yes," Scott agreed.

"As I recall from my biology, the telomerase has something to do with helping the telomeres function properly," Hiramatsu said. "Is that right?"

"Yes," Scott said. "The telomerase is a kind of natural, protein-related, biochemical paste that helps restore the telomeres over and over again during our lives. But in old age, the telomerase also gets out of whack."

"The protein paste fails to repair the telomeres properly?" Goldberg said.

"That's right," Scott replied. "With the same result. Cell death."

"And *our* death," Hightower echoed.

"Now tell us about that other word—*apoptosis,*" Pushkin said.

"Complicated," Scott replied. "But basically, it refers to a related issue—our built-in system of cell death. Our cells are programmed to die after a certain number of divisions. That's apoptosis. It's probably the reason you have mostly white hair, Professor Pushkin, and mine is still mostly brownish-blond. My hair color cells are still working, more or less, but yours have gone through apoptosis."

Pushkin responded with one of the few smiles Scott had seen from him in the previous twenty-four hours. But the smile quickly faded, and like the rest of the team, he lapsed into silence as he looked back at the introduction on the computer screen.

As Scott studied Pushkin's face, the Russian's eyes seemed to turn glassy, with a faraway look. Scott almost wondered if the man had gone to sleep with his eyes open. But then Scott forgot about the Russian as the mounting excitement in Jeffrey Hightower's voice grabbed his attention.

"Does all this mean what I think it means?" the Australian asked no one in particular.

"The end of aging," Hiramatsu said quietly.

"A fountain of youth," Goldberg said. "This is an offer of eternal life."

"All through an extensive program of genetic engineering," Scott agreed. "That does seem to be the message—though it will take a team of experts smarter than I am to confirm it."

"Scott, let me ask you one more question," Pushkin said, looking directly at him. "I know this is all very preliminary. But from what you have seen so far, does this material have the ring of truth?"

"For the most part, I've seen only what you've seen," Scott replied, trying to hedge his way out of a definite answer.

"But you're the only physician here," Pushkin noted. "You've done research in this area."

Scott nodded. "While we were spot-checking the other disks, trying to confirm their proper order, I did glance at one section on Alzheimer's disease. Now understand, I scanned the material for less than a minute. But the text clearly identified a couple of genes—and also multiple proteins produced by those genes—that purported to deal with the disease. There appeared to be a very involved guide as to how to repair and rejuvenate the genes and proteins that cause Alzheimer's. I have to admit, that excited me. So do I think this has the ring of truth? I'd have to say yes."

"I don't get this," Hightower said, scratching his head. "Who could possibly write all this stuff? And who could put it together this fast?" He looked at his watch. "It's been less than a moon day since we popped that original disk into our little wormhole. Now we get this back—written in perfect English, and I assume perfect Russian, Chinese, you name it. This has to be a trick."

"But how do you devise a trick like this?" Goldberg protested. "An impossible feat, I'd say. At least impossible by the standards of our most advanced technology."

"Scott, check another section, will you?" Hiramatsu asked. "In the limited time we have, we have to get the best reading on whether or not this material seems medically sound."

The others immediately agreed, and Scott began to scan ahead on another section of the first disk.

"The format is amazingly clear and usable," Scott said. "Look here. This part of the contents refers to a huge section on the thyroid gland. So I click on it and—" The picture on the computer screen immediately whizzed to information far along in the disk. "Look at that! Here, we begin a long, practical description of hypothyroidism, or an underactive thyroid. And there— look up there. You see a reference to the gene, and multiple proteins produced by that gene, that are involved in the problem."

"And it shows you how to do it?" Hightower asked. "A doctor could actually take this disk and cure that particular thyroid problem?"

Scott contemplated the next few screens before answering. Then he stopped, excitement gripping him. "Yes! Look at this! It outlines a specific method to use a retrovirus technique to do some genetic engineering to correct the problem. A family doctor might not be able to figure this out, but a medical specialist could definitely follow the explanations."

He sat back and stared at the screen. "This may be the most amazing information human beings have ever received," he finally said. "And I don't say this lightly. But from what we know about genetic engineering—and understand, we're still at the very beginning, in our scientific infancy when it comes to this kind of medicine—the explanation on the screen in front of you is precisely what we'd expect."

"But a hundred years from now," Hiramatsu said quietly.

"Or a thousand," Scott replied. "Certainly not today."

The entire group, including Robert Wang, the computer specialist, sat in stunned stillness. As the magnitude of what they were viewing sank in, there seemed to be no words to describe the response.

Finally, Scott looked at Pushkin. "What do you think about the source for this stuff?" he asked. "This can't come from anyplace on earth, can it?"

Pushkin shook his head. "Absolutely not. It's impossible. Completely impossible."

"Bolotov didn't have any background in genetic engineering, did he?" Scott asked.

"Of course not!" Pushkin said. "What, you think Bolotov may have concocted this?" He shook his head. "He knew enough fusion physics to help me with my work, but that was all. He was a trained cosmonaut, and he knew martial arts. But this would have been unintelligible to him. For that matter, making such disks seems well beyond any known human abilities."

"So where do you think this comes from, Dr. Pushkin?" Hightower pressed. "What's your best guess?"

"I don't like to guess in matters like this," Pushkin said, walking to the end of the computer console and then spinning around to face the other five. "But we are at something of a dead end, aren't we? So I suppose we have to speculate."

The Russian thought for a few seconds and scribbled some notes on his computer notepad as the others looked first at him, then at the computer screens, and then back in his direction. Finally, Pushkin slipped his computer into his pocket and turned to them.

"It can't be from earth," he said. "That much is clear. Our knowledge and technology aren't advanced enough to accomplish this in such a short time, even as a joke."

"Actually, the disks are enough to settle the question about whether these things came from the moon," Robert Wang piped up. "No disks like these are currently on the moon. They have been in experimental use for less than a year, but only in Washington. And one or two other places." He looked knowingly at Pushkin.

Russia, Scott thought. *And maybe Japan and China.*

Pushkin shrugged. "Without telling them the purpose, I asked my computer people to give me their most powerful disk with certain earth-related information stored on it, such as the human genome. So they prepared the one disk. That's the one we sent through the original wormhole. You all saw that. But I'm a fusion specialist and physicist, not a computer expert. I rely on our computer specialists to help me with my work, but I don't know the details of their technology."

"It's very new," Wang said cryptically, obviously deciding he had already said too much. "Anyhow, unless somebody smuggled these six disks up here, there's no way we could have come up with them on the spot."

"So the technology itself argues against a human agency having anything to do with these disks," Scott said. "And if the genetic instructions turn out to be correct, that would really seem to rule out any earth-based origination point. We simply don't have this kind of medical technology or know-how at the present time."

Once again, silence settled on the group. Because he didn't want to be the first to appear kooky, Scott resisted asking the question he knew was probably on everyone's mind. But when the silence had persisted longer than he could bear, he finally turned to Pushkin.

"Could it be aliens?" he asked. "Isn't that the only remaining possibility?"

Pushkin sat down heavily and looked up at the domed ceiling of the factory module. "I'm reluctant to get into this area, but I suppose we must," he said. "It's like demon possession. The responsible priest wants to eliminate all the medical and psychological options before he resorts to fallen angels and exorcism. From a classic religious perspective, that's always the treatment of last resort. It's the same with aliens when you move into the realm of space science or theoretical physics. You never choose the alien explanation when more reasonable options exist. But what *are* those reasonable options? I can't think of any."

"It's almost too pat," Scott said. "Too obvious. A complete program for genetic engineering designed to allow us to live forever—and explained in perfect, clear English. Like a plot out of a bad space movie. Look, I don't believe in aliens. I don't even believe in God or angels or anything beyond the here and now. But I'm stymied. This whole incident takes me completely out of any familiar frame of reference."

"Don't feel like the lone koala bear, mate," Hightower said. "Anyhow, does it really make any difference *who* sent this thing? The important thing is that we learn how to use it."

"I think it makes a *huge* difference who sent it!" Goldberg objected. "This obviously came from some intelligent source. If it's authentic, the intelligence is far superior to our own. But what's the motive? Who or what would want to do us such a good turn? What's in it for them?"

"Hey, Ruthie, why not enjoy it?" Hightower said, almost looking as though he would slap her on the back, but then thinking better of the idea. "Maybe we shouldn't worry so much. After all, what's so bad about living forever?"

The others laughed—a little nervously, Scott thought—and then Pushkin proceeded to help Robert Wang gather up the disks. It was agreed that Wang would take the disks under guard to Secretary Martin's office, where they would be locked up. A round-the-clock armed security team would be posted at the location.

As Scott watched Pushkin and Wang prepare the disks for storage, he couldn't get Ruth's final question out of his mind. *What's in it for them—whoever "they" really are?*

As the security detail entered to escort Wang and the disks to the storage locker, Scott hung back, still trying to sort through his feelings. For some reason, he couldn't get an old painting of the Trojan horse out of his mind. Something just wasn't quite right.

Then he noticed that Sergey Pushkin was also lagging behind—and was gesturing for him to remain in the room until all the others had cleared out.

48

When they were finally alone, Pushkin walked quickly over to Scott and leaned within a few inches of his face. "You and I must prepare for certain contingencies," the Russian whispered.

"What do you mean?" Scott replied, taken off guard by the scientist's secretive and anxious manner.

"I know you represent your government, and I know you are a committed American patriot," Pushkin said. "But I also sense you are an honest man. So let me ask, can I trust you to treat what I'm about to say as completely confidential? Just a matter between the two of us?"

Scott looked at him warily. "It depends," he replied. "I can't promise not to pass on information that may bear on the security of the United States."

Pushkin shook his head impatiently. "That's not what I mean. In fact, what I want to tell you could get me in trouble with my political superiors in Russia. I stand to lose much more than you. But I mustn't proceed with this discussion if you can't give me your assurances."

Scott relaxed, but his curiosity had been piqued. "Okay, I'll keep my mouth shut. This is for our ears only. What's the problem?"

"There are several potential problems," Pushkin began, motioning the American toward two chairs that were in a corner, well away from the door panel, which had been locked. "First, I am deeply concerned about the origin of these disks."

"You didn't mention that in our team discussion," Scott said.

"I know," the Russian said. "The reason is that I wanted to speak with you privately and not arouse undue concern or suspicion. But clearly, there is anxiety about the source of the disks, and I think it's justified. Think about what has been handed to us: six disks apparently completely filled with the most detailed human genome information. Yet we know that all the earth's writings and publications since the beginning of recorded history wouldn't fill up one of these disks!"

"Yeah, that comparison crossed my mind too," Scott said. "It's taken thousands of years to accumulate all our scientific and cultural knowledge. But all of a sudden, we find ourselves holding more than six times that amount of information on only one subject—and in seven languages, no less!"

"A higher intelligence—and advanced civilization—is clearly involved here," Pushkin said, worry deepening the lines on his face.

"So you've definitely bought the alien explanation?" Scott asked, somewhat surprised that the Russian had put aside any pretense of trying to be cautious.

"There is no other logical explanation," Pushkin said unequivocally. "Yet we have no idea about the intentions of that advanced civilization. They may have our best interests in mind. But then again, they may not."

"On the face of it, the prospect of getting rid of disease and living forever seems pretty positive," Scott said.

"That would be a common first impression," Pushkin said. "But think about it for a moment. Suppose everyone begins to live two hundred, three hundred years, or longer? What will that do to the earth's population?"

"We'd soon be packed elbow to elbow," Scott replied thoughtfully.

"With what consequences?" Pushkin asked. "Living forever won't automatically change human nature. There would still be crime, wars . . ."

"And probably the population pressures would aggravate those difficulties," Scott said. "The environment would go to pot. All that is certainly possible. Probably we'd have to do some serious social engineering to keep things on an even keel."

"On the other hand, suppose this information falls into the hands of only one segment of the population—and that segment refuses to share the secrets of eternal life," Pushkin said. "Can you imagine the hostility such selfishness would provoke?"

"The have-nots wouldn't stand for it," Scott agreed. "That's an interesting point. Hadn't crossed my mind."

"And then there is the question of accidental or violent death," Pushkin continued. "How could we humans handle the prospect of most people living virtually forever in perfect health, but a few others dying by chance? How could the average person deal emotionally with a loved one who died in an auto accident, or as a result of homicide? The long-standing emotional and spiritual support systems that allow us to handle the issue of death would be put under unbearable pressure."

"Subtle," Scott said, recalling Hiramatsu's observations months ago in Houston about Pushkin's spiritual proclivities. "I guess you are something of a philosopher. When did all this come to you?"

Pushkin stared at the American for some time before he spoke. "We are speaking frankly, so I'll hold nothing back," he said at last, leaning forward in his chair. "As we were evaluating the disks in here, I experienced a brief . . . experience. A spiritual experience. To be quite blunt, something seemed to grasp my thoughts and direct them toward these issues I've been sharing with you."

"Kind of a vision?" Scott asked, beginning to feel uncomfortable. "I have to confess, I did notice at one point that you seemed to be spacing out, you know, becoming distracted by something."

"You're right," Pushkin replied. "I did go on what our friend Hightower might call an 'inner walkabout.' But I believe it involved more than distraction or a flight of imagination. I believe something, or someone—in my opinion, God—broke through to me with a particular word about these events."

"You heard voices?"

"No, but the message was just as intense. Some might describe it as receiving a kind of prophetic communication. A warning about what may result from the use of these disks."

"Do you feel sure this wasn't just your own imagination?" Scott asked, his natural skepticism still making him suspicious about the turn this conversation had taken.

"I am quite certain," Pushkin said. "I know from what you've said during our conversations together that you are not particularly sympathetic to spiritual matters—to religious interpretations of life, prayer, and whatnot. At the same time, I sense that you are not completely closed to this area of inquiry either."

"Not completely," Scott said. "But as long as we're being honest, I have to say I can see more than one interpretation of this prophecy or message you feel you had."

"Of course," Pushkin replied. "But still, you are willing to entertain the notion that some of the points are worth considering. Is that right?"

"Absolutely," Scott agreed. "We'd certainly have to prepare people for a fast surge in population growth and all that. But that's no reason to withhold a fountain of youth when it's handed to us on a silver platter."

"If it were entirely up to you and me, we might work out a fair and equitable solution," Pushkin said. "But it won't be up to us—at least not if our political leaders get hold of those disks."

Scott looked at the Russian carefully. "So you're suggesting what?"

"I'm suggesting first of all that I wish these disks had never appeared," Pushkin said with some vehemence. "I personally don't think humanity is ready for this information. At the same time, I know that I can't keep them only for myself or destroy them."

"At least we're in agreement there," Scott replied incredulously. "You really mean you'd have considered destroying them?"

"Indeed, I would have considered it, though I'd probably have decided against such an extreme solution," Pushkin replied. "But if we do take the disks back to earth, we'll be left with some serious difficulties. Let me warn you about what's likely to happen.

"My government will insist that these are Russian property—to be shared with other nations only if our leaders decide that's appropriate. Now, suppose they decide *not* to share the information. Suppose they elect to bestow eternal life *only* on Russians—probably certain anointed, elite Russians. Or suppose they decide to sell the information at exorbitant prices to non-Russians. Remember, we Russians have been wrestling with serious national financial and economic problems since the end of the Cold War. These are very real possibilities. Believe me, I know because I understand how my leaders think. Ask yourself: How would you feel about the disks being used in such ways?"

Scott was becoming uncomfortable at the drift of the discussion. "What are you suggesting we do about this?" he asked.

The American watched every minute shift in expression on the Russian's face—every twitch, quaver, or eye movement—for any suspicious change in demeanor. He sensed he was being pulled steadily into questionable, even cabalistic dealings with a foreign national, and he didn't like the feeling one bit. The last thing he wanted was to be tricked into betraying his country under the pretense that he was really helping humankind.

But he wasn't ready for the Russian's response. "I want to give you a complete copy of the disks," Pushkin replied. "Given the current situation, I believe that's the only reasonable alternative we have to destroying them."

"Even though your government has a strong argument that it's their property?" Scott said, knowing that his eyes had widened considerably.

"Yes," Pushkin replied. "And there's one main reason. I want to be as certain as possible that this information will not fall into the hands of one narrow interest group."

"Such as the group headed by Prime Minister Martov," Scott suggested.

Pushkin nodded, a pained look now twisting his lips and narrowing his eyes. "Let me express what you're thinking," he said. "I know I could be accused of treason for this. I could be arrested as soon as I set foot on Russian soil. After that, I would probably be shot. Or most optimistically, I might be placed under close guard for the rest of my life—so that my scientific expertise would remain available to the motherland. But I'm willing to take these risks."

Scott looked deeply into the Russian's eyes, where he continued to see pain. "Given the scenario you're suggesting, I have to agree with you," the American finally said. "I'll go along with your proposal and take a copy back to the States."

"But we must say nothing of this conversation," Pushkin insisted, his voice falling to a whisper again. "If word gets back to my superiors that I have been trying to negotiate an arrangement with you, I could be . . . I could encounter an unfortunate accident, even here on the moon."

Scott looked at him curiously. "Who are you afraid of? Bolotov was the only one in our group who looked like an assassin to me!"

"It's not just a question of our scientific team," Pushkin said, waving off his comment. "The FSB deploys agents who can strike anywhere, anytime. Even on the moon. I'm sure there are Russian operatives among the lower-level scientists and technicians." He looked pointedly at Scott. "Even you are not safe, you know."

Now it was Scott's turn to scoff. "Tell me something I don't already know! I already have my battle scars."

He pointed to the spot on his side where Bolotov had injured him, but Pushkin ignored the comment.

"You know, there may be serious technological problems in trying to copy those things," Scott reminded the Russian. "Didn't Wang say there weren't any other nanodisks on the moon? And they were invented less than a year ago. How do we copy them if we don't have blank disks that can store such a huge amount of data?"

"There must be a way—but we need a computer expert," Pushkin said. "Is

Wang reliable? Would he agree to keep this matter confidential, or would he feel an obligation to report what we're doing to your government?"

Scott shrugged. "I've seen him around, but today was the first time I've worked with him. Your guess is as good as mine. For all I know, he's CIA."

They hesitated, each lost in his own thoughts. Then Scott spoke: "I could get a friend to do a quick check to see if he's connected with any other agency. If he's clean, I'll pull him aside and tell him I'm working on a national security matter. Then I'll draft him into our little three-man plot. By the time he starts having qualms, we should be finished making the copies—and may already be on our way back to earth."

"We must act quickly," Pushkin emphasized. "I have a window of no more than a few hours, maybe even less time, before my government begins to demand a detailed accounting from me. When that happens, I'll have no choice but to comply with their wishes. To defy them openly would jeopardize our plans—not to mention my life."

"Do you know for sure someone else is sending them information from here?" Scott asked.

Pushkin nodded. "They seem to be getting reports almost as events occur. My messages show that even before I mentioned anything, they were aware of Bolotov's disappearance and were asking about him. So I must assume that they know now, or will know shortly, of the contents of the new disks."

Scott pursed his lips, then snapped his fingers. "That could tell us if there's a mole in the immediate family."

"What do you mean?" Pushkin asked, a puzzled look on his brow.

"Think about it," the congressman said. "The only people who know the contents of those disks were in this room a few minutes ago. Five of us original top team members, and Robert Wang. If your government shows any knowledge of the genome material before you tell them, we'll know that the leak is coming from one of those six people. So read your messages carefully."

49

In response to a quick e-mail message from Scott, Colleen Barker confirmed that Robert Wang was a top independent computer consultant—but nothing more complicated than that. A natural-born American citizen, he apparently had no links with any covert agencies of the U.S. government, and no ties with foreign powers. In fact, his college record at Stanford showed that he was fiercely independent in his politics, an outspoken libertarian who had engaged in several antigovernment demonstrations.

Knowing that he and Pushkin were under tremendous time pressure, Scott decided to take a chance on the computer expert. He called a secret meeting for later that night with Wang and the Russian scientist in the revamped computer lab. At the same time, he arranged to have the six disks delivered to them by the security team.

When the three men had assembled next to the computer console—with the small, glistening gold disks stacked on a table in front of them, and a security detail stationed just outside the door—Scott immediately began to apply gentle but steady pressure on their new member. He knew he couldn't let Wang in on the international machinations that had been going on with the project. He certainly couldn't tell him about Pushkin's fears that the Russian government might misuse the information. But he had to make it clear that American national security was at risk, that Wang was essential to their objectives, and that he—Scott—was running this operation.

"Robert," he said, leaning over the slight young man and assuming the most authoritative tone he could muster, "you know I'm in charge of the top scientists here on the moon, right?"

Wang swallowed and nodded. "Sure, I know all about that," he said uncertainly.

"Okay, now I know you have a pretty high security clearance, but what I'm about to say is classified way beyond your level," Scott continued, keeping steady eye contact with the man.

He thought he could begin to see tiny beads of perspiration popping out on Wang's temples. *Good. Very good.*

"I want to be sure you understand that *nothing* said here can go beyond the three of us—got that?" Scott said, holding the other's eyes firmly in the most piercing gaze he could muster.

Again, Wang nodded.

"Good," Scott said. "Now we've got a potential crisis—a national security crisis—and we're going to need your help to resolve it."

Wang glanced at Pushkin nervously. "*Whose* national security?" he asked.

"He's working with us," Scott replied vaguely. "There have been some accidents around this outpost lately. Explosions, people disappearing. You've heard about all that."

Again, Wang murmured his agreement.

"What you don't know is that we have reason to suspect that the information on these disks may be in danger," Scott said, again keeping away from too many specifics. "You've picked up enough from our conversation today to know how important this material is. But we want to be certain that the disks don't get destroyed, either by accident or design. You follow me?"

Scott hoped this general explanation would play well, without provoking any probing questions, and he was heartened to elicit another nod from the man.

"Okay, what we have to figure out right now—and we probably won't have another chance after tonight—is how to make one complete copy of this material," Scott said. "And one person has to be able to carry that copy back to earth without drawing attention. Any ideas?"

With the conversation now turning from security matters to the nuts and bolts of computer science, Wang's uncertain demeanor changed to confidence. He contemplated the disks for a moment and then looked up at Scott.

"Actually, I've thought about this," he replied. "When we were working on the disks this afternoon, I was already wondering about possible ways to back up the system."

"So what do you think?" Pushkin asked. "We have no additional nano-disks. That's what you told us this afternoon."

"Right, and the amount of data on these six disks is humongous," the computer specialist said. "You know that the word on the street has been that one of these things can hold all the earth's knowledge and then some. That's probably an understatement. And far as I could tell, each of these things is filled up with data."

Wang shook his head, a look of wonder creeping into his eyes. "It would take more ordinary floppy disks or compact disks to download all this data than we have on the moon," he added. "Even if we had enough—with the greatest possible storage capacity—you probably couldn't pack them into one lunar shuttle. It would probably take a couple of railroad boxcars."

Scott felt his heart dropping through his stomach. "What other options do we have?"

Wang thought a moment. "Maybe we could e-mail these disks as an attachment to a computer on earth," he said. "Just a minute."

He inserted one of the disks into the special disk drive he had rigged and then tried to send the material to a separate computer across the room.

"No dice," he said, shaking his head. "I think the data is packed so densely into these disks that they won't feed into a regular electronic message like a normal e-mail attachment." He leaned back in his chair. "Either that, or the designers of these disks set them up so that the stuff couldn't be transmitted by ordinary means."

"Kind of an encrypted blocking device," Pushkin said.

"Sort of," Wang replied. "Also, even if I could figure out a way to transmit this data back to earth by electronic messaging, it would almost certainly take longer than you'd want. I'd estimate it would take at least nine months to a year to send all the information on these disks."

Scott stood glumly, watching Wang concentrate on the problem and hoping against hope that some answer to their dilemma would break through. Suddenly, energy seemed to infuse the thin young specialist. "Hold on! I've got an idea."

Wang pulled out his pocket computer and did some quick calculations. Then he leaned back again in his chair.

"Like I said, as many advances as we've made with our regular compact disks, they just don't hold enough data to act as a reasonable backup for these superdisks," he said. "Our hard-disk systems would come closer, but once you put all this data into them, they wouldn't be portable either. But our *data storage boards* are a different matter."

"You mean the technology for taking overflow or excess data off a hard disk and putting it into a data storage bank?" Scott said.

He had some vague knowledge of these massive data storage systems, which had begun to increase quickly at the turn of the century because of the heavy corporate demand for the service. In recent years, the outsourcing of electronic data storage had become a major industry. Scott really hadn't paid much attention to these developments because the whole field seemed too specialized for his interests. But now it seemed that this arcane field might provide the solution they were looking for.

"Exactly!" Wang said. "We have several state-of-the-art data storage vaults here at the outpost—just a few steps away from this office. Obviously, you couldn't take an entire vault back to earth with you in your luggage. One of them is the size of a couple of large refrigerators. But the memory-storage boards inside them are another matter. They're thin as a wafer and only about a foot square. I'd say fifteen or twenty of those—with my special configurations to juice up their storage capacity—would be enough to hold everything on these six nanodisks."

"And that number of storage boards would be easy for me to transport back to earth?" Scott asked.

"Sure! Small enough to fit into a protective case, and then you could put the whole package into a medium-size handbag, like the type you're allowed to carry with you on the different shuttle flights," Wang replied. "You might have to cut back on clean socks and underwear to make room. But it sounds to me like that's a sacrifice you'd be willing to make!"

Scott nodded, finally seeing a glimmer of hope.

"Of course, to retrieve the data you'd have to install these storage boards in a similar computer vault when you get back on earth," Wang said. "But that would be no problem. And bingo, you've got all the data at your fingertips."

"How long would this take, to set up the storage memory boards and download the data onto them?" Scott asked.

Wang shrugged. "Half hour to get the storage boards and reconfigure one to store extra data. Then, I could work on the others while the first batch of data is downloading. We've got plenty of extra boards lying around. And the total download time? Should go pretty quickly. These are very powerful machines we have here—and we use the latest laser-optic technology to transmit the data. Of course, we're talking about a huge amount of information. Still, I'd say a few hours at most." He looked at his watch. "I should be finished by breakfast."

Scott looked at Pushkin, and the Russian nodded. "Then let's do it!" Scott said.

Pushkin and Andrews agreed that one of them would always be present as Wang was working on the storage boards. The Russian volunteered for the first shift, noting privately to Scott that this would provide him with a little additional justifiable delay before he was forced to read and respond to his messages from earth. He fully expected that those messages would put him in the position of having to deal with difficult challenges from his political superiors, who he was sure were already in a panic, wondering what was going on at the moon base.

"I anticipate they will want me to return to earth immediately with the disks," he whispered, out of earshot of Wang, who was already working intently on configuring the hard drive.

"And Energy Project Omega?" Scott asked. "You have to be here when we go on-line."

"It will just have to wait, at least for a few weeks," Pushkin said, and then he pointed to the small gold disks. "I know this new data will be Prime Minister Martov's first concern. And he won't consider allowing anyone other than me to deliver these disks to him."

Scott bounded slowly back toward the moonwalk conveyor that would take him through the long Energy City passageway to the living module—and a few hours' sleep before he had to relieve Pushkin. As he moved, he became lost in speculation about what steps to take next. Questions and decisions came and went:

Should I tell President Dalton about the data we're copying?

No. Unfortunately, even though he was the commander in chief, he couldn't be trusted.

Should I tell anyone else?

He hesitated a while on this one. Shouldn't Colleen be informed? Finally, he decided in the negative. Absolute silence about these copies was imperative. Too many people were already in on the secret—Pushkin, Wang, and himself. Besides, Colleen really didn't need to know, and he was wary of trusting this information to moon-earth communications, even though he had every reason to believe the technology was secure.

What should Hiramatsu, Hightower, and Goldberg do, now that Energy Project Omega will be delayed?

Without Pushkin, their roles on the moon were limited. To ensure their continued healthy bone and muscle mass, as well as cardiovascular fitness and energy, they should return to earth with Pushkin. Anyhow, regardless of what he suggested, their governments would probably recall them for R-and-R. Then, they would be sent back up to the moon when Pushkin returned.

What do we do about the energy project?

For the time being, they would put the lower-level scientists and technicians to work on it. But final execution—bringing it on-line operationally—had to wait for the return of Pushkin, Hiramatsu, and the other top moon team members.

When should I return with the copied data?

Immediately.

What sort of opposition should I expect if the Russians learn I have a copy?

Serious and deadly. Very deadly.

50

When Scott returned to the computer lab four hours later, the same armed security guard, consisting of a female sergeant and two male corporals, was still standing outside the door. They admitted him without question, but he wasn't quite prepared for what he found when he walked inside and closed the door behind him.

Sergey Pushkin was sitting in front of a computer console, scrolling carefully through the Russian version of one of the disks. But one look at the man's face told Scott something was drastically wrong. The Russian scientist wore a haggard, haunted look, which Scott was certain involved more than mere fatigue.

Robert Wang was obviously well aware that there was a problem with the Russian. Even though he had apparently made considerable progress with the downloading process, he periodically glanced with a concerned look in Pushkin's direction.

Deciding to check the progress of the copying first, Scott glided over to Wang's side. "Things going okay? I assume they are because I didn't get a call in my quarters."

Wang looked in Pushkin's direction and then said, "I'm already into the fifth disk. Should be finished well ahead of schedule. But I'm a little worried about him," he added with a nod toward the Russian. "I actually thought I heard him sob at one point. I asked what was the matter, but he wouldn't say. Just waved me off."

Scott immediately bounded across the computer room to Pushkin and put his hand on his shoulder, but the man didn't respond. He just kept staring at the computer screen and slowly scrolled deliberately down the page, line by line.

"Find something interesting?" Scott asked.

The only response was a deeply pained look and a hand raised for silence. The scrolling continued.

"Look, how about letting me in on the secret?" Scott finally asked, trying to force a jocular tone. "Can't be all that bad, can it? Found a flaw in the fountain of youth? A little poisoned well water?"

Pushkin looked up at him abruptly. "What made you say that?"

The sharp reply made Scott hesitate for a moment. Then he tried to recover some of his casual air: "Just came to me, Sergey. What's wrong?"

"You may have spoken more truthfully and profoundly than you realize," the Russian replied, looking back at the screen. "Something beyond the both of us may have put those words in your mouth. I want you to examine this section in English. The Russian and English versions are in separate documents, so we can look at the passages simultaneously. Try the monitor next to mine so that we can talk."

In less than a minute, Scott was seated next to Pushkin, looking at the same passage in English that his companion was reading in Russian.

"You're the physician," Pushkin said. "So you tell me if I'm interpreting this correctly. We assumed that these disks were designed so that the human genome could be shaped to provide an end to aging—in effect, an infinite life span—correct?"

"Right," Scott said, still mystified about where the Russian was taking him.

"We believed that they were giving us only advanced instructions about genetic engineering—how to prevent cell death, specific diseases, and so forth?" Pushkin said.

"Yes, that's right," Scott replied.

"It's not true," Pushkin said vehemently.

"What do you mean?"

"It seems that our friends on the other side of the wormhole want to redesign us," Pushkin replied, shaking his head.

"I don't get you," Scott replied.

Pushkin pressed a couple of icons, and another part of the disk appeared on the screen. "Look at this section—something I found rather easily by using their table of contents. This material is amazingly well organized. Each new section is introduced by a clear summary—one even a nonphysician such as myself can usually understand. Now read this: they say our current level of intelligence is inferior—and will prevent us from taking the next major leap in scientific and intellectual development."

Two or three times, Scott read the short summary that the Russian had put on the screen just to be sure the man's interpretation was correct. Apparently, it was.

"Then they go on to claim that by manipulating our DNA in the way they describe, we can increase our mental powers many times over," Pushkin continued. "There is even a suggestion that we can develop the ability to communicate by telepathy. Not only that, they say we'll be able to change and move physical objects with our minds."

"Telekinetic powers," Scott said under his breath.

"Exactly," Pushkin replied. "Now watch this."

He pressed another combination of icons, and a different section appeared on the screen. Scott needed only to scan the summary once to see that the disk was outlining ways to increase the physical size, power, and agility of human beings.

"Unless I'm wrong, they seem to be claiming that with their program of genetic manipulation, we could all become star NBA centers or Olympic champions," Scott said.

"That's precisely the way I read it," Pushkin said.

Scott looked away from the monitor and reflected for several seconds before he spoke. "It's genetic engineering, pure and simple. This is the most comprehensive proposal for genetic engineering I've ever seen."

"It's more than a proposal, Scott," Pushkin said darkly. "It's a *program*. I'm old enough to remember the horrors civilized people experienced when they understood the full implications of the eugenics and human-breeding programs that Hitler and the Nazis attempted. This program on the disks is potentially much, much more dangerous because human scientific knowledge is far more advanced than it was in Hitler's day."

But Scott was reluctant to go that far. "I'm not sure I'd automatically place these disks in the same category as the Nazis' desire to create a superrace," he protested. "Maybe whoever these aliens are, they just want us to improve at a faster rate than we could achieve on our own."

Pushkin shook his head vigorously and brought up another section on the disk. "Don't be fooled, Scott! The beings who have sent us this disk want much more than that."

The Russian took control of Scott's cursor and pointed toward some lines in English. "Look here. This section deals with the process of human reproduction. Again, I found it by using a link in the table of contents. It says clearly that ultimately, the full success of redesigning the human genome—becoming superintelligent and physically superior, and conquering death—will depend on injecting some outside ingredient into our bodies. And that ingredient will be sent to us at some later time through a wormhole."

Scott examined the section carefully, rereading several explanations and diagrams to be sure he understood it. Then he looked carefully at Pushkin, who had been eyeing him closely.

"You're right—the focus of this text is on altering the X chromosome, which controls the determination and characteristics of the female gender," Scott said. "But curiously, nothing of substance seems to be said about the Y chromosome, which controls male sexual characteristics."

"Also, a large part of this section is devoted to the manipulation of the entire process of pregnancy, from conception through gestation," Pushkin noted.

"Yes," Scott agreed, still studying the text.

"It seems the unnamed outside ingredient—just referred to in the instructions as 'an additional force'—must in some way be supplied to the woman," Pushkin said.

"I think you're right," Scott finally said. "But this doesn't say what the force is supposed to be."

"Does it really matter?" Pushkin asked in a whisper, motioning to Scott to keep his voice low so that Wang wouldn't hear what they were saying. "These beings who sent us these disks are offering to interbreed with us."

"That may be a little strong," Scott murmured uncomfortably, not really wanting to believe what he was reading on the screen, or hearing from Pushkin.

"I don't think it's too strong at all," the Russian said. "In effect, they are proposing that we become a different species. Superhumans of some type."

"And if we follow their directions to the letter, we get to live forever," Scott said quietly.

"A Faustian compact," Pushkin replied.

"A deal with the devil," Scott echoed. "So let me get this straight. To put all this in blunt, tabloid-news terms, whoever or whatever is on the other side of that wormhole window wants to mate with us. That's where we're going with this?"

Scott's response came across half as a question, half as an incredulous statement.

"Yes, and evidently through some form of artificial insemination," Pushkin said quietly. "We must face the fact that this is a strong possibility. And we also have to consider more seriously the option of destroying these disks—and the hard-drive backup of the data."

"But you're a scientist!" Scott protested, a little too loudly for Pushkin's taste. As Robert Wang looked up from his work and glanced curiously at them, the Russian motioned for Scott to keep his voice down.

"I may be a politician, but I'm also a scientist," Scott continued more quietly. "How can we consider destroying new scientific discoveries just because . . . well, we think there may be some danger down the line?"

"We didn't *discover* this," Pushkin said. "This information was handed to us on a platter. You mentioned poisoned water in this fountain of youth. What if we are facing an advanced civilization with evil intentions, a group of beings who want to control or destroy us? What better way than to redesign our genetic makeup and our reproductive systems along lines that will place us under their thumb?"

For the first time, Scott began to feel a cold draft of fear—perhaps the same fear that had been racking his Russian companion as he had studied and contemplated the disturbing information on this disk.

"Strange we'd end up confronting such a problem," Scott said weakly. "After all, we're not heads of state."

"I don't think they meant for this to happen," Pushkin said.

"What's that?"

"The aliens, or whoever they are—I don't think they expected that just two human beings in our position would be sitting here evaluating this data along moral lines," the Russian explained. "I believe they assumed these disks would go directly to political bodies or health centers, where the new information would be accepted and processed without question. By the time anyone began to raise ethical issues, it would have been too late to do anything about it."

"But you and I aren't qualified to make a final decision on this," Scott protested. "I'm a legislator, and a nonpracticing physician, with some background in medical research. And you're a physicist, of all things! We may not even be reading this part of the disk correctly."

Pushkin sighed. "Of course we aren't experts on genetic engineering. But do you really have doubts about our interpretation of the data?"

Scott cast about for some other logical explanation, but he came up short.

Finally, he shook his head. "No. I'm pretty sure we've got the basic message on the disks right."

"I agree," Pushkin said. "Now let me ask you another question: Do you think it's likely that superintelligent, highly advanced beings sent this data with the intention of changing our genetic makeup, and even our reproductive processes?"

Scott hesitated again. Then he nodded. "Probably."

Pushkin nodded again. "Then that leaves us with a final question: What are the motives of these aliens? Is it possible that they want to harm us, rather than help us? Could they even intend to take control of us and our civilization through the channels of genetic engineering and interbreeding?"

Scott could see where the Russian was going, and he didn't like the direction one bit. At the same time, he saw that these horrific alternatives were at least as likely as the hope many humans still harbored that benign extraterrestrials would someday land on earth and permanently change lives for the better, bringing peace on earth and untold personal and societal benefits.

"Okay, I have to concede you have a point," Scott said. "It may be that these aliens—and I agree that there probably are aliens on the other side of that thing—want to improve our lives. But we can't take a chance on that. It's at least as likely that we'll be worse off if we give them a foothold."

Pushkin nodded. "So that leaves us with a choice. We're both responsible human beings, capable of making moral decisions. And it seems to me that we are confronted here with a very serious moral dilemma. I mean, you and I must decide if we should return these disks to earth—or destroy them immediately."

"I don't know . . . ," Scott replied tentatively.

Pushkin didn't respond. Instead, he looked down at his pocket computer. He seemed to have pulled up some text on the screen, but Scott couldn't tell what it was.

"Maybe there's a way to make use of *part* of this information, without buying into the whole package," Scott continued, knowing that he was grasping at straws. "In other words, we might be able to use some of the information on the disks to wipe out most diseases and extend our life spans by a few hundred years, even if not forever. That wouldn't be so bad! But we'll never know if this is possible unless we get experts working on this material."

Pushkin shook his head in what looked to Scott like a sign of resignation. "Human experts and knowledge are not always the best answer."

Before the congressman could reply, the Russian passed over his small computer. "Read this," he directed.

"It's in Russian," Scott said with an amused smile.

"Sorry," Pushkin said, reaching over and touching an icon, which switched the language to English.

Now, Scott could see that Pushkin had been looking at some ancient religious text. The words on the monitor riveted him:

When men began to multiply on the face of the ground, and daughters were born to them, the sons of God saw that the daughters of men were fair; and they took to wife such of them as they chose . . . The Nephilim were on the earth in those days, and also afterward, when the sons of God came in to the daughters of men, and they bore children to them. These were the mighty men that were of old, the men of reknown.

The LORD saw that the wickedness of man was great in the earth, and that every imagination of the thoughts of his heart was only evil continually. And the LORD was sorry that he had made man on the earth, and it grieved him to his heart. So the LORD said, "I will blot out man whom I have created from the face of the ground, man and beast and creeping things and birds of the air, for I am sorry that I have made them." But Noah found favor in the eyes of the LORD.

Scott paused and contemplated the words, a frown passing over his brow. "The Bible?" he asked.

Pushkin nodded. "Genesis, the beginning of chapter six."

Scott hesitated, searching for a way to be firm without offending his new ally. "Look, Sergey, I don't want to be disrespectful, but I really can't see what this Bible passage has to do with these disks."

"You saw the reference to the 'Nephilim'?" the Russian asked.

"Yeah, I wondered about that," Scott replied.

"I think it's possible that we are dealing with Nephilim," Pushkin repeated. "That's the Hebrew word for 'giants' in the Genesis passage I gave you. The word could also mean 'bully' or 'tyrant.' Strange references are sprinkled here and there throughout the Old and New Testaments about physically large, powerful supermen who are the offspring of these sons of God and daughters of men. Many feel that these sons of God may refer to fallen angels who have mated with human females."

Scott shook his head and smiled sardonically. "You're joking, right?"

"I'm completely serious," the Russian said.

"But Sergey, this is really . . . well, you know I respect you, and I'll listen closely to anything you say, but I have to tell you, this sounds pretty far out. Pretty, well . . . silly."

"Yet who would have imagined the incredible things we have witnessed here on the moon in the past few days?" Pushkin reminded him. "If I had told you a wormhole would actually appear, and that Bolotov would disappear through it, and that we would receive a message from an unknown source that purports to offer eternal life, you wouldn't just have called that silly. You would have told me I was crazy!"

Scott had to admit the Russian had a point. *But Noah and the ark? And fallen angels?* To any sophisticated, well-educated person in the twenty-first century—and certainly to any trained scientist—those were fairy tales. Then Scott remembered that the man whispering within inches of his ear was the world's leading nuclear fusion expert and probably one of the top three or four theoretical physicists.

So for the moment, Scott decided to take Pushkin's wild speculations seriously, even though he wasn't close to being convinced. He was sure the Russian was sane, even if eccentric, and that a few well-placed questions or points would demolish the fallen-angel theory.

First, Scott decided he would meet Pushkin on his own ground—the Bible. If the Russian could be convinced quickly that there was nothing to his interpretation of this passage in Genesis, then they could move on to a more productive discussion.

"I seem to remember that Jesus said angels don't marry or have sex," Scott argued, fishing deep through his memories of old Sunday school lessons.

"Actually, Jesus said that angels *in heaven* don't marry," Pushkin corrected. "The sons of God in this passage had *left* heaven—and that may mean that somehow they could interbreed with human beings. Anyhow, I think you and I would both agree that the alien beings we are dealing with through that wormhole are almost certainly not in any kind of heaven—though they may exist in some extradimensional realm. I mean, a place that has more dimensions than our four of height, length, breadth, and time."

"So you really think they may be . . ."

"They may be supercreatures who fit into the category that some theologians and poets have called 'fallen angels,'" Pushkin finished. "But let's not become distracted by religious terminology. Terms like 'fallen angel' carry too many negative connotations in our time. Think of another name. Perhaps we should call them 'flawed' or 'evil superbeings,' or 'superior intelligences.' In other words, they may have mental and physical capacities far beyond anything we can imagine as humans. And they may exist in a strange realm on the other side of that wormhole. Most important, we have to assume that their intentions may not coincide with our best interests."

"This is getting really weird," Scott said, looking toward Wang to be certain he wasn't eavesdropping on any of this outlandish conversation.

"Some people do discount these ancient stories as unfounded myths and fabrications," Pushkin conceded. "But others think there may be something to them, something we don't understand. For example, some have suggested there may be some historical basis for the stories about the ancient Greek gods and goddesses who mated on occasion with humans. Hercules, Achilles, and other superhumans of ancient times were supposed to be the products of those human-divine unions."

"So you're linking the Nephilim of the Bible and the superhuman offspring of ancient Greek and Roman gods and goddesses, such as Hercules and Achilles?" Scott asked, becoming increasingly uncomfortable. "You're suggesting they were really all the children of fallen angels, who mated with human beings?"

Pushkin shrugged. "We have to consider all possibilities. Many times, these ancient mythological accounts have some basis in fact. I think there are some disturbing parallels, don't you?"

Scott didn't answer immediately. In part, he didn't want to say anything that Pushkin might interpret as ridicule. Their ability to work together was too important to risk compromising their relationship.

Pushkin smiled—almost paternally, Scott thought. "I know it's hard to trust me with these disks," the Russian said, placing his hand on Scott's forearm. "That's understandable. Our nations' interests are often at odds. But remember: over Bolotov's objections, I insisted that you and the others be brought in on this experiment. And I also am quite serious that I want you to share in this decision about the disposal of the disks, even though by all rights they are Russian property."

Scott nodded. The man was absolutely correct about all that.

With his hand still squeezing Scott's arm, Pushkin continued: "I also know that what I am trying to tell you now may seem so bizarre and far-fetched, you may worry that I am losing my mind. At best, you may think I am—what do you say?—a religious nut. I don't expect to convince you in this conversation. I only want you to think about what you have just read and what I am saying—especially if something should happen to me. Remembering and acting on that memory may save not only you, but many others."

He paused and looked down at his pocket computer screen, which still displayed the Bible passages. "I feel strongly that you and I have been placed in this particular place for a reason. And I continue to feel that the best, wisest course would be to destroy every trace of these disks. But I also feel constrained not to act alone. I feel that we must act together, or not at all."

Scott shook his head emphatically. "I can't agree to destroy the disks."

"Then would you agree to have me present the original disks to the international community, and not just to Russia?" Pushkin asked.

Scott frowned, not sure he had heard the scientist correctly. "You mean you'd give the disks to, say, a commission from the United Nations, or something like that?"

Pushkin nodded. "That's precisely what I have in mind."

Scott's first reaction was that such a scheme would be completely unworkable. He didn't regard the UN leadership as any more trustworthy than that of Russia, or the current United States administration, for that matter. Most serious of all, he could see no way, once they had set foot back on earth, that Pushkin could do a successful end run around his own political leaders.

"But wouldn't your Russian leadership go crazy?" Scott asked in an intense whisper. "Your life wouldn't be worth a fake ruble if you tried that."

Pushkin smiled again. "I don't think my life will be worth much if I act wrongly or immorally. And giving these disks only to Russia would be quite wrong. You should know, by the way, that I have decided not to provide my country with any details about these disks. I have no doubt that they will learn something from other sources. But they'll learn nothing from me, other than the general fact that we have received information that could revolutionize human health and longevity."

Scott shook his head, not quite believing what he was hearing. "You may not have to stick your neck out that far," he protested. "After all, I'll have the storage memory-board backups. By giving those to me, you've already passed them on to the international community. We don't have to tell Martov or any other Russian leaders how I got the copies."

Pushkin shook his head with a tolerant smile. "We must be straightforward about this. Also, the information needs to be considered by *all* nations, not just yours and mine. I feel that we need to make a strong public statement to this effect. And please understand, Scott, if I am successful in transferring the disks to an international commission, then I would expect you to turn over the copies to the international community as well. Can we agree on that?"

Scott hesitated. He was not thinking about the moral implications of the issue as much as he was about the practical political advantages that the United States might achieve with sole ownership of the copy. After all, Americans had more money and scientific expertise than all the other nations of the earth combined. In a flat-out race, the United States would probably be able to outstrip all other nations with little trouble.

But to what end? Scott couldn't answer that question satisfactorily. After all, what was the point in having Americans live forever if the rest of the world was dying on schedule? Such a prospect not only struck the congressman as unfair, but also certain to provoke envy and probably violence from the "have-not" nations.

In the end, Scott nodded. "Agreed. Both your originals and my storage-board copies go to an international group. But there are a lot of UN branches and committees. Which one do you feel should get it?"

"To make it absolutely clear that this information is the property of all human beings, I would suggest that you and I together make a presentation to the United Nations General Assembly," Pushkin said. "The assembly is now in session. I propose that immediately upon our arrival, we travel to New York City and put the materials into their hands."

Scott could think of all sorts of arguments against the plan. First, he couldn't imagine how he and Pushkin could ever get from Florida to New York with the disks without being detained, searched, and divested of the genome information by some official agency or operatives, whether American or Russian. Even if they made it to the UN, he didn't know anyone there who would have enough moral fiber to take the lead in a venture of this type. Also, he expected that the UN's bureaucratic red tape, which more often than not strangled worthy causes, would do this one in as well.

Finally, just trying this UN ploy would probably cause both of them to be branded traitors by their respective countries. Scott had already decided not to tell President Dalton about his storage-board copies. Did he really want to take the next step and perhaps end up behind bars?

Scott couldn't honestly say he was happy about taking such risks. But it was obvious that Pushkin had drawn a line in the sand on this issue—one that

Scott couldn't cross without disrupting their delicate relationship and maybe even losing access to the duplicate data memory boards. Besides, they were running out of time.

So Scott agreed to go along with the Russian. At the same time, however, he resolved to leave the door open to making later adjustments in these plans if they were needed as events unfolded back on earth.

"Finished!" Robert Wang called out, interrupting the intense conversation.

In a matter of minutes, the computer specialist had assembled twenty thin memory storage boards and placed them in a nondescript container.

"Remember, to access these, you have to insert them in the same kind of data storage vault they came from," Wang said. "Here's the identification number. And good luck!"

Scott nodded, but he hardly heard what Wang was saying. He was already thinking ahead—to the trip back to earth and to the certain confrontation he faced with forces that he worried might be too powerful for a lone U.S. congressman and a quixotic Russian scientist to handle.

51

The preparations for the return to earth went quickly, but not smoothly—at least not for Professor Sergey Pushkin. When he returned to his room after meeting with Scott Andrews, the scientist transmitted an encrypted e-mail message to Prime Minister Martov, describing very briefly the team's plans to return immediately to earth.

Pushkin desperately wanted to prevent in-depth interrogation at this point about their discoveries on the moon, and he also was determined to avoid any possibility of disclosure about his plan to go directly to the UN. So he explained in his message that he felt it was best for security purposes not to be too specific about the results of the experiment. He mentioned only that they had received extensive information that could "revolutionize human health and longevity." He said that he preferred to provide a detailed description of his findings at a face-to-face meeting with the prime minister.

Within minutes, as he was finishing his packing for the return voyage, message alarms began to go off on his computer. Martov's fury practically leaped off the screen.

> You have violated the trust I placed in you. You have not informed me fully or in a timely manner about your discoveries and about important events related to the experiment. Why should I have to rely on others to learn about Bolotov's disappearance? You will immediately provide me with more information about these disks. And you will not leave your lunar post until I order you to do so. Any disobedience of these instructions will be treason.

As Pushkin read the message, he swallowed hard and felt panic well up in his throat. Obviously, he had provoked one of the most powerful men on earth and was now teetering on the brim of a chasm of professional and personal disaster. He continued to feel his primary allegiance was to a higher purpose. *But how can I satisfy Martov without ravaging my principles—or digging my own grave?*

Finally, he responded:

Forgive me, Prime Minister, for failing to communicate sooner with you, but events have been occurring so quickly that I have hardly had time to sleep. I believe you will be extremely pleased at what we have found, but the information we have received is too vast and complex to be sent to you as an e-mail attachment. As you will see when I return, we lack the technology to create such an attachment. A lunar shuttle is now prepared to take us to earth, and I request your permission to depart on that flight with our entire set of scientific findings.

Pushkin waited nervously as he watched for Martov's reply. If the prime minister ordered him to stay on the moon, he knew he would have to comply—or risk the gulag or even execution when he returned to earth. Finally, the response he had hoped for arrived:

You have permission to return to earth immediately. But remember that you must now prove anew that my trust in you has been justified.

Pushkin leaned back on his bed, heaving an audible sigh of relief. Fortunately, Martov had given him no instructions about what specific steps to take with the disks when he arrived back on earth. He knew the prime minister would initially be unhappy about his plan to turn the genome information over to the UN. But Pushkin was convinced of the righteousness of his mission and was determined to convince Martov of his position.

Then an idea came to him. He might be able to pacify Martov by giving the Russians the original disks at virtually the same time that he and Andrews turned over the copies to the General Assembly. Surely Martov would be happy to have the originals, and he would undoubtedly understand that the information on the disks had to be disseminated to all peoples on earth, and not limited to just a few. Pushkin resolved that he would discuss this possibility with Andrews, and together, they would work out something acceptable.

Feeling increasingly confident about his new plan for the disks, the physicist stood up from the bed and finished packing. He had no intention of waiting around for Martov to change his mind, and he also didn't want to delay the flight back to earth. The lander that would take them to the *Moonshot* shuttle, which was now docked in lunar orbit, was ready to blast off from the landing pad, and he had already been notified that all the other team members were on their way to the boarding area.

With *Moonshot* halfway home, most of the shuttle passengers were gazing out into space through the viewing portals, expressing their wonder about how the earth had grown considerably larger even as the size of the moon had shrunk. Even though they had seen similar sights on the first leg of the journey to the moon, it was still hard not to be impressed by the vastness of space and the relative insignificance of their beautiful but small home in the solar system.

As the others watched and chattered, Scott Andrews was distracted. Sergey Pushkin had informed him at the beginning of their return journey home about his plan to give the Russians the original copy of the disks. Now, Pushkin wanted Scott's copies to go to the UN, but the congressman still wasn't convinced. He didn't trust the UN officials, and he much preferred to have some American agency be in charge of them. But he wanted to avoid a confrontation with the Russian at this point. Instead, he got Pushkin to agree that immediately after they arrived back on earth, the two of them would retire to a private meeting room at the Kennedy Space Center to work out the details.

One thing that bothered Scott was that Pushkin appeared to have become increasingly impractical. He seemed to have no idea about the dangerous international game that he was playing. After all, he was only one man who was trying to match wits with earthly powers that could exterminate him in an instant.

His latest notion, which Scott also opposed, was to make some sort of an announcement to the entire team. Apparently he wanted to try to pull them all into his plan of giving the genome information to the entire world.

"You're being naive, Sergey!" Scott had protested. "We're sitting on a powder keg. The more people who know about our plans, the more dangerous it gets—for both of us, but especially for you."

"But we're on the way to earth!" Pushkin had argued. "Only a few more hours, and we'll be landing. What can anybody do in such a short period of time?"

Pushkin had refused to listen to Scott's warnings, and now he signaled that he felt the time was right for his special announcement. Before Scott could pull him aside and caution him further, the Russian called the top scientists on the moon team into the middle of the central chamber of *Moonshot*.

"Since we are all equals in this venture, there is something I feel you must all know," he began. "These disks, which I carry always close to my heart"—he reached into his pressure suit and pulled out the now-familiar container—"will not go just to one powerful nation or two, but will be shared with all peoples on earth."

The scientists murmured at this news, but Pushkin raised his hand for silence.

"Dr. Andrews and I have agreed on this approach to minimize any dangers associated with the disks," he continued. "We fear misuse of the information if placed exclusively in the hands of the few. Also, because the decisions about the use of this information will affect all human beings, one or two nations cannot be allowed to decide for all. So Dr. Andrews and I will take the disks directly to the United Nations General Assembly after we land at the Kennedy Space Center."

He paused, and after some hesitation, light applause broke out. It was obvious that the group hadn't been prepared for such an announcement, and they were still digesting the implications.

Scott wasn't so sure it was a good idea for Pushkin to have advertised the fact that he was carrying such valuable cargo unguarded in his front vest pocket. At the same time, he was happy that the Russian had been vague about exactly what the UN would receive and had neglected to say anything about the disk copies in Scott's possession. Still, Scott couldn't help thinking nervously about his copies, which were stowed away in a handbag that was locked in his gear compartment in the rear chamber of the shuttle. He almost wished he could float back into the storage area to check on it.

"Now let me propose a toast," Pushkin said, holding aloft a fruit drink container, with the usual microgravity tube protruding from the end. "To our friend Vladimir Bolotov, whom I fully expect to meet again!"

"Hear! Hear!" Jeffrey Hightower exclaimed.

All five remaining members of the team raised similar containers and silently drank to their missing colleague.

"And to the future of Energy Project Omega—which we expect to resume in a few months!" Scott said.

Again, all containers went up, and the drinking tubes disappeared in five separate mouths.

"And to a profitable future for the wormhole disks!" Ruth Goldberg said.

"May we all live forever!" Hightower said.

"*Hai, hai!*" Hiramatsu echoed. "And to the good health and long life of our dear friend Dr. Pushkin, who has been the guiding light for every phase of this work."

As the group drank the final toasts, Scott gazed silently back toward the moon. There were still so many unanswered questions. The whereabouts of the wormhole, which for all they knew might reappear at any time . . . the ultimate fate of Bolotov . . . the identity of the alien beings who had provided the genome information. Would they ever have all the answers?

Scott turned to stare at the earth, which seemed to have grown larger, even during the short time consumed by their meeting. *What does the future really hold for us?*

Pushkin's expansive approach to sharing the information on the disks still made him nervous. He was convinced that the man had at least one foot in Fantasyland if he really expected his Russian handlers to go along docilely with his decision to dump all rights to the revolutionary genome disks into the public domain. A world power just wouldn't play the global game that way. On the other hand, the Russians were limited in the action they could take on American soil.

So what can we expect when we land?

It was at this point that Scott made a fateful decision about the disposal of his own copies of the genome information—a decision that would have repercussions far beyond anything he could ever have anticipated.

52

Valery pulled on his dark blue windbreaker, emblazoned with the word *Emergency* in white on the back. Then he turned around twice as Klaudia inspected him.

"Good," she said. "Very good. You look official."

The stocky Russian responded with a broad smile, which abruptly disappeared at his taskmaster's next harsh words: "If you execute this assignment properly, you'll redeem yourself, and I may forget your lapses at the apartment building—which almost resulted in our capture."

Both of them knew quite well what she meant. She had reminded him daily that he had allowed the Americans to trail him back to the apartment. Then, to cap his transgressions, he had committed the unpardonable sin of acknowledging her with a wave at the front door. As a result, they had been forced to move quickly to new quarters in Satellite Beach, just south of Cocoa Beach.

But Klaudia wasted no time thinking any more about Valery. She had already turned away from him and was busy examining her own uniform, which was identical to his. Satisfied with the garb, she looked quickly through the equipment packs they would each be carrying. Some of the usual medical gear was scattered about the top. But within easy reach was an arsenal of submachine guns, pistols, grenades, and belts filled with rounds of ammunition.

"This should do," she said with some satisfaction. "The ambulance is ready?"

"Yes, Colonel," her companion replied nervously. "They are waiting right now for my call to bring it around back."

"Good," she replied, looking at her watch.

One of Valery's assignments while the two of them had been in hiding in Brooklyn had been to make contact with the American branch of the *Dolgos Mafiya* and line up reliable drivers, saboteurs, and gunmen in case they were needed. Now that their mission had become clear, Klaudia had summoned the team of mercenaries to central Florida.

"The shuttle is scheduled to land in three hours. We'll walk out of here in a half hour. Allowing for traffic, that should give us plenty of time to make it to the Kennedy Space Center."

"Yes, Colonel," he replied, not daring to look her in the eye.

"Now please leave me," she said brusquely. "I must send one last message to our superiors. And be sure that all our gear is ready to be moved on an instant's notice. Nothing must remain in these rooms. We won't be returning."

As Valery exited, Klaudia Ming-Petrovich adjusted her computer display screen and entered the required code to open communications with Martov. In seconds, his image was staring back at her—and he didn't look happy.

"You're late!" he said.

"Only by seconds, my esteemed colleague," she replied, using her eyes and a slight smile to calm him. "We have had so many last-minute responsibilities. So much to do. But everything is falling into place nicely."

"No further mistakes? No near-misses with the FBI?" he asked, a faint note of accusation coming through the audio.

"None at all," she assured him. "We leave our quarters in less than a half hour, and with our departure, the final game begins."

"This is not a game!" Martov chided. "This is very serious business. For you and for me. Indeed, for Russia and the entire earth. We must not lose control of events."

"Certainly not, valued one," Klaudia replied.

"You have enlisted sufficient reinforcements for the operation?" he asked.

"Yes," she replied. "They are the best that are available. Not *Pika* quality, of course. But still, seasoned *Dolgos* warriors."

"They seem adequate," he replied, signaling that he had checked on her choices himself. But that was to be expected. This operation was too important for him not to be deeply involved. "And the arrival scene has been prepared properly?"

She nodded. "We were fortunate in finding a space-center employee who was having problems with his women," she said with a smirk. "We learned through our government contacts that one of the worker's girlfriends had recently called to complain that he was unreliable. As a result, the officials at the center transferred him to another job, which he didn't like. So he was ripe when Valery and I approached him about giving us a special nighttime tour of the landing site—for a fee, of course."

She smiled slyly before proceeding. "These Americans always respond well when you wave money in their faces," she said. "Also, I had to take certain steps, shall we say, to distract this man, but that was easy. He likes women. That gave Valery the opportunity he needed to make his special preparations on the runway tarmac and around the ambulance holding area."

"Good, good," Martov said, nodding approvingly.

Klaudia was disappointed that the prime minister showed no signs of jealousy, but that was typical of these politicians. The more powerful they became, the more disconnected they seemed to become from ordinary human emotions.

"Now, I believe you have some important information to pass on to me," she prompted.

He cleared his throat. It was obvious that he had not been looking forward to this moment because the information would put more leverage in her hands than he liked. *We both know quite well that information is power*, she thought. Now she was gratified to see that he had no choice but to share his secret.

"You need the name of our undercover operative," he said.

She nodded expectantly—and couldn't contain a slight gasp when he revealed the name.

"I didn't know *you* could be surprised," he said, in an ironic but complimentary tone that elicited a broader smile from her. "Here's another surprise: our agent is *Pika*."

Stunned might have been a better description than surprised. Klaudia stared at him for a second or two, her mouth slightly agape at the news that the operative was one of the small cadre of elite *Mafiya* assassins. Now, it was Martov's turn to grin.

"How can someone be in *Pika* without my knowing about it?" she asked testily.

"You may be the senior member," he replied sternly, "but you don't control the group. Sometimes, for purposes of total security, certain information must be withheld, even from you. Especially when you are in the field. What if you should be captured and questioned under drugs? Even with your discipline, we couldn't count on you not to break."

His explanation made sense, but she refused to show she agreed with him. Instead, she shrugged sullenly and glanced away, but at the same time she made sure her body language conveyed her displeasure.

"There is more you must know," Martov said, ignoring her petulance. "Disturbing news that will change your assignment somewhat. Professor Pushkin has lost control of himself. There is even evidence he may have turned traitor."

"What?" she said, becoming increasingly disturbed as he told her about Pushkin and the new disks.

"The problem is that Pushkin provided the other top scientists—including the American, Scott Andrews—with access to the genome information," Martov said.

Andrews again! When would she be rid of the man!

"It gets worse," Martov said darkly. "Pushkin has just made it clear—even as they are en route to earth—that he and Andrews plan to give these disks to the United Nations General Assembly."

"You know this for certain?" she asked, momentarily forgetting her position.

"Of course I'm certain! Transmissions from the shuttle keep me updated."

"So Pushkin actually plans to give away our property?" Klaudia asked incredulously.

"Yes. That's exactly it." The prime minister's voice had started to shake; he was obviously growing angrier by the second as he spoke.

"He should be shot."

"There is another priority," Martov said. "To make sure no one else gets these disks. You must intercept the team before they get to the debriefing area."

Klaudia frowned and shook her head. "Quite a feat. Few places are more heavily guarded than the shuttle landing area."

"You *must* succeed!" Martov said.

"I'm the only one who could *possibly* succeed with such a difficult assignment," she replied in something of a huff. She was proud of her abilities and never hesitated to display her supreme self-confidence, even in the presence of one so powerful as Martov.

"I know your abilities," he replied, softening his tone somewhat. "They are legendary. But something else worries me. I've also learned from shuttle communiqués that the passengers and crew will be wearing not only pressure suits, but also helmets as they disembark. Something about heightened security. That will make identification of any individual much more difficult."

Klaudia frowned without answering.

"It's absolutely imperative that you make correct identifications," Martov emphasized. "If you're uncertain, look for distinctive *Pika* identification. You understand?"

"Yes," she said.

"Another thing," Martov said. "Keep Pushkin alive if possible. But the other top scientists, especially Andrews, should all be eliminated. Pushkin has told them too much. I have reason to believe that Andrews knows more about the potential of those disks than I do! Obviously, that is unacceptable."

"Andrews will be my pleasure," she said.

"And remember, if necessary, *everyone* is expendable—but *not those disks,*" he said. "We must be the only ones with access to that information. In many ways, our future—yours and mine—depends on the safe delivery of the disks."

"I understand," she said. "I understand perfectly."

Now, she knew all she needed to know. She had been authorized by the highest authority to finish this job on her own terms. She smiled grimly as she contemplated the possibilities.

After signing off with Martov, Klaudia immediately called Valery back into the room. "We move immediately," she ordered. "The end game has begun."

53

They're scheduled for touchdown in less than two hours," Colonel Spike Caldwell barked. "Let's go over the procedure one final time."

Colleen automatically joined the low groans that filled their makeshift operations room at the Kennedy Space Center Headquarters. The participating operatives had gone over the basic response plan and various contingencies so often that most of them were beginning to have one thought: *overkill.* They now knew the duties of practically everyone else, and an increasing, though unspoken, undercurrent of opinion was: *What's the point?*

"No bellyaching!" he ordered.

Then, as if in answer to their unspoken complaint, he said: "This repetition is designed to teach you chapter and verse about what the guys on your right and left are supposed to do. It's not just about nailing your own assignment. If there's resistance, any of you could be taken out. So you *will* be prepared to take over for any other person on the team! Got that?"

Knowing nods now replaced the groans.

"Okay, let's start with you, Barker," Caldwell said, his eyes boring a hole into Colleen and almost physically pulling her up to a straighter position in her chair. "Where are you going to be standing?"

Colleen couldn't figure out why he had singled her out first, but she didn't have time to think through the possibilities. Instead, she shrugged and replied, "At the end of the line of dignitaries and a few anointed members of the press. Close to Scott Andrews's family, and just behind and to the right of the vice president." She then raised the miniature but extremely powerful binoculars she had been issued. "And I'll be holding on tight to these."

Her quizzical tone in effect added: *Do you think I'm a little slow, Spike?*

"And you're going to *stay* there, right?" he emphasized. "No matter what happens?"

"Right, right," she replied.

Now she understood. Somebody, probably one of her erstwhile FBI friends, had put Caldwell on notice that she was unpredictable, something of a loose cannon with political connections. He just wanted to be sure that she didn't go off half-cocked and mess up the operation.

"Now, Commander James," he said, turning to the Wheaton Bible professor.

That was the first time Colleen had heard Michael James addressed by his old Navy rank. He was even wearing his uniform, with more rows of combat ribbons over his heart than she could count. *Is he legal?* She knew he wasn't on active duty, but she had never asked if he had remained in the reserves. Or if he retained some other status that gave him his unusual access to the higher-ups in Washington.

She found herself becoming amused now that it was the supremely self-assured James who was finally being put on the spot. She suspected that Caldwell was focusing on him because he recognized that James was even more of a loose cannon than she was.

"I'll be standing next to Colleen," he replied respectfully, but confidently. "The two of us will be there for two functions. First, we'll be sure that Andrews's family members don't bolt toward the disembarking crew and passengers. Second, we'll help provide instant identification of Pushkin and Andrews. When we locate them, we'll immediately pass on the information to Corporal Jefferson"—he pointed to a strong-looking young man in loose slacks and sports shirt—"who will, in turn, relay our message by radio to you."

"And why is instant identification of Pushkin and Andrews so important?" Caldwell asked pointedly, apparently not at all impressed by James's aplomb.

"Because the faster we identify them, the more quickly steps can be taken to protect them," James said, betraying no irritation with the security chief's didactic manner.

"And why are we concerned about taking unusual precautions to protect them?" Caldwell prompted with some mild impatience.

"Because we have reason to believe that Pushkin and Andrews may be targeted for an assassination attempt," Colleen interjected solemnly. The words almost stuck in her throat.

As Colonel Spike Caldwell questioned each of the other key players in the upcoming drama, Colleen found her mind wandering. Caldwell, one of the nation's top Special Forces operatives, obviously knew what he was doing. That gave her some confidence. But she remained deeply worried because she knew that when the shuttle touched down on the space-center runway, anything could happen.

She had memorized the expected sequence of events. The passengers—the top scientists on the moon team—and the shuttle crew would disembark at a point some distance from any spectators. Members of the special military response team would be scattered around the landing area, many of them disguised as ground crew personnel.

The members of the moon team would be physically wobbly because of their long stay in a low-gravity environment. There was a good chance they would need help making it the short distance from the orbiter-shuttle to an enclosed and reinforced holding shack, a prefabricated shelter that had been set up especially for this mission. So NASA had assigned two trained assistants to provide any needed help to each of the returning scientists.

Inside the shack, which had been built to withstand small-weapons fire and small-charge explosives, the scientists would be placed in heavily armored vehicles. When the vehicles were loaded, they would exit the back of the shack at high speed. Identical armored vehicles *without* any passengers would serve as decoys. They would leave the building at the same time as the actual transport vans in an effort to divert the attention of possible foes.

If everything went smoothly, the passengers would arrive in less than a minute at a reinforced concrete building complex. There, they would be placed under heavy guard and would spend as long as necessary—probably several hours—undergoing debriefings by a multinational team of inspectors.

At this point, no one really knew what to expect from the moon team. Contradictory reports and rumors from the moon, or from intercepted communications picked up by the Russians, Japanese, and Israelis, had conveyed a fragmented picture of the occurrences in space. There were reports that a return message of some sort had squirted into the moon outpost through a tear in the fabric of space-time. Some scientists were using the term *wormhole*, but others were pooh-poohing the description as impossible, a total fabrication.

There were also unsubstantiated—and most felt, laughable—reports that Pushkin was in possession of an entire set of disks from aliens, which he and Andrews planned to pass on to the world at large through a meeting of the UN General Assembly. Colleen smiled involuntarily when she thought of that one.

She couldn't imagine her boss agreeing to go "total cowboy," as she put it to the CIA official who passed the rumor on to her. The factor that caused Colleen and most other officials evaluating the situation to take these reports with a grain of salt was that none of them came directly from Pushkin or Andrews.

The last message she had received from Scott had hinted that the team had made some potentially explosive discoveries. But he had left it at that. Consequently, Colleen suspected more was going on than Scott had been able to tell her—but she was virtually certain that the facts fell short of the wildest rumors.

She sighed again, wishing that this real-time nightmare would come to a swift, happy end. She felt certain that once the team had passed on all they knew—and had demonstrated that they weren't sitting on priceless information that held the "secret to eternal life," as one supermarket tabloid had reported—they would become less vulnerable to outside attack.

But as Colleen had learned on several occasions in the past few months, any assumption about the future, regardless of how reasonable, could prove to be wrong. Dead wrong.

54

The transfer of passengers from *Moonshot* to the *Challenger II* orbiter had gone smoothly, and now the orbiter was beginning its reentry into the earth's atmosphere. The commander of the mission announced that weather at the Kennedy Space Center was perfect. As a result, they wouldn't have to consider the alternative landing sites at Edwards Air Force Base in California or one of the secondary locations in New Mexico.

Scott, who was strapped into a seat next to Hightower on this leg of the flight, was having second thoughts about his failure to pass on what he knew about the genome disks to any contacts back on earth—and that even included Colleen. He knew that Pushkin had also withheld information about the disks from his people—and that meant the two of them were perched together on a potential time bomb.

At this point, he and Pushkin knew more about the disks than anyone else. They alone were aware of perhaps the most important piece of information now available—the desire of aliens to influence the human reproductive cycle. That disturbing fact was something that could be dealt with only by a broad-based international commission, and not by one or two superpowers.

But Scott also knew that some reports about the wormhole and the six disks were bound to have leaked out. By now, wild rumors and speculation had to be floating about in every intelligence center on earth. To head off such rumors, would it have been better for him to push the issue to a crisis while they were still in the relatively contained environment of the moon?

He couldn't help but think that he and Pushkin would have been in a better position to influence world opinion from the relatively simple and secure lunar political platform. Instead, they would now have to make their case from the unpredictable political quagmire of earth.

He glanced around at the other passengers who were seated in the crew compartment. They had all been unusually quiet since *Challenger II* had disengaged from the Deep Space Station platform and begun its descent toward earth.

The team members were all tired—and they *looked* tired. Most had lost noticeable weight and muscle mass, despite efforts on the part of most of them to keep up a regular strength-training program. Only Ruth Goldberg looked about the same as she had upon her departure. If anything, she seemed stronger and fitter than when she had left. He wondered how much of a letdown it would be for her to return to her regular wheelchair on earth—after running rings around most inhabitants of Energy City with her moonchair and other equipment.

"De-orbit will begin in thirty seconds!" the commander announced.

Through the portholes, Scott could see the sky and earth spinning as the *Challenger II* orbiter rotated into a rear-first position for entry into the earth's atmosphere. He knew from his many briefings that this rotation was achieved by manipulation of the rocket thrusters on the reaction control system, which was located at the front and rear of the craft.

With the shuttle now rotated a full 180 degrees, the rear engines blasted into action to slow the movement of the craft and cause it to drop out of earth orbit from its current position, about two hundred miles above the earth's surface. Now, every movement of the shuttle followed a time-tested pattern for reentry. The reaction control system rocket spun the nose forward again for the return to earth, with the craft officially contacting the planet's atmosphere at an altitude of about 400,000 feet.

The angle of entry had to be just right. Too steep, and the heat generated by the atmosphere could burn the hull and its passengers to a crisp; too shallow and *Challenger II* could skip like a flat rock on a pond right back into space. But that was never a worry with a seasoned commander and pilot at the controls—not to mention one of the finest computer systems the earth had to offer.

As the minutes ticked away and the altitude and speed decreased, the passengers did more chatting than sightseeing. They knew that the time from the de-orbiting blast to landing always took just a little longer than one hour. When Scott looked at his watch, he was amazed to see that they had less than fifteen minutes before touchdown.

"You've been quiet, Jeff," he joked with Hightower over the intercom. "I haven't heard a 'mate' or a 'cobber' since we left the space station dock."

"Sorry to be bad company, Scotty my man," the Australian said. "I'm just wondering if I'll be able to walk in earth gravity."

"You and Goldberg are in better shape than anybody!" Scott said. "Both Hiramatsu and I were saying that we wished we had spent as much time in the Energy City exercise room as you did."

"Ah, well, you know us Aussies," he quipped. "Have to stay in shape to wrestle those crocs."

"Five minutes to landing!" the pilot called out.

Scott lapsed into silence as the air currents caused the shaking of the shuttle to increase. They were now approaching the upper range of the landing speed, or 226 mph. If they sank below 213 mph, they would be moving too slowly. Then he felt a jarring bump, and as so often happens on a commercial airliner, a cheer went up on his intercom. He could see Hiramatsu and Goldberg holding their arms up in triumph in their seats on the other side of the craft.

"Lady and gents, wait for my command before you unbuckle," the commander ordered.

Finally, the forward motion of the shuttle stopped, and soon they could feel slower movement, which was being generated by the tug of a runway tow truck. After interminable minutes, the craft finally came to a halt, and the pilot and commander unbuckled their own shoulder harnesses and waist belts.

The passengers began to stir, taking off their harnesses but following prior instructions not to remove their helmets until they reached the debriefing area. Suddenly, the side hatch popped open, and Florida sunlight and fresh air poured in as a member of the ground crew poked his head into the compartment.

"Who wants to be first?" he yelled.

"Professor Pushkin!" Hightower volunteered.

"No, no!" Pushkin said. "It must be Ruth. Ladies first."

Scott smiled to himself. He knew that the Russian's concern went beyond old-fashioned courtesy. Pushkin wanted to be sure that the only handicapped member of the crew didn't get shoved to one side in the rush to touch mother earth again.

So Ruth made her way laboriously across the crew compartment to the open hatch. Clearly, it was much harder going for her in the one-G environment of earth than in the microgravity of space, or the one-sixth G of the moon. He wondered what was going through her mind now. Was she longing for the freedom she had experienced off the earth during the past couple of months?

As she exited the open hatch with the help of two members of the ground crew, the remaining members of the moon team cheered yet again.

"*Now*, Professor Pushkin!" Hightower repeated, enthusiasm permeating his voice. "It's your turn!"

This time, the Russian didn't object, and Scott moved a step toward him so that he could get behind his seat to make a clear passageway to the hatch. But just as Pushkin neared him, he saw the man reach into the top of his slightly opened pressure suit—and he froze. He grabbed his chest, and his face went completely white.

At first, Scott's medical training made him think, *Heart attack!* But then the Russian grasped his shoulders and pulled him within a few inches of his face.

"It's gone!" Pushkin cried in a hoarse whisper.

"What's that?" Scott asked.

"The container with the disks—it's gone!"

At first, the words didn't register. Then, Scott's first thought was that the Russian scientist must have looked in the wrong pocket. "Check again, Sergey!" he said. "It has to be there. You've had it on you since we left the moon."

Pushkin frantically searched through his pockets again, and even unzipped the upper part of his pressure suit. But still, no disks.

"Hey, we have to move!" Hightower called from the doorway. "Our public awaits! Shiro and I are going on out onto the lift. Can't keep the fans waiting, mates!"

Scott waved him on and turned back to Pushkin. "Think!" he said to the Russian. "Did you take it out of your pocket at all on the trip back to earth?"

"Only when we were making those toasts on *Moonshot*," Pushkin replied, now completely distraught. "I held the container over my head, and then I put it right back in my pocket. I know they were there because I checked later, when I took a short nap in my sleeping compartment."

"Did you check again, after you woke up?"

Pushkin thought a moment. "No," he replied. "I got up only minutes before we docked at the space station. I slept more soundly than I have in the entire time we've been in space. I could hardly get up. The pilot had to wake me. Anyhow, after I awoke, things went so quickly, I didn't think about the disks until just now."

The sleeping compartments again, Scott thought, anxiety building inside.

"We'll have to do a thorough search of your pressure suit when you take it off in the debriefing area," he said. "But it's possible we have a problem."

Scott turned to the commander and pilot, who were waiting patiently. Pushkin and Scott were the last two passengers, and they had to exit before the crew could leave.

"We have a potential emergency," Scott said to the commander. "A serious security matter. I want you to notify the officials in the debriefing area to be on high alert, and hold everyone at debriefing until we've sorted some things out."

As the commander relayed the message to Space Center Headquarters, Scott moved over to the compartment where he had stashed his bag with the memory storage boards containing the copy of the genome information. He had kept this handbag in easy reach during the entire trip home, and he wanted to be absolutely sure that his copies hadn't disappeared along with the originals. To his relief, the bag with the case containing the memory boards was still there, exactly where he had placed it when he boarded *Challenger II.* He said a silent thank-you—to what or whom he wasn't sure. And he couldn't avoid another feeling of gratitude that Pushkin hadn't mentioned the copies to anyone.

Finally, the American and the Russian walked to the hatch and stepped out onto the lift, which was poised high above the runway in the bright Florida sunlight. Even with the help of the two landing aides who had been assigned to him, Scott had to concentrate on not losing his balance in the one-G gravity of earth. But even though he could feel the extra pressure bearing down on his muscles, the exercises he had done on the moon seemed to be paying off. At least he could walk unaided.

Pushkin, who was older and had neglected his conditioning routine, was in much worse shape. Unable to walk alone, he had to lean heavily on his ground crew aides.

Scott hardly thought about the adjustments that they had to make to earth's gravity. Pushkin's disks were all that was on his mind. *Did they slip out of the Russian's inside pocket—and maybe fall to the bottom of his pressure suit?* That would be the first thing he would check when they got to the debriefing area.

But an empty feeling in the pit of his stomach told him that something more might be involved. Pushkin had been vulnerable in his sleeping compartment, just as Scott had been on the trip to the moon. The Russian might even have been drugged. Almost sounded like it.

Clutching his priceless handbag, which he had secured around his body with a shoulder strap, Scott looked closely at the others on the lift. There were only three likely suspects—but he had to admit none looked too threatening. Ruth Goldberg was sitting to one side in her wheelchair, waving at the sparse crowd of greeters and dignitaries, who had been stirred up by the notes of a military band. Looking in the same direction, Scott could make out Sara, Megan, and Jacob, who were standing next to Colleen—and, yes, that was almost certainly Vice President Phillips waving a hand near them.

As he glanced behind Ruth Goldberg's chair, Scott noticed that Shiro Hiramatsu was also waving to the crowd, but a tired smile showing through his helmet visor opening suggested that earth's gravity might be taking its toll. Fortunately the Japanese scientist's rigorous athletic routine on the moon had prepared him to walk alone as they disembarked from the shuttle.

Jeffrey Hightower seemed the most vigorous of the lot. But after all, he had worked out more than anyone else, Scott thought with a twinge of jealousy. The Australian was standing toward the front of the lift, where he leaned precariously over the railing, waving and shouting to the crowd. As the lift reached ground level, Hightower, in the middle of a hearty wave, pivoted in Scott's direction. In that instant, the American noticed an out-of-place ornament on the man's chest, some insignia that wasn't part of their regular uniform.

No, it's not an insignia, Scott thought idly, shuffling a half step closer to Hightower. It looked more like a round disk, a coin dangling from a thin silver chain that was swinging back and forth outside the man's pressure suit. Scott had seen that piece of jewelry somewhere before.

Then, visor-to-visor, his eyes locked on Hightower's. And he began to understand.

55

The rush of impressions left Scott lightheaded. The noise of the crowd faded almost to silence. As they stepped onto the tarmac and headed toward the holding shack—which had been erected a short distance away—the passengers and crew members seemed to move in slow motion.

Hightower had turned and was now leading the way toward the hut, which stood about forty yards away from the parked shuttle. His two aides were walking in front of him. Since he didn't need them to support him as he walked, they had assumed the role of guides to usher the moon team quickly out of the open area. Ruth Goldberg was rolling in her motorized wheelchair slightly behind the Australian, and about ten feet to his right. Hiramatsu, Pushkin, and Scott were scattered out just behind the others. The *Challenger II* commander and pilot brought up the rear.

But Scott's eyes and thoughts were riveted on Hightower. The Australian turned and waved toward the dignitaries and other spectators who were standing behind the security line about thirty yards to the arriving team's right. But now, Scott could see that he was no longer smiling or cheering. His eyes were searching beyond the crowd, and his lips were fixed in a dead-serious line.

From somewhere, a single siren began to wail. *We're too far from town to hear sirens, unless . . .* At the sound, Hightower sank to the tarmac in front of Scott and simultaneously slapped his right thigh. A deep red fountain spurted from between his fingers.

Adrenaline surged through Scott's body a split second before he heard the first series of explosions, a distant rumble that quickly erupted in nearby blasts that ripped up the tarmac all around him.

The holding shack exploded in a ball of fire just in front of them, producing a shock wave that knocked Scott to his knees. Simultaneously, he felt something tear through the right side of his pressure suit. Looking down, he noticed with peculiar detachment that a rip had opened in the suit all the way to his ribs, and a red stain was spreading steadily on his side.

For a moment, the scene seemed fixed in a surreal, motionless tableau. Then, like a pent-up supervolcano, noise, action, and blood exploded everywhere on the tarmac.

Sara! The kids! He looked in their direction, but the entire line of spectators seemed to have disappeared. Then he saw the bodies, stretched out along the ground. Some were moving. Some were not.

He started to rise and move toward his family, but the pressure suit and helmet made movement difficult. Then he was thrown back onto his knees from the concussion of explosions that lifted whole sections of the runway. Behind him, the scaffolding and lift that had brought them down from the shuttle disappeared in crackling lines of smoke and flame.

The wail of the single siren had now become almost deafening, and the screech of brakes told Scott that help had arrived. Now almost prone on the runway, he saw that the ambulance had stopped only yards from where the members of the moon team now lay. An odd thought struck him: *Only one ambulance? Where are the others? They keep dozens on call!*

"Him, I think!" a woman's voice barked.

Vaguely, Scott perceived that the orders were coming from a female emergency-service worker, who had jumped out of the ambulance and was directing a male coworker toward Hightower. The solidly built, rather short man, who wore a jacket emblazoned with *Emergency,* ran over to the Australian and hesitated for a moment, looking intently down at the fallen scientist. Hightower sat up on his own, and they appeared to exchange words. Then Hightower stood, and the emergency worker rolled him over his shoulder in a fireman's carry, and jogged with his burden toward the waiting ambulance.

Scott, now coming back to his senses, struggled to sit up. He saw that another rescue worker, a woman, was checking Pushkin, who seemed to have been wounded by the blasts. Apparently satisfied the Russian could be moved, she hauled him off the ground and positioned him across her shoulder.

Unlike Hightower, the Russian scientist was a dead weight in the woman's grip, unable to help at all with his rescue. But she was obviously strong and athletic and seemed unfazed by the disadvantage. With hardly any hesitation, she moved quickly with her burden toward the ambulance.

Then, in what almost seemed an afterthought, she stopped in midstride and called out to the remaining wounded: "Lie right there. We have room only for these two. Other medics will be here for you shortly."

Just as she spoke, her eyes locked on Scott's, and for a moment she seemed frozen to the spot. Then she whirled back toward the ambulance with Pushkin on her shoulder. As Scott watched, she began to gesture and point back toward the downed moon team members who still lay on the tarmac.

Vaguely, Scott thought something seemed wrong about the behavior of the ambulance crew. He didn't realize just how wrong until he saw the stocky rescue worker jogging back in his direction with another male emergency worker—and a matching pair of submachine guns in their hands.

"Get down!" Scott yelled to no one in particular.

He immediately recognized the futility of his warning. Before he could react, the deafening discharge of their submachine guns seemed to shake the very earth where he was lying. As the first wave of rounds swept across the tarmac, Scott saw the shuttle aides fall like rag dolls around him. Most were armed, but the attack was so sudden they had no time to respond.

The two attackers paused and took more careful aim at the remaining members of the moon team, who were lying weak and helpless on the runway. An eerie wave of calm swept over Scott. He knew there was absolutely nothing he could do. It seemed his time had come. Then a strange thought flashed through his mind: *Am I ready?*

But for some reason, the phony emergency workers didn't fire their weapons. Instead, both flew awkwardly through the air. At the same time, their submachine guns squirted out of their hands and onto the ground in front of them.

Then Scott saw the reason for the odd, sprawling flight of the two attackers. They both had been knocked off their feet by a dark-blue blur that had emerged out of nowhere. The blur resolved into a man in uniform—U.S. Navy, a commander, Scott thought absently, as he focused for some odd reason on the man's rank insignia. In some inexplicable display of martial gymnastics, the commander had simultaneously used a foot to knock one of the gunmen senseless and the edge of a forearm to disable the other one.

Scott then looked back toward the line of spectators. He rose to his knees, searching frantically for some sign of his family. But smoke from the explosions, and perhaps from a smoke grenade, obscured his vision. He knew he had to stand up if he hoped to get a better view of the scene.

Then he heard a scream that somehow pierced through all the moans and shouts and explosions: "Scott! No! Down!"

Bewildered, he dropped back to his knees and watched as a ragged, disheveled figure emerged through the smoke that was now covering the tarmac. At first he didn't recognize her, with the torn blouse and soot-blackened face. But then it registered that he was looking at Colleen, lurching toward them out of the line of downed spectators. She was pointing to the location where the two gunmen had been firing. As he focused, he saw the problem.

One of the attackers was still lying motionless on the ground, knocked unconscious by the Navy commander's kick. But the other gunman had recovered and had managed to scoop up his automatic weapon. Now he was swinging it around toward Scott and the other scientists.

The commander, who was pulling himself off the ground several feet away, was trying to gather himself into a crouch. But he appeared slightly stunned, and perhaps wounded as well. Blood now covered his left arm, and his movements seemed slower. It was obvious he would never reach the gunman before the man pulled the trigger.

One thought hung suspended in Scott's mind: *So this is the way it ends.* But then he caught some movement out of the corner of his eye. The commander was reaching out, almost serenely, to his left, his open palm seemingly linked to an invisible cord that was pulling a streaking figure directly toward Scott.

The fast-moving figure materialized into Ruth Goldberg. But the amazing thing, Scott thought with a strange air of detachment as he watched the action unfold, was that she wasn't in her wheelchair. She was actually *running*.

The attacker got off a couple of rounds, and Scott saw Shiro Hiramatsu's body shake and quiver on the ground not far from him. But before the gunman could take aim at Scott, he seemed to hesitate in shocked wonder, watching as Ruth sailed directly on top of Scott. As another shot cracked from the man's weapon, Ruth's body shook at the impact, and Scott felt pain slice through his right leg. But by then, the Navy commander was on top of the gunman, hacking away with the edges of his hands until the attacker finally lay still on the smoky runway.

Scott, the breath knocked out of him by Ruth's dive, lay half-conscious under her still body. As the ambulance roared off the tarmac with siren wailing again, Colleen reached Scott's side.

"Check Ruth first," Scott directed.

The Israeli scientist was beginning to regain consciousness as Colleen probed here and there to try to determine the extent of her injuries. Then she turned to examine Scott's wounds on his side and leg. Before she had an opportunity to try to test her rusty first-aid skills, a couple of space-center medics, who were now swarming over the runway, took over the job.

"They blew up the other ambulances," Colleen said, her voice shaking with anger as she watched the medics work on Scott and Ruth. "I heard that on my hand radio. They're animals!"

"What about Sara and the kids?" Scott asked, almost afraid to put the question to her. He winced as the medic assigned to him began to cut away his pressure suit.

"Fine," she replied. "Shaken up a little, but fine. I told Sara to stay over there with Jacob and Megan while I checked on you."

Because of the heavy smoke screen, it was still hard to see what was going on with the spectators. But Scott took her word for it.

"Dr. Hiramatsu is dead," an authoritative male voice said.

They both looked up at the Navy commander who had just joined them. He was limping with superficial shrapnel wounds and some painful shoulder and hip bruises, which he said had resulted from the fight with the gunman. But otherwise he seemed to be functioning all right.

Scott looked in the direction where he had last seen the Japanese scientist. Now, the laser-expert's body was being zipped up in a body bag by medics and a physician. Scott felt helpless tears well up in his eyes. Memories of Shiro rushed through his mind . . . the man's patience and good humor when jokes were made at his expense . . . the knowledge about lasers Scott had gained in their informal discussions . . . the relaxed times they had spent exercising together on the moon . . . their common commitment to making Energy Project Omega a success.

"An honorable man," Scott finally said. "I'll miss him. And I'm determined to bring his killers to justice."

"Two are already in hand," the Navy commander said.

"Scott, meet Michael James," Colleen said.

"I should have known," Scott said, weakly reaching for a handshake.

"One of the men is dead," James said. "I guess I kicked him a little too hard. The other one has a bad headache, but he'll recover. He's the same one you and I were following around here in Cocoa Beach, Colleen. But I don't expect he'll be out on the streets again any time soon."

"Sorry we had to meet under these circumstances," Scott said. "Or maybe

I should be happy. You saved my life. Colleen's told me about you. But the uniform threw me off."

"The security response team insisted on it," James said. "Guess they figured I'd be easy to identify as an official in case something like this happened. Spike Caldwell's a stickler for detail. Anyhow, it brought back memories. I don't get to wear this monkey suit too often in my present incarnation."

Then a worried frown crossed Michael James's face. "They took Sergey. Was he alive?"

"Not moving," Scott said, shaking his head. "But maybe he was just knocked out."

James sighed. "This was an extremely well-planned operation. Far as I could tell, only four of them created all this havoc. We've met two of them before, Colleen—the woman and her stocky friend who's now in custody. They were posing as emergency ambulance workers. And there was another fake rescue worker—the guy who's dead—and the ambulance driver."

"So two of them escaped," Scott said. "And they took Pushkin and Hightower with them?"

"That's right," James replied. "Somehow, they got onto this facility and planted explosives under the runway tarmac and back where the vehicles and ambulances are parked. Then they set them off with remote triggers. Very sophisticated. We can just thank the Lord their plan wasn't perfect. At least you and Dr. Goldberg are alive."

"There's a big problem you're not aware of," Scott said. "Hightower is a mole. He was working with the Russians—or whoever this bunch is that caused all this chaos. He was wearing that Russian *Mafiya* coin and chain in plain view when he got off the shuttle."

"Are you sure?" Colleen asked.

"You bet I'm sure," Scott said. "You stuck pictures of the necklace in my face often enough for me to memorize what it looks like."

"So Hightower is *Pika*," she said.

Scott nodded.

"You're sure about that?" James said, alarm now evident in his face. From his reaction, it was obvious that he knew about the elite Russian *Mafiya* assassins. Scott was surprised, but didn't stop to question him about his knowledge.

"Yes, as sure as I can be," Scott replied. "But that's not the half of it. Since the saboteurs have got both Pushkin and Hightower in that ambulance, it's certain that they also have a set of disks that we absolutely must try to recover. I can't tell you more, but this is a matter of the most urgent national security."

"I hear you," James said, already moving away from them. "I've got to get the word out on that ambulance team."

As James hobbled off toward what looked like a makeshift command center that had been set up about fifty yards away on the runway, Scott pulled Colleen close to him so that he could whisper in her ear.

"See this bag?" He pointed to the handbag containing the memory storage boards that he had been clutching during the attack on the runway.

She nodded, a perplexed look on her face.

"I'll be going to the hospital directly from here. So you have to take this and guard it with your life. *Literally.*" He thought a moment. "You know our big safe-deposit box here in Cocoa Beach? The official U.S. government box? I want you to leave right now, and go directly there. Put the entire bag in the box. Don't let it out of your sight until it's locked up. Understand?"

She nodded again.

"By the way, you were giving Michael all the credit," Colleen said. "But she saved your life too." She pointed toward Goldberg, who lay half-conscious as a medic and physician worked on her injuries.

Scott looked in wonder over toward the Israeli, or Russian, or whatever she was. "I'm certainly grateful," he replied. "And I desperately hope she's okay. But she has some questions to answer. Such as how does an Israeli—who is really a Russian—and who is supposed to be a paraplegic from childhood—suddenly hop out of her wheelchair, sprint across a runway, and like a trained Secret Service agent, throw her body in front of a speeding bullet—and save the life of a U.S. congressman?"

Colleen just shrugged without attempting an answer, and Scott decided it was just as well. His chief of staff's exclusive concern had to be getting that handbag containing the copies of the genome information to a safe place.

Scott leaned back on the tarmac, waiting for his medic to make final preparations to move him to another ambulance. The pain from his injuries was really hitting him. Also, as a physician, he knew that the morphine injections were preventing him from thinking straight. Yet as he drifted into hazy half-consciousness, one thought stuck in his mind—a stop-frame vision of Ruth Goldberg flying through the air, intercepting a hail of bullets heading in his direction, and ensuring him of a little more time on planet earth.

56

As the ambulance sped out onto the highway, Klaudia Ming-Petrovich, who was sitting in the rear with her two patients, yelled at the driver: "Fast, but no accidents! And remember—keep the siren on until we're a block from the garage. Then turn it off and slow down!"

"Yes, Colonel!" he called nervously over his shoulder.

Klaudia was upset. She always expected to lose people during a dangerous operation, and this had been one of the most dangerous in her career. But she was not accustomed to having half of her hit team wiped out.

Despite Valery's weaknesses, she deeply regretted that he hadn't made it through the firefight. His expertise with explosives would be hard to replace. But, if he had survived the attack, he would be subjected to interrogation procedures that would almost certainly pry information out of him. Information about her and *Pika* operations on American soil.

At least she had been careful to send him out of the room when she was communicating with Martov. That was one thing to be thankful for in this mess. Most important of all, Martov would surely count this mission a success because she had managed to extricate both Pushkin and Hightower—and, she trusted, their valuable data—from the hands of the Americans. There was no time to worry about minor flaws in her assignment. They would be in serious danger until they could leave the United States behind them.

Her attention now turned to the two men lying on the cots on either side of her. Sergey Pushkin was still breathing but had not regained consciousness. He had lost a considerable amount of blood from two bullet wounds, but bandages and a tourniquet had stanched the flow. She felt the pulse at his carotid artery again and was almost sorry it remained so strong. Still, she knew if she could bring him back to consciousness, she might get something useful out of him. A quick search of his pockets had turned up nothing in the way of alien computer disks.

"Can I sit up now?" the other man asked in fluent Russian.

His unexpected query irritated her already frayed nerves beyond the point of tolerability.

"No!" she barked in English. "Someone outside may see you. A patient sitting up in an ambulance could raise questions. And stick to English, please. We are still in the United States. We cannot afford to be overheard and generate suspicion."

She didn't know what to call the man. He went by the name Hightower, but that was almost certainly not his real name.

"I'm under your orders—for now," the man replied with a humorless smile.

Klaudia recognized that look—the expression of one who was extremely confident, and quite arrogant. This agent wouldn't bend to her orders like Valery.

"Are you injured?" she asked.

He laughed. "Not unless you call this red paint on my pants an injury."

He pointed to the bloodlike coloring he had slapped onto his thigh to simulate a shrapnel or bullet wound. The man was obviously well-trained. He had flattened himself out on the tarmac immediately when the fireworks began, a preplanned move that had enabled him to avoid injury and signal to the *Mafiya* hit squad that he was on their side. Just as impressive, he had possessed the discipline to stay down and wait during the entire firefight.

"I know most *Pika*," she ventured. "But not you. You're really Australian?"

"Australian enough," he said cryptically. "And I *do* know you. At least *of* you."

She was slightly miffed by the remark. So Martov had taken this operative into his confidence, but not her!

"You have the disks?" she asked abruptly, changing the subject on purpose. This was not a man with whom she cared to engage in idle chatter.

That mirthless smile again. "Of course."

She looked over at Pushkin. "We couldn't be sure that you had been able to acquire the disks on the flight back to earth, so we had to take him as insurance. But now it seems that it really wasn't necessary to bring him along—except that he's still alive. We couldn't afford to have the Americans gain possession of him."

"Also, the prime minister wanted him alive if possible," Hightower reminded her. "I watched the man in operation on the moon. He's a genius—even if he's out of control. He can still be of use to us."

"Perhaps," she replied. "That's not my decision, nor yours. But if it were up to me, I would dispose of the garbage."

"You're as tough as they say."

She knew he was laughing at her. But at the same time, she thought she detected a note of grudging admiration edging into his voice. He had shifted his body so that he was now on his side, propped on one elbow. Obviously not one to take orders easily, he was pushing her command to lie down as far as he felt wise. At the same time, she thought with some satisfaction as she watched the movement of his eyes, he was surely trying to get a better look at her.

"I do what is needed," she replied coolly.

He fingered the *Pika* coin and chain, which had swung loosely to one side from his neck. "We have to get rid of these," he said.

"Oh?" she replied, feigning a lack of interest.

"Too many people have seen them," Hightower replied. "I could tell that somehow the neckpiece caught Andrews's attention as we were leaving the shuttle. He even seemed to recognize the ornament."

"How is that possible?" she asked.

"At least one was lost in New York during that Rensburg matter, correct?"

Klaudia hesitated as the thought of Valery sprawled out on the runway tarmac flashed through her mind. Then she caught herself, knowing that any sign of uncertainty would give away more than was wise.

"But it was never recovered," she replied quickly.

"At least, we *think* it wasn't recovered," Hightower replied, rubbing the coin hanging around his neck. "I'm not so sure. Anyhow, it's too Soviet. And too low-tech. That's all in the past. We are international. We're the future. Coins and chains are almost czarist."

"The necklace represents an honorable tradition," she protested.

"But why ask for trouble?" he argued. "Anyone can look at this thing and see the Cyrillic writing. We must carry nothing that will link us directly to the mother country. And certainly not to the prime minister. Why force him to deny us?"

Klaudia shrugged, now becoming tired of the conversation. She had harbored some of the same thoughts herself but had been reluctant to share them with Martov for fear of seeming disloyal. Anyhow, she had to admit to herself that the necklace, despite the symbolic link it represented to the elite *Pika* assassins, was outdated. She and this Australian were looking to the future, while the neckpiece embraced the past. This Hightower, or whatever his name was, fascinated her. He was something of a mystery, and she liked mysteries.

"The garage is just ahead!" the driver announced.

At the same time he shut off the siren and slowed the vehicle, as he had been instructed. In seconds, they rolled into a large mechanics' garage and the entry door closed down behind them.

"We must move very quickly!" Klaudia said. "You will change out of your space suit into a business suit, and I'll get rid of this uniform. In five minutes, we must all be in the limousine over there, heading down to the airport in Vero Beach, about an hour's drive south of here."

"And him?" Hightower asked, gesturing toward Pushkin.

Klaudia stared at the physicist for several long seconds before answering. "He will be with us in the limousine, along with a physician who is already waiting for us in the car."

"I assume that he's returning with us," Hightower said almost as a challenge.

She shrugged and smiled cruelly, in a way that she knew he would understand. "Yes. But Prime Minister Martov has left the decision about Pushkin's fate up to me—and I haven't yet made up my mind. We'll see if he proves healthy enough to survive these wounds. If he shows he can't make the rather rigorous trip back to the motherland, he will be terminated. The disks are our primary responsibility, not this traitor."

57

As the long, black, stretch limo pulled onto A1A and headed south toward Vero Beach, Klaudia placed her hand on the knee of the doctor who was accompanying them to the airport.

"It's time," she said. "Bring him to, and let's hear what he has to say."

The physician, who was sitting across from Klaudia and next to Pushkin on one of the side passengers' couches, turned toward the unconscious physicist with a needle. Hightower was watching the procedure with some amusement from the rear seat in the long vehicle.

After the injection, Pushkin began to stir. Then his eyes fluttered, and he coughed once.

"He's coming around nicely," the doctor said, who next waved some smelling salts under the professor's nose to hasten his return to consciousness.

Pushkin jumped at the pungent odor, gasped, and winced as the pain from his wounds hit him with full force.

"Hurts, doesn't it, Professor?" Klaudia said, without a hint of sympathy.

When Pushkin nodded, she placed a hand on one of his leg wounds and squeezed. A yelp from the physicist told her she had hit her mark.

"It will be much more painful for you unless you tell me what I need to know," she snarled. "What did you plan to do with those disks? Were you going to join the Americans and use them against Russia?"

He shook his head vigorously. "No, no! I would never betray Russia. But the information on the disks is for humankind. Everyone must benefit. So we've also arranged to give copies to the United Nations."

Shocked into silence, Klaudia leaned back and looked at Hightower.

"What do you mean?" Hightower asked, his lips now only inches from Pushkin's ear. "You didn't really copy the disks, did you?"

The physicist jumped at the question and turned his head abruptly around. "Dr. Hightower? Jeffrey? Is that you?"

"Aye, mate!" Hightower replied in his exaggerated Australian accent.

The Australian was obviously trying to sound casual, but Klaudia could tell from his strained tone that he was now feeling more pressure than she was. She suppressed a smile as she watched perspiration form on his furrowed brow. Although she knew her reputation would suffer considerably if this operation fell short of expectations, Hightower stood to lose much more. After all, Martov had given him prime responsibility for recovering those disks and keeping them out of anyone else's hands.

"Come on, Serg old boy, level with me," Hightower said again. "What's this nonsense about giving copies of the disks to the UN?"

"Scott Andrews is an honorable man," Pushkin replied. "He has the copies. He'll do the right thing for humankind."

Klaudia and Hightower looked at each other in alarm.

"You actually gave Andrews copies?" Klaudia demanded, hardly believing her ears. The American congressman's life had been in the palm of her hand out there on the tarmac, and she had let him escape—apparently with copies of the disks. Now, she began to perspire.

"We agreed that it would be best to give the information to the world at large," the physicist replied tersely. "I even announced our plan about the UN during the return trip on the lunar shuttle—though I don't think I said anything about having made copies." Then he gave Hightower a hard look. "But this isn't right. What are you doing here, Jeffrey? Why are we in this car with these people?"

For once, Hightower was speechless. He just shook his head and looked glumly toward the back of the limo.

"Where are Andrews's copies of the disks?" Klaudia asked Pushkin, shaking him slightly as she spoke. "What do they look like? Are they the same as the ones you made on the moon?"

Pushkin hesitated for a moment. "I think I understand now. Jeffrey, you stole the disks from me, didn't you? You're a spy with the FSB, aren't you? Or are you just a highly educated terrorist?"

Hightower continued to look away and shake his head.

"I believe I have nothing more to say," Pushkin finally said.

"Professor Pushkin, your life is now in my hands," Klaudia said, placing her hand on his chin and forcing him to look her directly in the eye. "The physician sitting next to you has two needles. One contains a solution that will put you to sleep. You'll then be put in that wheelchair"—she pointed to the folded vehicle that had been placed at the door next to Hightower—"and you'll wake up to enjoy a cruise with the rest of us on a nuclear submarine, which now lies near the Florida Straits. That vessel will take you back to a relatively pleasant life in Mother Russia."

Then Klaudia paused for effect. "The other needle will end your miserable life," she finally said. "If you fail to give me the answers I need, a body bag under this seat will serve as your final garbage container, you ungrateful traitor! Now let me ask again. Where are the copies of those disks? What exactly does Andrews plan to do with them?"

Pushkin stared at her so intently that she involuntarily dropped her hand from his chin and drew back from him. "Your spirit is not right," he said, shaking his head in almost a warm, fatherly rebuke. "I can say no more. If you must kill me, so be it. Perhaps I've lived long enough, but that's for God to decide. I know that God is good, and I forgive you, my dear. Really, from the bottom of my heart, I do forgive you—because I know you don't yet understand."

"You ingrate!" she screamed, slapping his leg wound again. But this time, she elicited no response—not even a grimace. They stared at each other, and then she made up her mind.

"That one!" she ordered, pointing to one of the two syringes that the physician was holding in his hand. "Give him that one!"

The doctor immediately jabbed the needle into Pushkin's neck, but again the physicist failed to acknowledge any pain. His only response was the same smile and a tender look—a look that so infuriated Klaudia that she had to look away from him to avoid losing control altogether.

When she turned back, Pushkin was sagging to one side, still and peaceful, his eyes half-open.

"Roadblock!" the driver barked over the speakers, shocking all the passengers out of the grip of the drama they had just witnessed.

"Use the diplomatic passport!" Klaudia ordered through a microphone. "The French one. If they argue, tell them we have a very sick diplomat in the backseat. Everybody speak French—beginning now!"

The limousine slowed, crept up to the blockade, and finally came to a full stop next to a phalanx of flashing police lights. Through an opening in the glass separating the passengers from the driver, they could hear bits and pieces of the conversation. At first, the police resisted because there was no diplomatic flag on the front of the car. The driver apologized profusely, and then he said, "The governor himself insisted that we take Monsieur LaFleur home immediately!"

Klaudia winced. What if the Florida governor was nowhere near their part of the state, and this policeman knew it? Fortunately, the ruse worked. The officers waved the limousine on through, and shortly, they cut over to U.S. 1 and pulled into the small private airport at Vero Beach.

The paperwork for their departure had already been completed by the time they reached the airport parking lot. The seaplane was warming up on the runway, with a flight plan listing their destination as St. Thomas. Of course, there was no mention of the unofficial stop on the waters of the Florida Straits, where the nuclear submarine awaited them.

All that remained was for the passengers to hurry from the limo to the aircraft. Walking quickly, Hightower and Klaudia Ming-Petrovich led the way onto the runway. Glancing over her shoulder, she saw that the driver was following with the rest of the bags. Bringing up the rear, the physician was pushing the wheelchair, which carried an unconscious but otherwise reasonably healthy Sergey Pushkin.

Klaudia reflected with some regret that the body bag remained folded up neatly under one of the backseats. Killing the physicist would have solved a lot of problems. But if Pushkin had died by her hand, the unpredictable Martov might have directed all his anger—and blame for the missing copies of the disks—in her direction.

She would still have to pay a price for the flawed operation. Perhaps a high price. But with Pushkin alive, Hightower was the leading candidate to face the brunt of the prime minister's wrath. She glanced over at the Australian and derived some satisfaction to see that he was still frowning and sweating.

58

Immediately after he had undergone surgery, Scott was sure he was well enough to walk directly out of the hospital. But Sara, who was the first person allowed in the room to see him, refused to let him even consider the possibility—at least for another twenty-four hours.

"Are you crazy?" she said. "You're a doctor! And you're talking about leaving before you get proper care? What about complications? What about infection? They haven't even removed all the shrapnel. Get serious!"

Finally, Scott relented. He even consented to remain flat on his back, with his injured leg elevated and his upper body mostly immobilized so that the wound to his ribs would begin to heal more quickly. But in return for these concessions, he insisted on a decided *lack* of peace and quiet in his schedule of appointments.

His first order of business was to get reacquainted with his children. Then, he reluctantly recognized that he couldn't put off the task of playing serious catch-up with his congressional work. He faced a huge backlog of paperwork from the months he had been on the Energy Project Omega. Also, he had been deluged with messages and questions from political colleagues and constituents about his moon voyage. To stack and sort the material, he had ordered two separate tables to be set up in his hospital room.

To answer the inquiries and demands effectively, Scott knew that he had to confer extensively with Colleen, Michael James, and others who could fill him in on the events that had occurred on earth since he had been away. Also, he wanted to take a better look at Colonel Spike Caldwell, who had been assigned to command a small security detail that would guard him and his family round-the-clock for the foreseeable future.

"I have to know I can trust the guy," he whispered to Sara, as the children occupied themselves with some moon rocks he had brought back for them. "You and the kids have been on my mind ever since I left. Maybe we're out of the woods now, but I want to be sure security around all of us is beefed up—and this Caldwell is the key. I've got to check him out more thoroughly, and I can't put that off any longer. Bring Colleen and Michael James in right now so I can talk to them."

Sara, still concerned that he needed to take his recovery more slowly, reluctantly complied. As she left with the children, she ushered in Colleen and Michael James.

"What about Pushkin?" Scott asked them before they even reached his bedside. "Has anyone heard what happened to him?"

James frowned and shook his head. "We've heard nothing since that phony ambulance crew picked him up."

"And Hightower?" Scott asked.

"Nothing on his whereabouts either," Colleen said. "But we have learned from preliminary intelligence reports that he was apparently a long-term sleeper agent planted in Australia years ago by the Soviets. From what we can tell, he was only a kid when they placed him in Sydney. His foster parents were really undercover Communist agents. After the Soviet Union fell, the renegade *Pika* operatives got him. He was a brilliant student and good athlete, and he easily made the grade as a top nuclear engineer. Then Energy Project Omega came along, and the rest is history."

"Amazing, isn't it?" Scott said, looking glumly away from them. "I completely misread the man. I really couldn't believe my eyes when I saw that *Pika* necklace dangling from his neck."

"A very professionally planned operation," James said, grudging admiration in his tone. "Hightower's an undercover terrorist agent of the highest order. Even an intelligence professional would probably have missed any clue to his real identity."

"Well, sometimes he did seem a little *too* Australian," Scott reflected. "But he pulled it off. I took his croc-hunter image as just a running joke on himself. Amazing, isn't it? They actually managed to plant a fine scientist as an agent right under our noses, in the middle of a major, highly publicized international expedition."

"Bolotov was a political operative too," Colleen reminded him.

"Yeah, but everybody *knew* what Bolotov was about," Scott replied ruefully.

"It's as though they stuck him there as a red herring, so we'd focus on him and forget about everybody else—especially Hightower. I never would have figured that an Australian scientist would be on the Russian payroll."

"Not really a Russian payroll," James corrected him. "Remember, the elite *Pika* wing of the Russian *Mafiya* is a supranational outlaw organization, which happens to have Russians in positions of top leadership. I shudder to think how broad-based and multinational this group is—and what power they may exercise with the science and technology at their disposal."

"All that is certainly important, but something else is much *more* important," Scott said. He looked hard at Colleen. "The handbag I gave you—it's still safe?"

She nodded and looked over at James.

"He knows about the bag?" Scott asked.

"Just that you gave me a valuable package," she replied. "As extra protection, Michael arranged to have one of Caldwell's guards accompany me to the deposit box. But neither of us knows the contents."

Scott didn't want to get into that just yet. "What do you know about this guy, Spike Caldwell?" he asked.

James nodded. "I know him by reputation. Trained as a Ranger. A lot of covert experience. Highly competent and reliable."

"Who's paying him?" Scott asked. "Who does he answer to?"

"He was called out of retirement by FBI Director Arnie Saunders," James said. "And he's been assigned to you at my request. I've known Arnie a long time. Since our days in the Navy together."

Scott shook his head. "You're full of surprises, Professor James. You're what, about fifty? And you leap through the air and destroy two assassins in one swoop? I thought I was in good shape, but you . . ."

James shrugged. "I work out."

Scott couldn't resist a gentle gibe: "Strange that a Bible scholar teacher could become so violent. I always thought it was 'turn the other cheek.' Don't get me wrong—I'm not complaining! I know I'm the main beneficiary of your Christian kung fu."

James smiled broadly, and without missing a beat he leaned almost in Scott's face: "I *always* try to turn *my* cheek. But I *don't* turn the cheek of those who can't defend themselves."

"Like I said, I'm not complaining," Scott replied.

"And by the way, only one of the assassins is dead," James said. "The other one, who was working with that Russian woman Colleen and I were following, is in custody under heavy security. He's recovering from a concussion, but he'll soon be good as new—and facing rigorous interrogation."

"I can imagine," Scott said wryly. "Ever figure out who the woman was?"

"We have a definite identification," Colleen replied. "Her name is Klaudia Ming-Petrovich. She has *Mafiya Pika* connections and is also probably an FSB agent."

"Any ties to Prime Minister Martov?" Scott asked expectantly.

"As a matter of fact, there probably are," Colleen said. "Those hours I spent cooped up with the FBI down here finally paid off. We learned that some mystery signals we were picking up were actually heavily encrypted computer-video transmissions between Ming-Petrovich and a Russian official, who we're almost certain was Martov. Unfortunately, we only unlocked the audio in the conversations, not the pictures. But voiceprint analysis and the context strongly suggest that Martov was the second party."

Scott smiled grimly. "If we can really nail down Martov's involvement, that will go a long way toward pulling President Bob Dalton into this mess."

"So we may have a real scandal on our hands," Colleen said.

"Yes, but back to Caldwell for a minute," Scott said. "You feel we can trust the guy with classified information—I mean, at the absolute highest level of national security?"

"Spike Caldwell can be trusted," the Wheaton professor said with finality.

"Okay," Scott replied. "I accept that. But if you ever have a doubt, let me know, understand? I'm putting not only myself, but also my family and U.S. national security, into Caldwell's hands. So call him in here, and let's see how he's doing his job."

A few moments later, Caldwell entered Scott's hospital room with James and shut the door behind him.

"Is this room secure?" Scott asked. "Has it been debugged?"

Caldwell nodded. "Yes, sir. I did that right after you were brought in here. You were sedated, so you didn't see us sweep the place clean."

"Find anything?" Scott asked.

"Not a thing," Caldwell assured him. "Of course, that wasn't surprising. Your room wasn't chosen until you arrived in the hospital, and we were up here before anyone else to check it out."

"How many on your detail?" Scott asked.

"Four besides me. Combat-trained veterans. All with covert experience overseas."

"You trust them all completely?"

"Absolutely," the Ranger colonel replied. "I've worked with them before, on a number of assignments."

"Okay. Now, what I'm about to tell you is as black as it gets—understand?" Scott said.

Then he summarized the events of the past few weeks, including the dramatic appearance of the genome disks, which on the surface purported to have the power to produce an unlimited human life span.

"And you think the disks were stolen by Hightower and are now with this renegade bunch of assassins, the *Pika*?" Caldwell asked.

"I'm sure of it, Spike," Scott replied. "And I'm also sure that the disks are on their way right now to Prime Minister Demitry Martov. But what neither Hightower nor any of the other *Pika* operatives know is that Pushkin insisted I have copies of the disks. We made the duplicates on the moon—and that's what's sitting in my government safe-deposit box right here in Cocoa Beach."

Scott derived some satisfaction from the looks of astonishment, and then the relieved smiles and murmurs that swept across the faces and lips of his listeners. But their expressions of relief disappeared at his next words.

"That's the good news," Scott continued. "The bad news is that I can't figure out how to get those duplicate memory boards into the hands of trustworthy people who'll make them available to the world's population. This material can't become the property of an elite few, and quite frankly, I'm convinced that our president can't be trusted with the information. We have reason to believe that he may even be in cahoots with Prime Minister Martov."

"If we can't go to the president or his administration, what's the alternative?" Colleen asked.

"Pushkin wanted to give the duplicates to the UN," Scott replied. "But too much shady, backroom deal-making and backstabbing goes on there. If we hand the genome information over to the General Assembly, I wouldn't be surprised if the memory boards ended up with some terrorist group. So the question is, who can we trust?"

"The director of the FBI," James replied without hesitation. "He can definitely be trusted with something like this. I'd stake my life on it."

Scott looked at Colleen. "Saunders answers to President Dalton's Justice Department," she noted, looking to James for confirmation. "But from all I can tell, he's remained reasonably independent of the president's administration."

Michael James nodded. "I trust Arnie Saunders completely. He runs an independent shop. The only way he'd reveal anything would be under congressional subpoena—and that probably wouldn't be so bad for us."

"Spike, I take it you'd also vote for Director Saunders?" Scott asked, turning to his new security commander.

When Colonel Caldwell nodded, Scott clapped his hands once to close the discussion. "Then Saunders and the FBI it is!" he said. "We'll have to trust that they'll help us make these genome disks available to everybody."

Then Scott became very serious. "At the same time, we can't allow ourselves to forget about the wormhole that started this whole mess. Granted, it's gone now, but I'm convinced we haven't heard the last from the other side of that dark window."

He paused for effect, scanning the eyes of each of his listeners before proceeding. "Make no mistake: these disks were not produced on earth, and we have no idea where they may take us. They embody the worst fears of those who have opposed genetic engineering, cloning, and the like. At all costs, we must prevent this material from falling into the grip of the power-hungry few. As Pushkin would have said, the rest is in God's hands."

Colleen looked at him curiously, but James responded with a knowing smile.

"I believe your words are prophetic, Dr. Andrews," the Wheaton professor said. "These appear to be times when signs and wonders beyond human understanding or analysis are increasing. As I believe you all know, I witnessed one of these phenomena more than a decade ago—a strange light in the eastern skies that I believe was a *positive* sign of things to come. Despite the upsets and chaos that followed in parts of the world, I know beyond any doubt that the Star was a message of goodness and hope. But I have a sense that this wormhole is a sign of danger—even evil. Perhaps we're approaching a time when the very worst elements of human nature are about to be unleashed."

Scott listened, but he elected not to respond. His opinions on these matters were still in an early, formative stage. Yet something resonated in him. Also, Scott knew that the words he himself had just uttered—his acknowledgment of the sovereignty and power of a deity—had some special meaning that he still couldn't articulate.

"I have just one more question," Scott said, forcing himself to return to the more mundane concerns of the present. "What's the deal with Ruth Goldberg? She saved my life, but frankly, I don't have a clue as to who she is and what she's about."

"Let her tell you," Michael James said, moving toward the door. "She's in the next room—and considerably more mobile than you are."

59

In a few moments, James opened the door again, and Ruth Goldberg marched into the room and over to the side of Scott's bed. She was limping slightly, but apparently not from any lingering paralysis. A bandage on her leg, which showed beneath the shorts she was wearing, suggested that she had suffered a leg wound when throwing herself between Scott and the flying bullets on the shuttle runway.

But Scott found he was focusing not on her legs, but on her broad smile. "Who exactly are you?" Scott asked. "Are you Ruth, or Tatiana, or someone else?"

"I can't tell you everything," she replied. "Matter of fact, as soon as I leave this hospital, you may never see me again. But I'll say this: I'm on your side. I've been on your side from the beginning. And I answer to the same authority you do—though my bosses, my controls, are not as public as yours."

"A double agent?" Scott replied in undisguised astonishment. "Or is it a triple agent?"

She shook her head. Obviously, she wasn't going to proceed any farther down this path.

"You should have no doubt that Sergey Pushkin always wanted to do the right thing—even though he wrestled with deep personal conflicts," she said, changing the subject to a topic that was clearly at the front of her mind. "Also, you as much as anyone should know that it's not easy for a committed patriot to subordinate his national loyalties to the needs of humankind—or even to his God."

Scott thought about that for a moment. He still wasn't so clear about God. But he did have to admit that over the past few months, as he had confronted momentous international and even interplanetary issues, his deepest personal allegiances had been expanding.

More and more, he had found himself looking beyond his local congressional constituency . . . beyond his political party . . . and even beyond his national interests. It had all started on the moon with Energy Project Omega, which was designed to provide the earth with unlimited power. Now, through unexpected events over which he had exercised little or no control, he was facing decisions that could have the most profound impact on basic human biology and the future shape of human history.

"Anyhow, you had me fooled," Scott said, shaking his head at Ruth. "You had us all fooled. Completely snookered. I could have sworn you couldn't walk. That story about becoming a paraplegic when you were a kid—that was masterful!"

"It was no story," she replied, a smile still playing about on her face. "And I certainly didn't fool you."

"What do you mean?" Scott asked, now completely serious. He was sure he had missed something.

"I *was* a paraplegic," she said. "I *couldn't* walk. Not a step. I was sent on this mission both because of my abilities with lasers, and also because my superiors felt that my handicap would make little difference in space. As it happened, they were right."

"But how . . . when did you . . . recover?" he asked, completely befuddled.

"On the runway," she replied.

"When the explosions and shots went off?" he asked. Then he found himself searching for some rational basis to continue the conversation. "I guess that happens sometimes, a kind of shock to the system, hysteria of some sort . . . some indications in the medical literature, you know, that such emotional trauma may change a patient's physical capacities . . ."

She shook her head. "It was nothing like that. I walked when Dr. James"— she pointed toward Michael—"held out his hand toward me. But something started happening in my legs earlier, after Dr. Pushkin prayed for my healing when we were on the moon. My thighs and calves seemed to be getting stronger, but I wasn't sure."

So Pushkin had told the truth. He and Ruth really had been praying when Scott happened upon the two of them in the Russian laboratory.

"When I saw you were knocked down and that emergency ambulance worker was still shooting in your direction, something cut through me, like a bolt of electricity," she said, her eyes now gazing at some faraway place. "Suddenly, I knew beyond any doubt that I could get up and run to help you. No, it was more than that. I knew I *had* to run to help you."

"And you're *still* walking," Scott said quietly, looking her up and down as she stood straight and strong before him.

"I don't pretend to understand," she said, her lip now quivering and tears running down her cheeks. "I just know that before, I was lame. But now, I can walk. Now, I can actually run."

James moved over and put an arm around her shoulder, and Colleen grasped her hand. Spike Caldwell remained near the door, tight-lipped and looking somewhat uncomfortable.

But Scott didn't feel uncomfortable at all. For the first time in months, he no longer felt alone. He was well aware that a profound mystery still surrounded that outpost on the Ocean of Storms. The ultimate intentions of whoever or whatever lurked on the other side of the vanished wormhole continued to be shrouded in uncertainty. And the prospects for enhanced health and a longer life span for the peoples of the earth remained in doubt.

But somehow, in his deepest being, Scott now felt at peace. Somehow, he sensed there were answers. Somehow, he knew there was hope.

Acknowledgments

S everal people have played important roles in helping bring this book to publication—though only the authors take responsibility for the content of the final manuscript.

Our editor, Janet Thoma, of Thomas Nelson's Janet Thoma Books imprint, has provided us with invaluable advice on character and plot development.

Stuart Woodward has contributed a cogent analysis of the plot development and has given helpful factual advice, especially with regard to new information technologies.

Pam Proctor has devoted many hours to reading and making editorial suggestions.

About the Authors

Dave Weldon

U.S. Representative Dave Weldon, a three-term Republican from Florida's Fifteenth Congressional District, is also a practicing physician, with a specialty in internal medicine.

His involvement in cutting-edge policy-making on space exploration is extensive. He is Vice Chairman of the Science Subcommittee on Space and Aeronautics; Cochairman with Governor Jeb Bush of the Florida VentureStar Pursuit Team, a group formed to bring the next-generation launch vehicle to the Kennedy Space Center; and Cochairman of the Congressional Space and Aeronautics Caucus.

A graduate of the State University of New York's Buffalo School of Medicine and a high honors graduate in biochemistry from the State University of New York at Stony Brook, Dr. Weldon served a three-year internship and residency in internal medicine at the prestigious Letterman Army Medical Center in San Francisco. He rose to the rank of major in the U.S. Army, and then entered private practice with the Melbourne Internal Medicine Associates.

William Proctor

William Proctor, a graduate of Harvard College and Harvard Law School, has authored, coauthored, or ghostwritten more than eighty books, including several national best-sellers. His books, which have sold in excess of ten million copies in more than forty languages, include the international bestsellers *Controlling Cholesterol* and the *Aerobics Program for Total Well-Being* by Dr. Kenneth H. Cooper; the *G-Index Diet* with Dr. Richard Podell; and *Beyond the Relaxation Response* with Dr. Herbert Benson. His latest publications are a novel, *The Last Star* (Thomas Nelson, 2000), and a nonfiction study of media bias published by Broadman & Holman.

Proctor has also served in the U.S. Marine Corps as an infantry-trained JAG officer (captain) in Vietnam and a military judge.

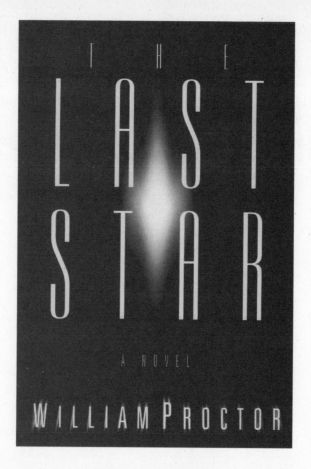

ISBN: 0-7852-6810-3

Is it the latest in spy technology, a meteor, a UFO, or a new star? No one—not even government leaders, military commanders, astronomers, or other scientists—can provide any real answers regarding the mysterious light that has suddenly appeared in the eastern sky. When a diverse group of scholars and scientists meets in Israel to investigate the phenomenon, they are soon caught in a web of political and spiritual intrigue, terrorist bombings, and sniper attacks. As uncertainty about the phenomenon causes worldwide panic, the pressure is turned up to find a scientific answer to the mystery of the light. Finally, the team begins to explore an unorthodox scientific question: Could the light be the return of the Star of Bethlehem . . . and a sign of Christ's Second Coming?